PRAISE FOR MARY BURTON

DON'T LOOK NOW

"With plenty of possible suspects, Burton's latest will appeal to readers who want light romance and heavy suspense."

—*Library Journal*

BURN YOU TWICE

"Burton does a good job balancing gentle romance with high-tension suspense."

—*Publishers Weekly*

"Scorching action. The twists and turns keep the reader on the edge of their seat as they will not want to put the novel down."

—*Crimespree Magazine*

HIDE AND SEEK

"Burton delivers an irresistible, tension-filled plot with plenty of twists . . . Lovers of romantic thrillers won't be disappointed."

—*Publishers Weekly*

CUT AND RUN

"Burton can always be counted on for her smart heroines and tightly woven plots."

—*For the Love of Books*

T0190975

"Must-read romantic suspense . . . Burton is a bona fide suspense superstar. And her books may be peppered with enough twists and turns to give you whiplash, but the simmering romance she builds makes for such a compelling, well-rounded story."

—*USA Today's Happy Ever After*

THE SHARK

"This romantic thriller is tense, sexy, and pleasingly complex."

—*Publishers Weekly*

"Precise storytelling complete with strong conflict and heightened tension are the highlights of Burton's latest. With a tough, vulnerable heroine in Riley at the story's center, Burton's novel is a well-crafted, suspenseful mystery with a ruthless villain who would put any reader on edge. A thrilling read."

—*RT Book Reviews* (4 stars)

BEFORE SHE DIES

"Will keep readers sleeping with the lights on."

—*Publishers Weekly* (starred review)

MERCILESS

"Burton keeps getting better!"

—*RT Book Reviews*

YOU'RE NOT SAFE

"Burton once again demonstrates her romantic-suspense chops with this taut novel. Burton plays cat and mouse with the reader through a tight plot, credible suspects, and romantic spice keeping it real."

—*Publishers Weekly*

BE AFRAID

"Mary Burton [is] the modern-day queen of romantic suspense."

—Bookreporter

ANOTHER
GIRL
LOST

ALSO BY MARY BURTON

The Forgotten Files

Morgans of Nashville

ANOTHER

GIRL

LOST

MARY
BURTON

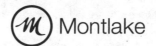

This is a work of fiction. Names, characters, organizations, places, events, and incidents are either products of the author's imagination or are used fictitiously. Otherwise, any resemblance to actual persons, living or dead, is purely coincidental.

Text copyright © 2024 by Mary Burton
All rights reserved.

No part of this book may be reproduced, or stored in a retrieval system, or transmitted in any form or by any means, electronic, mechanical, photocopying, recording, or otherwise, without express written permission of the publisher.

Published by Montlake, Seattle

www.apub.com

Amazon, the Amazon logo, and Montlake are trademarks of Amazon.com, Inc., or its affiliates.

ISBN-13: 9781662516030 (paperback)
ISBN-13: 9781662516023 (digital)

Cover design by Ploy Siripant
Cover image: © Sol Vazquez / ArcAngel; © Planner / Shutterstock

Printed in the United States of America

The eye, like a shattered mirror, multiplies the images of sorrow.

—*Edgar Allan Poe*

Chapter One

Detective Kevin Dawson

Saturday, July 20, 2024
Norfolk, Virginia
11:00 a.m.

Fear is a shape-shifter.

It manifests in dozens of different ways. Loud shrieks, righteous wails, angry denials, moans, nervous tics, tapping feet, even nail biting. Detective Kevin Dawson had seen all incarnations in his fifteen years on the force.

He'd also crossed paths with the rare ones who didn't show any signs of anxiety. They barricaded themselves behind an oppressive, icy silence that was difficult to penetrate. Discovering their secrets was always a challenge.

The woman sitting across the interview table from him now was one of the unusual ones. A rare breed. Scarlett Crosby had tucked herself under layers of a smooth, nonresponsive facade. Nonplussed— bored, even.

He'd yet to get under her skin, but she'd burrowed deep under his. Hours ago, he'd been pissed when he tightened the cuffs around her thin wrists, constricting the links until tension rippled through her body.

Scarlett Crosby had likely killed one woman and had been caught trying to murder another. She'd viciously attacked the arresting officer, and now Dawson, along with everyone else in the department, wanted a pound of her flesh.

Two hours ago, after the paramedics had patched her up, he'd stuck her in this small, windowless interview room. He'd dimmed the lights, knowing she'd stew in shadows and dirty grays. When he'd slammed the door behind him, he'd made a show of flipping the dead bolt. His message was clear: *You're locked in. Trapped. Get used to a cell.*

On his orders, she'd received no bathroom breaks, water, or coffee, and no human contact. He wanted her uncomfortable. Given her history, a little physical discomfort in a confined space might penetrate her silence.

Playing fair? Maybe not. But his job was to solve a murder, not coddle Scarlett Crosby.

When he reentered the room, her eyes were closed, and her bandaged hand rested on her thigh. If he didn't know better, he'd say she was meditating at a yoga retreat.

She wore gray scrubs, courtesy of the forensic officer who'd confiscated her blood-soaked T-shirt, jeans, and shoes. The garments swallowed her thin frame and cast an unhealthy hue on ivory skin stippled with traces of blood. She smelled of her victim's perfume, the back of the squad car, and the artist's paint she used daily.

When he flipped on the lights, she didn't open her eyes or move.

He angled the second chair at a diagonal close to her, the position a deliberate choice to foster a connection between them. No table separating them, they were allies, not enemies.

He sipped coffee as he set a cup of water in front of her. He shouldn't be the one talking to Scarlett Crosby. His perspective on this case was tainted, but he was the first to admit he had an on-again, off-again relationship with common sense. He wanted, needed, her to talk to him.

When she opened her eyes, there were no signs of gratitude or relief. If anything, annoyance simmered. He prided himself on sizing up suspects, but reading her was tough.

He tugged his jacket, sipped coffee. "How did we get here, Scarlett?" The use of *we* and her name was deliberate. Creating-connections, building-bridges kind of thing.

The suggestion that *they* were in this together seemed to amuse her. "I want my lawyer." Her voice rattled with a slight rasp.

When his investigation began almost two weeks ago, he'd recognized her name immediately. An internet search had unearthed ten-year-old images of a haunted, broken Scarlett staring blankly into a camera. A gash had run down her cheek, and bruises covered her neck and arms. That version of Scarlett had plagued his nightmares for a decade. He'd failed that Scarlett. She'd been the victim of Tanner Reed, who'd held, raped, and tortured her for three months. She'd suffered for those three months because when Dawson had interviewed Tanner weeks before her kidnapping, he'd not seen past the man's easy explanations and smile. It took three months for the dots to connect in Dawson's mind, and thanks to some dumb luck, he'd finally saved Scarlett. The world had seen him as her ultimate savior, and he'd been promoted.

This Scarlett sitting here now, the 2.0 version, had physically filled out in the last decade, softening those sharp bones. Her blond hair had thickened and grown glossy, color warmed her skin, and the old terrors radiating from her eyes had vanished.

Now, he believed, her fears hadn't gone anywhere, but had bonded with anger and embedded in sinew and bone. She'd remade herself into an artist, a businesswoman, and a volunteer who helped at a local recreation center, where she'd just completed a mural. Current publicity and public images captured smiles, but a detectable distance blunted her gaze.

"I'll call your lawyer soon," he said.

Scarlett drank her water and dug her thumbnail into the Styrofoam cup. "I'm only talking to Luke Kane, Detective Dawson."

"It could be a while. I'd hate for you to sit here any longer than necessary."

The cup creaked as she tightened her fingers. "I was locked in a basement for eighty-eight days, remember? You'll have to try harder to intimidate me."

He glanced at his watch, struggling to hide his rising frustration. "Scarlett, let me help you. I want to get this sorted out so you can go home. Talk to me."

"Lawyer first, Detective Dawson." Full lips flattened into a grim line, projecting experience well beyond her twenty-five years.

As if she'd not spoken, he said, "We have footage of you speaking to your latest victim, and we've also confirmed you were one of the last people to see her alive. You also stalked and kidnapped a second woman. You'd have killed her if you'd not been stopped."

She sat silent, barely breathing.

"And I can also link you to the human remains found entombed in a wall." He leaned forward, his knees less than an inch from hers. "What set you off? Why call in the location of the first body that's been hidden for a decade? Why kill again after all these years?"

She exhaled slowly, her face remaining a blank mask.

He sat back, refusing to acknowledge the frustration elbowing his gut. He lowered his voice and softened the tone. "Tell me about Della." He knew Della was a trigger point for Scarlett, their alleged relationship an open wound. "Tell me how she hurt you."

She settled back in the chair, her face cool and emotionless. "Not talking."

"You and me have history, Scarlett. You don't want another cop handling your case. I've seen you at your worst. Others won't understand you like I do."

"You understand me?" Bitter amusement vibrated under the words.

The first threats of anger. Progress. "We must talk, Scarlett. You helped kill a woman, murdered another, and tried to suffocate a third. You put a cop in the hospital with a vicious stab wound. You called that officer *Della* multiple times. And this isn't the first time you've confused a woman with this Della."

Scarlett's fingernail dug into the cup.

Dawson focused not on the dead women but the one currently in surgery. Scarlett's latest version of Della had elicited so much anger and rage, she'd attacked her with a knife. "Nineteen stitches. Your knife left a nasty gash on your victim's neck and chest. The doctor said a few more centimeters to the left and you'd have severed her carotid artery. If she'd bled to death, you would be facing another murder charge."

The cup creaked again.

He'd sat across from hardened criminals in this room. Gangbangers, drug dealers, and men who'd strangled their baby mamas to death. Some protested their innocence. Some tried to look bored or indignant when he accused them of attempted murder. Some cried. Scarlett barely blinked.

"I was there when the van crashed a decade ago. I shot and killed Tanner Reed when he drew on me. I helped pull you from the wreckage," he said. "I'm on your side."

She inhaled and exhaled slowly.

"Breaks my heart when I think about pulling you out of that torn metal. What happened to you in that basement should never have happened to any person."

Counselors he'd consulted in the early-morning hours said she managed the old traumas by disassociating. *Quiet. Distant. In her own world.* This was how she coped. The consultant had underlined *Detached* several times.

"Were you always like this?" he asked. "Withdrawn, I mean? As a girl, were you outgoing?"

"You want to talk about my middle school years?" Bitterness pirouetted with amusement.

"I want to start a dialogue with you. I want to help you."

"Then call my lawyer."

"At some point you and I are going to have to talk, Scarlett. You need to tell me what you know."

How did you scare someone who'd been tortured by the devil?

Dawson's fifteen years in the department had armed him with tricks and tactics. Fighting every urge to rail at her, he leaned on his patience. "When did you first meet Officer Margo Larsen?"

She moistened her lips. "Is this information for the case or your own personal reference, Detective?"

He almost protested, then slid back behind a blank stare. "What does that mean?"

"You know." A smile tipped the edges of her lips before she closed her eyes, released the cup, and drew in a deep breath. The muscles in her arms and hands eased, shedding the tension. She'd turned the tables.

"When did you decide to stalk Margo Larsen?" He shifted back to offense. "I've seen the portrait you left for her in her apartment. Odd."

Scarlett blinked. "Her name isn't Margo. It's Della."

"She's Officer Margo Larsen."

"When did you start screwing Della? Did you find her, or did she find you? What itch do you have that she scratched?"

"What's that mean?"

"Della found me. Her smile was so bright, it banished all my fears and worries. That smile lured me into Tanner Reed's van. That smile ruined my life."

"Margo Larsen isn't Della."

"You're wrong. She's Della, and she's come back for me."

Chapter Two

DAWSON

Almost two weeks earlier
Wednesday, July 10, 2024
2:00 p.m.

When Dawson's phone rang, he was eating a sandwich. He'd had an early call at court that morning, which had meant no breakfast. His stomach was ready to eat itself, and he almost tossed the call to voicemail. He chewed faster, then swallowed before offering a gruff "Dawson."

"This is Officer Margo Larsen." He didn't know the name, and the woman's voice sounded irritatingly young.

"Yeah."

"I'm at the scene of a homicide."

He took another bite of his sandwich. "Okay." He swallowed. "Where?"

"It's a home near the Ghent District." The neighborhood that bordered the Elizabeth River dated back to the 1890s, and it was filled with older homes with a European flair. "Dispatch received a call that there was a body on the premises behind a wall. Didn't take long to find it. Looks like it's been here years—a decade, even."

He grabbed a paper napkin and wiped his mouth. "Who called it in?"

"Don't know. Anonymous call to the nonemergency number on July 2. The report got lost in the shuffle."

Dawson sighed. "Male or female?"

"There are several layers of industrial plastic wrap encasing the body. However, the clothes appear to be female."

He dropped the second half of his sandwich onto the crumpled foil and wiped mayo from his fingers with the napkin. "Okay. I'll be there in fifteen minutes. Don't let the medical examiner or anyone else move that body or anything attached to it until I get there."

"Will do."

Dawson was forty-five, and during his years on the homicide team, he had worked hundreds of investigations, including murders, suicides, and unexplained deaths. Early in his tenure, he'd caught all the late-night calls that took him to abandoned buildings, crack houses, back alleys, and even the landfill. Most of the victims had been young, and many of the crimes had been drug related. A body embedded in a wall in the middle of the day was almost a treat.

Dozens of questions rattled through his mind as he grabbed his jacket. When he strode out of the station, he caught a couple of sideways glances. One or two coworkers waved, but the rest ignored him as if his sins were contagious.

It occurred to him as he moved toward his car that he was wearing his good suit because of morning court. Six months ago, he'd have swung by his house and changed because his wife would have given him shit if he messed up a suit fresh from the dry cleaner's. But the wife had kicked him out, and because the site sounded decent, he opted not to stop by his very depressing hotel room to change.

He hung up his jacket in the back seat and slid behind the wheel, and twenty minutes later, he rolled up on the Ghent District town house. He parked on the street behind the marked cruiser.

Centuries-old townhomes arched along the Elizabeth River and were sandwiched between the Norfolk Southern railyards and lower-income neighborhoods to the east. Renovations ranged from paint and plaster to total gut jobs.

He strung his badge around his neck, pushed up his sleeves, grabbed gloves and a notebook, and rose out of the car. He strode down the sidewalk toward yellow crime scene tape wafting around a brick brownstone. The air was moving, but instead of cooling, it churned the hot, humid summer breeze under plump gray clouds.

A uniformed officer, a stocky man with dark skin and bulky biceps, stood at the entrance to the town house. Dawson climbed cracked cement stairs and exchanged introductions.

"Officer Poole, you the first responder?" Dawson asked.

Poole shook his head. "Officer Margo Larsen got the call to check out the property. She's the one that slung the sledgehammer and opened the wall."

"How did she know where to look?"

"Caller gave specific instructions."

"Where is she?"

He nodded his head toward the door. "Near the kitchen."

"Thanks."

He stepped into the dim interior, disappointed it wasn't air-conditioned. If anything, it was hotter. He moved through the living room, past stacks of wallboard and two-by-fours toward skeleton walls displaying dangling wires, galvanized steel pipes, and wooden studs. On the wide-plank pine floors, pale strips hinted at old walls recently demoed.

Around the corner, he found a tall, fit woman wearing jeans and a sleeveless black blouse. Short blond hair accentuated a round face and large green eyes. Sweat dampened her brow. "Detective Dawson?"

"That's right."

"I'm Officer Margo Larsen, and it looks like you met Poole."

"I did."

She angled her head toward three forensic technicians. "I told the team to stand down until you arrived. They've taken pictures and sketched the scene; the others scanned the surrounding area for anything that might need collecting. Dawson, meet Sam, Bill, and Julie."

Dawson's gaze shifted to Sam, the shorter man standing behind her. He had the muscular frame of a weight lifter, thick black hair, and a sour expression. "We've crossed paths before."

"Been a few months," Sam said.

Bill and Julie, both dressed in hazmat suits, nodded. He'd worked with them all. "Can you show me the body, Officer Larsen?"

"Sure."

He followed her to the kitchen, where chunks of wallboard and dust were scattered across the floor.

As he stepped around a pile of dusty white fragments, construction grit kicked up on the shoes he'd polished that morning. Larsen handed him a flashlight, and he clicked it on and shined it up the largest hole. Wedged in between the wall joists was a body wrapped in multiple layers of plastic and bound with duct tape.

"You've completed photographing the scene?" Dawson asked.

"Yes," Julie confirmed. "We were waiting for you before we removed her."

To wrap a body that carefully and shove it into a wall suggested the killer never wanted it found. But time tended to strip away secrets. Buildings got demolished, backhoes dug into vacant fields, and lovers and family members no longer felt the pressure to hold old secrets.

"Any idea when the kitchen was last renovated?" Dawson asked.

Larsen glanced at a small notebook. "I called the real estate agent. He said the house was a flip ten years ago and a renovation was done then. It'll take digging to get the original construction crew's names."

Ten years ago—2014. Hell of a year. "Who currently owns the house?"

"An elderly couple. Both have recently moved to assisted living. The couple's son ordered the renovations. Work started last week."

"Okay." He clicked off the light. "Let's pull the body out."

The forensic techs spread a large blue tarp on the floor in front of the fireplace and then moved toward the hole as he and Larsen stepped back. Julie and Bill grabbed the wrapped legs and pulled. Plastic grated against joists and pink insulation. The shrunken and shriveled form gave way after the second tug. Larsen took hold of the torso as Bill held on to the feet. They lowered the corpse onto the tarp.

Dawson moved closer. The figure reminded him of a horror-movie prop. The arms were folded across the chest, and brittle blond hair twisted around the face.

In 2014, Dawson had been on the job five years. He'd been engaged, newly promoted, and believed he could do no wrong. He thought about the girl he'd been searching for that spring. "Any idea who this is?"

Larsen squatted by the body and surveyed the length of it. Her gaze wasn't rushed, and she didn't appear repulsed. She was intently curious. "The purse might help."

A small purse lay on the victim's chest. Whoever had stowed the body appeared to have cared enough to ensure the victim could be identified in the distant future. Killers, like most people, could have complicated emotions and motivations. Grief for a victim was not uncommon.

"The purse is a pseudo–grave marker," he said, more to himself. "Julie, can you open the plastic and get the purse out?" he asked.

Julie nodded. "Sure. Bill, be ready with the camera."

"Will do," Bill said.

Julie removed a small knife from a tool kit, but she waited until Bill was in position with his camera before she pressed the sharp tip into the brittle plastic. The wrapping cracked and creaked as she dragged the blade in a straight line.

When she had an opening that was about a foot long, she set the knife aside and gently pried open the plastic. Carefully, she removed the small purple purse; unwound the long, thin strap; and laid it on the tarp beside the body.

Dawson stared at the purse with anticipation as Julie opened it and pulled out six items: a silver vinyl wallet, a tube of coral-pink lipstick, a brown hair clip, a hair tie, a ring with three keys, and a silver bracelet.

"Can you check the wallet?" he asked.

As Bill's camera snapped, Julie pried open the wallet's synthetic material. Inside were three crumpled one-dollar bills in the side sleeve and a license in the clear slot.

"What is her name?" Dawson asked.

"Sandra Elizabeth Taylor," Julie said. She dropped the license into a plastic evidence bag and then handed it to him.

Dawson released a breath that had been trapped inside him for a decade. He could never remember his ex-wife's birthday or their anniversary, but he could recall vivid details of unsolved cases.

"Let me run a check on her," Larsen said.

"No need," Dawson said. "I worked her missing persons case in the spring of 2014."

He didn't need to see the DMV picture to visualize a young girl with thick blond hair and bright-blue eyes that sparkled with laughter. "Sandra Elizabeth Taylor was born in 1996. She was five foot four, pretty, Caucasian, and required glasses when she drove. She went missing April 1, 2014."

"That's some memory," Larsen said.

"Her foster family didn't report her missing until early June. After the report was filed, I chased tips for a week, but Sandra's trail was already cold. Foster care, combined with a history of running away, put her low on the priority list, and my boss pressed me to move to the next case. She was last seen at the Shore Drive McDonald's close to Cobb's Marina on a busy Tuesday night, and no one noticed her leave. Her foster mother said Sandra had gone out with several guys, including Tanner Reed."

"Hard to forget Tanner Reed," Julie said.

"Help the new girl out," Larsen said.

Dawson knelt and tried to make out the face obscured by thick plastic. Closed eyes. Tight, drawn features. A mouth pressed shut. "I never proved Tanner Reed was connected to Sandra Taylor."

"Another girl vanished about that time," Julie said.

"June 6, 2014. Tanner held and brutalized that girl for eighty-eight days and then used her to lure another woman into his van. But his captive called for help, so Tanner dragged her back into the van and took off. The van crashed. He came out weapon drawn." And Dawson had shot and killed Tanner before he could fire the first bullet at the growing collection of cop cars.

"Think Tanner killed Sandra Taylor?" Larsen asked.

Dawson sighed. "I wouldn't bet against it." Memories edged forward. "Foster mom had refused to let Sandra date Tanner, who was twenty-nine at the time. I stood at a construction site blocks from here when I interviewed him."

"What happened?" Larsen said.

"Tanner never blinked or appeared the least bit nervous. He had no police record. Said he'd shared a burger with Sandra but had broken any budding relationship off when she told him she was still in high school. The last time I had a conversation with him, he was walking back into the house he was renovating."

"What was the name of the girl who was rescued?" Julie asked. "It wasn't an ordinary name. Saffron. Serena. No, Selene."

"Scarlett Crosby," he said.

"Wonder if Sandra and Scarlett crossed paths?" Larsen asked.

"Very possible," Dawson said.

"Red flags had to have popped up when Scarlett vanished," Larsen said.

"Her mother didn't report her missing until August 2, 2014."

Larsen shook her head. "This case clearly stuck with you."

"It's not an easy one to forget."

When the uniformed officer had opened the van door and they found Scarlett Crosby crumpled on the metal floor, he realized how much he'd fucked up months earlier. Could he have saved Scarlett Crosby sooner if he'd taken a few more moments when he'd interviewed Tanner? If he'd been sharper, smarter, more tuned in to Tanner, he'd have learned of his farmhouse on the Virginia–North Carolina line or that Tanner had been seen flirting with Scarlett, who lived across from where Dawson had interviewed him. Maybe, if he'd kept digging, he could have saved both Sandra and Scarlett.

Dawson stood silent, wrestling with the weight of failure. Add another check to the Loss column.

Chapter Three

SCARLETT

Thursday, July 11, 2024
5:30 a.m.

Standing in the center of my warehouse studio, I stared at the portrait of the young girl. The painting portrayed her wide brown eyes rippling with worry. Coffee-colored hair framed a round face, and full lips were slightly parted, as if she'd been caught midsentence. Freckles dotted the bridge of her nose and her cheeks.

I set my brush down and wiped my hands on a rag already smeared with a mosaic of blacks, reds, whites, and greens. Stepping back, I locked gazes with those painted eyes, wondering what it was I'd missed. Della.

Why didn't Della's gaze align with my memories of her? I'd painted fifty-five versions of Della, but I never quite got the eyes right.

"Della," I whispered, "what am I missing?"

When I looked at her face, I saw kindness and sadness intertwined with a feral need to survive. I also saw my shame, terror, anger, friendship, and sometimes love. So many emotions tangled into one face that had clung to me for a decade.

Della had lured me toward Tanner Reed's van a decade ago. Her smile had drawn me close enough so he could grab me. After he'd clamped his hand over my mouth and dragged me into the van, she'd closed the sliding door and held me down while he jabbed a needle in my arm. Immediately, my vision blurred. I'd focused only on her face as panic scraped under my skin.

Over the years the details of Tanner had faded. His expectant look when he entered my cell, the sound of his whispered words as he pushed inside me, the smell of his stale skin, and the sting of a calloused palm slapping my face. All those horrors should've been permanently welded to him alone, but I could barely remember him now. All my memories had shifted to Della, his helper and my sometime cellmate, sometime friend. For a decade, she'd stalked my nightmares and lurked in my memories. She was the face of old traumas.

"Fuck you, Della."

The alarm on my phone rang. I drew in a breath, pushing through a wave of grief, and slowly turned from the painting. I cleaned my brushes, washed my hands, and changed into a clean black T-shirt, jeans, and boots. I grabbed my bag of paints and brushes and opened the back door to the alley where my truck was parked. After loading my supplies in the back, I climbed behind the wheel. Minutes later, I was on the road.

This early in the morning, the drive to the youth-recreation shelter took less than ten minutes. The facility didn't open until nine, but the security guard was expecting me, and he would let me in the side door.

I parked in the lot near the entrance, rose out of the truck, and shouldered my art bag. I never parked too close to other cars or any collection of trees. I liked a wide field of vision when I exited my vehicle. The other cars were empty.

Drawing in a breath, I locked my truck and walked toward the recreation center's metal doors. The morning air was already warm, and the humidity added weight that would grow oppressive when the day heated. Weather reports said low nineties today. I wasn't in love with the warm weather. My warehouse had fans and wasn't air-conditioned, but no matter what, I never opened a window. Give me snow, ice, and closed windows.

I crossed the lot to the side door and rang the bell, and seconds later it opened. The security guard, Simon, a midsize man with a round belly, salt-and-pepper hair, and a thick mustache, smiled. He'd worked police dispatch for most of his career but last year took early retirement. This part-time security job at the community center wouldn't make him rich, but as he said, it got him out of the house and gave him a place to be. 24-7 with the wife was too much for them both, he often joked.

The heat appeared to be getting to his knee, which had been scoped last winter. He wasn't ready to go under the knife, he'd said at least a dozen times.

"Scarlett. You're early today," he said.

I grinned, scooting past him into the air-conditioned building. "I need to finish the mural. Reception is tonight, and I want to make sure the paint is at least almost dry."

"Been climbing lately?" The familiarity in his tone was amusing and annoying. He thought we knew each other because I listened as he talked about his life. Though he'd shared most of his personal details, I'd revealed scant few. I had a collection of five I distributed. Born and raised in Norfolk. Artist. Rock climber. Astrology sign Aries. Played guitar badly.

Rotating between the five facts satisfied most people. Enough to create the illusion of a bond but not enough to invite more conversation. "Every chance I get. Are the rec room doors unlocked?"

"They are. And the first class isn't until nine a.m. Summer school reading. You've about three hours."

"Perfect. Thanks, Simon." I set my bag on the table to be searched and walked through the metal detector.

He pushed my bag along, not bothering to look inside. "I peeked at the mural. It looks pretty good."

"A few more hours today and I can declare my masterpiece done."

"That *Virginian-Pilot* reporter who was here last week released her story," he said. "The piece ran yesterday."

The Judge, a.k.a. Judge Marcia Thompson, had volunteered me six weeks ago to paint a mural in the cold, sterile cinder block room that did nothing to comfort children who found themselves here for tutoring, classes, or seeking a haven after school. The Judge had requested a mural of a dozen laughing cartoon children. I'd said yes because I'd never been able to say no to her.

I'd been avoiding that reporter until she'd shown up with the Judge as I was packing up my paints last Friday morning. I tossed out my standard fun facts about me and tried not to sound too rude. With each pop of the reporter's iPhone flash, I'd tensed. I'd have refused the interview, but the Judge had insisted. Thankfully, the Judge had done most of the talking.

"I didn't see the article," I said.

"I saved a couple of copies. I'll bring you one."

"You don't have to do that."

"Don't mind at all."

"Okay, thanks." I shouldered my bag, smiling. "Better get going. The Judge likes me wrapped up and out of the center before the kids arrive."

"Right."

"See you at the reception tonight?"

"I'll be here," he said. "I'll bring that article."

"Great."

I walked down the silent hallway, past the photographs of kids playing sports, creating art, reading, and playing board games.

In the recreation room, I found the lights on and the mural I'd been working on for the last month and a half illuminated. Painted bright sunshine dripped from the ceiling, and muddy, black earth rose from the floor.

The mural was a parade of cartoon characters all wearing brightly colored clothes covered in daisies, polka dots, or stars. Each wore sneakers, but many of the laces were untied, several shirts had ripped sleeves, others had scuffed knees, and two had clenched fists. Of the ten characters, eight kept their gazes forward. Only two—the one with curly brown hair and the one with straight blond hair—looked back. All were smiling, and most would label the characters as happy. But they each had challenges. I'd created backstories for them and knew all the kids were damaged and broken in some way.

I'd painted each of the characters as independent creatures. None were holding hands; even the two in the back kept their hands at their sides. Two lessons here: You only have yourself. And under the light, there's always darkness.

Far too much symbolism for ten cartoon characters, but the Judge knew I could get intense, and she was fine with it as long as I didn't put it on full display. The Judge had always been a guardrail for me. She kept me on course but accepted that from time to time, I bounced off a fence. And when I did, she helped mitigate the damage.

I was willing to bet some of the kids who played here would see some of the nuances. Their lives weren't easy or perfect, so it stood to reason their cartoon characters would mirror that. I wanted them, or at least some of them, to see that someone else recognized the imperfections behind the smiles.

When my life had been destroyed, the last thing I'd wanted was to see grins and laughing faces. But the Judge reminded me that smiles sent good and positive messages, and the kids needed that hope.

I spread my drop cloth under the last quarter of the mural and prepared my paints and brushes. Setup took a good twenty minutes. Today, I was putting finishing touches on the last kid, the one with curly brown hair and bright eyes. Technically, she was done, but like the portrait at my warehouse, I felt like I hadn't nailed her. She was a secret-keeper, and she hoarded bits of information from everyone, especially the girl in front of her.

Unlike the portrait, I would have to stop fiddling with this painting. With the opening reception scheduled in twelve hours, I needed to put the brushes down. Time to move on.

As my brush curved along the edge of the little girl's foot, darkening shadows for dimension, the door to the recreation room opened. I glanced over my shoulder, half expecting to see Simon telling me to wrap it up early.

The man standing at the door was about six feet tall and had a tapered waist and broad shoulders. He had an unusual look. A brawler's crooked nose, a square jaw, short black hair, and thick brows. He wore an expensive dark suit, a blue tie, a gold watch, and polished shoes; however, the man didn't quite jibe with the clothes. He was curating an image that wasn't really him.

I'd seen my share of people come through here in the last month, and I was good at guessing their professions. His suit was too nice to peg him as a victims' rights advocate, a state-appointed attorney, or a cop. Silk tie screamed defense lawyer, or maybe a corporate donor.

The guy's gaze searched the room, and it was clear he was in the wrong place. "Do you know where I can find Judge Thompson?"

"She keeps an office on the second floor." If he'd asked me about the restrooms, cafeteria, or basketball court, I could've directed him there, too.

A slight nod suggested he'd acknowledged my information and would leave. Instead, he moved toward me. "What're you doing?"

"Mural for the kids. A favor for the Judge."

"She's hard to ignore." He walked up to the painting. "Nice."

"I wouldn't touch anything. Paint's still tacky."

"Right." He leaned closer and studied the child with long blond hair. "She looks like you."

"Does she?"

"She looks sad."

"She's smiling," I corrected.

"If you say so." He nodded and shifted his gaze to the little boy with the torn pockets. "They're all smiling. But they don't look happy."

His observation surprised me. "It's meant to be fun. Bright and joyful."

"But there are nuances." He regarded me closely. "Risking the obvious, are you a professional artist?"

"I am. Primarily printmaking."

"I'm Luke Kane." He extended his hand. "Judge wants me to join the board of the center."

I held up paint-stained fingers. "Scarlett Crosby."

He lowered his hand as his gaze scanned me. I sensed he'd taken a mental picture of me and filed it away with my name, so that the next time we met, he'd connect the image and name. But we weren't meeting again. "How long have you been working on this?"

"About four weeks."

"I haven't seen you."

"I'm gone before the center opens."

"Looks like you're about finished."

"Ready for the opening reception tonight."

He shifted his gaze from me to the mural. "Lots of undercurrents, Scarlett Crosby."

Frowning, I stared at the smiling cartoon faces. "I thought I was being subtle."

He leaned forward a fraction, as if sharing a secret. "I'm paid to pick up on hidden messages."

"What do you see here?" I challenged.

He slowly pulled his gaze from mine. "The kids are trying to be happy. They're trying to feel normal, but it's hard."

"Wow."

"The work is great, and I don't think the average person will look past the bright colors. Your secret messages are safe."

Secret messages. I was sending out a warning that the world wasn't what we wanted it to be.

"Will you be at the opening?" he asked.

My focus shifted from bright-pink polka dots back to him. "The Judge has requested it."

Even white teeth flashed. "Command performance?"

"Yes."

"Looking forward to seeing you tonight, then."

Desire sparked in his gaze. To his credit, it was subtle. A classy kind of horny. I knew I was attractive. I'm tall, have blond hair and full breasts, and I realized men had noticed me since I was twelve.

Whereas some women understood this power and wielded it to promote or entertain themselves, I'd learned ten years ago that playing with fire risked third-degree burns.

"See you tonight." I knelt to my supplies and began to close paints and wipe off brushes. "I've got fifteen minutes to get cleaned up and out of here before the center fully wakes."

"Sure. I don't want to get in your way." He took a step back.

I reached for the cloth hooked to my belt and wrapped up my brushes, which I would clean thoroughly back at my studio.

"How many hours does something like this take?" Luke asked.

"Ninety to one hundred, give or take."

"All in the early-morning hours?"

"Basically."

"My hat's off to you, Scarlett. Great work."

"Secret messages aside."

He laughed. "They make it interesting."

Having him close and watching me so intently was disconcerting. It was normal for a man and woman in our age range to flirt, but nothing about my interactions with men had been normal. I'd gone from the occasional middle school sloppy kiss to nonstop violence. With no frame of reference or jumping-off point, I couldn't read the signals most women could.

I rolled up my drop cloth, not as neatly as I'd have liked, but I was working quickly because suddenly, I wanted to be out of here. If

I'd been more cautious a decade ago, if I'd made one decision that was slightly different, my life wouldn't have been shattered. Just a moment's hesitation might have allowed me to escape Tanner's grip. A slight pause could have been enough for someone to see him shoving me into the van, and that person might have called the cops. Another squandered moment and I might have missed the bus altogether that night and not been anywhere near Tanner's van parked by the Naro theater.

I'd put the pieces of my life back together, but healed fractures were never as strong as the original. I couldn't risk another hit—this time there might be no fixing me.

"Have a good one, Mr. Kane."

"Luke."

My pursed lips curled into what I hoped was a not-too-friendly but not rude (which could piss him off) smile. I didn't want to suggest any interest on my part.

When I moved toward the recreation room doors, Luke beat me to the handle and opened it. "Good to meet you, Scarlett."

He'd moved too quickly and quietly. It was jarring. "Yes. Right."

I walked past the security checkpoint, waved to the new morning guard on duty, and hurried out the front door to my truck. I slung my items into the back seat and then slid behind the front wheel. My mouth was dry, and my palms were sweating slightly only because I'd been alone with a man in a public space. I glanced in the rearview mirror. Flushed cheeks brightened my green eyes.

I started the truck and shifted it into gear. The drive back took longer in morning traffic, but eventually I parked in the alley behind the warehouse where I lived and worked.

Gray with large windows, it was three thousand square feet. Back in the day, it had been constructed to house goods shipped into the Port of Norfolk.

Located in the center of Norfolk, it was blocks from the NEON art district, a mile from the railyards and ports, and another mile from the tony Waterside District. The Judge had helped me find the space six years ago with the monies she'd raised for me on a GoFundMe page. The property had been in foreclosure, so it had been a steal. I'd had generous offers to sell the building last year, but I liked this once-forgotten and neglected space.

I held my breath as I unloaded my paints and hurried toward the back door. I punched a code into the digital panel and slipped inside. After flipping another half dozen locks, I allowed my gaze to wander to the print blocks, machine presses, paints, and canvases. I let out the breath I'd been holding since I'd left that morning.

As my supplies slipped from my fingers to the concrete floor, I glanced at the Della portrait. I walked up to the three-by-five-foot canvas, reached for a brush, and pressed the bristled edges to barely tacky paint. I was tempted to scrub around Della's eyes, dig into damp layers I'd piled on over the last few days, and rework both. Maybe I could add depth.

Or better, find a way to decouple our molecules that seemed forever cleaved together.

A fist pounded against my front door. Irritated by the distraction, I carefully covered Della's face and moved to the front window. I paused, looked out, and saw a stocky man on my stoop. He was wearing a dark suit that was a bit worn but clean, a white shirt, and a yellow tie. His hair was cut short, and the edges of his sideburns were sharp. At nine in the morning, he was clean shaven, but I bet he'd be sporting a slight five-o'clock shadow by noon. Good, practical dusty black shoes rounded out the look. Behind him, parked by the curb, was a nondescript dark-blue four-door.

I'd crossed paths with enough cops to recognize one. They had a way. Even the kind ones projected an arrogance when they told jokes or tried to be my friend.

After my rescue, I'd been treated as a victim initially. Most cops were nice or pretended to be. Some couldn't sustain eye contact with me because I embodied their worst nightmare. I'd slipped into the victimized versions of their daughters, sisters, or wives.

After I'd been released from the hospital to my mother's care, I'd not thrived. I'd been broken, battered, and very angry. I'd acted out. I drank too much. Did drugs. Got arrested. After my third arrest, alternative theories about Tanner and me arose like thorny weeds in a garden, and as often happened with each new telling, assumptions about me grew darker. By the end, the rumors had repainted me as Tanner's willing accomplice. We were both satanists, we imprisoned girls to breed an army of Tanner's children, or we were wannabe serial killers.

The rumors spread like a blight, tainting all my interactions with the cops over the next year. Each time a cold case grew hot, I received a visit asking me if I knew where to find a missing person. I didn't have any answers, which was always met with stony expressions or threats to lock me up. If not for the Judge, I don't know what would have happened.

The skin on the back of my neck tingled. Who had gone missing or died this time?

The cop's gaze flickered to the window, and for an instant our stares locked. Even as I considered leaving him to stew on his side of the closed door, avoiding him would snowball into more trouble. I was low-hanging fruit on the food chain and too easy to pluck.

I flipped the three locks and unfastened two security chains. Drawing in a breath, I opened the main door but left the mesh metal security door locked. "Can I help you?"

"Scarlett Crosby."

Not a question but a statement. "Who are you?"

He reached in his breast pocket, removed a badge, and held it up to the steel netting, giving me ample time to review his credentials. "Detective Kevin Dawson. We met years ago."

I wasn't going to make this easy for him. "Did you arrest me?"

He replaced his identification back in his pocket. "The first time our paths crossed, I was pulling you from Tanner Reed's van."

All I remembered about that day was heart-stopping panic, a bone-crushing crash, pain, and shots fired. My world had been spiraling. "I don't remember you."

"Not surprising. It was chaotic."

"Yes."

I suppose he needed to hear me say thank you, but I wasn't feeling grateful. "What do you want, Detective Dawson?"

"Wondering if you have a few minutes. I have several questions."

A dull headache formed behind my eyes. "About?"

His expression didn't give any hint to his thoughts. "Better if we don't have this conversation on the street."

"I don't know you, Detective Dawson. I'm going to need more."

His hand slid into his pocket. Change rattled. "Do you remember the second time we met?"

"No."

"It was about two months after you were released from the hospital."

I'd been so high in those days because all I'd craved was nothingness. "No."

"I asked you about a missing girl on that second visit."

"I've vague memories of a younger, thinner man talking to me, but I barely registered a word."

My brutal honesty prompted a half smile. "I was definitely in better shape a decade ago." When I didn't react, he cleared his throat. "A body was found. We believe she's a young girl reported missing in the spring of 2014. She went out with Tanner Reed once."

I stood still, barely breathing. Each time cops brought a query like this to me, I imagined a girl in a dark room screaming, begging for her mother or anyone to please find her. I'd lived as Tanner Reed's captive/whore for eighty-eight days, and I'd been the last to see him alive. The parade of detectives, uniforms, and forensic psychologists had always assumed my insight into Tanner's mind could be the key to all their unsolved cases.

"Was her name Della?" I asked.

He shook his head slowly. "No. Not Della."

The cops never really believed me about Della. They considered her a product of my imagination because I'd been so traumatized. "If it's not Della, I can't help you." A bus rumbled behind him, and a horn honked.

"I've read your file. I understand your hesitancy." He attempted to soften his tone, as if compassion were a rusty implement in his toolbox. I didn't open the door.

"It's important we talk. Now." Impatience bucked under his words, but he kept it reined in as if it had hurled him into too many disasters before. However, his rigid legs and braced back told me he would stand here and wait until I spoke to him.

I opened the lock. Hinges groaned as I pressed the door toward him. He grabbed the door's edge and pried it open until there was nothing separating us.

My heartbeat quickened. Blood rushing, my head pounded against my temples—both sensations harbingers of a panic attack. It had been a year since I'd had a bad one. That episode had been triggered by an envelope filled with newspaper clippings about Tanner and me. I never figured out who had sent it or why anyone would bother to taunt me after all these years. For the weeks after the envelope had arrived, I'd had trouble sleeping.

Drawing in a deep breath, I stepped back, giving him a wide berth. I closed the security door behind him but didn't lock it.

Dawson's gaze scanned the interior of my warehouse space. Old brick walls stretched toward a twenty-foot metal ceiling supported by steel rafters. Five large skylights allowed in bright sunshine that mingled with the light from ten round industrial pendant lights.

Some of my prints hung framed on the brick walls, but most had been sold either via commission or at local shows in the art community's NEON district.

He looked toward a portrait of a blond woman, her face turned away from the artist. "May I get a closer look?"

Impatience elbowed through rising panic. "Of course."

He walked up to within inches of the print and leaned toward it. "Detail's amazing."

"Thank you."

His attention remained on the painting another beat before he turned. "That one hasn't sold?"

"Some don't. I'll try again at the fall art festival. You interested?"

He smiled. "More of a framed poster kind of guy."

"Nothing wrong with that." Folding my arms, I waited for him to get to the point.

Some of the ease faded from his features. "Do you remember Sandra Taylor?"

"She's the girl you're looking for?"

"Yes. She'd be about your age. She's the one who vanished a few months before you."

"I don't know her."

"Did Tanner ever mention her?"

"No. He rarely spoke to me. He was never interested in conversation."

Dawson's jaw pulsed. "She looked like you. Did a little part-time waitress work. She went to East Norfolk High School like you."

"You keep referencing her in the past tense."

He drew in a breath. "We believe we've found her body."

The Other Girl. "Della mentioned the Other Girl when she was warning me about being defiant. But I never met or saw her. It was just me and Della."

He reached for his phone, pressed a couple of buttons, and then turned the screen toward me. "This is Della, correct?"

I'd drawn Della's face for the detectives who'd been interviewing me. No traces of the girl had been found in the incinerated remains of Tanner's house, and she hadn't matched up with any missing person cases. After a time, detectives stopped believing in Tanner's mystery girl.

Looking at the old cartoonish image with its immature pencil strokes, reminded me of how young I'd been when I drew the picture. I was amazed how crude my work had been a decade ago. Della sketch #1.

Re-creations of Della's face had been literal at first, but after years and multiple drafts, Della's face took on different incarnations. Queens. Fairies. Aliens. Sirens. No matter the form, the face and especially the eyes were the same.

"That's her," I said.

"Della never mentioned Sandra by name?"

"No. But she spoke about another girl."

"What did Della tell you about the other girl?"

He didn't believe in Della and must have thought my poor mind had broken and my personality split. "Della told me there'd been another girl in the house. Della said she vanished suddenly."

"Did Della tell you anything else about this other girl?"

The air palpitated with a dizzying energy. "We talked about a lot of things. We didn't talk about the Other Girl much. We both feared we'd end up like her."

"Why do you think Della was never found?"

"I don't know. Tanner's house burned to the ground after my rescue. Maybe she set off all the bombs he'd planted before she ran." I stood silent, staring at him, hoping to peel back a layer or two so I could discern what he was after. People rarely meant what they said. There was always a hidden agenda.

His brown eyes watched me closely. "Sandra Taylor's phone was found with her body. It's old and the techs are hoping to breathe life into it. Will I find any call exchanges between you two on it?"

I couldn't determine whether he was sincere. Cops weren't bound by truth when conducting an interview. All's fair in love and war, in a manner of speaking. "I never talked to Sandra Taylor. Ever."

"The house where we found her body is around the corner from your mother's, which I believe you now own."

"Tanner did several renovation projects in our neighborhood. He was working a job across the street from our house when I first saw him." On a bad day, bitterness would have dripped from those words. Today, my anger was in check.

"Did Tanner approach you, or you him?" Dawson asked.

I almost appreciated the brisk, efficient question. He wasn't dancing around my past. "I was sitting on the front porch of my mother's house and sketching. He asked to see the drawing. He said it was nice."

"Did he ask you out on a date?"

"No." But he'd been so charming, and for the first time in a long time, I'd felt seen. I'd have said yes to a date.

"How soon after that conversation did he take you?"

"Three days. It was a hot Friday. June 6. I was outside the Naro theater on Colley Avenue."

"You were selling your art."

"Trying to. I'd had no takers. And then Della walked up to me. That was the first time I ever saw her."

"She lured you to Tanner's van?"

"Yes."

"You got in willingly?"

The noose of his suspicions tightened around my neck. "I approached it willingly."

"After your run-in with Tanner, you were arrested multiple times."

Run-in. Eighty-eight days of torture and sexual abuse. Detective Dawson made it sound so simple. No mention of chains, isolation, or starvation. "You don't strike me as the clueless type, Detective."

"I'm not," he said.

"Then why are you trying to get under my skin?"

"I'm not."

"Run-in?" I said, more to myself.

"Maybe I understated it a bit."

His quiet judgment made me angry. I smoothed my hands over my hips. "I can't help you, Detective Dawson. I'm sorry about Sandra Taylor. I hope you find her killer. She deserves justice."

He reached in his side pocket, pulled out a worn leather case, and removed a card. He extended his hand, the card dangling from the tips of his fingers.

I hesitated and then took the card, careful not to touch him. Detective Kevin Dawson. City of Norfolk Police. Criminal Investigations. "I'll call if I have information."

Nodding, he moved toward the door. The mesh security door squeaked, but he paused. "There were four missing persons reports filed the spring you vanished. You were one of them and Sandra was the second. The other two girls were never found. But no Della."

"So I've been told."

"Tanner never asked you to help him lure another girl, other than Tiffany Patterson, correct?"

Tanner had targeted Tiffany, a young waitress with red hair who worked at his favorite diner. Ten years ago, Tiffany had been a thin, nervous girl with a strip of freckles splayed over the bridge of her nose. She was older, wearier these days, but basically the same. "Correct."

"When's the last time you spoke to Tiffany Patterson?"

"A few weeks ago."

"You're in contact with her?" No missing his surprise.

"She has a drug problem. She came to me about six months ago asking for money. I don't give her money, but I feed her every time I see her."

He surveilled me with a hawkish glare. "Why would she come to you for help?"

"She feels like I owe her."

"What did you say to her ten years ago to coax her outside?"

I suspected he knew the answer, but for the sake of this performance: "I recited the story Tanner gave me. I told her there were puppies in the back parking lot behind the dumpster. She got excited and followed me." Tiffany's upbeat chatter still could rattle in my head. Such optimism that I'd helped crush. "I don't remember what she said to me."

"Tanner was there waiting by his van."

"Yes."

"You coaxed Tiffany to within five feet of his vehicle, according to the surveillance footage."

"Yes." I pictured Tiffany moving toward me, a curious smile tweaking the edges of her lips. As when Della had beckoned me, there'd been no worry or concern. Tiffany's future, like mine, had boiled down to seconds. A delay of one or two determined whether her life would stay the same or descend into hell.

One moment.

"You saved her life," Detective Dawson said.

I remembered Tanner smiling. And the next word I'd said to her was *Run!* "Yes."

I'd saved the young girl with trusting eyes and a bright smile, but I'd also been seconds away from betraying her on Tanner's promise that Della and I would be freed. I'd been prepared to send a young girl, body and soul, into hell. And then at the very last second, for reasons I still didn't understand, I'd changed my mind. "She also saved mine."

The security door squeaked closed as he moved toward me, stopping a few feet short. Far enough away so I didn't panic but close enough to make it impossible for me to ignore him. He removed a notebook from his breast pocket. "And now you take care of her?"

"When I can. Yes."

"Tiffany communicated with you after your rescue, correct?"

"She wrote me a note expressing her gratitude." I'd torn up the note and thrown it into the trash, knowing whatever hero Tiffany saw didn't exist. I'd been a coward who'd had a lapse of decency. I'd also been furious and resentful of the girl who'd been gifted with that precious moment of hesitation denied to me. I might still be. "I didn't respond to any of her notes."

"How many did she write?"

"Three."

"No contact with her until last year?"

"Are you looking for a specific answer?"

A frown furrowed his brow. He was fishing, but not getting any bites. "Just the truth. You said Della was often locked up with you."

"Yes, but Tanner had a different relationship with her. She wasn't always confined in the room with me. Many times, he let her sleep upstairs with him. She had more freedom, if you could call it that."

Pages in his notebook flipped. "You said he treated her like a wife."

"Yes."

More pages turned over. "And Della never told you why he beat her up that last day."

"No."

"Had he beaten her that badly before?"

"Not that I'd seen."

"Tanner trusted you enough to lure Tiffany to the van?"

"Yes."

"Why was he so sure about you?"

Another mystery I'd not been able to solve. "Della said I could be trusted because I'd stopped fighting. I'd accepted my new life."

"Why did you stop resisting?"

"The less I fought, the less it hurt."

When I didn't elaborate, he said, "Why did you target Tiffany?"

"I didn't. Tanner did."

"He'd seen Tiffany before?"

"Della told me she and Tanner had been to the diner a few times that spring."

"Tiffany didn't remember them when asked by the detectives."

"They'd picked busy times. Easier to blend in, Della said."

"Why did you agree to do it?"

How many ways could I explain myself? My head spun, sucking in the circling shadows. "You make it sound like I had a choice."

"We always have choices." He drew in a breath.

"Live in Tanner's basement for eighty-eight days and then we'll talk about choices."

Suspicion tinted his gaze. "What did Tanner promise you if you got Tiffany to the van?"

"A hamburger. And he said he might let me go."

"And you went along."

"I didn't go through with it."

"You took it right up to the edge."

"I was desperate. And if you really were at the crash that day, you know I was in bad shape."

"I'm not denying you didn't suffer." His discomfort gave me some pleasure.

"But desperation doesn't warrant what I almost did, right?"

He was silent for a moment. "And Della, the woman who lured you into Tanner's trap, vanished just like that. And the house where he'd kept you both burned to the ground."

"Yes."

"Ever wonder what happened to Della after your rescue and the fire?"

When I'd heard about the fire, I thought she'd died in it. I'd no doubt the house and anyone in it had been obliterated, given how many gasoline bombs had been planted. I'd wept bitterly. Only later, when the arson investigators had sifted through the rubble, did I learn the police had found no bodies in the ruins. "I have."

How many times had I had Della sightings? How many times had I run after or screamed at women who'd borne a vague resemblance to Della?

"You filed six police reports over the last ten years, swearing you saw this Della."

The initial two reports were met with keen interest. After that, the officers took me less seriously. "The cops proved I was wrong every time."

"Would you say you were fixated on Della?"

"Maybe. I don't know." I swelled with a sudden hollowness. One psychologist suggested I was shifting blame to the fictitious Della to help me deal with the guilt.

"Do you dream about Tanner?"

"No, not really."

"Why not? He's the stuff of nightmares."

Get off me! Get off me! I still woke up screaming those words. "Easier for me to put him out of my mind."

"But not Della."

Before Della, I'd been a moody teenager who worried about homework and parties. After Della lured me into the van, I was distant and distrustful. I might have physically survived, but the girl I'd been had died.

A tension crept up my back and coiled around my neck. "I'm not sure what you're fishing for, but I can't help you." My head spun. "I've got an appointment in a half hour. I need to leave."

He hesitated. "I'll be back if I find out more about Sandra Taylor. And I'm sure there'll be more questions."

"And I still won't be able to help you."

He left, and as soon as the security door closed, I locked it and slammed the security door behind it. All locks were secure in under ten seconds, a drill I practiced often.

Detective Dawson walked to the curb to his unmarked dark-blue car and got behind the wheel. He sat staring at my building for a long moment before he started his car and drove off.

Della was real. I knew it. She wasn't a figment of a traumatized mind.

But the cops had never found her, and the more I'd told Della's story, the more they questioned my mental stability. So I stopped talking about Della after the last failed sighting three years ago.

After ten years, there was still no sign of Della.

But the cops were circling again.

Chapter Four

Scarlett

Then
Friday, June 6, 2014
9:00 p.m.

I didn't think of myself as an artist. I liked to draw. I'd even mustered enough courage to sketch the contractor working across the street. He had a Paul Walker kind of vibe (if Paul weren't dead), and when he smiled, I sizzled.

When he'd crossed the street on Tuesday and asked me my name, I'd felt special. Seen. He told me his name was Tanner Reed.

Tanner. Tanner. Tanner.

We kind of flirted even though he was older. He asked about my art, and I showed him my sketch pad. He looked impressed and said I should try to sell it. I mentioned trying to sell at the concert at the Naro theater. The venue was a mile from my house, and the show, an '80s band, was sold out. He told me to give it a whirl.

I was stoked this evening as I packed up my few drawings and took the bus to the corner of Colley and Shirley Avenues. I set up, which basically meant laying out a beach towel and placing my five drawings on the ruby terry cloth. The paper was flimsy and easily caught whispers of wind, so I placed rocks on the corner of each. However, random breezes teased the edges all night.

I felt lucky. The music drifting from the '80s concert was decent. A lot of old people came and went, but they were laughing and smiling. Even under the city lights, the stars were so vivid. Maybe Tanner would show.

As the evening passed, people walked by; a few glanced in my direction, but most looked at me as if they were afraid that I'd catch their gazes and chase them down. As time passed, doubt took root and grew quickly.

I glanced down at the self-portrait and drawings of the bay and homes in the area, and I realized this was a dumb idea. The air was hot, even at nine o'clock at night, and my feet ached.

"What do you have there?"

The young woman's attention drew my gaze up. She wasn't much older than me, and she wasn't someone I'd have noticed right off. Curly shoulder-length brown hair drew my attention to wide-set eyes and full lips. She wore cutoff jeans, a cropped T-shirt, and flip-flops. A belly button ring peeked out from her midriff.

I smiled, grateful to be seen. "I'm selling my art. Nothing fancy."

She leaned in and inspected each piece. "That's you in this picture, isn't it?"

"It is." I sketched a lot of self-portraits. I was an easy subject to find, and each time I drew a different version of me, I saw something different. I'd scribbled *Girl Ready to Escape* across the bottom. "I was practicing portraits."

She looked at me and then back at the picture. "It's really good."

"Thanks."

"I'm Della."

"I'm Scarlett."

Her hand trembled very slightly when she tucked a strand of hair behind her ear. "It's so nice out here. Better than inside the concert hall. Hot as hell inside, and the band has blown a fuse twice."

"What do you like about eighties music?"

"Not as much as I thought." Laughing, she picked up the drawing of me. "You've always been an artist?"

Artist was too pretentious. *Think you're something, don't you?* Mom often said. "I've always drawn. This is the first time I've tried to sell anything."

Della held up a sailboat on the bay. "Can I buy one?"

"Sure."

"How much?"

I'd never thought about how much to charge because I never thought I'd really sell anything. "Ten dollars."

Della fished a twenty-dollar bill out of her pocket. "Do you have change?"

"No, sorry."

"Come with me to my van. I have my wallet under the seat."

I glanced at my flapping sheets of art and then carefully collected them. I knew enough that if I left them behind, they'd get swiped.

When we rounded the corner onto the shadowed side street, I saw the open van door but didn't think twice about it. I didn't see it as a gateway or a portal to the underworld. It was just a door, opened to an empty space.

When I reached the door, I glanced past Della to the interior. It was a metal box with blacked-out windows, no seats or carpet. The interior smelled of urine, blood, and sweat-soaked bodies. I recoiled. In that split second, my instincts screamed, *This is wrong!*

Della's smile didn't falter as she climbed in the van's cab. "Come on. My wallet is right here."

Common sense flickered to red alert. Who leaves a van door open with a wallet inside in the city? A part of me needed to believe her. Della was nice, and she wanted to buy my art. I didn't scream or run. I followed willingly.

As I hesitated, strong hands shoved me into the van. I stumbled forward, and Della threw her body on mine. A needle pricked my arm.

A scream gurgled in my throat and then faded as invading drugs captured and silenced my voice. My vision blurred. The van door slammed closed.

As handcuffs clinked around my wrists, I looked up into dark eyes looming inches from my face. Confusion mingled with terror. I recognized the man, and at first, I was oddly relieved. He'd waved to me yesterday and smiled. Tanner. I'd been charmed. He was so nice. And hot.

I believed for a split second that I'd been saved. Close call. As my vision deteriorated, I still believed hell would have to wait.

But the eyes that once stared at me with so much warmth had cooled with the cruel amusement of a hunter trapping prey.

"Why?" I asked.

Tanner was already climbing behind the wheel as Della sat beside me.

She stroked my hair. "I'm sorry. I'm sorry."

A scream lodged in my throat, but when it escaped, it sounded like a sad moan. "Noooo."

As Tanner angled the van and shifted gears into higher speeds, Della nestled closer. "Shh. It'll be fine. You're not going to die."

The vehicle rumbled down the potholed side street. The drugs mingled with the hum of the engine, paralyzing me in a twilight. Awake, but unable to move or speak.

My head spun, my hands grew numb, and the metal van floor rubbed my bony spine. My pants grew damp, and color rose in my face when I realized I'd peed. I was humiliated.

The van kept driving for what felt like hours. Where were we going? Was he driving in circles? The constant rocking of the van made my stomach so uneasy. Bile rose in my throat. When the van finally stopped, I had no idea how long we'd been traveling. The side door opened. Fresh air rushed the cab. Stars glistened through trees.

Della hopped out as Tanner came around the side of the van. Her expectant smile faltered as she met his gaze.

He hauled me out of the van and hefted me on his shoulder. As I looked up, I saw Della slam the van door. Boots climbed three old wooden steps. Through the haze I saw an old gray farmhouse. We were in the country. How far were we from Norfolk? At least thirty or forty miles.

Tanner kissed Della on her cheek. "Good girl. You've earned a burger."

"You're going to let her go, right?"

"Sure, baby. Sure."

Later, when the drugs faded, and the trapped cries escaped, Tanner didn't let me go. And I screamed until my throat was raw.

Chapter Five

Scarlett

Thursday, July 11, 2024
6:00 p.m.

The dedication reception for the recreation center was packed. Judge Thompson had her fingers in a lot of political pies in this city, and when she said *jump*, the smart people asked how high. I was no exception. She'd saved me, and I could never turn my back on her.

Obligations aside, based on the laughter blending with the blues quartet, the guests were having a good time. *God. People. Crowds.* Tension radiated over my skin.

I moved toward the front door, where Simon stood checking names off a list attached to his clipboard. I held back as the line thinned, and when Simon looked up and saw me, he grinned.

"About time. I thought you were going to ditch," he said.

I smiled. "Running late. I was finishing up a painting." The truth was I'd been sitting in my truck for the last forty-five minutes, scraping together the reasons why I should attend.

"Everyone loves your mural." He reached for a newspaper.

"Nice."

"And there are already several bids on the print you donated."

"Wonderful."

"Reporters want to talk to you. Speaking of which, here's last week's article about you."

I glanced at the front page of the style section, glimpsed my frozen smile, and rolled the paper into a cylinder. "Thank you."

"Sure thing. I got your back."

I scanned the crowd. "Didn't I talk to a few of these people last week?" I'd been swamped by reporters before. All had had the glinting eyes of rabid coyotes.

He laughed. "Don't look so pained. This is all very positive. Publicity is never a bad thing."

"Speak for yourself." A couple exited the front door, laughing arm in arm. The casual way they touched each other was charming, and I envied their intimacy. But I'd crossed too many bridges and was too lost to enjoy that kind of closeness.

"Better get inside. Judge is asking about you."

"Right."

I moved past Simon into the crowded recreation center that had been so quiet and peaceful this morning.

"Finally."

I turned to see Judge Thompson, a tall, lean woman in her early sixties. She wore a black pantsuit with an aqua blouse that flattered a salt-and-pepper ponytail, dark skin, high cheekbones, and pearl earrings.

I had first met Judge Thompson when I was sixteen. I'd been in foster care since shortly after I'd run away from home, and though my foster mother had been kind to me, she'd had rules and expectations, two things I'd never had in my mother's home. I'd grown accustomed to setting my own hours, attending school when it suited me, and working on my art late into the night.

This foster family didn't believe in violence, so they locked offending kids in a windowless room called the Quiet Space. I was terrified of that room, so I was careful to follow rules.

There were other kids in the mix, and basically the girls and I got along well. One girl painted my nails a bright pink with sparkles. Another brushed my hair and twisted it into a bun. Another tried to teach me how to play guitar.

For thirty days, I'd focused on my drawing and pretended the pink sparkle nail polish, blue eye shadow, and music were important. Then a girl in the house named Serena had learned about Tanner, and she'd started gossiping about it. When she'd called me his slut, I'd punched her hard in the face, and when my foster mom tried to toss me into the Quiet Space, I'd really lost it. I broke her nose.

I ended up on the streets for a few days, living in doorways and avoiding the drug dealers and pimps. But I'd gotten arrested for shoplifting and landed back in the Judge's court. This time she'd suggested I live with her. She had had eight other foster kids before. I wasn't so sure, and neither was she, but I was tired of being hungry and surviving on little or no sleep. After a few tense days, I relaxed a fraction, and I think I stopped sleeping with one eye open. The Judge's house was my first brush with normal, and even though I knew I'd never be *normal*, I had an inkling of what it could be.

"You've got quite the crowd," I said to the Judge.

She smiled, satisfied. "Arm twisting is my superpower."

I rubbed my forearm. "I felt the pressure."

The Judge grinned. "You can endure a crowd for a little bit of time. And when you smile for the cameras in five minutes, I'll release you early for time served."

I grimaced. "Pictures."

The Judge laughed. "You'll survive. Don't go far. I have two donors to thank, and then it's showtime."

"Terrific."

The Judge placed her hand on my shoulder, and I only flinched a little. "Have a drink. The white wine is decent."

"Right." I crossed to the bar and got in the back of a line ten people deep.

"Are you the star of the evening?"

The familiar deep masculine voice had me turning toward the man I'd met here this morning. He still wore the same suit but had changed his shirt and tie. "I hope not."

"Why?" He looked genuinely curious. "You should be proud of the work."

"I am. Just not a fan of the attention."

Gray eyes appeared to be cataloging every detail associated with me, including a black silk blouse, faded jeans with a raw-edge hem, and Doc Martens sandals. Gold hoops winked from my ears, and most of the paint was scrubbed from my hands. This was as good as it got for me.

However, I wasn't so far gone that I didn't see the appreciation in his eyes again or that he was an attractive man. Oddly, I didn't mind his attention. However, the attraction was doomed to be metaphorically strangled in the cradle.

"Hard to say no to Judge Thompson," he said.

"You're right about that."

"Are you drinking?"

"Judge has ordered me to drink a glass of wine."

He turned, plucked a glass of white wine from a waiter's tray, and handed it to me. "Never ignore a judge's ruling."

"Thank you." I sipped my wine. "What hold does she have over you?"

He laughed. "Always good to support the judges."

"Do you handle a lot of juvenile cases?"

"I worked in the prosecutor's office for ten years. She and I crossed paths many times. I like Judge Thompson. Fair but tough."

"You said *worked*. What do you do now?"

"Criminal defense. I focus on adults. The kids are tough and heartbreaking."

"I can only imagine."

"That mural was a serious time commitment. You must really owe the Judge."

"Maybe a little."

The comment piqued his attention. What had I done to fall under the Judge's radar? No doubt he was compiling a series of crimes in his head.

"You can see my mind working, can't you?" he said.

"I'm likely not guilty of ninety percent of what you're considering."

"Now I'm curious about the ten percent."

He was flirting with me. Subtle. Charming. And I appreciated that. Wine always loosened my bowstring nerves, but as soon as the tension eased, I put the glass down. I knew a second glass of wine would stir an unwanted, dangerously enticing curiosity about couples who held hands casually and kissed easily.

"How did your early-morning meeting go with the Judge? Did she sell you on a board position?"

When he smiled, I churned. "She did."

"Ah. She'll keep you busy."

"So I've been told." A beat of silence hummed between us. "How did you meet the Judge?"

There'd been a time when I made up answers to hide the past, but this time I broke with the norm and told the truth. "She was my foster mother for a couple of years."

A brow arched. Did I not fit the mold of a foster care kid? "I've heard she does that." He didn't press me for details, but if he'd worked enough juvenile cases, he could fill in the blanks. "Looks like you turned out okay."

Normal uncoiled and tried to rise, moving like an old woman with bad joints. "Good to know."

Judge Thompson stepped up to a microphone in front of the mural. "Ladies and gentlemen . . ."

Finally, an excuse to turn away from Luke's sharp gaze and focus on the next challenge.

"I'm so thrilled you could be here for our dedication," the Judge continued. "Let me offer a special thank-you to Scarlett Crosby, the artist who painted this stunning mural."

Eyes shifted toward me, and several people clapped. I stood my ground, scrounged up a smile, and waited for them all to move on to the next thing.

"Scarlett, come up onstage with me," the Judge said.

Tension climbed up my vertebrae, coiling around my neck and settling heavy over my shoulders. Crowds came with lots of eyes and many memories. Someone would put the pieces together. Their whispers would stir uncomfortable questions that triggered inevitable nightmares.

"It's not a firing squad," Luke whispered.

Annoyance snapped when I looked at him.

He grinned. "Ouch. If looks could kill."

That tamed the anger and coaxed a smile. "That obvious?"

"Afraid so." He leaned forward a fraction. "They can't eat you. Find a smile on the way to the stage. Everyone is here to celebrate your work."

Thanks to Della, I could shove my fear down until I couldn't feel it. Later it would scratch its way to the surface, but that was a problem for another time. "You're right. Thank you for saying that."

His eyebrows drew together as I turned toward the stage and walked through the parting crowd. I kept my arms pressed tight to my body and my gaze on the Judge.

I stepped up on the stage, unearthed a brittle smile as the Judge detailed her dream to make this recreation center more approachable for children. She raved about the work I'd put into the mural, my dedication to my craft, *blah, blah . . .*

When the crowd clapped, I smiled on cue, fielded a few questions about my work, and did my best to provide answers that didn't sound surly or impatient. The reporters' questions stuck to the project, and none delved deeper. After a decade, I always hoped my former troubles were long forgotten, pushed out of the headlines by the serial killer on

Long Island and the plane that went down in the Atlantic last year. One psychologist called it "bread and circuses." I was one of a million sensational stories that grabbed public attention for a little while and then were soon forgotten. However, those who wanted to remember me only needed a five-second internet search.

A few folks in the crowd expressed their delight at my work and thanked me for my service. A few said they'd bid on the print I'd donated. All in all, it wasn't terrible, but the attention was too much. I made my escape out the side door less than an hour after my arrival.

As I crossed the dimming parking lot, a car's headlights flashed, drawing my attention to a black sedan to my right. The beaming bright lights dilated my pupils, effectively blinding me. The sedan's engine rumbled. The car didn't move. Odd. And I didn't like odd or being around cars.

My eyes adjusted, and I realized no one was behind the wheel. Then a thirtysomething woman with short blond hair, dressed in jeans, a silk top, and heels, weaved her way through parked cars toward the sedan. Her downcast gaze didn't dart in my direction as the confident click of her heels telegraphed an enviable nonchalance. Door open, purse tossed on the passenger seat, and a check of her lipstick in the rearview mirror.

I'd never seen the woman before, but a shrill of recognition rattled through my body. My thoughts skipped to the portrait of Della alive with dark curly hair, a round face, and wide doe eyes. Nothing about my Della jibed with this woman, but an oily familiarity coiled in my chest. My breath caught in my throat as my thumb slid to the button on the pepper spray attached to my key chain.

The woman closed her door, fastened her seat belt, and slid the car into gear.

I never walked through a parking lot without my keys and pepper spray in hand. And I never looked at my phone. Never. My focus was always on my surroundings. I never lost track of my truck. I memorized landmarks, remembered lot numbers, and counted spaces to the end of the row.

As the car zoomed past me, I wanted to yell out a warning. *Be careful! Pay attention!* But I didn't. I stood silent, wondering why I was suddenly so worried for a woman I didn't know.

"You all right?"

Luke's voice startled me, and I turned to see his gaze idling on me. His expression was part curious and a little concerned.

Smiles always defused worries, so I found a wry grin. "Lost my truck for a second. Not used to all the vehicles."

"Easy to get turned around." He moved toward me, his stride confident and steady. "You bugged out quick."

Absently, I threaded my keys through my fingers. "I did my due diligence. Time to jet."

"Have any other volunteer projects on the table?"

"No, time to focus on the paying work. Got a little behind." That wasn't true. I was caught up because all I did was paint and work out.

"What do you do when you're not painting or volunteering your time for the Judge?"

"Rock climbing is my latest challenge."

"I work out at a gym on Lindsay Avenue. There's a wall there."

"That's my wall."

"I can't picture you climbing."

"Why?"

"You strike me as the cerebral type. I see you visiting art museums and exhibits."

"I do, but that's kind of like work. On the rocks, it's just me, the crevices, and the present."

"Keeps you focused."

"Mind can't wander."

"Does it tend to wander?" he asked.

I'd said more than I'd intended. "You ask a lot of questions, Luke."

A hand slid into his pocket as bulky shoulders folded in a fraction in quasi contrition. "Hazard of the business. And I'm interested in you."

His awareness was part of the reason that I'd exited the party early. I'd been hoping to avoid this conversation. "That so?"

Luke stepped toward me until a few feet separated us. He made no move to touch me, but his energy pulsed against my skin.

I gripped the keys tighter.

"Would you like to grab a drink sometime?" he asked.

A drink. Easy if I kept it to one, which I would. A busy, public venue would ease my worries. And I would meet him. And then something would trigger me, I'd freak, and the date would go off the rails as they all did. But I'd spent too much time alone lately, so what the heck? Muscles puckered in my gut. "Where do you have in mind?"

"Pick a place close to your studio or apartment."

"Lito's?" It was a few blocks from my studio. Well-lit parking and several exits.

"Great choice. It's close to my office. Saturday?"

"I'm working until about five, but I can be there by six."

His lips curled into a smile. "You'll have to tell me all about it. See you then, Scarlett."

"Okay." I pressed my key remote and my truck lights blinked. "This is me."

"Excellent."

Shit. "Terrific."

Luke waited until I was behind the wheel, seat belt on, and the engine started. When I glanced in the rearview mirror, his attention had shifted to a black SUV.

Drive time provided the opportunity to nurture future regrets about Luke. If I didn't blow the date after drinks and conversation, he'd ask me out again. He'd try to kiss me. Then I'd panic, say no as a reflex, and vanish. Ghosting was my thing.

I parked behind my warehouse under the security light above the back door. This time of night, it wasn't hard to find parking. It could be an issue on weekend evenings, when people came into the area to drink at the breweries or bars and decided an open alley was fair game. But on a Thursday night, I had it all to myself.

Keys in hand, purse on my shoulder, I slid out of the truck and locked it immediately. I crossed quickly to the door and pressed in the door code. Scattered by the door was a pile of crumpled newspapers. As I collected them, I noted the headline referencing the recreation center. I unfurled a page and realized it was the article on me. I balled up the brittle paper, wondering if this was someone providing a copy or someone screwing with me.

Inside, I secured the main latch and then the secondary ones. I tossed the newspapers in the trash can, washed my hands, and kicked off my shoes. Residents on my block knew me well enough to kid me about my door locks, but the conversations generally ended there.

I fished my phone from my purse and realized Tiffany Patterson had texted me.

I paused and read the text.

I need to talk to you. It's important.

Tiffany. What did she want now? My guess was she was coming off a high and looking for a new hit.

Bracelets rattled as I ran long fingers through my hair. This was the fourth text from Tiffany in as many weeks. Each time I'd responded, she'd not returned my messages. She flaked often, so I never gave it much thought. **Where are you? Are you okay?**

I stared at the display, willing Tiffany to respond.

But the phone's screen remained blank. No words, no bubbles, no sign that Tiffany had seen my text. Dawson's visit churned fresh worries, and my mind drifted to darker places.

I sat on my couch and leaned back. Not so weird that someone would leave a copy of the article, but these had been balled up. It was likely innocent. Trash happened in cities. No need to panic, right? All normal.

But I wasn't normal. Hard lessons had taught me to make the difficult decisions so I could survive. Plenty would judge me for the decisions I'd made when I was with Tanner. They'd wonder why I got into the van, why I didn't fight harder, or why I didn't walk into Mike's Diner screaming for help immediately. People liked to believe that the world was separated into black and white or good and evil. But it wasn't so clearly divided. A spectrum of grays linked morality to sin. We all had the power to dip into the dark side if it meant living or dying.

I rose, changed into a large T-shirt and paint-splattered cutoff jean shorts, and tied my hair into a ponytail. In my studio room, I uncovered Della's portrait. I checked my paintbrush, scrubbing the dry bristles over the back of my hand as I stared into the dark eyes glaring back at me.

Della knew me better than anyone. Della knew my darkest secrets, the compromises I'd made to stay alive. She knew the shame I'd never shared with my mother, the police, the Judge, or any therapist. Della had witnessed what I'd do if driven to the brink, and she was the only person on this earth who wouldn't judge me, because she had also embraced the darkness to endure. We were two sides of the same coin.

Victim and captor.

Frenemies for life.

That night I dreamed of the dark, damp basement room and chains encircling my ankle.

Chapter Six

SCARLETT

Then
A day or two later in the basement

When I woke up, I blinked into the darkness. Confusion gave way to fear as I realized I was on a thin mattress in a small room. I was naked. My bracelet and necklace were gone. I sat up too quickly and my head spun. I toppled back, willing my stomach to quiet and the tightness behind my eyes to ease.

After several beats, my body steadied and calmed. My fingers ran over the coarse mattress fabric. No sheets. No blankets.

Slowly, I tried to sit a second time. I couldn't see anything in the room and was forced to feel my way to the edges of the mattress and then to a cool brick wall. I trailed fingers over the wall's rough, porous surface until they ran into the next corner. Maybe five feet. The next corner was ten feet away. A smooth metal door was on the third wall, and the fourth was blank.

A light clicked on under the door. Footsteps mingled with rattling keys. I scrambled to the mattress and pressed my back to the wall. A lock twisted, and the door opened. Light flooded, and I winced until my eyes adjusted.

Standing at the threshold was the girl from the concert. Della. She was wearing a yellow dress, and her feet were bare. She was holding a length of rope. "I'm sorry."

"What's going on, Della?"

She stepped into the room. "I'm sorry for yesterday and what's coming."

Fear spread, closing my throat. "What's coming?"

"You'll survive. Remember that."

Dread tremored through my body. "Let me go," I begged. "I won't tell anyone. I want to go home. I want to see my mom."

"I can't." She uncoiled the rope.

"Take me home! Please, take me home!"

The man from the van—Tanner, the flirting man with beautiful blue eyes from the construction site—stepped over the threshold. I looked directly at him. He had high cheekbones, thick wavy hair, and striking blue eyes. But there was nothing beautiful about him now. His smile was cold, his gaze piercing. Hands flexed slowly at his sides.

"Lay down," Della said. "It'll be easier if you don't fight."

Later, I would learn that the more I fought, the more it hurt. I would learn that if I lay still, he'd finish faster. Or if I smiled, he didn't hit me. But I didn't know any of those lessons. When I looked over at Della, she was crying.

Chapter Seven

Dawson

Saturday, July 13, 2024
8:00 a.m.

Dawson arrived at the small cinder block house on Pretty Lake Avenue by the banks of Little Creek. The grass in the yard was patchy, and what was there was weedy and tall. A couple of kids' bikes lay on the ground, two cars were parked in the gravel driveway, and the trash cans overflowed.

At the front door, he knocked on the metal security screen door. Inside, he could hear a television and then footsteps. When the door opened, he stood face-to-face with a woman in her early sixties. He'd met her at this house a decade ago, when he had darker hair and a slimmer build.

He held up his badge. "My name is Detective Kevin Dawson."

"I remember you. You asked me about Sandra."

"Yes, ma'am. You're Betty Gardner? Sandra's foster mother." She'd gained weight, and her salt-and-pepper hair had washed out to pure white.

"Yes. You come to tell me you found Sandy after all this time?" Mrs. Gardner shook her head slowly. "It's not good, is it?"

"No, ma'am. We believe we found Sandra Taylor's body," he said.

Raising her chin, she drew in her breath. Her fingers slipped into a pocket, and she removed a rumpled packet of cigarettes. She flicked a red plastic lighter and then pressed the flame to the raw tobacco edge. "Well, at least I know now, don't I? I'm sorry I couldn't help that girl. I tried, but she was stubborn and said she had all the answers."

"Kids can be tough." He wasn't sure what else to say. Mrs. Gardner had had seven foster kids at the time Sandra had vanished.

Mrs. Gardner's hands trembled as she raised the cigarette to thin lips. Smoke drifted out of her mouth and nose. "I been waiting for a decade for this news. I've imagined it a million times. Part of me hoped she'd just run off and found a new life. It's not easy working with kids like her."

"Yes, ma'am."

"You know, her mother and father both died of overdoses. I guess expecting her to recover from something like that was asking too much."

He'd heard versions of this story too many times. "When was the last time you saw her?" Time had a way of changing answers. What had seemed pressing or threatening in the past often faded. He knew Mr. Gardner had died two years ago.

"We fought." She shook her head. "I blamed her for the trouble in the house, but looking back I see she was just being a moody teenager."

"Did she ever run away?" Dawson asked.

"Three or four times. Always found a place to sleep on a friend's couch. After a few days she always came home."

"Did your late husband abuse her?"

"Not in that way." She puffed. "But he hit her. Sandra hated this house. Hated her foster brothers and sisters and hated her job. Always stirring chaos. She despised her life."

Which would have made her an easy mark for a charming young man. He checked his notes. "You didn't call in her missing person report for almost two weeks."

She shook her head. "My late husband told me to wait. He said she'd come back. I did contact her friends, and no one had seen her. And then her work called and said she hadn't shown in two days. That's when I knew something was off."

But Mrs. Gardner wasn't that concerned because she hadn't called the cops for another ten more days. "How did Sandra do in school?"

She laughed. "Terrible. If East Norfolk High School had a Most Truant Student award, she'd have won."

"Did Sandra ever mention a girl at her high school named Scarlett Crosby?" Same high school and possibly the same kidnapper—the girls had to have crossed paths.

"I've heard Scarlett's name, but Sandra never mentioned her."

He jotted notes. "You said in your report that Sandra was dating Tanner Reed."

"One date with him. But she was seeing a few guys. Tanner was the best of the lot, if you can believe it. I wasn't crazy about their age difference and told her that. She said the years didn't matter." Mrs. Gardner shook her head. "I've seen Tanner's kind before. Men like him use girls like her and pass them on to their friends."

Memories of Dawson's initial interview with Mrs. Gardner sharpened into focus. "You met Tanner Reed, right?"

"Yeah. He dropped her off. Gave me his card. Said he did work well and cheap. Pretty and charming. I'll give him that. But it was a matter of time before he knocked her up."

"Sandra was pregnant?"

"I don't know that. But I could see it coming. Sandra and I didn't talk much those last few weeks." Tears welled in her eyes.

He could still picture Tanner standing by his black truck, the dustless tools organized in military precision, the man smelling faintly of sawdust. Tanner had been so relaxed when Dawson had shown him a picture of Sandra. He'd admitted he'd met her at Mike's, they'd talked and flirted, but that was the end of it. Given a redo, could he have picked up on the red flags?

"I called her phone over and over, but she didn't answer. I left her dozens of messages. I also called Mike's Diner, but no one had seen her."

"She worked at Mike's Diner for five months."

"A few nights a week."

"Did she meet Tanner at the diner?" Dawson asked.

"I don't know."

"But the cops did contact you after Tanner's death, correct?"

"Yeah. Sandy had been gone five months at that point. The cops thought Sandy's case might be linked to Tanner, but no one proved anything."

By then Dawson had been waiting for the review board's ruling on his shooting of Tanner. He'd been forced to cool his heels on administrative leave for three months until the *Justified* verdict had been issued.

Mrs. Gardner inhaled deeply. "I put up dozens of missing persons posters. All the crank calls. People can be cruel."

The posters had lingered in restaurant windows and stapled to utility poles until weather, time, and people shredded them all. "Yes, ma'am."

"Where did you find Sandra?" Mrs. Gardner asked.

"In a house that Tanner had once renovated."

"A house? Where? Please tell me not a basement."

"Not a basement." He still wasn't ready to release any more case details.

"Do you think Tanner killed her?"

"I need more evidence to make that statement." He believed Tanner had killed Sandra, but all the assumptions in the world didn't add up to proof.

"How are you going to prove anything after all this time?"

"Time can help shake things loose in a cold case." He removed a card from his pocket. When she didn't open the door, he tucked it into the grate of the security door. "Contact me if you remember any new detail."

"Call me if you find anything."

"You'll be the first." When he looked back at the house, the solid door was closed, and his card remained stuck in the grate.

He drove to Mike's Diner and seated himself at a booth. The 1950s retro vibe, including dull chrome, red vinyl seats, and booth jukeboxes, hadn't changed in the last decade. The only difference he could see was that the laminated menus had been replaced by a QR code.

He scanned the code and was reading the lunch selections when a waitress came up. She was midforties, slender, and wore her dark hair pulled back in a tight bun. Her name badge read *Tonja*.

"What can I get you?" Tonja asked.

He pulled out his badge. "A soda and answers to a few questions about an old case."

"This connected to Tiffany?"

"Why do you ask?"

She shrugged. "No one who works here doesn't know about Tiffany's drama. She sure talked about it a lot. Always looking for an angle to make money off the incident."

"Remember Sandra Taylor?"

"Another example of pure foolishness."

He closed out the menu app. "What can you tell me about Sandra?"

"Sweet kid. Kind of naive. Flighty. Mike let her work for cash a few nights a week."

"Did she ever interact with Tanner here?"

"Sure. Everyone liked him. He was a regular. He drove Sandra home once after a shift. I happened to be walking out and stopped to say hi to Tanner. Great tipper."

"When was this?"

"I think it was late March. It was right after spring break."

No one had shared this with him in 2014. "Tanner remained a regular customer at the diner, right?"

"He came in a few times a week. He met his girlfriend here."

Dawson checked his notes. "Lynn Yeats."

"They met for breakfast right up until that last day."

While Scarlett, and possibly Sandra, had been trapped in Tanner's basement, Tanner was here, eating eggs and toast and shooting the shit.

"Did you ever see Tanner with any other woman here?"

"Not on my shift."

Dawson showed her Scarlett's original sketch of Della. "How about her?"

She studied the image. "Not really his type."

Killers could be creatures of habit. They chose the same kind of victim, hunted in the same places, and dumped bodies in familiar locations.

"Were you here the day Scarlett lured Tiffany to the alley?"

"I wasn't working that shift, but the owner was here then."

Scarlett Crosby had been rescued on September 2. "And the owner is where?"

"I'll get him."

"Thanks."

He sat back, his gaze scanning the front entrance, the breakfast bar, and the door that led to the back room and the lot behind it. He'd seen the security footage of a fifteen-year-old Scarlett walking through the front door. Wide eyed with fear, her body tense, her hands clenched. Nothing like the woman he'd met on Thursday.

Scarlett had told the cops that Tanner had already picked out Tiffany. Clearly, he'd been watching her when he ate his meals at the diner. Though Dawson had told Mrs. Gardner he needed evidence, in his mind Tanner had also chosen Sandra from this diner, kidnapped her, and killed her.

"Can I help you?"

Dawson looked up toward the deeply lined face of a burly man standing by his booth. He was wearing a Mike's Diner T-shirt, and his long gray hair was pulled back in a ponytail. "Mike Hart?"

"That's right."

"Like to have a seat?"

Mike glanced over his shoulder at the crowded bar. "It's going to have to be quick. Lunch rush is on the way."

Dawson reached in his pocket and pulled out a picture of Sandra Taylor. "Remember her?"

"She used to work here. It's been a while."

"Ten years. Can you tell me anything about her?"

"Employees come and go here all the time. I barely remember last week, let alone ten years ago."

Dawson showed Mike a picture of Tiffany. "Remember the day she was almost kidnapped?"

"I'll never forget it. Labor Day weekend. I was working the griddle that day because the cook hadn't shown up. I called out to Tiffany for an order and saw that she wasn't at the counter or in the dining room. I thought she'd gone to the alley for a smoke break. I remember being pissed. And then I heard a scream."

"It was Tiffany?"

"I don't know. She said later it was that Scarlett chick. Either way, I ran out, my spatula still in my hand. Tiffany just about ran me over when she came flying in through the back door. She was screaming we needed to call the cops."

"You placed that call, correct?"

"I did. And then I went out into the alley and saw Tanner Reed punch Scarlett. She dropped like a stone. He tossed her limp body in the back of his van and took off. I got the license plate."

That's what had led to the BOLO and the confrontation miles from here. "What did Tiffany tell you about the event?"

"At first, she didn't have much to say. She was in shock. But as time went on, she seemed to remember more, especially when a reporter was calling."

Memory was an odd phenomenon. It wasn't as reliable as people wanted to think. Minds weren't steel traps and most leaked. Folks also tended to embellish their memories with emotions or extraneous information later linked to the event. "How did her story change?"

"Tiffany was convinced that other girl was in trouble the minute she walked into the diner. Described her as thin, pale, and clearly nervous. No one else in the diner noticed the kid. Like I said, it was a busy day, and we were all going full tilt. I never saw Tiffany slipping out the back door."

"No one spoke to this girl, Scarlett?"

"No."

"What about Tanner Reed, the man driving the van?"

"He was a regular. I liked the guy."

A bell rang in the kitchen, and Mike raised a hand, signaling he was on his way. "Why all the questions now? Did you find a dead body or something?"

"We believe we've found Sandra Taylor's body."

Mike's lips flattened as he shook his head. "I'm sorry to hear that. You think Tanner did it?"

"I can't prove it. Just following up old leads. When did you see Tiffany last?"

"A couple of months ago, maybe last year. She hasn't worked here in years but still stops by."

"Do you have a number where I can reach Tiffany? She's not answering her cell."

Mike pulled out his phone and opened his contacts. He showed Dawson Tiffany's information. "That's my most recent update."

"That matches what I have."

Mike shifted. "I need to get back to work. Any other questions?"

"Did Sandra or Tiffany ever talk about Scarlett Crosby, the girl in the van?"

"Tiffany said she calls her when she needs money. Why she'd call Scarlett of all people, I don't know." Mike leaned forward. "I hear that Scarlett girl had that syndrome that makes victims attach to the kidnapper."

"Stockholm syndrome. Scarlett's actions don't match the definition." Dawson didn't doubt that Scarlett had suffered while she was

Tanner's captive. She'd been grossly underweight, malnourished, and badly battered when she'd arrived at the emergency room. But in all her interviews, she'd never expressed empathy for her captor or his goals.

"What about Della? You ever meet anyone by that name?"

"That's the make-believe girl, right?"

"So far."

According to multiple police interviews, Scarlett had asked repeatedly about Della on the way to the hospital. She'd never mentioned Sandra.

By the time the cops had located Tanner's home via a title search, they'd discovered the house had burned to the ground. Witnesses reported hearing explosions before the fire. If there'd been any evidence of other girls, it had been incinerated.

Ultimately, there'd been no missing persons reports matching Della's description. Social workers had decided that Della was a figment of Scarlett's imagination. Her eighty-eight-day imprisonment and torture had been too much for her to endure and she'd created Della as a coping mechanism.

It struck him as odd that after a decade, Scarlett still clung to Della. "Right. Thanks for your time." He handed Mike a business card.

Mike flicked the edge with a calloused thumb. "I'll call if I hear from Tiffany."

"Thanks."

As Dawson left the busy diner, it occurred to him that the day Tiffany and Scarlett had first collided had been a warm day like this. Summer might have been winding down, but the air had been hot and sunny.

The bells on the front door jingled, and he looked up to see a couple of young girls enter and move toward the bar. No one else looked toward the door or the girls, just as they hadn't when Scarlett first entered.

Outside, he walked down the side walkway toward the back alley. It was long and wide enough for one vehicle at a time. The wall overlooking the area behind the diner was windowless. There was a security camera, but it looked new. According to the reports, there'd been no back lot cameras ten years ago. A regular like Tanner would have known that. He'd been here enough because he was scoping out the location.

Dawson crossed cracked asphalt that fed into a parking lot, stood at the edge, and tried to visualize Tanner speeding away. When dispatch had issued a BOLO on the van, he'd been close enough and had caught the call. Lights on, he'd jammed his foot on the accelerator. He'd caught sight of the van when it suddenly veered off the road and crashed. Tanner had stumbled free of the wreckage, gun drawn. Dawson fired. Suspect down. And the broken girl in the back of the van had been found.

Weary of chasing ghosts, he got in his vehicle and drove back to the station. Out of his car, he was looking at his phone, lost in the puzzle of Sandra Taylor, when he walked straight into a woman. She stumbled back and tried to resettle her balance.

He reached out to steady her. A rich perfume wrapped around him. His gaze skimmed full breasts. He grew hard. Margo Larsen.

"Sorry," he said, releasing her and sliding his hand into his pocket.

"Deep in thought, Dawson?"

"Yeah, sorry."

A faint smile tipped the edges of her lips. Green eyes softened with amusement as she took in his befuddled reaction. "No worries. What has you so deep in thought?"

"Chasing stale leads in the Sandra Taylor case."

"Any luck?"

"Nothing. Sandra Taylor vanished, and no one noticed."

Margo shook her head. "I worked human trafficking in Northern and Central Virginia. Heard similar stories too many times. And technically she remains a Jane Doe."

Jane Doe. Margo was right. The wrapped body hadn't been formally identified as Sandra Taylor. A driver's license was helpful but not definitive. "You have any doubts she's Sandra?"

"No. But all the t's need to be crossed, right?" she asked.

"Right."

"Keep me posted. That case is going to be hard to forget. Any word yet from dispatch who called in the tip?"

"Caller used a burner phone. They're trying to pin the call's location. That might help." All numbers pinged through a cell tower. Find the tower and then the address.

"I'm here if you need help." Margo smiled, and when she continued down the street, his gaze drifted to her round, hard ass. She wore fitted slacks, a lightweight collared shirt, and heeled boots.

He couldn't hide his admiration as she vanished around the corner. "Too much time on your own, Dawson. Too much time."

Chapter Eight

SCARLETT

Then
A day later in the basement

My entire body hurt. My insides were on fire, and I felt as if I'd been ripped to the core. I was bleeding. The room was dark, and I was glad for it. I wanted to hide, close my eyes, and let the darkness consume me.

I rolled on my side and curled into a ball, and my stomach tumbled. I was aware of the *drip, drip* of a pipe and the sound of what resembled breathing. But the inky blackness made it impossible to sort out shapes.

It took several more seconds before I tried to sit up again. This time, I was steadier and my stomach more settled. My left leg felt heavy, and when I ran my hands down my leg, I skimmed the cold, rough edge of metal encircling my ankle. I tugged on the manacle and realized it was attached to a chain. My panic rising, I gripped the chain and pulled. There was a little play, but the slack quickly vanished. I yanked again and the links snapped taut. And again. Panic tightened my chest, and it took effort not to scream.

I was still alive, still breathing, and I knew I would survive this. Somehow. Last night was the past. I had hope.

Finally, I rose on my knees and followed the chain with my hands until my fingers brushed against the brick wall. I pulled at the metal links, but as they continued to hold, my fear grew. Tears welled in my eyes.

I shifted my focus to the link around my ankle. I pulled on the edges, but the forged metal remained stubborn and unyielding.

Above me I heard floorboards creak. Was that him? Or had someone found me? I couldn't risk not acting on the chance that help had arrived, so I scrambled to my feet and began to yell. I screamed until my throat was raw and my voice so hoarse, I didn't recognize it.

I reached for the chain again, pulled and yelled until I was breathless. Finally, I collapsed onto the mattress. "Where am I?"

"You're here now."

The familiar girl's voice, whispering from the shadows, startled me. Della. I stumbled to my feet and readied to fight whatever lurked in the darkness. "Where is *here*?"

"His basement. He left me here to make sure you're okay." She tapped metal against brick. "I have water. You must be thirsty."

I recoiled. "Get away from me. I don't want anything from you."

"You will." She sounded tired, almost bored. "We only have each other now. You need to live so I won't be alone again."

Tanner had come to me in the dark, not bothering with a light beyond what leaked in the open door. I never realized she'd entered the room behind him. My face warmed with shame as I thought about how I'd begged and cried. Tanner had left me a couple of hours ago—maybe it had been longer—and I'd been lying here crying. And she'd said nothing.

"You should drink water," she said.

"Fuck off, bitch. You put me here."

"It's not my fault," she said quietly. "He makes me do these things." She turned on a small flashlight, which glowed eerily under her pale, round face. Shoulder-length brown hair kinked with grease skimmed a strong jaw. Wearing an oversize T-shirt but nothing else, she looked more like a spirit than a human, and for a moment I thought I'd died.

Tears welled in my eyes. "Go away."

"He does it to me, too."

I tucked my knees toward my chest. "Is that why you tricked me? To get him off you?"

The flashlight shifted, and the light skimmed over the concrete floor toward me. She set a cup of water in front of me. "Drink it. I don't know when he'll give us water again."

With the light shining, I winced, but as my eyes adjusted, I saw the cracks in the aqua ceramic cup with a broken handle.

The light clicked off. "I have to save the battery."

I stared in the direction of that cup for an hour. I didn't want anything from the bitch who had lured me to this hell. I wanted to leave. I wanted to hurl the cup against the wall. But the thirst grew stronger with each breath.

Della didn't speak, but I could tell by her breathing she was awake. Finally, I became so thirsty, I fumbled for the cup and drank. The water was warm and had a metallic taste. And there was just enough to make me want more.

"Are you better?" she asked.

"What do you think?" I ran fingers over naked arms and cringed when they trailed over bruises. "Where are we? Where is *here*?"

"*Here* is a farmhouse in the country," she said. A southern accent added a moody edge to her softly spoken words. "You can scream all you want, but no one will hear. This house is in the middle of nowhere."

I glanced in the darkness toward the ceiling, more tears brimming in my eyes. No one was going to find me. "Why did you do it?"

Silence settled. "He made me."

"You knew what was going to happen to me, didn't you?"

"I did."

Rage filled me. I screamed and jerked hard against my restraint until I could smell the coppery scent of blood. Warm liquid ran down my ankle and puddled around my foot.

My memory swung back to the sliver of light illuminating Tanner's face twisted in an unholy mixture of desire and rage—a jackal ready to devour. There had been no hints of the lovely man I'd seen before. "I've seen his face. He didn't hide from me. I know his name. Does that mean he's going to kill me?"

"It means you must be smart. You must make him like you."

Disgust soured in my belly. "Never."

"Never say never."

My head dropped back against the brick wall. Hopelessness rose in me, tightening my throat. I thought I was going to be sick. Closing my eyes, I drew in deep breaths. As my stomach calmed, my thoughts cleared. I had to get out of here. "How long have you been here?"

"A year, maybe."

A year. "In this room?"

"Upstairs at first. Down here three or four months on and off."

Three or four months. Suffering in this hole. "I want to kill you."

Della's laughter held no mirth. "Killing me won't solve anything."

"Maybe not, but I'll feel better."

"Then you'll be all alone with Tanner. You don't want that."

"Do you have a chain on your ankle?"

"No. I've earned his trust," she said. "If you want that chain to go away, you'll have to do the same."

I sat in silence. And then a comment she'd made circled back. "You said you don't want to be alone *again*. Who else was here?"

"There is another girl."

Breathless, I stared toward the sound of her voice. "Where?"

"Upstairs somewhere."

"Is she a prisoner, too?"

"Yes. But Tanner said he'd let her go if I got you."

"And you believed him?"

Another girl. Most likely chained and hurting. Della had known this when she smiled at me on that street corner. "You could've run! Why didn't you find a cop? There were people around the theater. They would've helped you and saved all of us."

"They couldn't have protected anyone. He's very clever."

I ignored that hard truth. "You didn't even try!"

"We have to play the long game if I'm going to save us all." Della's voice softened.

"Long game? I'm not rotting here having him hurt me again and again like he did last night."

"He's done it to me thousands of times. It wasn't always violent, and if you manage him right, he can be nice."

"Manage him? He's a monster."

"Don't be mad at me. We're all we have. We must be friends."

"I don't have to be your friend."

Della was silent for a long moment. "You'll be my friend. You'll see."

Chapter Nine

Scarlett

Saturday, July 13, 2024
8:15 a.m.

The gym wasn't crowded. Not uncommon on a lovely summer Saturday morning. With the days longer and warmer, most skipped the gym workout for runs or bike rides in the parks or the paths along the waterfront or coffees in one of the local cafés. There were so many reasons not to work out. And yet here I was, clinging to a routine that kept me sane.

Dawson's visit had rattled me. My thoughts kept returning to Sandra Taylor and Della's old references to the Other Girl. Della had said she'd gone away but never once explained. Dawson had confirmed what I'd suspected. *Gone* meant *dead*. But I had no idea when she'd died. Vanished in the spring, according to Dawson, and never found until now.

Tanner had often taken Della from our room and kept her upstairs. Many times, he'd turn up the music, blasting rock that rattled the walls and seeped through the floorboards into the basement. If Della was screaming upstairs, I didn't hear it. The world ceased to exist beyond my four walls.

Della never fought Tanner and often smiled when he motioned her toward the door. I always was relieved when he didn't choose me, but as soon as the door closed and I was alone, I worried whether she'd ever return. In the eighty-eight days I was under Tanner's control, I never left that dark, windowless room until the day he and I went to the diner.

Rolling my head from side to side, I tried to shake off the thoughts, grateful that I would never have to see Tanner Reed again.

Blond hair bound in a ponytail, I was dressed in fitted shorts, a snug T-shirt, and athletic shoes. My muscles were tight. It had been a shit day yesterday when it came to my work. My hands had trembled as I'd etched the final curls of a Kangawa-style wave into a block of wood that would become the stamp anchoring my latest print series. A sailboat on rolling exaggerated waves with clouds dangling above. No matter how hard I concentrated, I couldn't shake Dawson's visit. Seeing him had unlocked the jail where my demons resided, and I feared they were now free and circling.

My hands shook only a little when I set my bag down and looked up the climbing wall toward the ceiling, which had always symbolized freedom.

It had been months since I'd had one of the darker nightmares. Those night terrors left me in a pool of sweat and screaming. One had woken me up in the middle of last night, so I spent the rest of the time at my computer searching Sandra Taylor. There were a couple of old short articles mentioning that the teen had vanished. A few weeks later, another recap reported she'd not been found. And then nothing.

Sandra Taylor had been swallowed up and no one had remembered her for a decade. A discovery like that would conjure curiosity for those who might have known her or the others who enjoyed salacious details. There'd be articles, reporters with questions, and there might even be a true crime podcast or television special. And then just like that, Sandra Taylor would be forgotten again.

Sandra's story could easily have been mine. The girl with a sketchy family life, a loner who dabbled in drugs, no doubt desperate for companionship and acceptance. I tried to remember the girl who'd attended my high school but couldn't picture her face. Even I'd forgotten her. I'd been too obsessed with Della to remember Tanner's Other Girl.

Let it go. Let it go.

I swapped athletic sneakers for rock-climbing shoes and reached in a chalk bag and rubbed white powder against my sweaty palms. I looked up the wall stretching one hundred feet into the air, focused on the rocks and the trail they created to the top.

Most of the climbers stuck to the lower levels, but my sights were set on the peak. As the rocks grew slimmer and sparser, my focus narrowed to a fine point, crowding out the past and future. As I clung by my fingertips up in the rafters, my brain couldn't process anything but the wall in front of me.

I caught the attention of another climber, Jeff, who I'd belayed for a few days ago. He was tall and lean, and his skin was deeply tanned from all the exterior climbs he'd tackled. Word was he had his eye on El Capitan in Yosemite. While he had climbed, I'd worked the safety rope until he'd reached the top. I envied the freedom. I'd never been able to stray too far from Norfolk for more than a day or two. Maybe I was still waiting on Della.

"Help a girl out?" I asked.

"Sure." He grabbed his bag and moved toward me.

"Did you climb?" I asked.

"Not today. I have a torn calf muscle, so I'm forced to go easy for a few weeks."

"Sorry to hear that," I said.

"Par for the course."

I wrapped a safety harness around my waist, secured it, and locked in the belay rope. The first time he'd touched my shoulder as I secured the harness, I'd flinched as if his fingers had scorched my flesh. He'd backed off, said nothing, but I'm guessing a Google search told him all he needed to understand my quirks. There was plenty to read about me.

After that day, Jeff didn't press for details and was careful to avoid skin-to-skin contact. I was grateful. There were still people from time to time who asked. A few second-guessed my past decisions, and one or two dug for the lurid details of my captivity. I ignored everyone.

"Going to the top?" Jeff asked.

"Always."

"Fearless. Adrenaline junkie."

"Takes one to know one." I'd rather be scaling real rocks and mountains, but right now there wasn't time for a three-hour drive west. But soon. Soon.

"Busted." He shrugged, smiled as he wrapped the belay rope around his waist.

"Can you time me?" I asked.

"Ah, personal best time today?"

"Why not?" I grabbed the first plastic rock and settled my foot on another. The bottom rocks were wide and steady enough. I'd have to reach the halfway point before the rocks grew narrower and farther apart.

Heart beating a little faster, I pulled my body up and began to ascend the wall and out of Tanner's dark hole. There were times I imagined Della following me up the wall, reaching for my ankles. Sometimes she gripped my foot and tried to pull me down. Other times, I was free and had the strength to extend my fingers and offer a lifeline to Della. Tyrant and redeemer linked forever.

With each new inch now, I gained distance from Della and that dark room. Images of her faded. My focus narrowed. The wall always refused to let my concentration wander.

My muscles felt good, and my fingers were easily finding the grooves and notches in the rocks. My feet were steady and my legs strong. The buzz of the few gym rats grew more distant as I rose, and my focus tapered to my feet and fingers on the slimming rocks.

Sweat gathered at the base of my back, and without looking up I sensed I was close to the top. The air was always warmer, cleaner at the peak. I stole a glance upward and saw the ceiling inches from my head. Fingers strained. My toes cramped. I edged up the last few inches. I touched the ceiling, pressing my fingers against other smudged prints.

"Way to go, Scarlett. Personal best," Jeff shouted.

I glanced back toward Jeff and caught his smile. As I swung my gaze back to the wall, a woman passed behind him. She paused and stared up at me. She was blond, tall, and in good shape and wore fitted black leggings, an aqua top, and bright neon shoes.

The woman's gaze pinned me. It wasn't the first time a gym member had stopped to watch me climb to the peak. But when my gaze locked on this woman's, I didn't see idle curiosity. I saw clinical assessment. Della had stared at me like that when Tanner opened our cell door.

The woman's detachment gave way to curiosity, pity, and sorrow.

I blinked.

Her expression mirrored the Della embedded in my memory.

Della . . .

Merely the idea of Della standing here now and staring at me was enough to break my concentration. My laser focus shattered, and my foot slipped. I immediately struggled to regain my foothold and tightened my grip. But my shoes skimmed over the smallest rock, and my fingers dislodged from the tiny indent above my head. I grabbed for another rock, but my feet slid over it. My body couldn't recalibrate fast enough.

Della.

My weight tipped backward, and my stomach rose in my chest. In that split second, I knew I was falling. I'd climbed to the top of the black hole, and like always, Della found a way to yank me back. No matter what I did, she always won.

Someone in the gym screamed seconds before my body went airborne.

Chapter Ten

SCARLETT

Saturday, July 13, 2024
8:45 a.m.

I free-fell fifteen feet before I hit the rock wall and the safety harness jerked my body to a halt.

Pain cut through battered muscles as I dangled from the rope. I'd fallen before, but I had always sensed the critical mistake as I made it, and I was somewhat ready to brace and recover. But this fall had caught me off guard.

Slowly the rope lowered, and I inched closer to the ground. When I rested against the mat, I struggled to draw in a breath as the ribs on my right side groaned.

"Scarlett, are you okay?" Jeff's face was now inches from mine as he studied my eyes closely. "Jesus, what happened up there?"

My thoughts skittered from pain to the woman I'd seen. Immediately, I tried to sit up as I searched for Della. However, my stunned body constricted, and a muscle spasm sent me back to the mat. "Damn."

He hesitated to touch me. "Lie still. Take it slow. Let's figure out if you're hurt."

A group of people gathered around me in a circle, their expressions a mixture of concern and curiosity. Some spoke to me, but the voices sounded distant and muffled.

I closed my eyes and drew in a breath. My ribs ached. But breath half filled my lungs before I had to expel it. Another pause, and the next inhale allowed more air. The one after that was even better.

"Scarlett!" Jeff said. "Are you hearing me?"

"I'm fine, Jeff. Ego is more battered than the body."

He shoved trembling fingers through his hair. "You scared the shit out of me."

When I rose onto my elbow, I winced. "I got distracted. Sloppy and stupid."

Jeff carefully put his hand behind my back. I tensed only a little as he helped me sit. "You never fall."

"I did today." I eased away from his touch.

"Don't get weird," he whispered. "I'm just trying to help you."

"I'm fine." I pushed back the panic rushing through me. I'd rather endure physical pain than touch. I stiffened and moved away. "Sorry about that, Jeff."

"What distracted you?" Jeff glanced up at the wall as if trying to figure out where it all went wrong.

"I saw a woman walk behind you. I thought I knew her." My gaze skimmed the room, but there was no sign of the Della look-alike. Dawson's visit had dragged me back in time, and I was now seeing ghosts.

"Who was she?"

"No one. I just got stupid." I planted my hands on the mat and drew my feet toward my body. The legs protested, but they worked. A win. I tried to push upward, but core muscles refused to work.

"I can help you," Jeff said.

I held up my hands. "I know. Thank you. But I can do this by myself."

"You don't have to do this all alone, Scarlett. Not all the time anyways."

Drawing in a breath, I pushed through pulsing muscles, climbed to my knees, and then staggered to my feet. "I know. Thank you for trying."

Jeff shook his head.

I watched the questions and concern swirl in his eyes. "I know I've got a few quirks."

He ran calloused fingers through his hair. "Hey, it's cool. We've all got them."

I pressed my hand to my bruised hip. "Some of us more than others."

He grinned. "There's the gal we know."

They didn't know me. Not even close. Reading a few old articles on the internet didn't cut it. But to point that out would only prolong this exchange. "Thanks again. I think I'm going to grab my bag and call it a day. No more walls for now."

"Cold plunges for the first two days. Aspirin."

"I know the drill. Not my first fall."

I walked gingerly across the mats toward my bag. A few folks were staring. A couple asked how I was doing. I assured everyone I was just fine.

Glancing around the room again, I realized the Della look-alike was gone. I leaned toward the handles of my bag, winced when my left hip pulled, and then wrapped my fingers around the handles.

"Do me a favor and just hang out here for a while," Jeff said. "I'll get you a bottle of water."

"I'm solid, Jeff." I'd developed a high tolerance for pain a long time ago.

"You can still drink water."

I bristled at the command behind the words, but I simply nodded and smiled. He was trying to help, not manage me.

He trotted across the gym, grabbed a bottle from a vending machine, and brought it to me. Condensation dripped down the bottle and I realized my mouth was dry. "Thank you."

"You're our star climber," he said.

"And now I'm a cautionary tale to everyone," I said, smiling.

"We all fall. The trick is to recover as quickly as possible."

"No truer words." I pressed the cool bottle to my temple. "Thanks for having my back."

"Can I drive you home?"

"I walked." I scanned the growing crowd again in the gym for the Della look-alike. No sign of the pink shoes and blond hair. I needed to stop searching for this woman. My imagination had almost been my ruin before. "And moving will do me good."

"You do have your phone, right?"

"Yes. All good."

"Okay."

Drawing myself up, I ignored the stiffness tugging along my spine and smiled to the group of people still lingering and watching. "Alive and well. Thank you."

A few smiles flickered before the crowd slowly dispersed. With as much dignity as I could muster, I walked out of the gym. My irritation grew as I stepped outside. I took a long drink of water. My meltdown was due to Dawson's visit. He'd arrived Thursday with his notebook and suspicious gaze and pried open the can of worms I kept sealed most of the time.

I stepped off the curb. A horn honked and I looked up to see a truck driver glaring at me. He raised a hand as if to ask, *What gives?*

Smiling, I waved my thanks for his patience and not running me down and continued. I reached the next intersection. When I got the green light, I crossed and moved down the block past industrial warehouses.

At my building, I fished keys from my purse and unlocked the two dead bolts on the screen door. Next, more locks on the metal door before it pushed open. Inside my place, I secured the locks and walked to the portrait I'd been painting of Della. She stared at me with the eyes reflecting cunning, hurt, and love, depending on the angle. The eyes. I could never get them right.

The woman I'd seen today was tall, lean. She was not the plump, dirty girl I remembered. She looked nothing like my Della. Not *My Della. The Della.* So why had her gaze spooked me?

I knew I should spend the day working, but my nerves hopped with anxious energy, and my thoughts kept returning to Sandra Taylor. Was she the Other Girl? Had Tanner killed her?

The online articles I'd read about Sandra last night had offered scant details: Sandra had lived off Nineteenth Bay Street, and she'd worked at Mike's Diner.

I'd only been to Mike's once. That diner had changed my life, but I could barely picture the place. My single overwhelming memory of Mike's was the smell of food. Burgers. Fries. My mouth had watered even as my heart rammed my chest so hard, I thought my ribs would crack.

It made no sense for me to return to Mike's. Better to stay away from anything that could trigger the nightmares. But I still grabbed my keys and exited out the back of the warehouse to my truck. I plugged the address into my phone and drove the twenty miles to the diner. As the city melted and gave way to more green space, my unease grew. There was a comfort in the steel walls and concrete floors of my warehouse. Green spaces and open blue sky never comforted me. Too many places to get lost.

Thirty minutes later, I pulled up in front of Mike's Diner and stared at the long, cigar-shaped silver building reminiscent of a 1950s diner.

The parking lot was nearly full. Made sense. It was ten on a Saturday, and folks tended to enjoy a later breakfast or early lunch. I sat in my truck for a good half hour, watching people come and go. No one noticed me now, and no one had seen me ten years ago. They were all living their lives. I didn't register.

Finally, I shut off the engine and got out of the truck. The rising summer heat warmed chilled skin as I crossed the lot to the restaurant. My hand on the front door, I hesitated. A woman behind me cleared her throat. I opened the door and stepped into the diner buzzing with busy conversations, the rattle of plates, and Elvis Presley's "Blue Suede Shoes." *Go, cat, go.* Tanner's music choices had always been hard rock.

"Do you want to sit at the bar or a booth?" The waitress's question blended with the background noise.

I didn't remember the red leather tops to the barstools, the strip of yellow neon behind the bar, or the rows of booths to my left and right.

"Ma'am, do you want to sit down?" the hostess asked.

"Yes."

"Bar or booth?"

"Bar."

"Great."

I followed her to a stainless-steel stool at the end of the bar. She set a menu in front of me. "Enjoy."

"Thanks."

When I'd been here before, I'd walked up to the bar. I'd watched the redheaded waitress move back and forth between the kitchen and dining room. I hadn't known her name as I'd fingered a sugar packet with hands still stained with grime that soap and water couldn't remove. I'd told Tiffany about the fictitious puppies and then followed her through that kitchen door. No one had paid any attention to us. The back door was open, and through it I could see Tanner's van pull up.

"What can I get you?" a waitress asked.

I looked up to a woman's lined face. She held a full coffeepot as if she'd predicted exactly what I wanted.

"Coffee would be great."

With an effort, she found a smile as she filled a stoneware mug, dropped a couple of creamers, and asked, "Know what you want to eat?"

"Scrambled eggs and toast."

"Great choice, hon."

I sipped the hot, bitter coffee, watching as the cooks in the kitchen placed hot plates of food on the counter and rang a bell. They moved with controlled efficiency and barely looked up from the griddle.

"Do I know you?"

I shifted my gaze to the waitress who'd taken my order. This time I noticed her name tag: *Tonja*. "I don't think so."

Eyes narrowed. "You look familiar to me."

"I have that kind of face."

"Pretty distinctive." Her head shook slowly as recognition flickered in her gaze. "I'd almost forgotten about you until that cop came here yesterday."

I didn't respond.

She leaned forward and dropped her voice. "You're the girl that worked with that weirdo Tanner."

I'd been accused of working with Tanner before. Many cops, especially after my arrests post-escape, didn't totally believe me. But it had been a long time since the accusation had been hurled at me.

I'd learned not to engage. "Can I get my meal to go?"

"Don't you want to talk about it? Don't you want to know what I remember?" She looked past me. "Do you have a reporter with you? A book deal?"

I reached in my purse, fished out a twenty, and tossed it on the bar. Rising, I shouldered my bag. "On second thought, keep the food."

"Did Tiffany finally rope you into a story? She's been trying to cash in for a long time."

"When's the last time Tiffany was here?"

Her lips flattened. "I don't know. Why do you care?"

Tiffany had been on fragile ground mentally before I'd waltzed into this diner with conflicted dreams of escape. When I shouted for Tiffany to run, I thought I'd saved her. But she'd shattered. She'd survived, but not really.

"Why did you pick her?" Tonja asked. "The kid was always struggling. And you sent her over the edge."

Guilt clawed at my insides. "If you see Tiffany, tell her to give Scarlett a call."

I spent the afternoon carving my print stamp, zeroing my focus in on one arching wave. The small detail required my full attention, and finally the fine print work, like the climbing wall, narrowed my thoughts.

The alarm on my phone went off. Date with Luke. Shit. That was the last thing I needed. I wanted a hot shower and to curl up under the blankets on my small couch and sleep.

But I also wasn't keen on having a nightmare. And given Dawson, Sandra Taylor, and the Della look-alike, I was ripe for one.

I'd seen enough shrinks to know my tendency to self-isolate wasn't healthy. I had a date with Luke, and I'd keep the date.

I moved to the back of the warehouse, where behind a silk screen was my bed and beyond it a small bathroom. I turned on the water, waiting and waiting for it to heat up. Experience had taught me I had about five minutes of heat before the water turned cold. I could call a plumber, but plumbers took forever to arrive, and when they did, they were expensive. So I got used to quick showers.

I downed two aspirin and ducked under the spray, quickly working shampoo and conditioner into my shoulder-length hair. I'd just rinsed the last of the soap when the heat vanished and sent a cold chill down my spine. Instead of jumping out of the shower, I braced and let the ice slide over my skin. The cold would help with the bruising and stiffness from the fall, and it reminded me I was alive and could step out of the shower anytime I wanted. I was in control of this special brand of misery.

Finally, I shut off the water, grabbed a gray cotton towel, and dried off. I dressed in jeans and a sleeveless light-blue silk top. I slid my feet into black open-toed sandals before walking to a mirror and fluffing my hair dry until the natural waves sprang to life. Makeup wasn't a normal daily thing for me, but tonight I swabbed on red lipstick and then a bit of mascara. The goal was to look pulled together but not sexy.

I'd been on a few dates in the last decade, but they'd all ended within the first hour. The unsuspecting guy would try to hold my hand, or God help him, kiss me, and I would freeze, or worse, shove him back. I'd only punched one man, but that was years ago.

Odds were good this drink with Luke was going to be quick. He wasn't a kid. A guy in his midthirties wasn't interested in women acting like stiff matrons.

I grabbed my purse and carefully edged it onto a rigid shoulder. The aspirin was kicking in and hopefully would hold the line against the real stiffness that would come in the next twelve hours. This wasn't the first time I'd been battered, and I understood the patterns of pain the body endured as it tried to heal.

The evening air was warm, and the streets weren't that busy. This time of night, most of this area cleared out. There'd be pockets of people near the restaurants around the corner, but this block was always quiet.

My phone buzzed. I would have hoped it was Luke canceling, but we hadn't exchanged numbers. When I glanced at the display, I was disappointed and relieved. It was the Judge. I stopped walking and angled my back toward a brick wall—one of the million random safety tips I practiced all the time. Walking while talking on a cell created a sense of connection and safety, but the reality was the brain could concentrate on only one thing at a time. If I was listening to the Judge, my attention wasn't on the streets around me.

"Thank you for coming to the opening." A chair squeaked in the background, and I pictured the Judge still in her office. She always worked late.

"Of course," I said.

"Did I see you talking to people?" she asked. "Maybe a man?"

That teased a smile. "A few."

"Luke Kane?"

"That's correct." The Judge missed so little. "What's his story?"

"Why do you want to know?" Curiosity mingled carefully with amusement.

"Just curious."

The Judged chuckled. "Interest is a positive sign."

"You don't have to tell me anything."

"No, no. I'm happy to. He's a tough attorney. Used to work as a prosecutor in the Commonwealth's Attorney's Office. For the last two years he's become one of the Tidewater's best defense attorneys. Too good. I've seen the best prosecutors lose to him."

I'd often wondered if Tanner had lived and Della had been found, how their trials would have played out. I'd have been forced to testify and retell the story that I'd recited to dozens of cops. But Tanner was dead, and Della had vanished into the wind. Maybe the universe had done me a solid when the police had killed him and saved me from more scrutiny.

"Would you say ruthless?" Oddly, I was comfortable with predators. They wanted what they wanted and went after it. I knew what to expect.

"I'd say so. But he's also turned down cases that could have landed him a lot of money. The guy has a personal code."

"Okay."

"Did he ask you out?"

"He did. I'm on my way to Lito's wine bar now. A glass of wine won't kill me."

"Ah, that explains it."

"What?"

"He bought your print at the auction."

"Did he?"

"The man has good taste."

"Don't get too excited. My longest date lasted sixty-two minutes."

"Here's to breaking the sixty-two-minute record."

Another smile teased my lips. The Judge checked in often, but she never pushed or badgered unless I was teetering toward a downward spiral. Thankfully, I'd not really lost my shit in a few years.

"Thanks, Judge."

"I'm proud of you," the Judge said.

Compliments always made me uneasy. I never felt like any of them were deserved.

"Give him a chance," the Judge said. "Not an order, but a humble suggestion from an old, growingly sentimental friend."

"You're neither old nor sentimental."

"I might be softening in my old age."

"Don't. Stay tough." I needed the Judge to be strong. I needed her boundaries. I needed to know there was at least one rock in my life.

"I'll shake off any tender feelings immediately."

"Thank you."

"Have fun?"

"To be determined."

I ended the call, gripped the phone, and moved toward the wine bar. I wasn't more hopeful about this date, but some of the weight that had settled on my shoulders had lifted.

Lito's had opened its large front doors and pushed back sliding windows to bring the outside in. People were sitting at cocktail rounds chatting and laughing.

Sweat pooled on the back of my neck.

I tightened my hand on my purse, walked inside, and checked the time. A minute after six. I looked around, searching for Luke, still hoping he'd changed his mind and hadn't shown up.

A broad-shouldered man stood by a round top, and I realized it was Luke. He wore a suit, but he'd removed the tie. If he was trying to soften the image, he'd have to work harder. Slicked-back dark hair and the lights above sharpened the angles on his face.

I raised a hand and cut through the crowd, doing my best to avoid contact with anyone. One man backed away from the bar and bumped into me, driving an elbow into my battered ribs. My first reaction was to shove back hard and tell him to back off. But I caught myself. My fingers balled into fists as people flooded around me. Pulse pounding, I drew in a breath and kept moving. The goal tonight was a date that lasted sixty-three minutes.

Luke watched me as I approached, and I felt his appreciation stroking over me. At twenty-five, I should be making the most of my youth, but reaching beyond my walls and putting myself out there seemed like an impossible mountain to climb.

He'd expect a kiss on the cheek. A small casual touch. Bracing, I found a smile and leaned forward slightly as he kissed me on the cheek. Hints of expensive aftershave swirled around me. When his hand slid casually to my waist, I tensed.

"You okay?" he asked.

"I had a fall on the rock-climbing wall today." I skidded away from his fingers and took the seat across from him. The table between us helped ease some of the tension away. "Ribs are a little tender."

A frown furrowed his brow as his gaze skimmed over my body. "What happened?"

"I made it to the top and grazed the ceiling with my fingers, and then my concentration broke. Too cocky for my own good."

He settled across from me. "Why did your concentration break?"

"Sometimes it just happens."

Light from a candle nestled in a small votive glinted in his gaze. "Nothing just happens."

I shifted, smiling through a grimace. I was grateful now I'd fallen. It was something to talk about, and it would explain why my body tensed when touched.

"I assume you had a safety harness on," he said.

"I did. It was quite effective."

When the waitress came to the table, he ordered a bourbon neat, and I selected a white wine. "I've never tackled the wall. I focus on the treadmill and weight room. It's not exciting but it's efficient."

"You have a busy schedule?"

"Sure. But par for the course when you're in practice for yourself. You're self-employed. Any words of wisdom?"

"You never work a day in your life if you work for yourself."

His quick laugh was hearty and rich.

I relaxed a little. "Truthfully, the job never stops."

"No truer words." He leaned back as if he were talking to an old friend. "The Judge told me you purchased my print at the reception."

"I did."

"Thank you."

"It's a stunning piece."

The waitress arrived with our drinks, and I held mine up, toasting him, and took a sip. The cool, buttery liquid tasted good. I always allowed myself one drink when I was out. If I wanted more, I went home, locked the doors, and had a second.

There were moments like now, when I wondered what kind of person I would've been if not for Tanner and Della. Surely, I wouldn't have been this paranoid or nervous. My ability to relax and enjoy was one of the many things that duo had stolen from me.

"So you're on the board of directors for the Judge's recreation center," I said.

He nodded thoughtfully. "I had several good reasons why I wasn't the best choice, but she wouldn't hear my arguments."

"Tried and sentenced."

"Correct."

"What do you owe her?" I asked.

He scratched his jaw. "I represented a kid on drug charges. When I argued my case to her, I detailed several extenuating circumstances. Instead of sending the child to juvenile detention, I asked the Judge to remand her to foster care. She took the kid in herself."

I had met a couple of the kids who'd been under the Judge's care. Based on his recap, I suspected he must be talking about Marissa. She was in college now.

"Happy ending?" College was a long way away from the finish line. So many pitfalls.

"Is there such a thing?" he asked.

"Good point. But if you don't take the first step, you'll never finish."

"The Judge has fostered a dozen kids over the years."

"I was number nine, I think. I believe Marissa was number twelve." I smiled when the slight surprise sparked in his gray eyes.

"You mentioned that at the reception. How long did she foster you?"

"For a couple of years. Marissa was an angel compared to me. I tested the Judge often in the beginning, and then she sat me down and pointed out that I was headed to a bad place if I didn't course correct." I understood the true depth of darkness in bad places.

Luke raised a brow. "You pushed back against the Judge?"

"Once. Maybe twice. She talked to me like an adult, and for whatever reason her words clicked with me." The Judge had been the first island of sanity in my life, and I didn't want to be ejected. If not for eighty-eight days in hell, I might've pressed.

"How'd you get from there to here?"

"Art. It was a lifeline. It helped me focus and dream bigger."

"Did you go to art school or were you self-taught?"

"A bit of both. Mostly just a lot of practice." I sipped my wine.

He peered at me over the rim of his glass. "What broke your concentration on the climbing wall?"

"Didn't you just ask me that?"

"You dodged the answer." He didn't like unanswered questions, puzzles, or unclosed loops.

I skimmed a calloused finger along the glass's delicate stem. "I saw someone I thought I knew. It had been a long time since we'd crossed paths. I fell, and after that fuss and drama, she was gone, if it even was her." I sipped my wine, desperately ready to shift the conversation toward him. In under five minutes he'd touched on my foster care stint and Della. "You said you never climbed the wall?"

"I have not. I usually have less than an hour for my workouts, and the wall looks like it would take time to learn."

"It takes practice."

Luke was attractive, and I liked the cut of his jaw, his broad shoulders, and the tuft of dark hair in the V of his shirt. Hints of his aftershave reached me as someone walked past and stirred the air. If I were a normal person, I'd kiss him by the end of the evening and maybe wrap my arms around him. But I wasn't normal. There were a million invisible fissures running through me, leaving me more fragile than I wanted to admit. What remained whole and intact was the darkness lurking inside me.

"When you're not practicing law or doing an express workout, what do you do?" I asked.

"Not much," he said ruefully. "But when I do get a day or two off, I drive to the beach. I like swimming in the ocean."

"No lying on the hot sand and soaking up the sun?"

"I don't sit still well, and after reading thousands of pages of briefs, the idea of reading anything isn't appealing. By the time I escape to the beach, I've had my fill of words."

"And the ocean forces you to concentrate on exactly where you are."

"It tries."

"Like my wall."

The waitress came to our table with menus. "Would you two like to order dinner or appetizers?"

Luke looked at me. "What do you think?"

Food meant more time, more conversation, and more interaction. "Sounds good."

Without glancing at my phone, I estimated we'd been here about twenty minutes. I'd become good at judging time in the basement. To avoid being swallowed by an endless abyss, I'd started to collect all the clues hinting to the passage of time. When I heard Tanner's steady footfall on the floor above, I paid attention. The rising volume of the radio news suggested he was getting ready for work. I guessed it was about 7:30 a.m. because he'd always shown up at the neighbor's house for work at 8:30. During the day, while Della slept, songs on the radio blaring upstairs fell into a predictable pattern of morning, midday, and late day. Occasionally a bird chirped or a delivery truck pulled into the driveway and dropped a package.

According to my internal time gauge, I was only a third of the way into my sixty-three-minute date-night goal. I glanced at the menu, my gaze scanning words but not really processing. So much food. So many options. I never got tired of food.

Twenty more minutes here with him could prove I wasn't such a big mess. "How about the fruit and cheese board?"

Luke looked up at the waitress. "That work?"

"Coming right up," the waitress said.

"You're tense," Luke said. "Everything all right?"

Maybe he knew my backstory. The Judge wasn't one to talk, but word got around. Normally, I didn't care who knew about my past. I'd done nothing wrong. But in this moment, I hoped he didn't just for a little while. I rarely experienced normal, and it was kind of nice.

"Am I that obvious?" I asked.

"Only a little."

I smiled, wondering if he was simply playing his cards close to the vest. "You're very diplomatic."

"I try." His gaze swirled with more questions, but he employed silence to entice unsaid words.

"I don't date much." My awkwardness danced between us.

And if anything, it only deepened the mystery of me. "Why is that?"

Never default to truth if there's a believable alternative. "I'm the classic absent-minded artist who spends most of her time in the studio."

"Why did you say yes to this date?"

"I don't know. Sometimes I get tired of being awkward and alone." The key to a good lie was to thread in the truth.

"You're not. Awkward, I mean."

"Wait until you get to know me."

He laughed. "What's the biggest challenge when you're painting a portrait?"

Felt good to switch to a safer topic. "Getting the expression right is always tricky. The goal isn't to just re-create a person's face but to show who they are on the inside."

"How do you do that?"

"I talk to them. Ask for ten favorite candid pictures of them."

"Candid photos?"

"They can be shockingly accurate." Maybe that was why I was never satisfied with Della's portrait. I didn't know the real person behind the mask.

The cheese and fruit board arrived, and I was relieved to have something to occupy us for a few minutes. The food was good. This restaurant was now on Luke's Favorites list. Havarti cheese rocks. *Blah, blah, blah.* The platter bought me about ten minutes of mindless conversation, which I suspected Luke was also using to evaluate me. I understood he liked what he saw.

And I liked what I saw. But I had no idea what to do next.

I glanced out the window as a couple walked past arm in arm. Another loving couple. Shit. Were they everywhere?

A splash of red caught my attention, and I looked out the window. A woman wearing a red coat walked toward me on the sidewalk. She was the woman from the gym.

She looked up, her gaze meeting mine, and for a moment the eyes trapped me. I'd seen those eyes before. Not only in the gym today but also in Tanner's van and basement room. I'd been trying for a decade to re-create those eyes. Della. She was no look-alike. She was the real deal.

My pulse quickened, and my stomach soured. Twice in one day. There was no way I was wrong about this woman.

"Everything all right?" Luke asked.

I rose so quickly, the table shifted, my wineglass tipped, and it would have fallen if Luke hadn't caught it. Fumbling in my purse for a twenty-dollar bill, I stood. "I'm sorry. I need to go. I see someone outside." I tossed the money on the table.

"Are you sure you're okay?"

A sour taste settled in my mouth. "I'm fine."

I hurried through the restaurant, bumping into a couple of patrons and nearly knocking into a waitress sporting a platter of drinks.

Outside, heavy, humid air rushed my lungs. The crowds on the street had thickened, and Della had vanished again. I hurried to the corner and looked left and right, but there was no sign of her. How the hell had she vanished so quickly?

A hand touched my elbow, and I whirled around to see Luke. His gaze was a mixture of curiosity, apprehension, and maybe some annoyance. "What's going on?"

I carefully pulled my elbow from his grip. "I'm sorry. I saw someone I thought I knew." Shit. I scanned the street again but there was no sign of Della. "I'm sorry."

"Don't be sorry." He stepped toward me in a way that felt possessive, or maybe it was just concern.

When he reached out for my hand, I stepped back. "I can't."

"What's wrong?"

As first dates went, this one wasn't the worst, but it was in the bottom three. "Just rattled. Luke, thank you, but I need to go."

"This doesn't have to end now."

"It does. I'm sorry." Before he could speak again, I turned and hurried around the corner. I followed sidewalk after sidewalk down darkening roads until I found myself facing a dead-end alley near my warehouse. I heard a man talking to himself and saw shadows move toward me.

I rushed to my warehouse front door, unlocked the dead bolts and secondary locks on the metal screen door. Inside, I slammed the doors and closed my eyes. My breath came so quickly I thought I'd hyperventilate. I slid to the floor and buried my face in my hands.

"Della, why are you back?"

Chapter Eleven

Dawson

Saturday, July 13, 2024
8:00 p.m.

Dawson sat at the bar and smiled as the bartender set his favorite draft beer in front of him. He'd spent most of the afternoon on the Sandra Taylor case, rereading his notes on the teen's missing persons investigation, which felt woefully incomplete now.

A decade ago, his sources had described Sandra as a troubled young woman who partied hard and hated her homelife. So much like Scarlett and Tiffany Patterson when they'd been teens.

Next, he'd keyed in on his notes about Tanner. Polite. Neatly dressed. Seemed concerned. Tanner had grown up in a two-parent middle-class family. His father had been a carpenter and his mother a clerk in a hardware store. There were no siblings—just some distant cousins and a few aunts and uncles. He'd opted out of college for trade school and by nineteen was earning a six-figure income. He bought the house in Moyock, North Carolina, when he was twenty-one. The kid was a success.

No arrest record. No missing family animals, no complaints filed against him for sexual assault. Whatever he'd been planning, he'd kept it locked in his head until he was ready to act it out.

On June 12, 2014, Dawson had gotten a tip that Sandra had gone on a date with Tanner. Following the lead, he found Tanner at a jobsite—a home renovation project. What he'd not realized was that the jobsite was across the street from Scarlett Crosby's house and Scarlett had already been missing for six days. There'd been no missing persons report, so no red flags. Maybe if he'd knocked on more doors, someone might have mentioned Scarlett hadn't been seen in nearly a week. If he'd realized Scarlett was also in trouble, he'd like to think he'd have zeroed in on Tanner and saved both girls. However, *maybes*, like unicorns and birthday wishes, didn't mean much.

Since he'd separated from his wife last winter, he came here often. The bar was dark and didn't really attract tourists or the younger crowd but working-class folks who were either cops, navy, or dock or construction workers. The drinks were strong, and people left him alone. Most patrons were midthirties or older, and most were like him: they wanted to drink and hook up. He could always count on a cold beer and better-than-average odds that he'd find a woman close to last call.

A woman took a seat next to him and ordered a white wine. He caught the whiff of perfume, and peripheral vision revealed a thick shock of blond hair swept away from an angled face. Long, elegant fingers accepted a glass from the bartender.

The woman beside him now didn't look like the kind to linger, but he'd been fooled before. When she twisted in her seat and faced him, he damn near fell off his stool. "Margo Larsen?"

A smile curled the edges of her lips. "Detective Dawson. I thought that was you."

"What brings you here?" Her blouse was fastened above her breasts, but discretion made the look sexier.

She smiled. "Same as you. How's the food?"

"Burgers aren't bad, but beyond that I'd be careful."

"Not the kind of place to get a salad."

A smile tugged at his lips. "No."

Margo traced the stem of her glass. "You know this place well?"

"Well enough."

"But you come here often." She nodded thoughtfully. "You look comfortable, as if this is your place."

The observation was slightly unsettling. "Maybe."

She raised the glass to her lips. "Why do you come here so often?"

He shifted toward her. Their knees faced each other and were inches apart. "Same as the rest."

"Then I chose well, I suppose."

He wasn't thinking about her as a cop or colleague. And they both were off the clock, so what the hell. "Where did you live before here?"

"I was in the DC area; loved it, but I like the beach and decided to mix things up."

He tried to imagine a couple of her blouse buttons opening. If she were interviewing a suspect dressed like this, she might ask great questions, but anyone with a heartbeat wouldn't hear a word she said. Hell, he was having trouble concentrating himself.

Her tongue barely skimmed the edge of her glass as she drank.

He cleared his throat. "How do you like being near the water?"

"I like it. Town is smaller. Finding a place to live is turning into a challenge. But I'm getting by. What about you?"

"I've always lived here. Can't imagine anywhere else."

She nodded slowly, as if this weren't a surprise to her. "Any word on our Jane Doe?"

Jane Doe. In his mind, the victim was Sandra Taylor. "Waiting for the autopsy. DNA, X-rays, dental records."

She leaned a fraction closer, ensnaring him in her soft perfume. "If there are any records for Sandra Taylor, they shouldn't be too hard to find."

He didn't want to talk to her about the case. That was part of the reason he was here.

Margo moistened her lips. "Can you do me a favor, Dawson?"

"Depends."

"I swiped right on a guy, and he's just arrived." She glanced over her shoulder and then leaned even closer to him. "Let's just say, not as advertised." Her shoulder brushed his. "Mind backing me up if he comes this way?"

He'd hung up his white hat a long time ago. "I'm just having a beer."

"Oh, come on, Dawson. Help a girl out."

He didn't want to know what shit pile she'd fallen into. But he also wasn't anxious to send her along. Nice to have the company of a sexy woman. "That sounds like trouble."

Her laugh was throaty, deep. "You're intrigued by me, am I right?"

"Am I?"

"Sure. I saw the surprise on your face when you recognized me."

"How do you know that?"

"I'm a cop. I'm good at summing up people."

He caught the approach of the man in the corner of his eye. Out of habit, he shifted, freeing his jacket from his weapon. "Don't count on me."

"Oh, I don't. But I figure my chances are better if you back me up."

The man approaching Margo was tall and dressed in jeans and a blue shirt. He had a phone in hand and was glancing at the picture and then her. "Margo?"

Margo sipped her wine. "No, sorry."

"I'm Brad."

She shook her head as if the name meant nothing.

The man's eyes narrowed. "You sure? This picture looks just like you."

"You got the wrong gal."

The man's quizzical expression hardened. "Are you fucking with me, lady?"

Margo stilled but didn't flinch. "You've got the wrong lady."

"Why would you drag me here?" the man demanded. "Is this a game?"

"She's with me," Dawson said.

The man directed his attention to Dawson. "Who the fuck are you?"

Dawson shifted so the badge clipped to his belt buckle was visible. "I'm the guy that's going to cause you trouble if you don't back off."

"Is that badge supposed to scare me?" the man demanded.

Dawson stood and glanced toward the bartender, who reached below the bar and pulled out a bat. "He's a former cop. And there are about ten other cops in this bar I know. We'll all happily escort you out of the establishment, or better, to a holding cell."

The man held up his hands. "I haven't done anything."

"You're harassing me," Margo said. "Detective Dawson, what would you like me to do? Do I press charges?"

A few men around them stood at their tables. None moved toward the bar, but it was clear they were paying attention.

The man's eyes narrowed as he stared at Margo, but finally his hands raised. "Fuck you, bitch."

"A man of words," Margo said.

Brad turned and left the bar. Margo reached for her glass, as if the matter were closed. Dawson remained standing in case Brad doubled back.

"What're you doing tonight, Dawson?" she asked.

"Trying to stay out of a bar fight."

Margo tossed a twenty on the bar. "My hotel is across the street. Care to join me, or would you rather wait until last call and see what's left?"

His gaze settled on her face. Fuck, she was a stunner. Women like her didn't go for men like him. "Are you playing games with me now, Margo?"

She wriggled off the stool, drawing his gaze along the thin column of her neck. "Nope. Just a gal who doesn't have the best taste in men."

That teased a smile. "But you want me?"

She arched a brow. "Is that a yes or a no, Dawson?"

Maybe he wasn't the cream of the crop. He sure as shit had been passed over for promotion, and his ex-wife's drama had likely tanked his future in the department. But he was smart enough to understand a lucky break. He took a long pull on his beer.

"How did you pick a dump hotel like the one across the street?"

She arched a brow. "Are you familiar with it?"

"I am." What were the chances they were staying in the same hotel? "And I don't picture you there."

She laughed. "Yes or no?"

"It's a yes."

She trailed long fingers over his shoulders and walked toward the door. He tossed a couple of twenties on the bar and followed. She had a tight ass, and when she walked, it swayed seductively. He grew hard.

Outside, she didn't glance back as she crossed the street toward the hotel. It wasn't fancy, midgrade at best, and he'd been honest when he said he didn't place a woman like her here.

In the lobby, he glanced toward the reception desk. The clerk was watching his phone screen and not paying any attention to them. Margo moved with ease down a first-floor hallway, and he followed her to room 109 as she fished a key from her purse. Despite the many warnings of on-the-job complications his left brain was all but shouting, he continued onward.

She unlocked the door located five doors from the emergency exit and twenty feet from the lobby and the distracted clerk.

Her hair framed her face, highlighting a relaxed profile as she pushed open the door. He lingered back a step, watching as she flipped on the light.

His hand on his weapon, he followed, glancing in the bathroom and confirming there was no one there before closing the door. Old habits.

She sat on the edge of a bed covered in a paisley-print comforter and pulled off her high-heeled boots. Her toes were painted a bright pink.

"You aren't scared, are you?" she asked.

"Cautious."

She stood and wrapped her arms around his neck. Her hard nipples pressed against his chest. "Think I'm going to hurt you?"

He ran a finger along her cheek, neck, and down to her narrow waist. Her muscles were firm. "Like I said, cautious."

"This isn't an HR sting." She unwrapped her hands, stepped back, and unfastened her blouse. The fabric fell open, bracketing a red lace bra cupping full breasts.

He clung to reason, but his grip was slipping.

She wriggled out of her skirt, leaving her wearing only red panties, the bra, and the blouse. "Getting undressed, or are you going to just stare?"

"I like looking at you."

"There's more to see, but you have to undress first."

Dawson shrugged off his jacket and tossed it on a chair. He moved to the door, threw the dead bolt and security lock, and then dimmed the lights. He removed his weapon and put it in the top dresser drawer, along with his badge, handcuffs, and keys.

He closed the distance between them and rested his hands on her shoulders. Slowly, he traced her collarbone with his thumb and then pushed the folds of the blouse apart until it slid down her arms. She moistened her lips as his hand cupped her breast and squeezed. He suckled the taut swell. She hissed in a breath and arched into him.

"Tell me what you want," she said.

"What's that mean?"

"Tell me what you want, Detective Dawson. Name it."

Was there a hidden camera? That would be his luck. But she was asking and consenting. And the more he looked at her, the more he wanted her.

He looked down at her body and skimmed a finger over the panties. What did he want? An old boss had warned him to always keep his dick out of the payroll. He'd stuck to that, and still it all went sideways. "Take your bra and panties off."

She reached behind her and unfastened the bra, letting the straps fall down her arms. As she tossed it aside, she slid off the silk lace panties and let them fall until they ringed her ankles. She stepped out of them. "Now what?"

"Lie on the bed."

"Okay."

He watched as she slowly settled in the center of the bed. His erection throbbed, and it was all he could do not to climb on top and pound inside her. He removed his shirt, unfastened his belt buckle, and toed off his shoes. He fished a condom from his wallet and let his pants fall.

She piled the pillows against the headboard and leaned back. "What now?"

Naked, he climbed on the bed. His hands slid up her smooth legs. "Spread your legs."

A smile flickered over her lips as she teased her nipples with her fingertips and then slowly opened her legs a little for him. "Like this?"

Her compliance was intoxicating. "Wider."

She spread her legs wide and slid her manicured fingers over her belly. "Do you want me to touch myself?"

"Not yet."

He wasn't sure what kind of fantasy she was acting out, and it didn't matter. She'd picked him as easily as the guy she'd swiped right for. This was a onetime thing, but he didn't care.

He moved between her thighs, again stroking his fingers over her pale skin. Her gaze didn't waver from his, and he was slightly nervous as he slid latex over his erection. He positioned himself at her moist opening.

"What do you want?" he asked.

She tilted her pelvis upward, pressing against his tip. "Do I have to say it?"

"Yes."

"Fuck me."

Dawson shoved inside her with more force than expected. He halted, waiting a beat. "Good?"

"Harder."

When she cupped his ass, he slammed into her.

Chapter Twelve

SCARLETT

Saturday, July 13, 2024
8:30 p.m.

Fifty minutes.

My date with Luke Kane had lasted fifty minutes. And then the Della look-alike had appeared, and I'd lost my mind. Again. This wasn't the first time in the last decade that I'd spotted "Della." But at least I'd not made a total ass of myself or filed a police report. I'd only screwed up a date.

Over the years, I'd questioned whether Della was real and whether I was sane. Maybe my mind had broken in that locked room, and I had created her to shoulder my mistakes and pain? Maybe the cop psychologist had been right. Maybe Della never existed. Inventing Della, the doctor had said, was my way of coping and surviving. Maybe I had gone a little crazy.

I changed into paint-splattered jeans and an oversize T-shirt and pulled my blond hair into a ponytail. I uncovered the canvas and sat in front of the Della painting.

As I stared at the eyes, I willed Della to come to life and admit she was real. To tell me I wasn't crazy. But the eyes stared at me with stony, frustrating silence.

Maybe I'd never been able to get these eyes right because Della hadn't existed. Maybe I was trying to catch a fantasy that was fading with time. You can't capture what never happened.

I squeezed fresh paint from several tubes and then picked up my brush. I dabbed the tip into the colors and swirled them on a clean palette until the color seemed right. Brush raised to the painting, it hovered over the eyes that dared me now to fix them. But I had no idea how to remedy the eyes. I had nothing else to spark memories or inject life.

I tossed the brush down, rose, and flexed my fingers. Walking to the window, I stared out onto the quiet sidewalk illuminated by streetlights.

There'd been no word from Dawson since his visit. No updates on the case, and I wanted to take that as a positive sign, but silence was not always golden. The wheels of progress were slow, and they did churn with narratives and incorrect conclusions.

I fished my phone out of my back pocket and glanced at the screen. I'd not given Luke my phone number, but my website was easy to find. However, given my behavior, reconnecting would have to come from me. I shoved the phone back in my pocket. Ghosting him was for the best. I was saving him a lot of grief—getting tangled up with me was a no-win situation.

I rolled through my voicemail messages from numbers I'd not been able to identify and had ignored. I'd been ambushed by one too many reporters, so I'd made it a practice never to answer or even listen to messages from strange numbers.

I pressed play on the first, the second, and the third. All were robocalls. The last message was different. I recognized Tiffany Patterson's number. Static silence hummed for thirty-eight seconds. A horn honked. This message lasted nearly a minute and had come in at noon four days ago. I'd been in my studio that day, my phone on silent. Now, for whatever reason, I imagined her standing on the sidewalk across from my building watching me as I worked and wondering when I'd answer. There was no way of proving that scenario, but it took little for my imagination to run wild. I'd stayed sane in that basement room because I could imagine other places and people sitting beside me and offering comfort. That same imagination now spun stories that were a bit terrifying.

Had Tiffany seen the article in the local paper about my painting at the recreation center? Had she run out of money, or was she in trouble?

Tiffany had visited me at the hospital a decade ago. She'd told me she was worried about me. She said she was surprised we'd gone to the same high school. She was three years ahead, but small world, right? She'd cleared her throat often. Her faltering smile faded in and out, and she said quietly that she would never forget how I'd risked my life to save her. Carefully, she'd laid her bundle of flowers on the table by my bed. "Thank you."

That moment had stuck with me, and when she'd shown up on my doorstep six months ago, pale, thin, and high, my heart had softened for her. I'd fed her, allowed her to shower, and given her clean clothes. She'd thanked me and asked me for a few bucks. That first time, I'd given her a couple of twenties. Which I later realized she'd spent on drugs.

And now she was calling my phone and not asking me for money. That was out of character for her.

I turned from my warehouse window. According to Dawson, Sandra had gone to our high school, too. Two girls chosen from the same area could be random, but three made it a pattern.

Had Tiffany heard about the discovery of the young girl's body? Did Tiffany know something about Sandra? What was she trying to tell me?

A quick internet search of Tiffany listed her three last known addresses. I picked the most recent and searched it on the map before I crossed the room and grabbed my purse.

After I'd sat in my truck and started the engine, my heart pounded as I drove through the city, across the bridge, east toward the country. I knew basically the general area where she lived, and finding the two-story building wasn't difficult. I parked out front and for several minutes watched as people milled around the building, their laughter mingling with music blaring from several speakers. Out of the vehicle, I climbed the stairs to the second floor and found 2B. Inside, more music pulsed. Drawing in a breath, I knocked on the door. For nearly a minute, there was no response. Finally, footsteps moved toward the door, and it snapped open.

I didn't recognize the tall woman with dark hair staring at me. Midthirties, with a long, sallow face, she wore a loose-fitting T-shirt that draped off her shoulder, exposing a butterfly tattoo on her bicep.

"Yeah, what do you want?" the woman asked.

"I'm looking for Tiffany. I was told she lived here." I rushed to add, "We were friends as kids, and I'm in town for a few days and wanted to say hi." The lies tripped off my tongue so easily. "I tried to call her, but her number was disconnected."

"That sounds like Tiffany," the woman said with a smile. "Tiffany isn't here. She hasn't been here for days."

"Do you know where she could be?"

"She might be working. She might be getting high. I never know with her. Give me your number and I'll have her call you."

"She's got my number."

A brow arched. "You aren't a cop, are you?"

That startled a chuckle. "No. Not even close. I'm an artist." As proof I held up my ink-stained fingers.

That seemed to satisfy her. "Tiff's known for going MIA. Give her a few days and then worry."

"She ran away a lot when we were in high school," I lied, hoping to learn more about Tiffany. "A lot of times she came to my parents' house." Fabrications swirled around me, and if I wasn't careful, they would tangle, ensnare, and trip me up.

"Why are you in town?"

"My mother's funeral." In for a penny, in for a pound. "That's why I'm here. I wanted to tell Tiffany because it would have meant something to her. We talked a lot about our moms. And I want to make sure she's okay."

"Tiffany doesn't have many friends. She's always been wired tight."

"I remember," I lied. "She was a skinny little kid."

"Yeah."

I dug a pen and scrap paper from my pocket. I scrawled a note and my number asking her to call me. I wrote my name in bold block letters and underlined it. "Just in case. Can you give her this?"

"Sure." She flicked the edge of the paper with her finger. "When she's gone for more than a few days, she's usually at Jeremy's."

"Her boyfriend?"

"Really her drug dealer. He has a house in the Fairmont Park area. I don't know the address. But ask anyone near there and they'll tell you how to find Jeremy."

I knew the area. I'd been to a house in that neighborhood a few weeks ago looking for Tiffany after she'd texted me asking for help. I'd found her. We'd argued. She'd been so high. She'd wanted money, not help. Finally, I'd left without her. "Thanks."

As I walked to my truck, a man called out to me. He said he needed a favor. I moved faster, gripping my keys. His shouts grew louder and angrier. When I slid into my truck, I locked the door immediately and started the engine. I didn't bother to look back to see who'd been shouting.

Tiffany really knew nothing about Tanner, but maybe she had something to say about Sandra Taylor. Could she have overheard Tanner and his girlfriend, Lynn Yeats, when they'd shared so many breakfasts at the diner? Maybe Tiffany called in the tip. Maybe she knew something about Della? Maybe I was simply fishing.

Regardless, I needed to find Tiffany.

Chapter Thirteen

DAWSON

Sunday, July 14, 2024
2:00 a.m.

Dawson stood at the foot of the bed watching Margo sleep. In the five hours they'd been in this room, they'd gone for round two and then three. He couldn't remember the last time he felt this satisfied. This validated.

HR problems aside, he worried about the fantasies he'd tapped into tonight. He'd harbored dark needs, but this was the first time he'd given them life. Neither his wife nor his few girlfriends had ever voiced Margo's shadowy desires, which had dovetailed with his perfectly.

God help him, he'd liked it all. Liked knowing he was in control. As the ropes tightened around her wrists, power had triggered a sensation of pure euphoria that banished the failures that had been circling since he'd been pegged as the cop who'd talked to Tanner Reed and not picked up on any whiff of trouble.

Control was a precious commodity in his world. His ex-wife had used him to whitewash her drug problem, and then she'd tossed him out. And on the job, he chased the missing and the dead. Many of the missing didn't want to be found, and the ones who did were often already dead. He closed some homicides, but too many remained open. The wins were rare, and most days he felt as if he were running in quicksand. The harder he struggled, the deeper he sank. Unlike the old-timers on the job, it would be decades before he could grab a pension. Rudderless. Hopeless. Trapped.

Margo rolled on her back, and the sheet fell below her breasts. She made no move to cover herself as she studied him. "That was fun."

"It was." He shrugged on his shirt and began to fasten the small white buttons. "You come to that bar often?"

"First time. But I liked it a lot. Maybe we'll see each other again outside of the office."

"Or I can call you."

"I like the randomness of meeting you in the bar last night." She shoved a thick shock of short blond hair away from her face. Red finger marks rimmed her slender wrists. Now that her makeup had faded, he realized she was younger than he'd originally thought. Thirty, late twenties, maybe.

"I can't say when I'll be back to the bar," he lied. "Running down the Taylor murder is going to take time."

"Let me know if you need a hand with that?"

He sat on the edge of the bed. "Walk me through your response to the 9-1-1 call."

"Dispatch said there was a possible body on the premises. The caller said the body was hidden in the wall near the kitchen. I keep a sledgehammer in the trunk of my car, so it was easy to break the drywall."

"You keep a sledgehammer in your trunk?"

"It comes in handy more often than you think."

"Okay."

"When I showed up, the house was empty. No signs of anyone. When backup arrived, I went into the kitchen, took my jacket off, and got to work." She smiled. "For the record, I found the body after the fourth hole. Have you listened to the 9-1-1 call?"

"I did. Sounds like a woman, and there's lots of background noise. I put a trace on the number. It's a disposable phone."

"Do you know the location of the call?"

Most assumed a burner was totally anonymous. Though the caller's name wasn't available, the location of the call could be traced. Soon he'd also have the device's point of purchase. "Working on that."

A smile curved her lips. "Do you have a recording of the message on your phone?"

He opened the texted message from dispatch. He hit play. *"Go to the house at 922 Hanover. There's a body in the east wall near the kitchen."*

"Direct and to the point." She sat up, letting the sheet drop as she stood. "Keep me in the loop."

Hard to concentrate with two lovely breasts less than a foot from his fingertips. "Sure."

"See you in the bar sometime?" she said.

"You know me that well?"

She slid on her blouse and faced him as she slowly buttoned it. "You're relaxed in that bar, like it's your second home. Bartender refilled your beer without asking." She wrinkled her nose. "Guessing divorced recently."

When it came to hiding his emotions, he was a skilled practitioner. The ex-wife had complained about his distance often enough. "What else do you know about me?"

She pulled up sheer panties. "You like giving orders. I would say that gives you a sense of mastery in your chaotic world."

He blistered under her intense gaze. He'd revealed a secret part of himself to her and now wasn't sure if that was very smart. "And?"

"I can't tell if you have children, but I'm thinking no. I don't get the vibe of a tortured soul missing his kid."

"I don't have kids or a tortured soul."

She raised a brow. "That makes divorce easier but not painless. Been there, done that. Kicked my ex to the curb last year."

Of course she'd had other men, but the image annoyed him. She felt like his. "Sorry to hear that."

A shrug lifted her shoulder. "You're married to the job, aren't you?"

"Maybe more than I realized. What about you?"

"I'm a hopeless addict. I loved my work to the exclusion of my marriage."

He ran his hand along her jaw. He didn't want to leave her. "Be in the bar on Tuesday night. I want to see you."

"You can give orders in here, but out there, I'm my own woman."

Irritation swarmed, ominous and disturbing, as he realized he needed to see her again. "Is that a yes or no?"

"It's a wait and see if it suits me to return."

A smile tugged at his lips, belying any fears that she could be slipping away. She liked taking the orders, but she was the one running this show. "Okay."

His gaze skimmed over her smooth thigh. There was lean muscle there, but she wasn't too slim. He liked a woman with muscles.

"See you around, Dawson. And keep me posted on that case."

"Are you kicking me out?"

"I've got to get some rest. Got an early call tomorrow."

"What case are you working?" He didn't question that he was curious about her.

"Who knows? I'm the new guy."

She'd dominate whatever case was tossed her way. "I'm sure you'll run the room in a few months."

"We shall see."

He chuckled. "Tuesday night, Margo."

Dawson left her hotel room, feeling buoyant. For the first time in weeks, he believed he could make a difference and maybe could solve Sandra Taylor's murder.

He strode down the hallway, wishing he were still in bed with Margo. He punched the elevator button and, when the doors opened, stepped inside. He rode up to his room on the fifth floor, waved his key in front of the lock, and pushed open the door. He glanced toward his neatly made bed. A few hours of sleep would be nice, but he was too jazzed, too optimistic to sleep, so he opted for a shower instead. He stripped and turned on the hot water. As the room steamed, he hesitated, raising his forearm to his nose. The scent of Margo still clung to him, and he wasn't keen to wash it off.

"Get a grip," he muttered and stepped into the shower. He buried his face in the hot spray, savoring the heat, willing it to give him more energy. Finally, he shut off the tap, toweled off, shaved, and dressed in suit pants and a clean shirt. He made a strong cup of coffee on the little one-cup Keurig machine he'd brought with him when he'd moved out of the house. The cup brewed quickly as he flicked on predawn news. Another hot day. Two gang-related shootings. A kid killed.

He sat at a small round table and flipped through the case file to an old picture of Scarlett taken after she was rescued, when she was still in the hospital. Her blond hair hung in oily strands around her pale, gaunt face. The first time he'd seen this picture, he'd felt a punch of regret. She'd been an at-risk kid for most of her life, and she'd been ripe for a guy like Tanner. And he'd spoken to Tanner and missed it all.

Scarlett's medical file detailed the horrors: scars from repeated whippings, vaginal tearing, malnutrition, and a hairline fracture on her right wrist.

Many in the press called her lucky, but this kind of abuse created a damage so deep it never really healed. The Scarlett who'd been snatched died spiritually, and what had been rehabbed and released from the hospital after her rescue might have Scarlett's DNA, but that was about it.

The Scarlett he'd seen yesterday was reserved to the point of cold. If she had any emotions or feelings about Tanner, Sandra, or Tiffany, they were buried under ice so thick, no amount of sun or heat would ever fully melt it.

Hers was a common reaction to assault. The reserve was a form of protection. He found it slightly unnerving, but he didn't blame her.

But he did fault Scarlett Crosby for lying, and she was lying to him now. Despite her nonreactions to his questions, he could tell she knew, or at least suspected she knew, more about the other girl in Tanner's house.

He shifted his attention to Sandra's file and cross-checked for similarities to Scarlett. Both had known Tanner. Same age, similar appearance, lived within three miles of each other, and they went to the same high school.

The crimes against the two girls hadn't initially been connected ten years ago because there'd been significant delays with the filing of their missing persons reports. After Scarlett's rescue, he'd tried to reopen Sandra's investigation, but by then he was on administrative leave.

He opened his laptop and searched for East Norfolk High School. The yearbooks for the last twenty years had been digitized and put online, making it easy to find the 2013–2014 school year and Sandra Taylor. She'd been a junior. Her smile was bright and wide and her eyes were vibrant blue and wary. She'd been in the social service system since she was twelve and had been in six homes in four years. Many kids had clubs or activities listed under their names, but she had nothing.

As he stared at Sandra's face, he thought about the nearly mummified corpse now lying at the medical examiner's office.

He scrolled back through the years and found Scarlett Crosby's picture in the freshman class. Like Sandra, she'd been a fresh face. Written under her name was *Art Club*.

Had the two girls crossed paths? With a thousand kids in the school, a year's difference could have created a gulf between them so they never hung out. However, it was possible they'd had a general knowledge of each other. Passed in a hallway. Saw each other in the principal's office. Ran in similar circles.

All three girls lived in the same area and attended the same high school. Tanner had found his hunting ground. But how?

For curiosity's sake, he typed in the name *Della*. Nothing popped up. He considered formal variations on the name, typing *Adele*, *Adaline*,

Del, and *Cordelia* into the search box. One Adele popped up in the senior class, but she was Black and didn't remotely resemble the sketches Scarlett had done ten years ago. There still was no proof of the mysterious Della.

His phone dinged with a text. For a second he thought it might be Margo, but he realized she didn't have his number, nor he hers.

The text was from his estranged wife. Kevin, our meeting with the attorney is tomorrow at 11. However, you've yet to sign the property settlement. We can't move forward until you do.

He glanced at the clock and realized it was nearly six. His soon-to-be ex-wife had always been an early riser, and he could picture her writing up the to-do list for the day.

Drawing in a breath, he sat and rubbed the back of his neck with his hand. Property agreement. He didn't have a pot to piss in. On paper, she was getting the house, the furnishings, and the limited savings account. But he wasn't in a rush to make it official. He texted back, Blood from a stone.

Kevin, just sign the damn papers so we can end this.

He didn't respond, annoyed that she wasn't satisfied that she'd gotten it all. She wanted his complete capitulation. Maybe he'd been an asshole and grown too distant, but his days of apologizing were over.

He rose, slid his weapon into his holster, grabbed his jacket, keys, and wallet, and with the television still on, left the Do Not Disturb sign on the door. Soon, he'd have to find a permanent place. This hotel room was hardly home, but it did the trick for now. And it was close to Margo.

Outside, the rising sun splashed bright shades of ginger and tangerine across the sky that dripped onto the cracked parking lot. In his car, he entered Tiffany's address, located in a small neighborhood off a bleak section of Shore Drive.

After a twenty-minute drive, he parked in front of the two-story apartment building. The strip of grass between the building and lot was filled with tall weeds, beer cans, and trash. The lot was half-full, but this early on a Sunday, whoever was out partying likely was still there.

Tiffany still worked in the food industry, and he guessed she worked long, odd hours. The apartment looked quiet. Time to wake up.

He pounded on the front door, then stepped to the side, waiting. When he didn't hear any sign of life inside, he banged on the door with his fist.

A gravelly feminine voice echoed from behind the door. "What? Who is it?"

"Detective Kevin Dawson." He held up his badge. "I have questions about Tiffany Patterson. You are?"

The door opened on a thirtysomething woman with brown hair and bloodshot eyes. "Bonnie Bartley. What's the deal with Tiffany? Why is she so interesting now?"

"Who else has been asking?"

"A friend of hers."

"You got a name?"

"Scarlett."

He motioned her forward, and when she approached, he selected a picture of Scarlett on his phone. "That her?"

She leaned in. "Yeah."

He slid the phone back in his pocket. "What did Scarlett want?"

"Trying to find Tiffany. Said they were friends from school. Said her mother had just died and her mom had taken care of Tiffany when she was a kid or something."

That was a lie. Scarlett's mother had died six months ago. "When did you see Tiffany last?"

She yawned. "It's been days. I don't keep up with her schedule."

"Where does she work now?"

"At Talley's Bar on Ocean Drive."

He removed his notebook and scribbled down the name. "Tiffany dating anyone?"

"She hooks up with Jeremy Dillon once in a while."

"The drug dealer?" Jeremy was well known in the department. He moved a lot of drugs but so far had avoided jail time.

"Yeah."

"That where she gets her drugs now?"

The woman shifted. "I don't know."

"I don't care about the drugs. I'm trying to find Tiffany. She's a witness in a key case."

She shoved out a breath. "Like I told Scarlett. Check out Jeremy."

"I'd like to see Tiffany's room."

The woman hesitated. "My roommate, Stephanie, is still asleep."

"I promise to be quiet." He edged over the threshold. Whatever he noticed lying around the apartment was admissible in court. He couldn't open doors or closets without her permission or a warrant, but he was amazed what people left lying about.

"Do you have a warrant?" Bonnie asked.

"I can get one, Bonnie." Likely not true, but she didn't know that. "If you let me look at Tiffany's room now, I'll turn a blind eye to anything not related to finding her."

She shoved out a breath. "How can I trust you?"

Dawson wanted to tell her she couldn't. He wasn't here to make her life better. "I'm not here to bust anyone on drugs. Like I said, it's the least of my concerns."

"Or anything else?"

He regarded her. He didn't have the patience to return to his car and run a check. "Are there weapons in the house?"

"No. But my boyfriend sometimes drops off stuff here."

"What's your boyfriend's name?"

Her face tightened. "Why do you care?"

"Anyone who interacted with Tiffany matters to me."

"Jeff's been out of town for a couple of months. He'll be back soon, and he'll want to pick up his stuff."

"Then Jeff doesn't matter." Dawson didn't know what kind of fish he was letting go, but he wanted to see Tiffany's room.

"Okay." Bonnie turned, and he followed her into the dimly lit apartment. The living room was furnished with a few worn love seats, a coffee table covered with pizza boxes, ashtrays, and a bong. The place had a funky smell, and he wondered when they'd last cracked a window.

She opened the bedroom door to a small room furnished with a twin bed. The sheets were rumpled, and the bed was covered with cast-off clothes, as if she'd been trying on outfits and then discarding them.

He pulled on latex gloves and moved to a box crate that doubled as a nightstand. He saw a full ashtray, loose cigarettes, a blunt, and a warm half-full can of soda. "Any bad breakups?"

She leaned against the doorjamb, folding her arms over her chest. "They all were. She didn't make the best choices."

He turned toward a small dressing table covered with makeup, brushes, and curling irons. There was a square-shaped mirror with necklaces hanging off one corner and scarves off the other.

On a side table were stacks of bills, junk mail, and notices to pay. "She was behind on her bills."

"Who isn't?"

"What kind of car does she drive?"

"A red Honda. I haven't seen it in days."

He noticed a newspaper article peeking out from the bills. He pulled it out and realized it was a recent article on Scarlett Crosby. He had read it three times when it had been published last week.

Dawson studied Scarlett's strained expression as she stood with a grinning Judge Thompson in front of a cartoonish mural.

"Did Tiffany mention this article?"

"No."

Laying the paper down, he took a picture of it before moving to a closet. Hanging clothes packed the small space, and in the back, there was a bookshelf stuffed with purses, shoes, and hats. On the bottom shelf, he noticed the spine of a scrapbook. The scrapbook's laminated cover creaked when he opened to the front page, revealing a newspaper feature about Tiffany.

The article was dated ten years ago and spotlighted an interview about Tiffany's escape from Tanner. He turned the page to find a few more articles about her near kidnapping. The writers asked Tiffany about her impressions of Tanner, his death, and Scarlett's rescue. No connections made to Sandra's disappearance.

As he thumbed through more pages, the articles shifted to notices of Scarlett's art shows. Clearly Tiffany was keyed in on Scarlett.

He showed the scrapbook to Bonnie. "Have you ever seen this?"

She leaned closer. "No."

"Did Tiffany ever talk about Tanner Reed or what happened?"

"Sometimes, when she got drunk. She said she had nightmares for years. I know a reporter called about six months ago, and Tiffany was excited to talk to her. She liked the attention."

"Do you have a name for the reporter?"

"No. She never called back." Bonnie shook her head. "As creepy as what nearly happened was, it made her feel special."

"Special?"

"Not invisible. Noticed." She nodded to the book. "I didn't realize she kept the articles. That's a little weird."

Tiffany's brush with Tanner had given her life meaning. And now Dawson's own meeting with Tanner was giving him renewed purpose.

He removed his card from his pocket and handed it to her. "Mind if I take the scrapbook? I'd like to study it."

"I guess. It's not mine."

"I'll take good care of it." He removed a plastic bag from his pocket and slid the scrapbook inside. "Call me if you hear from her."

"Yeah, sure." She flicked the edges of his card.

"Do you think she'll come home soon?"

"Hard to know. She comes and goes."

He looked around the living room. "Do you have any security cameras here?"

"No." She folded her arms over her chest. "They're expensive, and who would want to take our shit, right?"

"Right."

Chapter Fourteen

SCARLETT

Then
Maybe thirty days later in the basement

By my count I'd been in this room for at least a month. The bones in my hips were sharp, and my stomach always grumbled for food. I'd stopped fighting him. Tried to smile when he took pictures. It wasn't a conscious decision, but I was tired of the bruises. Tanner had left us a lamp last week, and now we had light to punch into the darkness. Better to see the four brick walls, the crawling June bugs, and the grate across the basement window. Who knew how long the bulb would last? He'd also removed my chain. Maybe Della had been right. Be nice. Survive. Escape.

I'd found a pebble and started scratching into the wall each time Tanner made me do it. Weekdays I'd usually scratch two hash marks, but those numbers doubled on the weekend. He liked having Della present when he did it. Most times, she sat in the corner, her gaze averted. At first, I didn't look at her, but in the last few days I'd made myself stare at her until she saw me. I wanted her to see what she'd done to me. I was here because of her.

Many times, he took Della upstairs. Strangely, he needed privacy with her. I wouldn't see her for most of the day and night, and oddly, the small space felt empty when she was gone. I hated her constant chatter and singing. And I missed her.

Now as I lay on my side, carving another hash mark into the wall, Della smoothed her hand over my hip in an almost affectionate way. "You're doing a better job."

"What's that mean?"

"You're not fighting as much. He hates resistance."

"How much does the Other Girl fight him?" We'd not talked about her in weeks, but I hadn't stopped thinking about her. I so wanted to believe she'd escaped and was doing well.

"Don't ask him about the Other Girl. It makes him mad."

I stared at my scratches. How many hours had I studied these growing marks, wondering if I'd eventually fill all four walls? "I'm asking you. Who is the Other Girl?"

She smiled as if we were buddies. "Why do you care?"

I rolled on my side toward Della and stared into her resolute expression. "Tell me."

Della's smile always had a tense, clownish vibe. "I only saw her a few times."

"Did you trick her like you did me?"

"I didn't lure her here. Tanner did."

I tipped my head against the brick wall. "How did he fool her?"

"Same as you and me, I guess. Charming. He's a pretty man. Sweet words. You must've noticed him out there."

"Yeah."

She laid her hand gently on my hair and began to toy with the greasy strands. "We aren't so different. I wanted someone to love me, too."

I shook off her fingers, annoyed her assessment hit close to home. "Is the Other Girl still upstairs?"

"He won't tell me where she is."

"Do you think he let her go?" I sat up and stared at her.

Della shook her head as she took my hair again in her hands and began to divide it into three thick strands. "Not in the way you think."

"How do you know?"

Her gaze grew distant as she coiled my hair into a braid. "I just do."

"He's going to kill me." In my gut, I'd known this day was coming. There were moments I'd welcomed it. But faced with death, I realized I didn't want to die. "How many girls have there been?"

"I'm not sure."

I shook my head. "He likes you. He must talk to you upstairs."

"Sometimes he talks. Most times he doesn't." She released my hair and leaned against the wall.

"What does he talk about?"

"Random stuff. His work. The projects he has. His plans to be rich and famous. Problems with his girlfriend."

I shifted away from her. I winced when my insides pinched. "He has a girlfriend?"

"Yeah. I've seen pictures of her. She's not super pretty. Tanner says she adores him. He says she'll do anything for him."

"I can't believe he can be normal with a woman."

"He's not exactly normal. He sometimes will lock me in a box under his bed when he's doing it with her."

"He puts you in a box."

"Being upstairs isn't always great." A soulful grin tugged at the corners of her lips. "It's nice to have you here. It's nice to have a friend."

"We're not friends," I said.

"But we are," she said. "No one will ever understand you better than me. We've become sisters in here."

We were both walking the same path right now, but she was mistaken if she thought this was friendship. An enemy-of-my-enemy kind of union.

I closed my eyes.

"One day, you'll help him get another girl," she said. "And when you do, you'll understand me better."

I understood what she was saying. Tanner knew how to hurt me. How long could I endure this and stay me? Tears welled in my eyes. "I won't. Never. I can't."

She wiped away a tear with her thumb. "You can. Don't worry, it won't be as terrible as you think. I'll show you how."

I looked at her as if she'd lost her mind. I'd beaten on the walls of this room for days, maybe weeks. But they were impenetrable. Tanner was my only chance to get out of here.

Della smiled. "You're thinking about it, right?"

"He'll never let me out of here."

She kissed me gently on the cheek. The touch was so tender, I had to fight back tears.

"He will as soon as he knows you won't run," she said. "He needs to believe you're loyal, like me."

I didn't argue, which for me was close to an agreement. "Why didn't you run when you had the chance?"

"He said he'd kill the Other Girl if I did."

"But you didn't save her, did you?"

Her jaw tensed. "No, I didn't save her."

"Why are you so calm?"

"I'm not," Della said. "But I have to be patient for now."

Chapter Fifteen

SCARLETT

Sunday, July 14, 2024
8:00 a.m.

My morning run was rough. My legs were stiff and my back ached, and both fought me for the first couple of miles. The heat of the day was already rising, and humidity quickly soaked my jog top with sweat.

As I moved down the side streets near Lito's, where I'd met Luke last night, I shoved down a surge of anger and disappointment. After my crazed exit from our date, he'd have been wise to write me off as unstable.

Normally, I didn't care about a date gone sideways. He wouldn't be the first man who'd seen me lose my composure. One guy had called me "batshit crazy." I'd blown up my share of dates and never once looked back. But still. Luke had been nice. And I kind of liked him.

I ran past the restaurant, stopped, and searched his name on my phone. His office was close, so I ran in that general direction. Shoving the phone back in my pocket, I dashed past several side streets and looked up and saw the 2317 Building. I paused, resting my hands on my hips, and stared up at the five-story brick building. I didn't get this way very often. So close, but I never ventured this far northeast because it wasn't the safest area. Made me wonder what kind of people Luke defended. But innocent until proven guilty, right?

I tugged on the front door and was surprised it opened. Inside, I searched the directory and discovered Luke Kane & Associates was on the fifth floor. I was sweating and my scent bordered on ripe. Not exactly sexy. But maybe that was a good thing.

I punched the elevator button, and as I waited, I fluffed my shirt, trying to dry out the sweat. The doors opened, I stepped inside, and the ride to the top took seconds.

When the doors opened again, I walked down the hallway past darkened offices, toward the one with a light on. It was Luke's. My heart thumped faster as I took a step back from the door and glanced toward the elevator. I could leave now. End all this and return to my life.

Instead, I tried the doorknob, which twisted, and slowly, I pushed open the door. The outer office was decorated with modern furniture fashioned out of metal and glass. There was a receptionist desk topped with clean, sparkling glass, and a low midcentury-modern couch and two chairs gathered around a coffee table. No magazines. Luke either didn't like to keep his clients waiting or he didn't care to entertain them. A partly opened door led to an office. I shifted, ready to leave. The floor creaked.

"Is someone out there?" Luke's deep voice drifted from the office.

Shit.

Why was I here? Dawson's visit and my own trip to Tiffany's apartment had rattled the foundation of my carefully curated life. I wasn't sure why, but I needed to prove to myself that the past didn't matter as much and I still had a chance at a normal life.

I cleared my throat, walked up to the door, and pushed it open slowly.

Luke sat behind a long glass desk covered with piles of neatly stacked papers. Bookshelves were filled with leather-bound law books. Four sleek chairs encircled a round conference table.

When he looked up, he didn't seem to recognize me at first, but quickly the tumblers fell into place. He stood. "Scarlett."

I remained in the middle of the room. "I figured out that your office was in the 2317 Building."

He didn't speak, but his gaze remained squarely on me.

"I wasn't planning on stopping by, but I was out for a run, and I realized I was close."

Again, he said nothing.

I took a small step toward him. "I'm sorry I flaked on you last night." Drawing in a breath, I wondered if he thought I was as unbalanced as I probably looked and sounded. "I thought I saw someone on the street, and I kind of freaked out."

"Why?"

I ran my hand over my slicked-back ponytail. "That's a long story. I have a kind of weird past and sometimes it comes back to bite me. Kind of a PTSD thing." I managed a thin smile. "I just wanted you to know I'm sorry."

When he didn't speak, I turned to leave. I was nearly at the threshold when he said, "Thanks for stopping by."

I faced him. "I owed you that much."

"You really didn't."

"I kind of did. Again, apologies."

"Want to try again?" His tone was casual, but his body language radiated authority and confidence.

Did I want to try again? That had to be a yes—I was here. But another attempt would mean a greater level of intimacy. Shit. Nothing had changed. I was still so easily freaked out. "I would."

A brow arched. "You don't look convinced."

"I am."

He regarded me a moment. "Drinks? Dinner?"

"You pick."

"How about dinner? I know a restaurant located on a quiet side street. And there are plenty of marked exits if you need to make a break for it."

His easy charm disarmed me a fraction. "I like lots of exits. Where?"

"Ben's?" He came around the desk, moving slowly toward me but stopping a few feet short.

"I know the place."

His hand slid in his pocket. "Try for six tonight?"

"I can do that."

"Meet you there, or do you want me to pick you up?"

"I'll meet you there."

"Fair enough. Maybe you can tell me a little something about this PTSD."

"Better, just google my name. There's more on the internet about me than you'll ever want to know. Key in *2014*." I fished my phone out of my pocket and held it out to him. "Text yourself a note from my phone. Then we'll both have each other's number."

He typed in a text. "I won't change my mind."

"Google me first. I won't blame you."

He handed me back the phone. "See you at six."

I was feeling a tad more optimistic when I left Luke's. Instead of going home, I swung by a bakery, picked up a dozen doughnuts, and drove to the Judge's house.

I knocked, and when she opened the front door, I held up the box of doughnuts. The Judge was already dressed, hair done and makeup applied. I'd often joked she slept this way. "You said anytime."

She motioned me inside. "And I meant it."

"I'm kind of sweaty. I was out for a run."

"Ah, something is bothering you."

"Maybe a little." I walked down the center hallway and set the doughnuts on the marble countertop next to an open copy of the *Washington Post*.

The Judge removed china covered in roses, as well as cloth napkins and forks from a drawer. Only the Judge ate a doughnut with a fork. She filled a rose-trimmed cup with coffee for me and topped off her own.

I opened the box and turned it toward her. I'd selected six glazed, two powdered, and four chocolates—all three were her favorites. She selected a glazed.

"I've been thinking a lot about Della," I said.

The Judge opened her napkin as she sat at the barstool by the island. Carefully, she smoothed the napkin over her lap. "Why? That was a decade ago."

I selected a doughnut and set it on the rose-trimmed plate. "You know a Detective Kevin Dawson?"

She frowned. "I do."

"That sounds ominous. What does that mean?"

She shrugged. "Let's say he cut a few corners to help his ex-wife. He's lucky to have his job. Why are you asking about him?"

"He came to my warehouse." I explained about his questioning and the discovery of Sandra's body. "He thinks Tanner might have killed her."

The Judge nodded slowly, sipping coffee. "I wouldn't bet against that. What does Sandra Taylor have to do with Della?"

"I searched Sandra on the internet. She went to East Norfolk High School like me. We were there at the same time. She was two years ahead of me. She also worked at Mike's Diner and vanished about two months before me."

"And?"

I pinched a piece of doughnut and popped it in my mouth. I wasn't a fan of sweets and found it cloying. But I was trying to think my thoughts through before I tossed them at the Judge. "What if she was the Other Girl, the one Della talked about?"

She sighed. "Keep talking."

"I went by Tiffany's yesterday. I thought I'd find her, but she's been gone for days."

She angled the edge of her fork through the soft doughnut. "Tiffany. Are you still trying to help her?"

"Yes. I feel like I owe her. And I feel like she needs my help."

"You saved her life."

"She's not doing well. Last I saw her, she was so high she could barely focus."

"That's not your fault."

"But I helped Tanner. I was willing—"

She laid her hand on mine. I stared at the dark, wrinkled hand that exuded so much quiet confidence. "You saved her life."

"But she's in a bad place and has been for a while. Did I contribute to her issues?"

"We all make our own choices, Scarlett."

"I chose to move toward Tanner's open van door because I wanted validation. I also chose to lure Tiffany toward the same van so I could escape."

"You suffered greatly, but you didn't let him break you. Tiffany might have always been broken and is using you to justify her own self-destruction."

"Maybe."

"No maybe about it."

I hesitated before the next confession. "I saw a woman twice in the last couple of days. Her hair was short and blond, but she reminded me of Della."

The Judge exhaled. She'd defended me to the cops when I'd filed reports swearing that I'd seen Della. She'd likely ended up with egg on her face for it.

"I know it's a little messed up," I said. "But maybe if I find Tiffany and I can help her, I can finally let it all go."

She understood I wasn't seeking her approval. I needed her help locating Tiffany. "Would it help you if I asked around about her?"

"Could you?"

"I know a few cops who can shake the bushes."

"That would be great."

"What're you going to say to her?"

"I don't know. She called me but didn't leave a message. She's reaching out, and I feel like I need to help her."

"And then what? What if she doesn't stay clean?"

"I don't know. Maybe she will this time and maybe I can finally forgive myself."

The Judge's expression softened. "There's nothing to forgive."

"I wish I could believe that."

Chapter Sixteen

SCARLETT

Then
Maybe six or seven weeks in the basement

"What's your mother like?" Della asked.

Della and I sat in the dimly lit room. Upstairs, AC/DC blared. Tanner hadn't been in this room to see either of us today. By my estimate it was a Saturday—maybe the sixth or seventh I'd spent down here. Normally, he took Della out of the room at night, but not last night.

"I don't like to talk about my mother." Absently, my hand went to my naked wrist where I'd worn the bracelet Mom had given me. Tanner had stripped me of everything that linked me to the outside world.

I wondered if Mom had called the cops. Did she realize I was missing? Because the hard, pounding rock music had been on a loop for days, there'd been no radio or news.

"My mother is a bitch," Della said. "She can go days or weeks and never say a word to me. She does the silent treatment when she's mad. Does yours do that?"

Bitterness bubbled. My mother wasn't evil—she was an addict. And addicts flaked. But I couldn't throw my mother under the bus. She was the only person out there who might realize I was gone and call the cops. "Mom does the best she can."

"That's not saying much. I'm doing the best I can, but what good is that right now?"

I drew in a breath, wishing I were in my room eating the last of the Rice Chex cereal. Maybe I'd not been the best daughter. Maybe she was glad I was gone and she didn't have to fight me about school or homework. I'd thought my life had sucked at home, but I'd had no idea how bad it could get. "She's probably called the police and told them I'm missing. People are looking for me."

Della leaned forward and began to braid my hair. "Tanner says your mom hasn't called the cops."

I turned and studied Della's eyes. "How does he know my mother?"

"He's still working on the project across the street from your house."

My mouth began to sweat, and my stomach churned with acid. "That's not true."

"It's true," she said mildly. "He talks to his girlfriend about that job after they do it—*blah, blah, blah*. All I can do is lie in my box and listen to the pillow talk. I bet I know more about him than anyone right now."

I pushed away, pulling my hair from her hands. "Did he talk to my mother? How would he know?"

Della seemed pleased to have cracked through my silence and won my full attention. "He said there are no 'Lost' posters, no cops. She likes to sit on the front porch, smoke, and stare into space."

I turned away from her, picturing my mother sitting on the floral porch glider, her bare, dirty feet tucked under her body. Unmindful of the heat, she liked to sip a cola and watch the traffic pass as she came down from a high. "She's going to call the police."

Della ran her fingers over my knotted hair. "Sounds to me like she's using and hasn't put the pieces together yet."

That could be very true. She was never sober long. But just as I had when I was little, I believed deep down she loved me more than her drugs. "She'll get clean and call."

"Tanner said a cop stopped by his jobsite. He was looking for a missing girl. Not you or me."

"The Other Girl?"

Della shook her head. "I guess."

I didn't know the Other Girl's name. I only knew she'd been in this house and now she was not. "Did the cop talk to my mother?"

"No." Dangling answers hovered in the damp, dark air. "After the cop left, your mom asked Tanner what was going on. He told her nothing to worry about."

"Tanner spoke to my mother?" I massaged a tight muscle in my neck.

"Yeah, he got a kick out of it," she said softly.

"When was this?"

"Weeks ago."

As easy as it was to imagine Tanner charming my mother, blinding her with that smile, I refused to focus on the image. Tanner controlled my body, but not my mind. I tipped my head back against the brick wall. "You're lying."

"I'm not." She dropped her voice a notch. "No one is looking for you. Or me."

Tears swelled in my eyes and spilled down my face.

"Maybe it's better you're here. At least you're safe."

"Safe?" I flexed my fingers and winced as pain shot up my arm. I'd balked the last time he came at me. I'd not meant to, but my body had refused to play along. As a lesson, he'd nearly broken my wrist.

"How's your hand?" Della said.

"It's fine."

"Liar."

"You don't know me that well."

"I do." She scrunched up her face. "You look like this when you lie."

The expression was ridiculous. And I felt so lost and alone that it was oddly amusing. "I don't."

Della touched the grim line of her own lips mirroring mine. "You do. But it's okay. I notice these little things about you, but he doesn't."

"What do you mean?"

"You're trying to be nice to him, and you were doing well until you snapped the other day. I know you hate it, but you must try harder if you're going to get him to trust you."

"He's never going to trust me. He knows I hate him."

"Maybe. Maybe not. Men are easy to fool. We ladies are the tricky ones. We're the best liars."

She was right. I could be even nicer. Be smarter. But the knife-edge of my hate cut deep into my bones. If I could kill him, I would.

"How did you meet him?" I asked.

"Tanner?"

"Who else?"

She smiled. "I was at Waterside. It was a pretty day, and I was walking along the boardwalk eating an ice-cream cone."

My stomach rumbled. I couldn't remember the last time I'd had ice cream. "I bet his smile was charming."

"It was. He saw me and asked me my name. I know I'm not supposed to talk to strangers, but it was kind of nice to be noticed. Let's face it, he's cute when he tries."

Della was right. Tanner was a good-looking man. And when he'd first smiled at me, I'd felt so special.

"Admit it, you had a little crush on him at first?" she said.

Confessing proved I'd been stupid. "I did."

Della relaxed back against the wall. "I thought he was super sexy. The first time for us was in this house. And it was nice. Not earth shattering, but nice."

"He didn't kidnap you?"

"No."

I understood what attraction to Tanner felt like. "Did you do it with him the first time down here?"

"No, upstairs in his bed."

I'd never seen the upstairs.

"He couldn't get it up," she whispered. "I told him it was okay, but that made him mad. Then he tied me up. It hurt. And then he was rock solid."

I rubbed my aching wrist. "That's your idea of nice?"

"He said he liked me. He said he wanted us to live together. I liked that idea. And then he locked me in the house when he went to work. And then one day, he came home with a girl tossed over his shoulder."

"The Other Girl?"

"I was so pissed. I told him I didn't share. That's when he started locking me down here. For a couple of days, the music blared upstairs. I heard screams."

"Did he lock her in here with you?"

"No. He said he kept her chained somewhere in the house."

"How long?"

"The last time I saw her was right before you came here." She scooted her body closer to mine. Our shoulders brushed. "I haven't seen her since."

I didn't move away this time, but suddenly I wondered if Della was working with Tanner. Was this one of his tests? But I couldn't not ask. "How did he hide her from his girlfriend?"

"Some of us see what we want to see."

"You mean his girlfriend knew there was a girl here suffering?"

"I don't know how she couldn't have seen something."

Chapter Seventeen

Scarlett

Sunday, July 14, 2024
6:00 p.m.

Date night: part two.

I'd walked around the block a couple of times. There had been no more Della sightings, and I was beginning to wonder if my obsession with her painting was now playing tricks on my brain.

I entered Ben's, the small Italian-style eatery, taking in the white tablecloths, intimate tables, and long mahogany bar backed by hundreds of glistening liquor bottles. The servers wore dark pants, white shirts, and neat green aprons. I saw three marked exits. Luke, to his credit, wasn't taking a shortcut tonight.

A young hostess greeted me with a smile. "May I help you?"

"I'm meeting someone. Luke Kane."

The hostess glanced at an iPad. "Yes, he's here. Let me take you to his table."

I was a couple of minutes early, but he was already here. I couldn't decide whether this was a good thing. He didn't strike me as the anxious or eager type.

When I saw him, he was sitting with his back to the wall and reading something on his phone. Dressed in a blue button-down rolled up to his elbows, he wasn't wearing a tie. A tuft of dark hair peeked out from the V created by the few unfastened buttons.

As the hostess and I approached, he looked up, our gazes locked, and he turned his phone face down and rose. He smiled but didn't move around the table. Instead, he allowed the hostess to pull out my chair. I'd bet he'd done his internet search.

"You look amazing," he said.

I'd been working nonstop after I left the Judge's house and, when I'd realized the time, had showered quickly and scrubbed hard to remove the paints from my hands and arms. I left my hair loose around my shoulders and now it curled softly. The dress was a simple sapphire sheath, the crystal necklace a find at an art show, and the gladiator sandals a go-to. "Thank you."

He waited for me to sit before he retook his place. A bourbon neat sat in front of him, and there was a white wine at my place setting. "You drank white wine last time."

A detail man. Good memory. Also, quick, efficient, and ready for this date to end sooner rather than later. "That's perfect."

He didn't appear in a rush as he sipped his bourbon. "How was your day?"

My back was to the front door. Not ideal, but at least I wouldn't have any Della sightings staring at Luke and the framed picture behind him.

I glanced at the glass of wine he'd ordered me. I never took open beverages from strangers. But I was tired of always being on guard, always afraid. I took a sip of wine, savoring the soothing, buttery smoothness. "I'm making a series of prints. Each of these prints will require a total of five colors. Today I applied the first color." I glanced at my hands and the faintest flecks of blue. I waggled my fingers. "Blue."

"Let me guess. It features the waterfront."

Norfolk was surrounded by water, so the guess was logical. "It does. It's a popular design with tourists, and I get a lot of visitor foot traffic at the art fairs. They'll sell well."

"A marketing decision."

"In part. It's a little abstract, but any artist who wants to eat on a regular basis needs to keep her eye to what sells."

He sat back, and I sensed he was methodically ticking through the small talk until he could breach the bigger questions on his mind.

I sipped my wine. "You looked me up."

"I did." He swirled the caramel liquid in his glass. "Quite the story."

He was a hard one to read, and that was unsettling. Della had taught me to dissect facial expressions down to the micro level. A slight frown, a heavy sigh, a hardening of a gaze could all make the difference between living or dying.

I drew in a slow, steady breath, rummaging for the forgiveness the psychologists preached. "Any questions?"

Sharp hawk eyes peered over his glass. "Why did you run the other night? Was it something I said or did?"

How could I explain that desperation had captured me in an iron muscled grip, making refusal impossible. "I saw a woman. She reminded me of Della, the other girl locked up with me."

"Della was never found, according to the articles. The cops concluded that she wasn't real."

"Lately, I've had my own doubts. But when I block out all the noise, I know she was real. I don't know how she got away or what happened to her. But I thought I saw her that night. Likely, I was wrong. I've been mistaken a lot over the years when it comes to Della sightings." Could a measured tone make crazy words sound a little less insane?

"Did you find the woman you saw?"

"I did not. I lost whoever it was I was chasing." I drew in a slow, steady sigh, determined to keep calm and not cling to my frustration.

"I'm sorry for what happened to you," he said. "That kind of trauma would leave a mark on anyone."

"I do have a few quirks."

"Such as?"

"I spend a lot of time alone. I'm obsessed with exercise and fitness so I'm always capable of running if necessary." Did I want to tell him there'd been no man before or since Tanner? No. TMI. Dawson's visit regarding Sandra Taylor's death and Tiffany's disappearance might also be a bridge too far. "I rarely date. Lots of locks on my door."

"Are you in counseling?"

"I have been many times. It helped, but when it's all said and done, I had to find a way to live with it all."

"You look like you're winning."

I tipped my glass toward him. "Except for the occasional freak-out."

That prompted a slight smile. "I've had dates that ended worse."

I frowned. "Why would you even bother with me? You're a good-looking guy and seem to have your act together."

"I was a prosecutor, and now I'm a defense lawyer. I'm used to looking at the other side of an equation, the side no one else wants to see."

"Justified motivations lurking under the bad actions."

"Something like that."

Tanner does this because he cares so much about you. Della's words rattled. "But sometimes good motivations can be twisted. They don't always excuse the actions."

"Is that how you felt about Tanner Reed?"

Hearing Tanner's name was jarring. First Dawson and now Luke. Twice this week.

"Does my directness bother you?" Luke asked.

"It's unexpected. Few ask about him anymore."

"If you'd rather not . . ."

The trailing comment belied the intensity in his gaze. "Most of my recollections of Tanner are tangled with my memories of Della. It's as if they became one. His words became hers. She kept telling me he was saving me from my mother, who had substance abuse issues. Della often explained and justified what he did to me. She encouraged me to be nice to him."

"How did Tanner know about your mother?"

"Tanner was a carpenter working on a renovation project across the street from my mother's house. He was nice to me. Charming. He showed interest in my art. It felt good to be noticed. And after he took me, he apparently spoke to my mother often."

Luke nodded. "He liked having a secret and seeing her distress."

"That's the thing: she wasn't distressed. The drugs threw off her sense of time."

"How old were you?"

"Fifteen."

"A child."

"Ironically, I thought dealing with my mother's addiction had made me worldly and careful. I thought I had it all under control. But Mom's disinterest made me incredibly vulnerable. Looking for love in all the wrong places kind of thing."

Luke nodded slowly. In the prosecutor's office, he'd likely seen his share of groomers. I didn't need to fill in the gaps for him to see a bigger picture.

"He was nice to me at first, and he got me talking, I guess so I'd become more relaxed around him. I looked forward to seeing his truck. I told him about my dreams of being an artist, and he encouraged me. It was nice to have someone care. Or seem to, anyway." I had accepted that only raw curiosity was keeping Luke in the chair. I understood when the questions were satisfied, he'd pay the tab, wish me my best life, and leave. There was something freeing about not feeling as if I had to try to be normal.

"Why did you get in his van?"

"Della," I said. "Della, the one no one believes existed, coaxed me to the van. I was selling my art on a street corner, and she convinced me to follow her. The rest is available in the interviews I gave to the cops."

"You were very detached in those interviews."

"You pulled up my interviews? They aren't available on the internet."

A slight lift and fall of his shoulder. "I know people."

"Detective Dawson?"

He frowned. "I wouldn't reach out to him, but there are others."

"I suppose that makes sense." I sipped my wine. "Detached is how I survived—survive. Some survivors get caught in loops of fear, some race toward trouble with a death wish, keep dating abusers praying for reform. Some scream and yell. And some slide behind a wall of ice and keep the pain at arm's distance."

"You're the latter."

I tapped the tip of my nose.

"Doesn't that get lonely?"

"Maybe. Sometimes. Lonely might not always be fun, but it's safe."

"Why are you here?" he asked. "Why swing by my office?"

"Like I said, I owed you an apology."

"Do you always apologize to the dates you ditch?"

This candor was oddly relaxing, and yet I was very aware that he'd made a career of drawing out the truth. "No. You're the first. But there haven't been that many dates. The record for my longest date is sixty-two minutes."

"We didn't break that record."

"No." I slid my finger through the condensation on the side of my glass. "How are we doing for time now?"

He checked his watch. "Thirty-one minutes if we count the moment when you entered the restaurant."

"I didn't think you noticed when I arrived."

"I noticed."

A warmth spread through me. Exciting to really be seen, but also unsettling.

"What's special about me?" he asked. "Why do I win an apology?"

"Maybe I'm tired of . . ." I couldn't find the word.

"Your loneliness?"

"I'm not sure."

The waiter appeared with menus. "Would you like to order dinner?" Luke looked at me. "What do you think?"

"Dinner would be nice." We each accepted menus.

When we were alone, Luke raised his glass and said, "Here's to breaking the sixty-two-minute record."

Chapter Eighteen

SCARLETT

Sunday, July 14, 2024
8:30 p.m.

I'd proven I could withstand a date for two hours and fifteen minutes. There'd been no kiss or hug. Not even a handshake. Luke hadn't pressed for anything beyond conversation, and I'd relaxed a fraction. And at the end of our date, there'd been no talk of another night out. Oddly disappointing. And comforting. But all in all, it was a victory for me, and I took wins when they presented themselves.

Luke had offered to drive me home, but I'd politely declined and walked the five blocks to my place, my pepper spray clutched in my fist. As I punched in the code to my front door, the streets around me were slipping into the shadows.

Inside my locked concrete walls, I felt safe staring at the sea of partially made prints now drying from clotheslines. Alone in my warehouse, I wasn't hurting, I had plenty to eat, and I could leave anytime. Tension drained from my body.

However, staying here sealed behind my own doors reinforced that I needed a prison to feel safe. I was maintaining the oppression with my own locks and self-isolation.

My runs and rock climbing, even painting the mural, were my ways of proving I was free to come and go. But I was never totally at ease outside. And most of my activities remained solitary and brief. All forms of self-imprisonment.

I glanced out my front display window and looked toward the apartment complex across the street. I knew all the windows and the people who lived in each unit. The man on the first floor closed his curtains the moment he entered. The guy on the second floor cycled every night on a stationary bike. The third floor was always dark, and the woman on the fourth floor danced and strummed an air guitar as she drank wine in the evenings.

The top floor, which had been dark for months, was now lit up. A new neighbor. Another person on a long list of people I would not meet. I pulled my shade down, closing out the world.

Removing my shoes, I tugged off my dress and walked toward my bedroom behind the large screen. Pulling on an oversize T-shirt, I pulled my hair into a loose ponytail as I moved toward my studio.

I flipped on the lights and uncovered the painting of Della. Until now, I'd kept this painting and all the ones like it hidden away. And when I was satisfied with the latest, I would take it into the back alley and set it on fire. I always stood alone for this, watching the flames eat at the canvas and Della's face. But maybe this time I wouldn't burn the portrait. Maybe I would save it, display it in my studio, so the world could see Della and maybe someone would recognize that face.

"Are you afraid to have your face shown?" I asked.

The portrait's eyes looked off to the side, and as I stepped back, the eyes seemed to follow me. Della was always present. Always watching.

I stared back at Della. We both got away from Tanner. I'd been tossed into the spotlight after Tanner's death, whereas she had faded into the shadows.

A week after my rescue, I left the hospital, and the police took me to the site of Tanner's house. Wearing borrowed sweats, a jacket two sizes too big, and purple lost-and-found sneakers, I stood before the smoldering remains of my former prison. The roof and first and second floors had collapsed, filling in the basement and obliterating all traces of my cell.

The flames, the cops had said, had destroyed the DNA evidence of Della, me, and anyone else who'd been in the house. There was no physical evidence of any of us. Like it never happened.

Anger and disappointment had twisted around each other. I'd felt abandoned. Della, who had said we'd survive together, had left me.

Months later, I'd taken my mother's car and returned to Tanner's house alone and walked around the scorched ruins. The fallen timbers had cooled, but it was difficult to approach the foundation. Still, I'd worked my way close to the blackened bricks, hoping to find something in the charred remains. I'd found nothing in the rubble.

The summer of 2014 had passed in most people's lives without being noticed, or if it had been, it was sunshine, beaches, and cool drinks. But those months had passed for me with aching slowness. And they were forever burned into my soul.

Chapter Nineteen

SCARLETT

Then
Maybe sixty days in the basement

There were ninety-eight hash marks on the wall, and the radio DJ was talking about back to school.

As I deepened a hash mark with my little stone, Della smoothed her hand over my hip, patted my bottom in an almost affectionate way. "He sees the marks. He knows what they mean."

I stared at the cracked wall and my white scratches. How many hours had I studied the growing number of marks? "I need to remember. I need evidence."

"Who's ever going to see it?"

"The cops might walk these rooms one day. I want them to see."

She edged toward me, trying to smile as if we were buddies. "He's wired the house to explode. There's dynamite in clusters all over the house."

I rolled on my side toward Della and stared into her resolute expression. "When did he do this?"

"He's been working on it since the Other Girl left."

"Why?"

"He'd rather we all die together. He doesn't want to go to prison and worries about it more and more."

I turned back to the wall and deepened the hash mark. Maybe some of this would survive. They found things that dated back ten thousand years. Why couldn't some of my marks withstand an explosion?

Della laid her hand gently on my arm. "You want this to be remembered, and all I want to do is forget it and move on."

"He's not going to let either one of us move on. One day we'll be gone, too," I said, more to myself. "If he did it to the Other Girl, he'll do it to us." In my gut, I'd known that day was coming. There were even moments when I welcomed it.

"I'm getting out of here alive."

"He likes you," I said. "I can tell. If anyone can escape, it'll be you."

"Make him like you and we'll escape together."

I burrowed deeper into the hash mark. "I'll try."

"I knew you were smart."

Chapter Twenty

SCARLETT

Monday, July 15, 2024
9:30 a.m.

I was running late for my appointment with the real estate agent who I'd hired to sell my mother's home. My mother had died of a stroke six months ago. A stroke wasn't normal in a fifty-one-year-old woman, but Mom's doctors had theorized years of alcohol and drug abuse had taken their toll. My mother had lingered longer than anyone had expected. She'd been transferred to assisted living, where her body had been atrophying. She was trapped in her own dark room. And then she'd died suddenly in her sleep. The doctors said that she'd simply stopped breathing.

Because there was no will, the home had been put in probate, but it had finally cleared, and I was free to sell the house.

When I pulled up in front of the brick three-story home, the Realtor was waiting. She was dressed in a red linen suit, and she'd swept her black hair up into a styled ponytail. My mother loved that color of red and often talked about the fancy clothes she wore and how she used to dress up before she met my father. When Dad moved out, I was about four, and Mom was left with only me to hear her complaints about a life lost to marriage and motherhood. Oddly, in that dark basement prison, I'd missed those complaints.

I glanced at my graphic T-shirt, ripped jeans, and Converse sneakers. My mind buzzed with Mom's guaranteed comparisons of my outfit versus the Realtor's.

Ragamuffin. The word would've drawn out slowly as she'd sipped a gin gimlet, her go-to after too much coke.

"Ms. Crosby," Elaine said.

I smiled, glancing toward the old house across the street where I'd first seen Tanner. The grass was freshly cut, the gardens weeded, and pansies filled the iron planters on the front porch.

I had decided to sell Mom's house immediately. I'd ordered a dumpster and hired moving crews. What didn't go to the Goodwill ended up in the trash. I'd been oddly detached as I'd tossed all the old clothes from my mother's closet, the few family pictures, and all the decorative knickknacks. I'd ripped down the thick satin curtains my mother had adored and tossed them into the dumpster along with dozens of throw pillows and rugs. The movers and I had worked for two days, pitching everything.

My mother would've been horrified seeing her frippery discarded. She'd said her things were like anchors that kept her rooted to this world. Only, they'd failed her. She'd lost touch with the world when I was missing.

"The place looks great."

Elaine smiled. "I did a bit of sprucing up. Cleaning crews went through the inside and made it sparkle. It now smells like pine cleaner and fresh air."

Scents of vodka and cigarettes long trapped in the closed house had finally been released. "That's great. You're having the open house soon?"

"The listing went live yesterday, and the open house is on Saturday. I expect the property will sell quickly."

"Wonderful."

"I was sorry to hear about your mother. I know it must be difficult."

"Thank you." When I heard she'd died, I hadn't reacted. I guessed one day I would, but so far nothing. She hadn't missed me, and I wasn't missing her.

The house still needed major renovations, but it was good enough for a buyer in search of a fixer-upper.

The real estate market was decent, and I hoped the house would sell before prices tumbled as all the pundits predicted. The money would cover the remaining hospital and nursing home bills. In the end, the goal was simply to break even.

"Would you like me to give you the grand tour?" Elaine said.

"If you don't mind, I'd like to walk through the house by myself. Kind of a last goodbye."

"Of course, hon. I know this must be emotional."

As I walked through the front door, footsteps echoed. I was amazed at how the light had transformed the interior. It looked larger, but there was a great deal of familiar—the molding, the arched doorways, the iron on the windows. They all reminded me of the house I'd lived in from ages ten to sixteen.

Before Tanner took me, I'd been drawn to him. As I'd sat in my room in my mother's house, I didn't expect, but kind of hoped, to find him watching my room. His attention in the before days had been exciting.

When I returned to the house after the eighty-eight days, I'd look out the same window. This time I'd imagine Della standing on the street corner, coaxing me outside. I don't know how many times I rose and searched the darkness for her. When I realized she wasn't there, I'd cry tears of relief and sadness.

Often, I'd find my mother standing in my doorway, sipping a cocktail and staring at me as if I were a stranger.

"Young girls get fooled by pretty men all the time," my mother said.

I pulled my blanket up around my shoulders as I curled my feet in the chair by the window. "Go away. I'm tired."

"It was a hard lesson, but you'll never forget it. Better to learn it when you're young."

I burrowed deeper. "Go away."

"Watch your tone. This is my house."

"Fuck you."

In the next instant, footsteps thudded across the floor and my mother grabbed my chin, forcing my eyes to lock on hers. "If you don't like it here, you can always leave. Those three months you were gone were some of the best of my life."

I'd left the next day.

This house had never been a place of comfort or love, and it needed to go. It was just another tie to the past, and maybe once the house was gone, I'd be one step closer to normal.

I stood at the bottom of the staircase, my hand resting on a bullnose banister. I could climb and see my old room, inspect the Realtor's work. But I didn't care. I just wanted to bury the past before it buried me.

"Thanks, Elaine," I said as I stepped outside. "It looks great."

If she was surprised by my very quick visit, her smile gave no indication. "Glad to hear it. I'll keep you posted."

"Thank you."

I strode onto the sidewalk and glanced up and down the street. I realized how little had changed. Of the dozen square little neat yards, half were well maintained, a few passable, and a couple in poor shape. They were the same yards, the same patterns. As I walked down the sidewalk, I paused and allowed myself to study the house across the street. The yard was well kept, but back in the day, it had been pristine. The white paint had been refreshed, vibrant marigolds were planted by the mailbox, and the porch furniture was wicker instead of wrought iron.

Reporters had swamped the area after my release. They'd interviewed neighbors, who were all universally shocked. Tanner had worked for many of them. They'd all described him and his work with glowing comments: *Meticulous. Always on time. Reasonable prices. Great attitude.*

I'd been portrayed as moody and distant. Some thought I'd been tricked by Tanner. Others assumed I'd gone willingly. "Scarlett."

I turned at the sound of my name. Standing to my left was Mrs. Rose. She'd lived in the neighborhood when Mom and I moved in fifteen years ago. I remembered she'd brought us a plate of cookies after my return.

"Mrs. Rose."

The lines on the woman's face deepened. "I heard about your mother. I'm sorry."

The polite words vibrated like buzzing flies. "Thank you."

"We haven't seen much of you in a long time," Mrs. Rose said.

"Not a place I like to remember."

"No, of course not." To her credit, Mrs. Rose met my gaze. "How are you doing?"

"Getting along. I love my warehouse."

"You look well."

Looking good or at least above average was always a win. "Thank you."

"You still doing your art?"

"I am. I run a printmaking business now."

"Honey, that's great."

"I hear the cops found a body nearby."

"Right around the block." Mrs. Rose nodded to the east corner. "The old Robinson house. I spoke to an Officer Larsen. She seems determined to solve the murder."

"That's great." I cleared my throat. "Who were the Robinsons?"

"An older couple. They hired Tanner to flip the house so they could resell it. He did great work on the renovation, from what I hear."

"Did they ever sense the house was off after Tanner had finished with it?"

Mrs. Rose frowned. "They did. But when they thought to complain, Tanner was dead."

"That was ten years ago. Who owns the house now?"

"A young couple. They're nice people, but they're a little upset."

"I bet."

"They're staying in a hotel now."

"I understand." I shifted my stance as a sudden surge of anger cut through my center. Most days, I kept the fury on a leash, but today it growled and snapped. "Did Tanner ever do anything that you thought was off? Were there any warning signs?"

Redness brightened her skin. "He was always nice to me."

"He was to me, too, until he wasn't."

"Scarlett . . ."

I could see she was on the verge of shutting down. When I opened too much, people scattered. I found a smile and made it as warm as I could. "I'm not mad at you, Mrs. Rose. I just don't understand how he went unnoticed for so long. How I went ignored for so long." The police hadn't been surprised by this. One officer had commented that no one really knew their neighbors.

Mrs. Rose sighed. "We really don't know people, do we? We think we do, but we don't." She shook her head. "I even met his girlfriend, who brought him lunch when he was working. She seemed to adore him. No hints of trouble. What was her name?"

"Lynn Yeats," I said.

Whereas Tiffany didn't know Tanner, Lynn had. She might have insight into Tanner and maybe could explain him. Maybe not. Maybe he fooled her like everyone else. But I'd never reached out to her because I thought slamming the door to the past would help me heal. But the voices of Tanner, the Other Girl, and now Lynn had grown as loud as Della's.

"Do you know where Lynn lives?" I asked.

"Honey, why would you want to talk to her? She's as much a victim as you."

I'd never seen Lynn Yeats locked in the basement with me. She might have suffered at Tanner's hands, but not like I had.

"I know," I lied.

Tanner had taught me in that basement room that lying was a useful skill. And when I escaped, I realized it was easier to lie when any cop or doctor dug too deep into my head. I became adept at coating every answer with just enough truth until the worry vanished from their faces.

Tanner had had his date nights with Lynn thirty feet above my head. How was he able to separate his two worlds so easily? Upstairs. Downstairs. Light. Dark. Did it make him harder as he pressed into Lynn knowing he had two girls locked in his basement? He certainly was more aggressive with me when he forced Della to watch.

My smile was quick and easy. "I better get going."

"You take care of yourself, dear."

"I will, Mrs. Rose. Thank you."

"Of course, honey."

I walked past my truck and around the corner. At the end of the block, I saw the yellow crime scene tape flapping in front of a brick house. I moved slowly down the sidewalk until I stood in front.

A car door opened and closed, and I glanced over my shoulder to see a woman get out of a blue van and lift a baby from the back seat. As she moved toward her own house, she cooed to her child.

When she saw me standing there, she frowned, and when her baby squawked, she held her closer and hurried inside.

A house, I reminded myself, was bricks and wood. It wasn't blood and bones. It wasn't Tanner. Or Della. It deserved better memories.

I climbed the front steps and noted the police seal on the front door. When I tried the front door, I discovered it was unlocked. Did the cops think their seal would keep trouble out of the house? I twisted the knob and pushed the door open, tearing the seal.

This house was almost identical to my mother's. Wood floors, a kitchen that dated back to the seventies, and small chopped-up rooms. Moving around the corner, I saw the fireplace had been reduced to piles of bricks, crushed mortar dusting the floor.

Following scattered yellow evidence markers, I approached the opening in the wall by the kitchen. The wall space was small, and I couldn't imagine a body jammed in the gap. Tanner had been doing the reno work alone, so if the house smelled of decomposing body, no one knew but him. And maybe Lynn. How could she have missed the smell if she'd been in the house?

When I left, closing the door behind me, the police seal dangled, a silent witness to my invasion. I looked up and saw the young mother standing at her window watching me. A phone was pressed to her ear. I'd bet she was calling the cops.

As I moved to my truck, my phone buzzed with a text. I glanced down, relieved at the interruption. It was from Tiffany's number. We need to talk. Someone is watching me.

Blood rushed to my ears as I stared at the words for a long moment.

Who?

I don't know.

Text bubbles rolled and rolled, but then they stilled and vanished.

Where are you?

There was no reply.

Chapter Twenty-One

SCARLETT

Then
Maybe day seventy in the basement

I curled my knees close to my chest and closed my eyes as the radio upstairs blathered on about August heat. We'd been in this room alone together for two days. There'd been no sign of Tanner, and neither of us had eaten and the water jug he'd left us was empty. My head pounded, and my stomach felt like it was eating itself.

"We're in this together, you know. We need each other," Della said.

I looked up and I wanted to rail on her and remind her I was here because of her. But I was becoming a practiced liar. I could smile when all I wanted to do was scream. "I know."

Della crawled toward me. As she got closer, I could see her eyes, shadowed by dark smudges, sparkle with need.

"He's scouting another girl."

I stilled. "Who?"

"I don't know her name. He calls her the redhead."

Disgust ricocheted through me, and I struggled to keep my face neutral. What if I helped him but couldn't escape? What if I not only failed to get away but also condemned another girl to this hell?

Della took my hand and kissed it. "You're worrying. I can see the line creasing your forehead."

I pulled my hand back. "I'm not."

"I can almost see your brain turning. You think we'll fail. And we'll all be trapped here together."

I wanted out of this room more than anything. And I'd do whatever I could to get free. I would risk another girl's life to save mine. I was becoming Della. A cold chill slipped through my bones. "Why does he do it?"

Della shook her head. "He's on a mission, Scarlett. He sees this as his calling." She wrapped her arm around my shoulder and pulled me close.

Oddly, her touch was comforting and untangled some of the fear inside me. I relaxed into her.

Another girl was a chance to get out of here. A chance at freedom.

Chapter Twenty-Two

DAWSON

Monday, July 15, 2024
1:30 p.m.

Dawson's office chair squeaked, and the left armrest wiggled. When he'd been on administrative leave over the winter, HR had ordered him a new chair, but on his return, this outdated piece of crap was waiting for him. Someone else in the building had his new chair, and he was stuck with this piece of shit. An FU from someone. His desk had no pictures, plants, or specialty mugs. It was a blank slate. All salt in the wound after his morning at the attorney's office and the official end of his marriage.

"Dawson."

He looked and found his captain standing at the door of his cubicle. Chief Monroe was tall and heavyset and had wavy white hair. He was nearing retirement and doing his best to get to the finish line without stirring up too much trouble.

"How is the case?" Chief Monroe asked.

"Like them all. Bit by bit."

"We have a new officer, and I'm partnering her with you."

The good thing about being in purgatory was no one wanted to work with him. And he'd grown to like setting the tone for all his days. "I don't need a partner."

"Well, you got one. And she's a ballbuster."

"What's that mean?"

"Worked human trafficking in Central and Northern Virginia. Had a bit of a reputation for catching bad guys, though some suspects were a little worse for the wear when she handed them over."

"Terrific."

"Time to get up and meet her."

Shit. He rose from his chair and looked toward the bullpen. He spotted Margo Larsen immediately, talking to a uniformed cop. Cradling a cup of coffee, she was smiling. Relaxed and confident, as if she'd always been here.

Adrenaline rushed him. His heart rammed his chest.

"Officer Larsen," Chief Monroe said.

She slid her phone in her back pocket, looked up, and smiled. "Chief."

"Meet your new partner, Detective Kevin Dawson."

"We've met," Margo said. "At the Jane Doe crime scene."

"Which is why you're here," the chief said. "Two heads are better than one. I want every and all links to Jane Doe and Tanner identified."

His boss was pushing him to pin the case on Tanner Reed. The implied order was simple: *Close the case and move on.* Tanner was the logical suspect, but logic didn't always go hand in hand with homicide. And working with Margo Larsen was . . . complicated.

"The more the merrier," Dawson said.

"Good," the chief said.

When he walked away, Margo leaned closer to him, dropping her voice so only he could hear. "I don't feel the love, Dawson."

Tension rippled through him. "I like to work alone."

She winked. "Not this time, Lone Ranger."

As he weaved through the building, she followed, her clipped heel strikes telegraphing she wasn't the least bit intimidated. When he pushed through the front door, air swollen with heat wrapped around him. "We can take my car."

"First stop is the Tidewater medical examiner's office?" she asked.

"Correct."

"I'll meet you there. Who knows which directions we'll have to go after. Give you a chance to absorb this new twist in your life." The mockery was subtle, but it hummed under her words.

"Did you know about this assignment at the bar?" Dawson asked.

"I'd heard whispers, but nothing was etched in stone."

"A heads-up would have been nice."

She arched a brow. "How would that have changed anything?"

Knowing she was angling for a position in his department could have changed his decision to sleep with her. Could have, but likely wouldn't have. His dick had taken over for his brain as soon as she'd sat next to him in the bar. "I'll meet you there."

"Will do."

He was relieved to be alone as he drove to the medical examiner's office. He could think better without her so close. As he pulled onto the quiet, tree-lined campus of Eastern Virginia Medical School, near the banks of the Elizabeth River, he had regrouped from the shock of having Margo on the case.

When he parked in front of the medical examiner's office, he refused to look in his rearview mirror and search for Margo. He never liked having a partner, but all the others had been easy to ignore. Not Margo. Out of his car, the heavy summer shrouded him as he walked to the front doors. Heeled boots drummed into concrete behind him.

Door open, he paused until she caught up. Inside, the building's air-conditioning coiled around him. He'd been in and out of this building more times than he could count, and he should have been used to it by now. He was a homicide detective. Death was part of the bargain.

It came for us all, but he still resented the hell out of it when it took young kids.

With Margo behind him, he weaved his way through the building to the autopsy suite. There he found the medical examiner, Dr. Alex Malone. She was midthirties, had a solid reputation, and was considered a straight shooter. Tall, thin, with dark hair that accentuated her brown skin. *Reserved*, to the point of cold, was the word that came to mind when he saw her. But he got it. Better to toss up as many defense barriers as possible or this job could eat you alive.

Dr. Malone stood by a stainless-steel autopsy table where skeletal remains were carefully laid out. "Good morning."

"Dr. Malone, this is Officer Margo Larsen," Dawson said. "She's new to the department and will be working with me on the Taylor case. Larsen, Dr. Alex Malone."

Margo plucked latex gloves from a box resting on a stainless-steel table. "Dr. Malone. It's a pleasure. Though I can think of nicer ways to meet."

Dr. Malone's tense features relaxed a fraction. "Me too."

"What do you have for me . . . us?" Dawson said.

Dr. Malone flexed gloved fingers. "Your victim was female and in her mid to late teens, judging by the cranial sutures on the top of her skull, which as you know don't completely close until about age twenty-five."

"That age estimate matches the description on the driver's license found with the body," Margo said.

"I understand the remains were discovered inside a wall," Dr. Malone said.

"In the Ghent District."

"Whoever wrapped her up did a good job. Meticulous. It was an airtight seal."

"I spoke to a dozen people who lived around the crime scene," Margo said. "Tanner worked for many of them, and his customers raved about his detailed carpentry work."

"Why bother to wrap this body so carefully?" Dawson asked, more to himself. "He lived in the country and could have buried the body so deep it would've never been found."

"The body was his version of a trophy," Margo said. "His memento of his time with her."

Dawson studied the drawn figure with dried gray skin reminiscent of a Halloween prop. A decade in the elements would have decimated a corpse, but the plastic wrap and insulation around the body had mummified the remains. "Let's not get ahead of our skis. Tanner's farmhouse was reduced to cinders. There was no way of proving if he held this victim or any other."

Margo shook her head. "Wonder what's in the walls of Tanner's other former customers' homes?"

"One case at a time," Dawson said. "Dr. Malone, how did she die?"

Dr. Malone placed gloved hands on the skull and gently turned it. Blackened blood stained the strands of straw-like blond hair. "She was struck in the back of the head. X-rays reveal spiral fractures across the occipital bone. This was a brutal strike. It would've caused extensive hemorrhaging. She might not have died right away, but without surgery, she'd have bled out in a few hours, maybe days."

"Could she have been alive when Tanner wrapped her in plastic?" Margo asked.

"No way of knowing," Dr. Malone said.

"Can you confirm this is Sandra Taylor?" Dawson asked.

"She meets the description on Taylor's driver's license. She was five foot four, small boned, blond, and Caucasian. That suggests this is Ms. Taylor; however, I pulled DNA from her back molars and sent it to the lab. DNA will work if I can find a family member to compare to. Social services are trying to track down her two siblings. I've also reached out to the foster care system for dental records, but no results yet."

When kids like Sandra Taylor fell into a black hole, it was hard to pull them out. "Okay."

"I will say this victim's teeth were riddled with cavities, suggesting malnutrition."

"I looked up Taylor's file," Margo said. "If this is Sandra Taylor, her parents died of overdoses when she was young, and she was placed in six different foster care homes."

Too many kids who fit that profile. Each added more weight to Dawson's shoulders. "What else can you tell me about the body?"

"Not much to say until I get my test results back," Dr. Malone said.

"Ball's now in our court," Dawson said.

Outside, Margo kept pace with him, matching him stride for stride. "What are the chances that that's not Sandra Taylor?"

"Anything's possible."

"But."

"If I had to bet the mortgage, I'd say it's her. But important not to jump to conclusions."

"No one in the neighborhood remembers a girl fitting the victim's description," Margo said. "I also spoke to the high school, and no one really remembers her."

He glanced at her. "You've been busy."

"You have a problem with me being proactive?" she asked.

"No."

"Then what's eating you?"

He shrugged. "I don't know how to take this. Us."

"Us?" She laughed. "Take it as it comes, my good man. We're cops, professionals, and what happens off-hours is no one's damn business."

"Tell that to HR."

Her keys jangled in her hand. "I won't if you won't."

Red Hot Chili Peppers' "Under the Bridge" played in the bar as Dawson settled on the stool. Retro, but appropriate. He was in a foul mood. He'd not expected to see Margo Larsen today or that she'd be assigned to the Jane Doe case. Shit. He'd been playing with fire and now was feeling the heat.

He wasn't surprised she was sharp. Not many officers would have taken a sledgehammer to a wall on the rumor there was a body behind it. She asked good questions. Took the bull by the horns. But shit, what were the chances? "Pretty damn good, you dumb son of a bitch," he muttered.

He called a cop buddy in Northern Virginia and asked about Margo. There'd been a long pause, and descriptors like *ballbuster, steam-roller, don't ever fuck that, like grabbing a tiger by the tail* rattled over the line.

Shit.

He was having trouble shaking the frustration and impotence that enveloped him now. Eventually, he'd find a way to ball up the bad shit and bury it deep, with the other atrocities that came with the job, but for now the details of the autopsy and screwing Margo were too raw and fresh. He took a long sip of beer.

The bartender set a basket of shelled peanuts in front of him. It was their nightly ritual. He was good for three beers and a large basket of peanuts. Something about the crack of the shell that was satisfying.

He angled a peanut between his index finger and thumb. *Crack.*

He'd told Margo to meet him here tomorrow night. Funny, he'd been so full of himself. But she'd been a random stranger. Now she was a ball-busting steamroller and his partner on this case.

The irony of their hookup wasn't lost on him. At this point it would do little to hurt his career, but if Margo wanted to grow her own, she'd learn quickly he wasn't the guy to help. He could barely help himself these days.

Dawson still couldn't picture Margo in this dark, shabby place that suited him so well. He snapped a shell. And another. The pile of shells grew. In an hour he'd be back at the office piecing together all the leads accumulated in the Taylor case.

A whiff of perfume caught his attention. Not the cheaper scents that he associated with this place. Expensive. Nice. Margo. She took a seat beside him.

He didn't look in her direction. He wasn't anxious to let her know just how glad he was to see her. "Thought we said Tuesday night."

"Do you turn into a pumpkin on Mondays?" She took a sip of his beer, seeming to savor the cold, salty flavor. "I have a few tidbits about Sandra Taylor, but that can wait for an hour. Ready to go?"

He forced himself to remain still. "You in a rush?"

"Well, we could braid each other's hair and nurse this beer longer."

That coaxed a smile. "Point taken." He cleared out his tab and, aware a few fellow cops were watching, followed her out of the bar. Let 'em gossip. And if he lost his job over it, fine. Life moved on.

They crossed the street to the hotel and then the lobby. He punched the elevator and rode it to the fifth floor, where his room was located.

Neither spoke as they moved toward his door. As he opened it, she checked messages on her phone. The bright light in the bathroom was enough to highlight a pile of dirty clothes, pizza boxes, take-out containers in the trash cans, and stacked Styrofoam coffee cups. Tiffany's scrapbook sat next to a laptop on the round table by the window.

The beds were made, and fresh dry cleaning hung in the closets. A football game played on the television screen because the sound of voices created the illusion someone was waiting for him. He closed the door behind him and then secured his weapon in the bedside table drawer.

She let her purse drop to the dresser and kicked off her shoes.

When he faced her, she was unbuttoning her blouse. Keeping distance between them was now a challenge. "You're that sure of me?"

She paused and raised a brow. "We ruled out hair braiding. Want to discuss feelings? Or the case?" She unfastened another button, drawing his gaze to her full cleavage.

His throat tightened. "No."

"Good." She shrugged off her jacket, revealing a black lace bra that skimmed full breasts. She unfastened the zipper on her pants and shimmied out of them.

It was Christmas morning for him. And judging by the way she smiled at him, she knew it.

"What do you want me to do?" she asked.

He allowed his gaze to linger on her body for several beats. This close to her, his skin rippled. The helpless outside chaos faded, and for this moment, he savored a sense of control. He closed the distance between them and skimmed the top of her lacy bra. "Lie on the bed."

"How did you know I'd be there tonight?" Dawson asked. Staring at the ceiling, he casually stroked Margo's thigh.

She drew in a deep breath and released it slowly. "Where else would you have been after a tough day?"

"Point taken. But why me?"

"Figured you'd help me blow off steam. When I attend the autopsy of a young girl, I get on edge."

Dawson was a grinder. He'd never make chief. Now he was with a woman who'd just let him know he was a means to an end. "You knew I'd be handy, ready."

"And you were."

"Yeah. I suppose so." Surprised by the rush of bitterness, he shifted the conversation. "This isn't your first murder investigation."

"They never get easy for me. And the more I asked around about Sandra Taylor, the angrier I got. No one cared she'd vanished."

"What did you learn about her?"

"I knocked on doors near her foster home this afternoon. A few had vague memories of her. I'm trying to track down a couple of the kids she fostered with, but so far dead ends."

"Anybody mention Tanner Reed?"

"No."

He ran his hand down her leg, liking the muscled curves. And then, as much to convince himself: "Someone will remember her."

"Ever the optimist." Her gaze skimmed his hotel room. "Why are you still here? Don't you think it's time to get a big-boy apartment?"

"Wasn't ready to jump into the next life until the door closed on the last." His fingers rubbed over the rough edges of a burn scar on her leg. "How did you get this?"

Rather than explain, she rolled on her side, facing him so that he had a clear view of her breasts. "Long story."

He traced the scar, mentally cataloging its dimensions. "I'm in no rush."

"You were frowning when I entered the bar tonight. Upset that I'm on the case with you?"

"Call that shock. The frown is linked to the visit to the medical examiner. Never a fun time."

"It's not. Only my second autopsy."

"Tell me about the first one."

Not a request but an order. And she didn't hesitate to comply. "A young girl was killed by her trafficker. He beat her to death."

He followed the rise and fall of her chest. "Did you get a conviction?"

"Involuntary manslaughter." The words dripped with bitterness. "Hoping the system is tougher on guys like that here."

"Even if we identify Sandra Taylor's killer, getting justice now is going to be tough."

"It would be nice to prove it."

Dawson's mind drifted back to the high school picture of the young, smiling girl. Sandra Taylor deserved justice. "You have a reputation as a ballbuster."

She laughed. "I know. By the way, what's the deal with the scrapbook on the table? Secret hobby?"

"Belongs to Tiffany Patterson. Her roommate gave it to me."

"Tiffany Patterson. The girl Tanner tried and failed to kidnap."

"That's a good memory."

"Been reading up on the case." She sat up and pressed her back to the headboard. "I learned you're the cop that shot and killed Tanner."

Dawson tightened his jaw. The scene still could play back in his head when he least expected it. If he'd been a second slower . . . "He drew on me, didn't get off a shot before I fired and killed him."

"He wanted to die."

"Tanner knew he'd spend the rest of his life in prison. I'm sorry I'm the one that gave him the easy way out."

"There's nothing easy about firing a weapon at someone."

"Yeah."

"Mind if I look at the scrapbook?"

"Have at it."

She rose and moved across the room, her stride confident, unashamed. She carried the scrapbook back to the bed, sat on the edge, and turned the pages. "Her run-in with Tanner certainly made an impression."

"Her claim to fame."

"She's been in contact with Scarlett Crosby. These days, she's looking for money so she can score," Margo said.

"She'll press anyone if she's desperate enough," Dawson said.

She closed the scrapbook and set it back on the table. As she stood there, she opened his case file, flipping through pages of notes and then the photographs taken of the items found on Taylor's body. She held up the picture snapped of the bracelet. "Interesting."

"What's that?"

"Why would Sandra Taylor have a bracelet with the letters *SC*?"

"Let me see."

She walked back to the bed and handed him the image. "SC. Scarlett Crosby."

Dawson traced the photo, irritated with himself that he'd missed this detail. "If this was Scarlett's bracelet . . ."

"Then you have a solid link between the girls. Or proof that Tanner took Scarlett's bracelet and put it with Sandra's body. His version of an inside joke."

"Fuck. I missed it."

"Don't beat yourself up. Sandra is lucky to have you. Scarlett Crosby was fortunate you intercepted Tanner's van so quickly."

"Lucky?"

"Most don't give a shit about girls like that." A practical statement riddled with practiced traces of empathy. "You'll piece this all together."

He'd never discussed cases with his ex because he wanted to keep the job from tainting her life. But Margo wasn't the kind of woman who needed coddling.

Margo lay beside him, trailing her fingers over his belly and around his dick, which twitched to life instantly. Whatever this was between them, it was temporary at best. Too bad. He could get used to Margo.

When he and his wife had sex, it had been quick and practical in the latter years. A scratched itch. No talking. But Margo was in no rush. She was content to linger, listen, and her achingly intimate touch stripped the last of his reservations. Suppressed doubts bubbled to the surface. "I'm not sure I'm that smart."

She straddled his groin. His erection hardened in anticipation as she guided it inside her.

"Is this my pep talk?" he asked.

"Is it working?"

He gripped her hips. "Maybe a little."

Her lips curled into a sly smile. "Do you feel out of control?"

His breath caught in his throat. "I do."

Margo studied him as if she'd seen him a thousand times before. "Where are your handcuffs?"

His voice was so rough, he almost didn't recognize it. "On my belt buckle."

She climbed off him, leaving him feeling exposed. She moved to his pants, grabbed the cuffs from his belt, and returned to the bed, links dangling from her fingers. "Do you want my hands in the front or the back?"

On the job, he always savored the snap of the cuffs as they locked around wrists. In those moments, when he knew the threat was neutralized and he had control, relief flooded him. But the cuffs had never made their way to the bedroom. "The back."

She snapped one silver cuff around her wrist and then clasped her hands behind her back. He reached around and locked the second cuff. He tightened it until he knew it pressed into her skin. She winced.

"Too tight?" he asked.

"No." She rose and hovered over his erection. With her arms pinned behind her, her breasts jutted out more. He guided himself inside her.

"What next?" she asked.

"Ride me." His whispered words were rough, raw.

Desire and orgasms were only a temporary fix. Once the glow faded, the darkness came back. But that problem existed in the future. Right now, he had a beautiful woman riding him. He ran his fingers up her flat belly and squeezed her breasts. The outside world fell away.

If life had taught him anything, it was to take one problem at a time. Let them all gang up on you at once, and they'd eat you alive.

Chapter Twenty-Three

SCARLETT

Monday, July 15, 2024
8:30 p.m.

I arrived at the gym near closing time. I liked the evenings because the place was quiet. Most were either in the showers or enjoying a summer evening. I had a full hour until the place closed. Plenty of time to climb.

I set my bag by the wall, changed into climbing shoes, and doused my hands with chalk. Looking up at the jutting rocks, I identified the spot that had nearly cost me big-time the other day. I'd scaled these rocks a hundred times before and never fallen. However, that was then. Now it was quiet, and I would not be lulled into looking back. If there was a Della look-alike lurking around, she wasn't here now. I'd been obsessing about her today, but on the wall, I didn't have the brain space to think about her. Later she'd return to my thoughts, but for now it was just me and the wall.

Without a belayer, I'd be arrow focused. No, it wasn't safe, but it was an effective way to keep my mind in the moment.

I worked my fingers into the groove of the first stone. The initial twenty feet were easy going. My feet found footholds effortlessly, and my hands slid into the ruts I knew very well. I continued the climb upward, anticipating the more difficult holds and slippery footings. My fingers ached as I pinched the rocks and hauled myself up another few inches. How many times in Tanner's basement had I dreamed of climbing to freedom?

My fingers cramped around a rock, forcing me to pause and loosen my hold. Against the wall, my breathing was fast. Sweat trickled down my back as I pushed closer to the hot lights.

When I'd stared at Tanner's basement ceiling, I memorized all the cracks, learned the pattern of the pipes that leaked, and trailed the paths taken by the bugs. That ceiling had become its own world. I'd spent hours pushing past it, climbing up, ripping away insulation, and breaking through the living room floor I'd never seen. I would imagine dashing to the front door, twisting the knob, and stepping into the hot sun. And then I'd run until my lungs and legs burned.

The lights above me hummed, popped, drawing my attention back to the present. I finished the last ten feet and scraped my fingers against the acoustic tiles.

The trip down was always risky. The stones were out of my field of vision and I had to rely on my memory. Slowly, I inched down, gripping and digging toes into plastic rock.

When I reached the floor, a rush of adrenaline flooded me. I'd escaped again. This feeling was a temporary fix. It would get me through the evening, but it wouldn't last. Peace, harmony, love—none of it ever lingered. I supposed there were people who lived in a state of bliss, but I wasn't one of them.

"You move like a pro."

The familiar male voice had me turning to find Luke Kane. He was wearing a faded Naval Academy T-shirt, shorts, and athletic shoes. "Thanks. When did you get here?"

His gaze steadied on me, warmth settling in the curve of his smile. "I was on my way out of the weight room when I looked up and saw this crazy woman climbing to the top without a spotter."

"And you thought, 'I know that woman.'"

He chuckled as a flicker of awe shimmered in his dark eyes. "You do this often?"

"Five or six days a week. Reminds me to keep my mind in the moment."

He seemed to file the detail away with all the other facts he had amassed on my story. "Did it work tonight?"

"Well. Real well."

"I'm sorry I haven't texted. Big case prep."

"I get it. We all have busy lives."

"I'd like to go out again."

I rubbed my chalked hands together, watching as the remains of the white powder floated to the floor. "I assumed you'd wised up and moved on."

"I won't lie. I've put some thought into it."

"And yet you just happened to be here randomly?"

"Nothing random about it. I remembered you said you climbed in the evenings. I took a chance."

"You could've texted."

"I hate texts." His deep tone added traces of humor to the confession. "Nothing beats face-to-face conversation."

"Very stalker-like." There was nothing desperate or angry about him, like there had been about Tanner once the mask dropped. Tanner had needed to control, hurt, and conquer. Was the man behind Luke's mask the same charming guy?

"Strategic." He jammed his thumb toward the locker. "I was going to shower and grab a burger. Care to join?"

I'd bought food earlier in the day thinking I might find Tiffany, but I hadn't, so I still had plenty in the refrigerator waiting for me. "I could eat. Let me change."

"Meet you here in fifteen?"

"Deal."

I moved into the dressing room and dumped my gear by the last shower on the left. It was the farthest stall from the door, which I liked. Also, its water pressure was the best.

I showered, taking time to wash my hair and shave my legs. Not sure why I felt like both were necessary to share a burger with a guy, but I did.

After swapping my climbing clothes for jeans and a blouse from my bag, I slipped on sandals. I combed my hair, ran a dryer over it quickly, and headed out of the changing room.

I found Luke by the front desk, talking to the attendant, Marty. The gym closed in five minutes, and normally Marty, in a rush to get home to watch basketball replays, got pissy when clients lingered. But he was laughing as Luke talked. I didn't think I'd ever seen Marty smile.

When Luke's gaze shifted to me, Marty turned, shrugging. "The fearless climber. You're going to give me a heart attack."

"I've signed all the waivers," I said. "You're in the clear."

"I don't like mopping up blood," Marty said. "I've done it before, and it isn't pretty."

This strange newfound directness was endearing. "That's why I'm careful."

"That's what the last guy said," Marty grumbled. "And then *splat*."

"Ready?" Luke asked.

"I am."

"Same time tomorrow?" Marty asked.

"Most likely," I said.

The air outside was cooler thanks to an afternoon rain shower, but it was still heavy with humidity. "Where do you have in mind?"

"The burger place five blocks away. Likely safer if we drive."

"Okay."

"I can drive us both."

He was offering it up to me, leaving the final decision in my hands. I rarely rode in a car with anyone other than the Judge, but the endorphin high from the climb still lingered and I was feeling optimistic. "Okay. You drive."

"I'll bring you back to your car when we return."

"I walked from my place."

"Brave woman."

The doors unlocked, and I sat in the front seat with my backpack wedged between my legs. Sitting forward, as if ready to spring free, I slid on the seat belt. When Luke sat behind the wheel, the car felt very small and cramped. He hit the auto lock. I flinched only a little. He clicked the lock off.

"Thanks."

"No big deal."

If Luke took note of my shifting energy, he pretended not to notice. "You ever been to AB's Burgers?"

"Driven by, but never stopped."

"You'll love it." He frowned. "Didn't think to ask. You eat meat?"

"I do."

"Okay." The ride in the car was smooth, and I barely noticed the rough road the city never got around to paving.

That close, I noticed little things about him. The way his rolled-up sleeves hovered just above his thick wrists; how his fingers gripped the steering wheel, relaxed but ready to jump into action; and the silver shimmering in the damp hair brushed back from his face.

"What attracted you to this neighborhood?" I asked.

"I know the area. I know the local dealers, the cops, and the dive bars. I grew up on these streets."

"I would think a defense attorney would want to go uptown and start fresh."

"Maybe. Eventually. One major life change at a time."

"You seem fearless to me."

He laughed. "I'm putting one foot in front of the other like every other slob in this world."

"Is there a story there?"

"Not really. I just like it better here."

"Fair enough."

He glanced at me. "You're the first person who's accepted that answer without suggesting I'm making a mistake."

"Why would it be a mistake to stay here? I live here. We only get one life. Do what you love."

"You haven't pressed for many details. Most dates want my full CV."

I laughed. "Not my style. And I tend toward silence and stony stares, rigid crossed arms."

"You weren't rigid on that wall. Your body flowed."

"But everywhere else, I'm tense."

That teased a smile. And to his credit, he didn't try to sell me on being comfortable with him. He didn't tell me I could trust him. Or that I shouldn't worry.

He parked in front of a dive of a burger place that I'd never been in because it looked so sketchy.

"What prompted you to try AB's?" I asked.

"Hunger. It was one a.m. and I'd just finished working. It was open. First bite and I was in love."

I rose out of the car and waited for him to come around. He moved one step ahead, opened the door, and waited for me to pass. The space was small, with just four red booths. Behind the narrow counter stood an older guy with thick gray hair and a mustache. There was no marquee displaying all the selections—just a few laminated menus on the counter.

"How's it going, Charlie?" Luke asked.

Charlie nodded. "Hanging tough, counselor. The usual?"

"You know me too well. Scarlett?"

I glanced at the menu. There were only twelve items, and they were all basic. Nothing fancy here. "I'll have whatever you're having."

"Make it two, Charlie."

Charlie called out the order to a cook and then filled two soda cups with cola. "Burgers on the way."

Luke took the booth farthest from the door and sat in the seat facing the exit. As I settled, a couple of guys walked in, laughing and shoving each other. They were drunk—but then, this place was designed to feed late-night drinkers. One of the men glanced back and leered at me. It was a feeling I'd never gotten comfortable with but could manage. I scooted closer to the inside of the booth.

Luke's jaw pulsed. "How long have you been in this area?"

"Eight years," I said. "At the time, places like this were cheap and what I could afford."

"And the prints sell well?"

"They do." I sipped my soda, grateful for the sugar and carbonation. "I've started a new series. I'll be making fifty prints. Each day is a new color. Today was the second color."

"Let me guess: green."

I glanced at my hands. "I thought I did a good job of cleaning up."

"There's a speck of green on your neck."

My hand rose to my neck. "Hazard of the business."

"Do you enjoy it? Working for yourself, I mean."

"I do." I relaxed a little.

"And for fun, you climb walls and risk your life."

"I also paint. And run. The days are full."

"Sounds pretty solo."

"It's good."

Charlie brought our burger orders as the two intoxicated men sat in a booth. I could feel their gazes on me, but I kept my focus on the food. "Enjoy, Luke. Loaded you both up with extra fries."

"Thanks, Charlie."

Charlie looked at me. "He's a good one. Best defense attorney in town."

I smiled. "Good to know."

"I know you, right?" Charlie said.

I shrugged. "Do you?"

"You own the art studio. I read the article in the paper. You painted a mural or something."

I'd never met Charlie, and realizing he knew me wasn't a great feeling. "That's me."

Charlie's eyes narrowed. "Where else do I know you?"

"I have one of those faces," I said.

Luke cleared his throat. "Thanks, Charlie."

"Got it. Enjoy." Charlie walked back to the counter.

"He's currently putting the pieces together," I said. "Old articles on the internet never die."

"You didn't give an interview. At least, I didn't find one. Tiffany Patterson received the most airtime."

"But articles were written. And Tiffany seemed to like the attention. Reporters called me dozens of times, but I never spoke to any one of them. I still don't answer unfamiliar numbers." My business number was widely published, so it wasn't hard to find me. But voicemail screened my calls. "I also make it a point to know what's being said about me. A fifty-fifty chance someone doesn't believe me."

"Really? What don't they believe?" he asked.

"That I was Tanner's victim. Some think I was his accomplice."

"How do they square that peg?"

"He worked a construction project near my mother's house. I did flirt with him once. I did willingly follow Della to his van. I did try to lure Tiffany into the same van. Those facts can sway anyone—including a few cops—against me." My chest still tightened when I thought about someone questioning my story.

The drunks laughed, and the short one looked toward me and winked. I curled my fingers into a fist.

"I see him," Luke said. "He's not going to bother you."

I looked up to find Luke staring at me. Hints of steel mingled with an odd kind of softness. "I'm fine. Sometimes guys just stare." I bit into my burger. Another Tanner lesson: eat when food was presented. The days of deprivation were always still too close.

"It's good," I said.

He wiped his hands carefully with a paper napkin. "I like Charlie. He became a client, and long story short, I'm glad to give him the business."

"Support small business. We must look out for each other."

"I think we did it," he said easily.

"What's that?"

He glanced at his watch. "If you count the time that you were climbing the wall, I think we've almost broken your date-night record."

I grinned. "We already set that record."

"And it's now broken."

The differences between us were noisy and rowdy. We weren't an *us*, but I saw possibilities. "I'm on a streak."

Carnal desire, knotted with control. He'd not made one move to touch me or uttered any suggestion that was remotely sexual. Poor guy was trying to figure out what to do with me.

I set down my burger, struggling to get my arms around my own blurring emotions. I liked him. Wanted more. But I still didn't know how to define it. "When anyone knows my history, they treat me as if they're expecting me to shatter or freak out."

"You've already freaked out, so we can check that box."

A smile tugged my lips. "All the more reason to wonder how I'll react in the future, right?"

He balled up the napkin. "Never a dull moment."

I chuckled, but I worried that I would see another "Della" and lose it. "That's a positive outlook."

"How does it feel to be in uncharted waters?"

Unwieldy and choppy as the waves in my print. "I can't promise how fast I can move. I have zero experience in this world."

"You seem to be doing okay," he said.

"That's not what I mean."

"I know what you mean. One step at a time."

I didn't want to panic when he touched me in the bedroom or when I woke up screaming from a nightmare while he slept beside me. For him, I wanted to be a little normal.

"I asked for curly fries!" the drunk shouted to Charlie.

"And I told you I don't have any," Charlie said.

Luke tossed his crumpled napkin beside his almost-eaten burger.

My nerves tightened and inwardly I winced, preparing for the violence that always came with resistance.

Luke rose slowly. "Pal, hit the road."

The man looked toward him. "Who the fuck are you?"

Luke's mild expression melted instantly. "I'm the guy that's going to crush you."

The man sneered, but the quiet intensity in Luke's tone caused him to pause for a moment. "Try."

Luke moved forward a step. "Are you sure? A man can't hold down a job if he has two broken kneecaps and a crushed eye socket."

"How you going to do that?" the man growled.

Luke's gaze didn't flicker or waver. "I can show you."

Charlie chuckled. "This is going to be good."

The drunk glanced at Charlie. "I want curly fries."

"Leave," Luke said. "Counting to five."

The man swayed, his eyes narrowing. He was intoxicated enough to strip away what few safeguards he had in place but not so lost that he couldn't imagine what broken knees and eye sockets would mean.

He flipped his plate on the floor and stalked out of the restaurant.

Charlie knelt and cleaned up the mess. "Thanks, Luke. That'll be the last time I serve him."

"Good plan."

"Dinner is on the house," Charlie said.

"Thanks." Luke sat back down across from me and fished three twenties from his pocket. He carefully stacked the neat bills and set the saltshaker on them as his gaze rose to meet mine. "You look pale."

I drew in a breath. "What can I say? It was a little jarring."

"He was all bluster."

"How do you know that?" How did anyone know what another person was capable of? How did I really know what Luke wanted?

"I make my living reading people."

"And you knew he wouldn't fight?"

"His T-shirt tells me he works for an HVAC company. Hard to do the work with broken knees, and paying the medical deductible will hurt."

"I doubt his brain is as logical as yours."

"We've all got the lizard brain, that primitive part of us that boils all decisions down to survival. He can't survive without his knees."

His unshakable confidence was enviable. "What if he'd called your bluff?"

Luke picked up a fry and bit into it. "I don't speculate on might-have-beens. He didn't. End of story."

"What if he's outside?" *What if I lose my shit one day and disappointment darkens your gaze when you look at me?*

His head cocked. "Do you always borrow trouble?"

I smiled. "The burden of potential overdue library fines is incredible."

He chuckled. "No reason to worry."

"Should I write that down?"

"Yes."

"Duly noted."

"Ready to get out of here?" Luke asked. "I can drive you back to your apartment."

"Thank you."

I slid out of the booth, and he followed behind me until we reached the door. He opened it, took the lead, and held the door. Despite his casual comments, he seemed very aware of his surroundings. So was I. But then, hypervigilance was how I rolled.

Back in his car, I relaxed into the leather seat. This time when he slid behind the wheel, only a little nervous tension rippled through me.

"What's your address?" he asked.

Again, panic. Stupid. My business was listed online. I rattled off the address.

He plugged it into his phone and drove.

"I could've directed you."

"That would've also worked."

When he pulled in front of my building, he looked up, studying the structure. "It's a warehouse."

"Home sweet home, with plenty of space to work."

"And you live here?"

"There's a small space in the back that's mine. Not fancy, but it works. The front is for art."

His gaze settled on me. "Drama aside, I had fun."

"I did, too."

"Did you?"

"Yeah, I did," I said honestly.

"Would you be open to a kiss?"

A question. A choice. I was in the driver's seat.

Beyond kisses from young boyfriends in my early teens, this kind of experience was somewhat warped.

"It doesn't have to be complicated," he said.

"It's been a while."

"How long?"

That jostled loose a laugh. "Middle school."

He didn't seem shocked or disappointed. "I've got a move or two I can teach you. Nothing complex."

I moistened my lips. "Okay."

He leaned toward me but paused. "Close your eyes."

"Why?"

"Close your eyes."

Heartbeat kicking, I lowered my lids. I felt his face nearing and then the gentle touch on the center of my lips and then the left and right sides.

It felt good. Stirred feelings. Tanner had been obsessed with me enjoying sex. Della had told me to show him affection, to kiss him like I meant it. She had told me to tell him that I loved him. And to my shame, I'd played the part of the whore so he would relax and trust me.

One of my therapists pointed out that I wasn't a bad person because of it. I'd survived, and I needed to be proud of that.

I leaned into Luke's next kiss, and when he raised a hand to my chin, I didn't flinch.

His face hovered close to mine. "Not bad."

I was all stumbling adrenaline. "Thank you. That was nice."

"We can do it again sometime."

I could feel my brows furrowing, knowing what was supposed to come next.

"Don't look so worried. We'll take this at your pace."

"You'll become impatient with me."

"Let me worry about that."

My therapist had also said to trust my instincts. If I felt fear, honor it. If I felt attraction, embrace it. He'd also said there would be transition people in my life. Men who showed me how to finish a date or gave me my first real kiss. Those interactions weren't meant to last, he'd said. More likely than not, that person would leave my life as quickly as they appeared. "Okay."

Chapter Twenty-Four

SCARLETT

Tuesday, July 16, 2024
12:30 p.m.

I was finishing up the third color in my current piece. Blue, green, and now black. Not an ink black, but a brownish, darkish tint that reminded me of the color of aging blood.

I'd traded texts with Luke, but no new date on the calendar. That suited me. I liked the time to process my reactions to him.

As I wiped my hands, I walked to the window and tipped my face toward the sun. When I opened my eyes, I noticed someone sitting in the entryway of the apartment building across the street. Her eyes were closed, and she leaned against the wall, a curtain of red hair covering her face. She looked thin and strung out. Was that Tiffany?

I stepped outside, locking the door behind me. I approached her slowly, knowing anyone coming off drugs could be easily startled. "Tiffany?"

At first, she didn't move. Her body was still, but when she looked up at me, I recognized her very pale face.

"Tiffany."

The woman's eyes blinked, and her stare was blank and lost before it slowly focused. "Scarlett."

I nodded and knelt in front of her. "It's been a few weeks."

"Has it? That's right. You were at Jeremy's."

"What're you doing here?"

"I came to see you."

I smiled. "Why?"

"I wanted to warn you," she whispered.

"About what?"

"I need to warn you about Tanner."

"Tanner." Hearing his name was jarring. And she knew that. "He's dead, Tiffany."

"No, he's not. He's alive. He's been texting me. And he's back for you."

Her confusion was unnerving. "You're playing me, Tiffany."

"I'm not." She stared directly into my eyes. "I swear."

The drugs could make someone believe anything. "What do you want?"

"To warn you."

"Tanner is dead," I whispered.

She shook her head as tears welled in her gaze. "He's not."

I'd dreamed for years that Tanner's cold hands could reach out from the underworld and grab me. How many times had I woken up screaming and brushing away imaginary fingers? "Tiffany, what have you been taking?"

"I don't know. I don't care. I need money. I need to get out of town."

"I'm not giving you money. Let me help you." I moved closer and carefully laid my hand on her arm. She tensed. "Let me help you stand."

"I can stand by myself." She tried to rise but lost her balance and tipped back. A second attempt brought her to her knees, and then she staggered to her feet. She leaned against the wall. "I need money."

"Why didn't you text me back?" I asked.

"I lost track of time."

She didn't lose track of time when she wanted money from me. I'd stopped giving her cash, but maybe this was a new ploy to stoke fears and guilt. She must have sensed I'd never absolved myself of my sins against her.

Tiffany stumbled. I took her elbow and steadied her. I owed her something, but what, I wasn't sure.

She pulled free. "How do I know you're not trying to hurt me?"

"You don't."

She blinked and rubbed her red nose with her fingers. "I shouldn't have come here."

"Why did you?" I'd spent the last decade wallowing in Tanner's wreckage. I'd climbed free of most of the debris, but Tiffany hadn't. "I want to help you."

"Why?"

"I owe you."

She sniffed. "Then give me money."

"I told you months ago, no more money."

Tiffany scowled. "I'll buy food."

"No, you won't. If you need a meal, knock on my door. I'll feed you."

"I need cash. Not a stupid sandwich."

"I'm not giving you money."

"Bitch."

I raised my hands in surrender. "I'm not giving you money."

Slowly, I turned and walked across the street. As I opened my front door, I half expected to see Tiffany following me. But when I looked back, I saw someone pause in front of Tiffany. The woman was nicely dressed, blond hair, large sunglasses. She handed Tiffany money, which she quickly pocketed. Enough for her next hit. Damn.

Gold bracelets winked from the woman's wrists as she started walking. Recognition flickered. Was she the woman from the gym and the one who'd passed by the restaurant the other night? My latest Della doppelgänger?

I trotted across the street, dodging a delivery truck, and rounded the corner. The woman was pressing a car remote, and the lights of a dark sedan blinked. I hurried toward her. "Excuse me! Ma'am!"

I wanted her to pause, glance in my direction, and give me a good look at her face.

The woman hesitated, her hand on the driver's-side door. When she turned, she was smiling, but large, dark sunglasses shaded most of her face. "Yes?"

I desperately searched her features for any signs of Della. The angle of the chin and the cheekbones were similar, but this woman was at least thirty pounds lighter than Della. The glasses and blond hair made it difficult to superimpose the two faces.

"I'm Scarlett. I live around the corner in the warehouse."

The woman smiled. "I'm Margo. I just moved into the Belmont building."

"Across the street from me." The lights I'd seen on yesterday. "Did you take the top unit?"

"I did."

"Your apartment has a view of my place."

"I guess that makes us roommates," she said, grinning. "We should get a drink sometime. Be nice to get to know my neighbors."

"That would be great."

Margo handed me her phone. "Text yourself from my number."

Heart striking my breastbone, I typed. "There you go."

As I handed Margo's phone back to her, my phone pinged with a text. "Now you have my number."

"Terrific." My brain continued to process details, but I couldn't assemble all the puzzle pieces into Della. "That girl you gave money to."

"The homeless girl."

"She shows up when she's out of money and needs a hit. I give her food but never money anymore."

The woman stilled and grimaced. "And I just gave her money."

"It's a natural reaction. But she's not going to use it well."

"She'll spend it on drugs." She shook her head. "Clearly, I'm tired. I should know better."

"It's an easy mistake to make."

"I'll remember, no more money for the redhead."

"Thanks."

"Let's grab a drink tonight? You can give me the rundown on the area."

I hesitated, remembering most offerings of a drink or lunch never happened. "Sure."

"Text me a place. About seven?"

"Perfect."

"Nice to meet you, Scarlett."

"You too, Della."

Her smile froze. "My name is Margo."

"Sorry. That's right. You remind me of someone I knew once."

"Hopefully she was a fantastic person."

My stomach tightened. "She was. Is."

Even white teeth flashed. "See you soon, Scarlett."

She vanished into the sedan, and I watched as she drove east.

Margo.

Not Della.

Margo.

Not Della.

I hadn't screamed. Reached for my phone and called 9-1-1. Sure, I'd called her Della, but on Scarlett's Unbalanced Scale, it registered low.

I hurried toward the Belmont and pressed the intercom button.

"Yes?" The static male voice sounded annoyed. It had to be Dave.

"I just met Margo, and I've already forgotten her last name."

"I can't give out resident information."

"Come on, Dave. It's Scarlett from across the street."

"You need to stop feeding Tiffany. She's ruining the look of the building."

"I know. I'm trying to help her out. Margo just gave her cash. I thought that was so sweet." I hoped my emphasis on *sweet* didn't sound too fake.

"You do-gooders are going to be the death of me."

The groaning complaint had an endearing quality. He complained about Tiffany, but he'd never chased her off. "Dave. What's Margo's last name?"

"Larsen. Margo Larsen."

"She's in the unit that overlooks my place, right?"

"Yeah."

"When did she move in?"

"Signed the lease two days ago. She's got a move-in scheduled for next Friday. And for the record, she's a cop."

"A cop?" That was very unexpected.

"A detective or investigator."

"Okay. Thanks."

I walked back toward my place and punched the code into the lock. Inside, I secured the doors and at the window stared up at the Belmont's top unit.

Super weird that my latest Della double lived across the street and had a bird's-eye view into my place. She'd called us roommates, like Della and I had been in that basement.

But Margo was a cop, which didn't jibe with any scenario I'd ever written for Della.

Still, it felt a little like we were cellmates again.

Chapter Twenty-Five

DAWSON

Tuesday, July 16, 2024
1:30 p.m.

Dawson had identified the convenience store where the burner phone used to call in Sandra Taylor's body had been purchased. It was a small place, located in the east end of Norfolk, did a lot of neighborhood transactions, and the security cameras weren't working. The buyer had bought five phones on a busy Friday night. Whoever picked this place had made a smart move. Only one of the five phones had been activated.

Dawson wondered when or if the other phones would be activated as he parked in front of Jeremy Dillon's house and paused to stare at the crumbling brick, tilting front porch, and broken windows. Jeremy was Tiffany Patterson's drug dealer, and he had operated out of this house for almost a year. Jeremy kept a low profile but was known to the cops in the area. As the pattern went, there'd be a police raid and Jeremy would make bail and set up shop somewhere else. The guy had nine lives, surviving five or six stints in prison, drive-by shootings, and countless up-and-coming drug dealers who wanted to take over his business.

This area had once been a decent working-class neighborhood, but the economy and rising crime had driven out those families. Areas like this reminded him how fast life could go sideways.

A dark sedan pulled in behind his, and in the rearview mirror he watched Margo get out of her vehicle. Dark slacks and a sleeveless blouse skimmed her fit figure. Boots and a detective's badge clipped to her waistband finished the look.

Dawson got out of his car, adjusted his sunglasses, and did his best to look at ease even as tension rippled through him. His right hand rested close to his weapon. "Have any trouble finding this place?"

"No. I have a stunning sense of direction."

"I don't doubt it."

"Why are we here?" Margo asked.

"The call that led you to take a sledgehammer to that wall came from here."

"Interesting."

"Jeremy Dillon isn't the public servant type. But he or someone familiar with this place made the call from this location."

"Who do you know who hangs out here?" she asked.

"Tiffany Patterson."

"Ah, Tiffany. Linked to Tanner Reed, Scarlett Crosby, and by a few degrees of separation, Sandra Taylor."

As they approached the porch, he spotted a young man sitting on a rusted glider. He wore threadbare jeans, a white shirt that rode up on his big belly, and no shoes. His eyes were closed and his mouth agape.

Dawson recognized him. Marco. He'd been in and out of the system since he was fourteen. Dawson had busted him a few times himself. He pressed his fingertips to the man's cool skin. A heart thumped faintly.

"I hear someone calling for help," Margo said.

"Me too." Even if he hadn't heard anything, no one could prove otherwise.

Fingers tightening around the grip of his weapon, Dawson waited for Margo to position herself to the right of the door before he opened it.

The inside was dimly lit, and the air was thick with smoke and the scent of unwashed bodies. There was an old, stained cloth plaid couch in the center of the room and a couple of metal chairs. Three people sat on the floor. All thin, heavily lidded eyes, bodies limp.

When Dawson had first joined the force, he'd thought he could make a difference in so many lives. And he'd done some good, but he'd since learned there were too many lost souls.

"Jeremy is always in the kitchen," he said. "It's his office."

"Heart of the house, right?" Margo asked.

Dawson crossed the thin green carpet and rounded a corner. Jeremy was sitting at the kitchen table with one of his lieutenants leaning against an avocado-green stove.

Jeremy, a large man with a thinning goatee, grinned when he saw Dawson and then Margo. "Been a while, Detective. Heard you had a rough time of it this winter."

"We all got shit, right?" He'd told Margo more about himself than he had most, but there were still plenty of secrets.

Jeremy whistled. "Some more than others. You still have the edge? I hear getting benched for a few months rattled you."

"You can press and find out," Dawson said.

Jeremy smirked, shaking his head. "Not today. Maybe some other time." There were no drugs on the table. But Jeremy always kept the space in front of him clean. The drugs were either in the refrigerator or the oven. Place your order, pay, and the goods materialized.

"What can I do for you, Detective?" Jeremy asked.

"Remember Tiffany Patterson? Late twenties, bright-red hair."

"I might. Why are you asking?"

"I'm trying to find her. She might have information on a case I'm working." There was no code of conduct that dictated truth or full stories.

"What kind of case?" Jeremy asked.

"She's an addict," Dawson said. "The usual. When's the last time she was here?"

"It's been a few weeks, I think. I don't keep up with my clients."

"When she was here, did she linger?" Margo asked.

Jeremy splayed his fingers to admire several gold rings. "She knows some of the guys. She hangs around sometimes to chat folks up. She loves to talk."

"Does she have clients that come and go from here?" Margo asked.

"I'm not her daddy."

"Can you give me names of her regulars?" Dawson asked.

"She don't work for me."

"You know what happens in your house and block, Jeremy," Dawson said carefully. "You always have. Was she acting differently?"

"She's always strung tight, but yeah, she might've been more on edge lately. But I didn't mess in her business. As long as she has cash, I don't care."

"You sleep with her?" Margo asked.

Jeremy shifted his gaze to her, allowing it to slide over her body.

"I'll take that as a yes." Margo took a slight step forward.

"You a mind reader?" Jeremy asked.

"I know body language well," she said easily. "Yours is screaming that you slept with her. And you might know more about her than you're saying."

He tugged at his pants and sat a little straighter. "What if I did? It was consensual."

"I'm not saying it wasn't," she said. "She's a pretty woman. Held it together, considering. But if she were connected to a murder, that might implicate you as well."

"What's she saying about me?" Jeremy demanded.

Shrugging, Dawson let the lie roll off his tongue. "She's made some suggestions that you have a temper."

He laughed. "Now that's a lie. I love everybody. Enemies are bad for business."

Dawson opened his phone and found a picture of Sandra Taylor. "You remember her?"

Jeremy sighed and looked at the picture. "No."

Dawson swiped to Scarlett Crosby's image. "What about her?"

Jeremy yawned and then looked at the picture. Recognition flickered. "Her, I do know. Came looking for Tiffany a couple of weeks ago."

Dawson flipped through his notes on the 9-1-1 call. "July 2?"

"That's exactly right," Jeremy said.

"That's a hell of a memory," Margo said. "I can barely remember yesterday, let alone two weeks ago."

"I remember the date because it was my birthday. I'm about to blow out the candles when I hear two bitches going at it in the backyard. Nothing worse than hearing a chick fight."

"What were they fighting about?" Dawson asked.

"Scarlett wanted Tiffany to leave. Tiffany refused. Started screaming that Scarlett wanted to kidnap her. She thought she was going to finish the job the Basement Guy started a long time ago."

"Tanner Reed?"

"That him?" Jeremy asked.

"That's right," Dawson said.

"Yeah, she thought Basement Guy had sent Scarlett to get her."

"Tanner Reed is dead."

"Tell that to Tiffany. When she's really messed up, she sees that fucker."

"Why's she so rattled?" Margo asked. "She was never kidnapped."

"She knew the guy before all the shit went down. Used to come in the diner, and he liked to flirt with her. She said once or twice she thought he was hot and would've gone out with him if his girlfriend weren't hovering so close."

"Girlfriend?" Dawson flipped pages. "Lynn Yeats."

"I don't know. Ask Tiffany."

"I will if I can find her," Dawson said.

Jeremy reached in his pocket and pulled out a packet of cigarettes and lit up. "Good luck getting a straight answer out of her."

"If anyone else talks about Tiffany, you'll let me know, right?" Dawson asked.

"Yeah, yeah, sure. I like to maintain a good relationship with the police."

A rail-thin guy with shoulder-length hair came into the kitchen, and Dawson shifted to the right, his hand tightening on the grip of his weapon. Steps behind the man was a pale redheaded woman. When she looked up, Dawson almost laughed. He'd take lucky over smart any day of the week. "Tiffany Patterson."

"Speak of the devil," Margo said.

Tiffany tensed and stepped back. "Leave me alone."

As she ran toward the front door, he dashed after her and grabbed her arm. "Hold up, Tiffany!"

She whirled around, her eyes wide. "Leave me alone."

"I'm a cop." He tightened his fingers.

She twisted her arm, trying to free herself from his grip. "You're hurting me."

He relaxed his fingers but didn't release her as he guided her outside to the front lawn. "Do you visit Jeremy a lot, Tiffany?"

"No."

Dawson cleared his throat. "I'll arrest you and pull your record. Save me the time and the paperwork."

She scratched the side of her head. "I haven't been here for a while. I was settling a bill with Jeremy."

Dawson shook his head. "I want to ask you a few questions about Scarlett Crosby."

"Ask her," she said, nodding to Margo. "She met her today."

Dawson looked at Margo, who showed no signs of stress. "That true?"

"I did meet Scarlett. She lives across the street from my new apartment. She scolded me for giving Tiffany money. Said she'd use it on drugs. Small world."

"What was Tiffany doing at Scarlett's?" Dawson asked.

"Trolling for dollars, I imagine," Margo said.

Tiffany jerked. "Leave me alone!"

Annoyance snapped through Dawson. "Answer a few questions and I will."

Margo smiled. "We'll be gone in no time if you just cooperate."

"Fine. What?"

"What do you know about Sandra Taylor?" Dawson asked.

Tiffany's eyes narrowed. "Who?"

He deliberately softened his tone. "You went to high school with her. She was a year behind you. She also worked at Mike's."

She shook her head. "High school was a million years ago."

He pulled up a picture of Sandra on his phone. "This is from the yearbook."

Tiffany studied the picture. "Yeah. She wanted to be a cheerleader."

"Doesn't say that in the yearbook." How many other dreams had Sandy had that died with her?

"She told me that when we were in between shifts. She had big dreams, or some shit like that. And I don't know what happened to her," Tiffany said. "Why do you care?"

"I think she was Tanner Reed's first victim," Dawson said. "I think he killed her."

Tiffany's face paled as she shook her head. "I don't know about that."

"If you hung out with her during your breaks at Mike's, you must have liked her," Margo said.

"That was a long time ago."

"Did she think Tanner was cute?" Margo asked.

"We all did."

"Didn't he have a girlfriend?" Margo asked.

"Yeah. Sour-faced bitch." Tiffany's eyes blinked very slowly, and Dawson knew whatever she'd taken was kicking in. He reached for his cuffs.

"What are you doing?" Tiffany asked.

He clasped a cuff on one wrist. "You're intoxicated. And we are in public." He read her the Miranda rights.

"I'm not high!"

"I disagree."

"You're a cop, not a social worker." Tiffany tried to pull free.

He held her arm, amazed that she had a strong pull. "In this moment, I feel more like a social worker. When you sober up, we'll talk again."

"Is this a shakedown? What do I have to do to get out of this?"

"Nothing."

"You want to know more about Scarlett?" she challenged. "She's been my new best friend for the last couple of years."

"How did something like that happen?" Margo asked.

"She feels bad. And I let her. She used to give me money—now she just gives me food."

He walked Tiffany toward his car and opened the back seat door. "You been playing her?"

"Sure. We all need an angle."

"When she showed up here two weeks ago, what did she want?"

"Got on my ass about getting high."

"She make any calls?" Margo asked.

"I don't know. Maybe."

"What does *maybe* mean?" Dawson asked.

"I don't know. She could've made a call. There was a lot going on."

Calling from a location like this was smart. With no cameras, a good defense attorney could argue any number of people could've placed the call. "Okay."

Tiffany leaned toward Dawson, bloodshot eyes wide with drugs and fear. "Scarlett's got a portrait in her warehouse. It's weird."

"What's it a portrait of?"

"Some girl. Bizarre. Dark curly hair. Pale skin."

Sounded like Scarlett's description of Della. "Did Scarlett say who it was?"

"No."

"Why were you at her place?" Margo asked.

"I needed money. Thanks for that, by the way."

He put his hand on Tiffany's head and guided her into the back seat. He'd be doing paperwork for an hour. "We'll talk tomorrow. I'll wait until you sober up."

When he tried to close the door, she balked. "I don't want to be put in a box."

"You'll be in a holding cell."

"I don't want to be locked up."

Dawson closed the door and looked at Margo. "Sounds like you were busy today."

"I was measuring for curtains at my new place," Margo quipped.

"Which happens to be right across from Scarlett Crosby."

"Didn't realize Scarlett Crosby lived in a no-go zone."

"She doesn't. But it's usually not that small of a world."

"I'm having drinks with her tonight," she said. "Have any questions you want me to ask?"

Could any of Margo's conversations with Scarlett be used in court one day? A good lawyer would get them thrown out, citing entrapment. But he didn't care. He wanted answers. "You move fast."

A brow arched. "You just noticed?"

"Keep me posted on the conversation."

"Of course."

Trust with a partner took time, and he and Margo didn't have much history. She'd slid into his personal life and his work world so easily. And if life had taught him anything, it was to be suspicious of easy.

Chapter Twenty-Six

Scarlett

Tuesday, July 16, 2024
6:45 p.m.

As I washed the murky black ink from my hands, a restless urge passed through my body. My thoughts kept returning to Margo.

She'd texted me two hours ago. Drinks at my place tonight?

Sure.

A glance up toward her apartment told me the lights were on, and I saw Margo pass in front of the window. I showered and changed into clean jeans, a black graphic T-shirt, and sandals. I didn't have a bottle of wine or anything to bring. So I set out across the street, waved to the front desk attendant, and entered the building.

"Hey," I said. "Me again. I'm meeting Margo Larsen."

"Fifth floor. Apartment 512."

"Thanks. How's it going?"

"Can't complain. You talk to that redhead?"

"No."

He grunted. "When you do, tell her not to sit on my front door-step. It's not a great look."

"I'll do my best." Tiffany flaked often and it could be weeks before I saw her. Maybe I'd never see her again.

I strode toward the elevator and stepped inside. As the doors closed, I drew in a breath, easing the tightness. Glancing up, I watched as the buttons ticked toward the fifth floor. I had no idea what I was going to say to Margo or why I was here. She was a cop, but she had Della's demeanor.

The doors opened, and I walked down the hallway to 512. I knocked, took a step back, and slid a nervous hand into my jeans pocket. Booted heels echoed in what sounded like a hollow space.

The door snapped open. Margo wore dark pants, a fitted top, and low-heeled boots. Her badge was hooked to her belt and her hair was brushed back. "Scarlett. Right on time."

I looked into her eyes, and suddenly felt as if I was looking at Della. "Hey."

"Come in."

I stepped past her. The unit was stripped bare and was all hard angles, metal, and glass. It bordered on cold, but the soft glow of the evening sun streaming through the windows warmed up all the dark-ened corners.

"So, this is my new home," Margo said. "What do you think?"

I cleared my throat. "Nice."

"I'm lucky to have found it. I hear units in this area get snapped up quickly. Apparently, the last tenant just took off without warning and broke her lease."

"It happens." I crossed to the window and stared out over the ware-houses across the street to the river beyond. People walked past my building, going about their lives, never really paying attention to their surroundings.

From this vantage, I could see directly into my warehouse. If Margo wanted to watch me, she could do it easily from here. Good. Let her watch.

"How did you find the place?" I asked.

"Nothing like staying in a second-rate hotel to motivate a house search. Found it online. My timing was perfect. The unit had only been listed for an hour."

I faced her, staring into her eyes. "You're a police officer?"

"That's right." She walked toward a granite countertop to an open bottle of wine and two paper cups. "For eight years now. I started in Northern Virginia, got a little tired of the traffic, and decided to move closer to the water."

"You originally from the DC area?"

"Newport News." The city was located across the Hampton Roads Bridge-Tunnel on the mainland and in light traffic took twenty minutes to reach.

"So, like coming home."

"If that's possible." She held up the wine. "Can I pour?"

"That would be great."

Margo grabbed the wine bottle and filled the two cups. Joining me at the window, she handed me one. "Cheers to me and my new home."

"Welcome," I said. The wine was decent if not a tad bitter. "What kind of police work did you do in Northern Virginia?"

"Human trafficking." She sipped.

"That must've been tough."

"It was. But I'm very good with those cases. I have a knack. Nothing jazzes me more than really busting up a trafficker."

"Arresting?"

"Sure. They also end up incarcerated." Margo took a liberal sip. "I have a confession. I know your story."

The comment was alive with too many unspoken meanings. "Do you?"

"I'm working with Dawson on the Sandra Taylor case. He told me about you."

I tried to picture her with Dawson and couldn't marry the two together. "Okay."

"Tough break for you."

A powerful understatement. "Nothing you haven't seen on the job."

"Still, never easy."

"No."

"Your backstory with Tiffany Patterson makes your interest in her odd."

"Why's that?"

"Seems you two would keep your distance. You feel like you owe her, don't you?"

"Why do you say that? I saved her."

"But you weren't planning on it, were you? Something broke inside of you in the last moment?"

The assessment hit too close to home. "That about sums it up."

"And now you're trying to balance the old wheel of karma, am I right?" Her curiosity was palpable, layered with agendas I couldn't define.

"Just trying to do the right thing." The words traveled on a breathy whisper.

"Did you know Sandra Taylor?"

I marshaled a fake smile. "Is this a meet and greet or an interrogation?"

Margo grinned like Della. It was the way the left side of her mouth lifted in a half-sheepish and half-humorous way. "Both, I suppose."

I set my cup on the counter. "I came to meet my neighbor, not to be interrogated."

Margo was nonplussed. "We're drinking wine. We're getting to know each other. And you're right: I focus on work too much."

Hidden agendas bounced between us. "Tell me about yourself."

"Nothing extraordinary. Divorced. I live to work." She sipped her wine.

"Why do you do it?" I asked. "The police work, I mean?"

Margo shrugged. "That karmic wheel. Like you, I keep it tilted toward the positive."

"You get what you want?"

"Always."

Her unswerving gaze propelled tension through me. "And what do you want now?"

"To solve this case." She raised her glass. "To get a big promotion. Rule the world, basically."

"Keeping it simple?"

She laughed. "Exactly."

I sensed I was a small, expendable obstacle on Della's and Margo's paths. I set my cup down. "Thanks for the wine, Margo. I better get going."

That smile faded. "No need to rush off. This is just a friendly chat, Scarlett."

"No such thing with a cop during an investigation."

"That might be true. But I'd like to have your help. I'd really like to know what happened to Sandra Taylor."

"So would I. I hope you find her killer." I started toward the door.

"Do you think Tanner killed her?"

I stopped. "I don't know. Seems possible."

"You never saw her when you were in his house?"

The air grew thick, dense, and I could almost imagine the *drip*, *drip* of the pipes in Tanner's basement. "No."

"Why did you call in the location of the body to the cops?" Margo asked.

The comment rattled warnings. I faced her immediately. "I didn't."

"You were at Jeremy's on July 2, right?"

"I was looking for Tiffany in early July. I don't remember the exact date."

"The call came into dispatch July 2, and Jeremy remembers you that night because it was his birthday. And you were fighting with Tiffany."

"There were a lot of people there that night."

She sipped and then set her cup down beside mine. "You and Sandra went to the same high school at the same time."

"If you check my school records, you'll realize I wasn't the best student. I missed a lot and didn't mix much with the other kids."

"You had to know Sandra."

"How many kids do you remember from high school?"

Again, the lopsided grin. "Point taken."

"I can't help you."

"See it from my perspective. Sandra was seen with Tanner. She vanishes. Tanner took you for eighty-eight days. Someone on July 2 called in the tip from a location where witnesses can place you. I found Sandra's body. See how you and Sandra keep showing up in this story?"

"I didn't place that call. I never met Sandra in high school or in Tanner's house. Della had told me about the Other Girl, but no one thinks Della is real."

"You believe she's real, and that's all that matters."

"I'm not delusional."

"No one is saying you are."

Time compressed, superimposing Della over Margo. "I have a piece of art that I think you might like. It would look great on the south wall."

"I couldn't." Curious amusement sparked.

"Of course you can. Consider it a housewarming gift, and when you've found Sandra's killer, reach out to me. We'll do this again."

I opened the door, and she followed me into the hallway. "Thanks for the wine."

"Will we find your DNA on Sandra's body?" Margo asked.

If Sandra was the Other Girl, we'd never spoken or touched, so it didn't make sense that my DNA would be on her body. However, the tone rumbling under her words triggered an alarm bell. "Have a good evening, Margo."

"Were you wearing any jewelry when Tanner took you?"

Why ask now about my bracelet and necklace? "I'm sure if I was it's in my police file."

Margo left her front door gaping as she followed me toward the elevator. "Lynn Yeats. When's the last time you saw her?"

Lynn Yeats. Tanner's girlfriend. "You're full of questions."

"I've only just begun."

As I punched the elevator button, I felt her gaze on me. When the doors opened, I stepped in and faced her. She smiled and waved. Dawson might be the louder of the two, but she was the more dangerous.

Lynn Yeats. She was my closest living link to Tanner. According to Della, she'd been in his house many times, and if anyone might have known about the girls in the basement, it would be her.

Back in my warehouse, I glanced up toward Margo's unit, still lit up. There was no sign of her when I reached for my phone and opened social media.

I kept an account for my business and used it to post pictures of my art and interface with clients. However, I never posted anything personal about myself. On my page, I noticed a couple of direct messages and responded to potential client queries.

I searched Lynn Yeats. There were a half dozen of them, but only one in this area. Oddly, her page wasn't private, because maybe she no longer worried about anyone associating her with Tanner. And why would she? It had been a decade, and life had moved on for everyone but me. The world didn't really remember Tanner, Sandra, Della, Tiffany, or me. I could almost imagine people when one of our names came up. *Oh yeah, I remember that case. The girl survived. But she must be messed up. How could she not be?*

Lynn Yeats, according to her page, liked wine tastings in New Kent County, lingering on the narrow beach rimming the Chesapeake Bay, and riding bikes along the Capital Trail. She worked at the local hospital as an oncology nurse. I guessed she'd always been a nurse, but that factoid had never reached me. Mrs. Rose had said Lynn brought lunches to Tanner at the renovation jobsite where Sandra's body had been found. Della said she'd met Lynn once when Tanner had introduced her as his cousin.

Maybe Lynn had finally decided that she no longer had to keep Tanner's secrets.

The sun dipped closer to the horizon as I drove to the hospital located fifteen minutes away. I didn't know Lynn's work schedule, but I was curious about her. I wanted to know what she knew about Della.

As I parked in the lot, I stared at the gray building, remembering this was where the rescue squad had taken me. I recalled the rumble of the gurney wheels, the quick conversations of the paramedic who gave the attending doctor my stats, and the curious stares of the nurses.

Officer Rogers, a six-foot-six man with graying short hair, had escorted me to an examination room. He'd said nothing to me, jogging alongside the gurney as if he were a football defensive end ready to block trouble. Officer Rogers was the kind of guy who kicked down doors, not a caretaker of a sketchy, broken girl suffering with injuries from a car accident and months of sexual assault. I didn't look fixable, and that had made him feel helpless. When he looked down at me, I saw pain etched in his hard features. I suspected he had a daughter or a sister and saw his worst nightmare in me. His voice had been gruff, as if annoyance trumped tears. "Hang tough."

Oddly, I'd appreciated his words.

I finished my coffee. Cool air gusted from vents, and soon my skin chilled and gooseflesh puckered the surface.

Out of the truck, I moved with a steady pace to the main entrance. I walked up to the front desk to an older woman sporting a gray bun and a blue hospital volunteer jacket. I remember someone just like her coming in my room when I'd been here and offering me a copy of *Seventeen* magazine.

"Hey, I'm looking for my next-door neighbor," I said, smiling. "I don't have her phone number or a key to her house but I'm hoping you can get a message to her."

"I can't give out the names of hospital personnel."

"I know. I get that. But can you tell Lynn Yeats that I think a pipe burst in her place. I could hear water gushing. I don't know how to reach her. We've chatted a few times and I know she works here. Maybe you can let her know."

The older woman frowned. "Has anyone else tried to shut the water off? Most homes have a shutoff at the street."

"A few guys were trying to figure that out. I think the meter at the street is fused or something. My job was to tell Lynn."

"I'll get word to her."

"Thank you."

I returned to my truck, turned on the engine, and sipped the cold dregs of my coffee. I figured I had a 25–40 percent chance Lynn would come running out of this door or one of the ones to the right or left. If this didn't work, I'd find her some other way—I needed to discover what she knew. How could she not have known Della and I were in the basement?

Five minutes later a tall brunette wearing scrubs came running out the exit on the right. I watched as she hoisted her backpack on her shoulder under the parking lot's rising lights and pressed a remote. The lights of a Jeep blinked.

The Jeep barreled out of the lot, pausing only briefly at a stop sign before heading east. I followed, keeping a reasonable distance. She didn't appear to be worried about speed limits. No doubt the woman was imagining soggy rugs, ruined wallboard, and soaked wood floors. I shouldn't have been enjoying her distress, but I was. A bit of payback for living her clueless life while metal rubbed my skin raw.

She took several rights and lefts, and we wound away from concrete toward tree-lined streets. Her brakes came to a screeching halt in front of a town house. The house wasn't particularly interesting or memorable. The brick was new, the shutters green, and the wrought-iron rails thin. The number *6240* was painted on the front door.

Scrambling with her keys, she shoved one in the lock, turned the handle, and vanished inside. The keys dangled in the lock.

I parked across the street, shut off the engine, and lowered in my seat. I pictured her running from room to room searching for water, wetness, or damage. She'd find none. And soon relief would give way to anger and frustration: *It's a hell of a joke to play on a person. How could someone be so cruel?*

If she thought this was unkind or unfair, she didn't understand the true meaning of either.

When Lynn came outside, she was scowling and muttering to herself. She went to her neighbor's door, banged on it, and waited until a young man appeared. Her animated hands pointing to her place said more than her words could. The guy shook his head, looking confused.

When she finally got back in her Jeep and drove toward the hospital, I sat in the silence, staring at the house. I knew where Lynn Yeats worked. I knew where she lived.

Chapter Twenty-Seven

Dawson

Tuesday, July 16, 2024
9:45 p.m.

As Dawson lay beside Margo, he savored the warmth of her body and smell of her perfume.

"Tell me what's bothering you," she said. "And don't tell me you're worried about HR. You couldn't give a shit. What's on your mind?" She held up her wrist ringed with the red marks of his cuffs. "I know when something is bothering a man."

He traced the red circling her wrist. Instead of smoothing his fingers over it, his hold tightened around the bone. "How did your visit with Scarlett go?"

"She's very closed. She doesn't remember Sandra, and she helps Tiffany because she says she owes her. She's had no contact with Lynn Yeats."

He relaxed his hold. "Do you believe her?"

"I don't know. Survivors of captivity are very good at hiding their true selves. I've seen it dozens of times before. It's a survival mechanism."

"She's completely closed off to me, but I have that effect."

"She stares at me as if she's searching for something. The first time we met, she called me *Della*."

"Della? Really?"

"I've read enough of the files to know Della isn't real, but it's odd she'd confuse her with me."

"You're not the first. She's called in reports on three different women over the years."

"Interesting."

"What does that mean?"

"If I could play into her fantasy, she might be more open to talking."

Dawson had no doubt that Margo could handle herself; still, he couldn't resist the warning. "Tanner might have turned her into a monster."

Frown lines etched deep in her forehead. "How's she a monster?"

"What if she knew Sandra? What if she killed her or helped Tanner hide the body? The timelines work. There's the SC bracelet found on Sandra's body. Sandra vanished nine and a half weeks before Scarlett, but the medical examiner can't lock down a time of death. Maybe she struck Sandra in the head or saw Tanner do it. Maybe she helped him wrap the body."

"Would you hold her responsible for the things Tanner forced her to do?"

"That's for the jury, judge, and lawyers to sort. My job is to find out who killed Sandra. She was a kid."

"You already believe it was Tanner. Why go after Scarlett?"

He shoved out a breath. "She was willing to help Tanner kidnap Tiffany. And we can place her at the site of the call to dispatch July 2."

She was silent for a moment. "Maybe she slipped the bracelet in Sandra's purse as a call for help."

"You believe that?"

"How else was she supposed to let the world know she was alive?"

"If the bracelet is hers."

"Ask her," Margo said. "You interviewed Tanner a decade ago, correct?"

"Yes."

"And you dropped the ball."

Her bluntness cracked across his skin like a whip. "Yes."

"Scarlett wasn't the first kid to make an impossible choice. And you're not the first cop who didn't see the entire picture immediately. It's called being human." Her hand slid down his leg.

"Do you believe in coincidence?" he asked.

"No. Why do you ask?"

"What're the chances that the past and present collide right now?" She rolled on her side and climbed on top of him.

"Someone called in the location of Sandra's body for a reason."

"From a burner near Jeremy's drug house, where Scarlett happened to be. Scarlett knows more than she's saying."

"Maybe. But I'd wait for the medical examiner's final report. There will be more details there."

Dawson stared into her eyes, trying to see what Scarlett saw. "Why did she call you Della?"

She shook her head. "You said yourself, she's called in reports before. I bet there are dozens of others you don't know about."

"You a psychologist or something?"

Teardrop earrings swayed as she shook her head. "Or something."

"Maybe you should push her. She might say or do something that'll break this case."

"I can do that."

Her hand slid to his groin, and she angled his growing erection toward her entrance. His hands gripped her hips as he savored her warmth. The case clung to him even as her body pulled him away.

Chapter Twenty-Eight

SCARLETT

Wednesday, July 17, 2024
5:45 a.m.

I'd barely slept last night. And after staring at the ceiling for a few hours, I rose and turned on the lights and moved into my studio. I glanced up toward Margo's apartment. No lights on. No sign of movement.

I crossed to the Della painting and uncovered it. Rubbing sleep from my eyes, I reached for the tubes of paint. I gripped the stylus and mixed the blues with hints of white. The color I mixed was not from an old, rusted memory but from the vivid blue of Margo's eyes. I dabbed a clean fine-tipped sable brush into the paint and regarded the canvas. I carefully began to reshape the eyes and shift the color. Slowly Della's eyes faded, and Margo's took their place.

Margo had said she was from Newport News. She'd been a cop for eight years in Northern Virginia, and now she was back. Not to Newport News, but to Norfolk, right across the street from me.

Was it an accident that she'd been the cop who'd found Sandra's body? Randomness was a big part of the universe, but I'd grown suspicious of it since Tanner. Was it a twist of fate that put him in the house across the street from my mother's house, or had he chosen it because he'd already selected me? He was familiar with the neighborhood and my school.

I wiped my hands, shifted focus to my laptop, and searched Margo Larsen. She was listed as a new hire with the Norfolk Police Department and according to her bio was highly decorated. She would be working violent crime and homicides in her new position. She had a two-year degree from community college and her BS from Virginia Commonwealth University, both in the Richmond, Virginia, area. Her degree was in criminology. No record of her high school. She had no social media presence. One article I found said she was a "wrecking ball" in human trafficking.

I sat back and regarded the painting, reconnecting with an awareness that had slowly waned over the last decade.

When my phone rang, I didn't recognize the number, but for the first time in a long time, I answered it. "Yes."

"Scarlett."

The woman's scratchy voice was barely recognizable. "Tiffany?"

"Yeah. Can you come get me?"

I hesitated, wondering why the shift in attitude. "Where are you?"

"Jail. I was arrested for being intoxicated in public."

I rose. "I'm surprised you called me."

"I don't have anyone else. My roommate isn't answering. Can you bail me out? I can pay you back."

She couldn't. But that didn't matter. "I can be there in a half hour."

"Thanks."

"Sure."

The drive across town to the regional jail took a half hour, and then it was a series of administrative procedures. I showed my driver's license and was directed to the magistrate, who then put me in touch with a bail bondsman. Two hours passed from the moment Tiffany called to the instant I saw her move through the double doors, hugging a plastic bag stuffed with her belongings.

When she saw me, she nodded but didn't smile or look grateful. Maybe she saw this as one more stone in the rebalancing of my debt to her. Maybe she was so tired and hungover she couldn't summon any emotion.

She followed me out the front door and to my truck. "Where do you want to go? You can crash at my place if you need to get it together."

"I have an apartment."

"I can take you there."

"I guess."

"Why don't I buy you a meal first? You've got to be hungry."

"Sure. Okay." Inside my truck the scents of jail and the streets hung heavily in the air. "Why did you do it?"

The simple question came too loaded for me to respond. "Do what?"

"Bail me out."

"Ah," I said, relaxing. "Because I meant it when I said I wanted to help you."

She scratched her pale, freckled arms. "That asshole Dawson arrested me."

Dawson. He got around. "What did he want?"

"To know more about you. But I was high." She shook her head. "I don't remember what he said."

"Where did he arrest you?"

"At Jeremy's house."

"You just happened on him?"

Nervous laughter bubbled, but it held no joy. "I'm there a lot."

"Do you remember the night I saw you there? It was early July."

"Kind of. It was really crowded."

"Whoever called the cops that night and reported the location of Sandra's body did it from Jeremy's block."

"It wasn't me."

"You sure?"

"Yes. How would I know something like that?"

213

"Okay." I drew in a breath. I didn't know what to believe now.

"You believe me, right?"

"Sure."

I drove back toward my place and parked behind the warehouse. Out of the truck, I started walking, and she followed. I could feel the tension radiating from her body. Down the block from my place was a Chinese restaurant. "Anything you want?"

"Whatever is fine." She leaned against the brick wall, tipping her face.

Ten minutes later I came out with a bag filled with three different entrées. "Come on."

Again, Tiffany followed me to my warehouse, and after punching in the security lock code, we were inside. She sat on a barstool at the small kitchen counter while I unloaded the food. I set out plates, opened the container, and handed her a fork and a cold soda from the refrigerator. We both ate in silence for ten or fifteen minutes, and when she finished off her soda, I grabbed her a fresh one.

"Your coloring is better," I said.

"My head is pounding, but not as bad as before."

"Good." But it wouldn't be long before fresh cravings started.

"I need to get to my car."

"Where is it?"

"Parked at my place. I caught a ride to Jeremy's."

"I can drive you."

"Thanks."

"Can I ask you a question? I don't like bringing it up, but I need to ask."

"Sure. Why not?"

"We've never talked about Tanner," I said.

"I try to forget him," she said.

"He came into Mike's Diner a lot, right?"

"A few times a week. Sometimes he lingered."

"Did he talk to you?" I asked.

"Mostly to Mike. But I could see him eyeing me when he didn't think I was looking. They liked to shoot the shit."

"Did Mike tell that to the cops?" I asked.

"I guess."

"Was Mike surprised when the truth came out about Tanner?"

She pushed back a thick shock of red hair. "We were all shaken."

"Any idea what Mike and Tanner talked about?"

"Sports. Construction. Women."

"Did you hear any names?"

Tiffany shook her head. "I make a point not to get into anyone else's business. I don't know any more than I told you."

I wasn't sure I believed that. I fished an egg roll out of a wax paper envelope and took a bite. "You like Mike?"

"He's cool. Cut me a lot of slack after what happened. I was late a lot after that."

"Tonja wasn't crazy about me visiting the diner a few days ago."

Tiffany shook her head. "Tonja is a mama bear. She took care of us all, including Mike."

That might explain why she was so tense and why she identified me so quickly. "Want a shower?"

"Do I need one?"

"You do."

Tiffany shrugged. "Do you have anything to drink here?"

"Beyond soda and water, no."

She frowned. "I'm going to need something soon. I really can't stay."

"You can leave anytime. Or you can shower and get some sleep."

"Can you just take me to my car?"

"What are you going to do?"

A small shrug lifted her shoulders. "Get my act together and get back to work. If I'm not fired already."

"I know a shelter where you can stay if you want to get your feet under you. It's more support than being alone in an apartment."

"Shelters have rules. And assholes."

"Everything in life has rules, and there are always assholes," I said.

"I don't like being locked in at night at the shelters."

"At least take a shower here. Get a little sleep." Opening my home to her would create levels of complications I wasn't sure I could handle. "I have fresh clothes you can wear."

"I like my clothes."

"I'll wash them and give them back, but that takes at least an hour."

"Okay."

"I'll put my clothes outside the bathroom door."

I walked her to the small bathroom, handed her a towel, and let her close and lock the door. The water started running almost immediately, and I imagined her looking around the space for any kind of pill. I'd been on antidepressants for a while, but they'd made me feel foggy, and I'd lost interest in my art, so I'd tossed those years ago. I didn't even keep aspirin here now. I laid a pair of jeans, a long-sleeve shirt, and underwear by the door.

When she emerged ten minutes later, the coloring in her skin was better and her damp hair looked a shade lighter. She looked so young. "How old are you?"

"Twenty-eight. Why?"

"Just curious." Only a few years older than me. "The washing machine and the dryer are small and old, so it'll take at least another hour. You can crash on the couch in the meantime."

She looked around the space, her gaze drawn to the tall windows and the afternoon sun casting a glow on the drying prints. "Why are you in such a big place?"

"I like the space and the light. I also make prints."

She walked up to a nearly finished image. "It looks weird."

"It's not finished. I can only screen print one color at a time. Two colors to go."

"People buy this?"

"They do."

She turned toward the easel where the Della picture lurked under the canvas. "Is that the painting of that girl?"

"Yes."

"Why's it covered?"

"I don't like looking at it."

"Why?"

No one had ever asked me about these paintings. "It drives me nuts because I can't finish it."

Her brow knotted. "What's wrong with it?"

"I'm not sure."

"How could you not know?"

"I just don't. When it's right, I'll know."

"Can I see it?" she asked.

A knot coiled in my gut. "Sure." I drew back the cloth, careful not to disturb the newly retouched eyes. With Tiffany standing beside me, Della's image didn't seem to hold as much sway over me.

She stared at the painting for a long moment.

"Do you recognize her?" I asked.

"Kind of. Maybe."

I swallowed, refusing to be excited. "Did she come into the diner?"

"Yeah, maybe. Once with Tanner."

My heart pounded. "You're sure?"

"I'm not sure about anything. But I feel like I know her," Tiffany said.

"Her name was Della. She's the one that lured me into Tanner's van."

Tiffany leaned in until she and Della were inches apart. "She was never found."

I folded my arms over my chest, refusing to allow Tiffany's half-hearted sighting of Della to matter. "No. Everyone tells me she's not real."

"I think she was," Tiffany said.

My fingers curled into loose fists. "Do you remember the last time you saw Della?"

Tiffany shook her head. "A few months before you came into the diner. Spring, but I'm not exactly sure."

"How could you remember her? It's such a busy place."

"I don't know."

"But you always noticed Tanner and who he was with."

"That's probably why I kind of remember her."

Here I was holding on to the maybes of a woman coming off a drug high. "Did the cops ask you about Della?"

"I think so. I don't remember."

Ten years ago, the cops' number one suspect was dead; his house destroyed, taking with it all the forensic evidence; and I'd been rescued. Case closed. Time to move on. "Okay."

"Maybe you should ask his old girlfriend. She might have seen her."

"Lynn?"

"Yeah. Tanner and Lynn came in the diner a lot. She seemed tight with Tanner."

"Why do you remember Lynn?"

"I was jealous of her. I kept wondering how a guy like him wanted to be with a plain woman like her."

Swallowing anticipation, I asked, "You said they were tight? How so?"

"She was really into him. They were always talking. I caught her staring at me once or twice."

"Why?"

"I've no idea."

"How did Tanner treat Lynn?"

"He was Tanner. Smiles. Eyes always roaming when he didn't think anyone was watching." Tiffany pressed her finger to the edge of Della's jawline and carefully traced. "They were fighting a lot that summer."

"About what?"

"She was tired of doing shit for him."

"She ever say what the shit was?"

"No." Her gaze settled on the portrait. "What are you going to do with the picture?"

"Normally, I'd burn it, but I might give this one to a friend."

"Burn. That's very weird."

"It is." I covered the painting with the drop cloth. Not having Della's eyes on me was always a relief. "Do you want to stay or leave?"

"When my clothes are done, you'll take me to my car?"

"I will."

She looked toward the door and the locks. "And I can leave at any time?"

"Yes."

"Why all the locks?"

My oddest habits were so ingrained, they'd slipped into the background. Tiffany's assessment reminded me I was far from normal. "Better safe than sorry, right?"

"I guess."

"I'll get you a pillow and blanket."

"Okay."

The drugs draining from her system, food in her belly, and locked doors surrounding her, she yawned. Exhaustion would take her now, but I wondered how long it would be before she couldn't resist the lure of another hit.

When I came back, she was sitting on the couch. Her head was tipped back, and her eyes closed. "Tiffany."

The woman didn't move, and from here it was hard to tell whether she was breathing. I leaned in, saw the subtle rise and fall of her chest, and set the pillow at the end of the couch. I lowered her toward it, lifted her feet, and covered her with a blanket.

Moving to the front, I stared at the building across the street. A light flickered on in Margo's unit. My breath caught in my throat as I waited for her to appear. When Margo passed in front of the window, she paused as if she felt my gaze. She looked toward my building, but I couldn't tell whether she saw me or not. She waved, then turned and left.

"Who the hell are you?"

Chapter Twenty-Nine

DAWSON

Wednesday, July 17, 2024
11:45 a.m.

Dawson parked in front of the hospital and walked through the main entrance doors. Inside, he found the receptionist desk, showed his badge, and located Ms. Yeats's floor.

"Can you ask her to come to the lobby?" he said to the receptionist.

"Sure." She lifted the phone and quickly relayed his message.

A tall woman with mousy-brown hair pulled into a ponytail pushed through the swinging doors. She was wearing scrubs, white sneakers, and a name badge that read *Lynn Yeats*. It struck him that she wasn't what he'd considered Tanner's type. Sandra and Scarlett had blond hair. Tiffany was a redhead but young, long, lean, and attractive. Maybe Lynn was the kind of woman Tanner thought he needed to cover for his secret life.

Lynn's gaze was cautious as she looked at Dawson. When he raised his badge and introduced himself, her flat lips deepened into a frown. "Are you here about that woman?"

Dawson asked, "What woman is that?"

"I don't know, and no one got her name. She came by the hospital and said my house flooded. I left a patient and raced home. There was nothing wrong with my house. It was all bull."

"Not cool," Dawson said. "Why would someone do that?" If he were Scarlett, he'd pull a similar stunt to find out where Lynn lived.

"I've no idea why people do what they do."

"Having trouble with anyone? Boyfriend? Neighbor?"

"No. At least not that I'm aware."

Dawson shook his head. "I'm not here about that. I came to ask you if you remember a Tiffany Patterson or a Sandra Taylor."

Lynn groaned, shaking her head. "This is about Tanner, isn't it?"

"Yes."

"I've had nothing to do with anyone associated with him for a decade. I've worked hard so people forget I was the girlfriend and alleged accomplice who helped him brutalize those women. I had no idea what he was doing."

"You've not spoken to Tiffany at all?" Dawson asked.

"The cops asked me about Scarlett, Della, Tiffany, and this Sandra chick, but like I told them years ago, I never met any of them except for Tiffany, briefly."

"Did the officer show you any pictures of these women? Did he say anything about them?"

"He showed me pictures, but I didn't know any of them." She shoved her hands in the pockets of her pale-blue smock. "The media linked me to Tanner, and that story rolled around the internet for years. Tanner did a fantastic job of screwing up my life. You know how many men want a woman who dated a guy like that?"

"I don't know," Dawson said.

"A lot. And they're all weird as hell. One boyfriend wanted to simulate strangulation with me. Another asked if I liked being tied up."

He shifted. "Must have been rough."

"You've no idea. What kind of guy likes tying up a woman?"

He stilled. "Did you ever meet Scarlett Crosby?"

"No."

"You sure?"

"Why would she and I meet?"

"I looked over your old interviews. Did Tanner call you *Scarlett* once?"

Her face reddened. "Once. He realized what he'd done immediately and apologized. Said it was a volatile ex. Said what he loved about me was that I was so normal. I was mad, but I never could stay angry at him long. The bastard was charming."

"Scarlett Crosby never reached out to you?"

Her brows furrowed. "Why would she?"

"Might help her make sense of what happened to her."

Lynn shook her head. "I didn't know anything about her. I had no idea she was in the basement." She shifted her stance.

"Nothing ever hit your radar about Tanner?" Dawson asked. "Nothing?"

"No. He was normal with me."

Many men like Tanner could cleave their dark and light worlds in two. Some could live a double life for years and no one noticed enough inconsistencies to sound an alarm bell. But in most cases, Dawson found if he pressed, family members or loved ones could look back and identify warning signs.

"Never heard muffles, odd sounds, or even banging on the pipes?" he asked.

Lynn slowly shook her head but stopped. "The pipes," she said, more to herself. "The pipes clanged from time to time. Tanner told me he had bad pipes, but after I mentioned it, I never heard the sound again."

"What did you hear exactly?" Dawson asked.

"Random clanging. It only happened a few times."

"You were at the house often?"

"A couple of times a week in the spring of 2014. We usually made dinner and watched television. Tanner wasn't always the most amorous guy, if you know what I mean."

"He didn't want to have sex with you?" Dawson asked.

"Sometimes he did, but it was never really super sexy." Lynn glanced toward Dawson. "I offered to spice it up many times."

"How, if you don't mind me asking?"

Her gaze flickered down. "I don't know. The usual ways."

"What're the usual ways?"

"Role-play, costumes, devices."

"But that was tame for him, wasn't it? He had girls locked in the basement to satisfy his spicier needs," Dawson said.

Her fingers curled into fists. "I thought he had a problem with me or was a prude."

"When exactly did you hear the pipes?"

"April or May. I don't remember the actual day."

Sandra was last seen April 1, 2014, so if Tanner had her, that fit into the time frame. "How did he seem after you heard the pipes?"

"Annoyed. Said he'd have to fix them."

The fatal blow to Sandra's head could have been unintentional. She'd tried to alert Lynn for help, and he'd lashed out and killed her in the process. "You're sure it was April or May?"

"I remember it was spring. Still chilly outside."

June 2014 had seen record-high temperatures, so chances were if someone had reached out for help, it wasn't Scarlett. "What can you tell me about Tanner?"

She threaded trembling fingers together. "I told all this to the cops ten years ago. Can't you read the files?"

"Humor me," Dawson said. "Sometimes the passing of time jostles memories. Whatever might have stressed you out then might have faded. It's understandable you'd have been under a great deal of pressure after Tanner's death."

Frustration tightened her face before it melted into resignation. "That was the worst time of my life. I could barely think."

"It had to have been horrible." The comment was rote, but he managed to make it sound sincere. "And I appreciate your help. This can't be easy."

She flexed her fingers. "What do you want to know?"

"How did you meet?"

"We met at Mike's Diner. I ate there every morning before my shift at the hospital. We were always the first two in the diner most mornings, and it got to be a regular thing. Then one day he invited me to join him. I was charmed."

"That's the same diner where Sandra Taylor and Tiffany Patterson worked."

"I don't remember Sandra at all, but I remember the waitress with red hair."

"Tiffany Patterson?"

"Yes. She was my waitress. She served me and went about her job. We didn't chat beyond 'Is there anything else I can get you' to 'No, thank you.' I do remember Tanner joked with her. She smiled at him like so many women did."

"What did he talk to her about?"

"The regular flirty-guy stuff. Said he appreciated her. Asked her what she would order even though he always ordered the eggs over easy. Asked her if all redheads had a temper. He left her a good tip. When I asked why he was flirty with her, he told me once she reminded him of his sister."

"Tanner had distant cousins but no siblings."

"I didn't know that at the time."

"Did he talk about his past?"

"Beyond the ex, not much. Said his parents were dead. I never pushed."

"You ever go into the basement?" Dawson asked.

"I never, ever went to the basement," Lynn insisted.

"You weren't curious about the basement?"

"Maybe a little. But the door to it was locked. He said the stairway was steep and he was afraid someone would open the door, not realize the steps were there, and fall."

"Sounds reasonable," Dawson said.

"That's what I thought," Lynn said.

"Mind if I double back for a second?" When a witness relaxed a fraction, he often returned to touchier topics.

"Sure."

"I apologize, but I must be direct again," Dawson said.

Lynn stiffened. "Okay, sure."

"You said you tried to spice things up. Was there any kind of aggressive play when you two were romantic?"

Lynn shook her head. "Nothing weird happened. He wasn't interested in that kind of thing. I kind of wanted him to be more aggressive."

"It's been ten years," Dawson coaxed. "Tanner's dead, and honestly the Sandra Taylor homicide isn't high profile. I got a day or two more to work it, and then I'm going to have to move on to a new case. My point is, you're not getting dragged into anything."

Lynn drew in a breath. "Why does our sex life matter?"

"Because guys like Tanner do their best to keep their worlds separate, but the darkness often leaks into the light."

She shook her head. "I just made suggestions I'd read about in novels. Nothing super violent."

Everyone wanted to believe they were in the normal range, including himself. But *normal* was relative, until it wasn't. "But a little violent."

"He put his hands on my neck. His hold was loose at first. Then his fingers tightened. It was scary, I kind of panicked. He squeezed until I couldn't breathe, and I was forced to relax. My acceptance seemed to turn him on."

"He liked to be in charge," Dawson said.

"I guess so."

"That was the only time?"

"Yeah. He said later he didn't know what had gotten into him. He apologized."

Dawson cleared his throat. "When was this?"

"August 29. A dating milestone. Five months." Her fingers absently rose to her collar, as if covering red marks that no longer existed.

Scarlett had been in the basement August 29, 2014, and Tanner's attempt to snatch Tiffany would happen days later. "Is that the day he called you Scarlett?"

Her breath was ragged. "How do you know that?"

"Just a guess."

"Yes, but he brought me flowers after." She spoke quickly, as if she needed to defend him and even herself. "I forgave him. I loved him. He died days later."

"Have you ever been back to the diner?" Dawson asked.

"No," Lynn said. "I don't go to that part of town at all. I would've moved away, but my mother is still in Norfolk, and she's getting old."

"Okay, Ms. Yeats. Thank you for your time."

"Are you going to investigate my false alarm?"

"I'll ask around," he lied with a smile.

As Dawson left, his smile faded into a deep frown. He knew enough about people to know that Lynn Yeats was lying—or at least holding back. He wasn't sure whether the information was small or large, but she was hiding something. In his car, he started the engine. Rattling pipes. Aggressive sex play. Heightened interest after she submitted. Calling her Scarlett. A locked basement. People saw what they wanted to see. Confirmation bias. She wanted a steady guy who made a decent income. So she ignored all the signs that he might have other issues.

He called Margo. First ring. Second. Third. Was she blowing him off?

She answered on the fourth ring. "Detective."

"What are you doing?" He pictured her in her hotel room wearing black silk.

"Talking to movers. Logistics irritate me. What about you?"

"Thinking about you." Gravel in his throat roughened his voice.

"Are you?" She sounded disinterested. She was making him work for it.

"You free?"

"You can come to my hotel room in an hour," she said.

"I thought you moved."

"Working on it."

He checked his watch. He'd have to leave now and hope there wasn't much traffic. "I'm on the way."

"Don't be late."

Tension coiled in his gut as he drove across town to her hotel room. When he arrived, he took a second to tuck in his shirt and smooth his fingers over his short hair. Not wanting to appear so stiff, he shrugged off his jacket, removed his tie, and rolled up his sleeves. He knocked.

When she snapped open the door, she was standing on the threshold wearing a raincoat and heels. "You're late."

He wasn't. "Sorry."

She nodded for him to enter her room. When she closed the door, anticipation buzzed in his body. "Why the nooner?"

Tension was building inside him. Separating the light from the dark was getting trickier. "Take off the coat."

She moved toward the bed, carefully unknotting the cloth belt. "No sweet words or a warm-up?"

"Want me to braid your hair?"

She chuckled as she shrugged off the coat, letting it drop and pool around her black high heels. She wasn't wearing anything underneath.

For all the power she gave him, he'd never felt more out of control. The more she gave, the more he wanted. In this moment, he understood Tanner, and that scared the shit out of him. "Get on the bed."

Chapter Thirty

SCARLETT

Wednesday, July 17, 2024
3:30 p.m.

I drove Tiffany to her car, a small red Honda parked on a side street. Her clothes were clean and her skin a healthier pink. I feared, however, whatever good path I'd just put her on wouldn't last.

"Thank you," she said.

"Sure."

"I'm going to make it to court. I'm going to do good."

I hugged her. "I'm glad."

I watched her slide behind the wheel and fire up the engine. I didn't move as I watched her drive off and her little red car vanish behind a corner.

All this damage went back to Tanner. The remaining two tangible connections to Tanner were Lynn Yeats and Mike Hart. I'd start with Lynn Yeats. Next, I'd figure out what to do about Mike. Twenty minutes later, I was parked in front of Lynn's town house.

I'd only been on the street for a few minutes. In that time several people had driven or walked by my truck. And though no one said anything, I'd been noticed.

When Lynn's front door opened, I slid down in my seat. I watched as the woman, now dressed in jeans and a loose-fitting top, quickly got in her car and started her engine. Lynn pulled out and headed west.

I wasn't sure what I hoped to learn from her, but she had to know more than she'd told the police. I'd been hesitant to be totally honest with them when they'd interviewed me. The detectives' soft-spoken words had never felt totally genuine, and I found myself policing all my statements. Lynn couldn't be that different.

I didn't know where she was going, but wherever it was, I would find a way to cross her path, whether it was to a grocery store or a café or on a sidewalk stroll. What's the opening someone like me can pitch to a woman like her? *I'm the girl in the basement. Did you know about me? No? How did you know nothing about me?*

I followed Lynn down Shore Drive, running a couple of yellow lights so I could keep pace until she pulled into the parking lot of a café. She parked by the front entrance, whereas I chose a spot in the back of the lot.

As Lynn moved inside the shop, I followed, keeping a reasonable distance. Entering the store, I watched as Lynn ordered a large cappuccino with double whip and a doughnut. As Lynn took a seat by the window, I ordered a coffee, paid with cash, and sat behind her so she couldn't see my face.

Lynn kept her gaze on her phone, only looking up as far as the doughnut or her coffee. Several times she licked cream from her lips or wiped sugar from her fingers.

A fortysomething woman with a flushed, expectant look on her round face hurried toward Lynn. Salt-and-pepper hair was pulled back into a rushed ponytail, and her oversize T-shirt hung over jean shorts. The woman leaned in toward Lynn for a casual hug that mimicked intimacy. "Hey, girl. What's going on?"

Lynn looked up and grinned in a sad kind of way as she stood. "Debbie, thanks for responding to the SOS. I just needed a friend and an ear to bend."

"Of course. Let me grab a coffee and I'll be right back." Debbie's voice sounded ripe with excitement, and I sensed she found Lynn's connection to Tanner, the beautiful monster, titillating.

"Sure."

Debbie didn't glance in my direction as she hustled toward the register to place her order. Lynn finished her doughnut and wiped her hands clean. She was tapping her finger on the table and staring out the window as Debbie returned. "So, what's up?"

"Been a week," Lynn said.

"I saw the article in the paper about Scarlett Crosby. I know you saw it." Her tone bordered on glee.

"I did."

I didn't dare look up, sensing old angers bubbling to the surface. "God, it must be so hard on you to go back to all that. And then the water thing."

"It's not been easy."

"Do you think it was Scarlett? Is she trying to drag you back into the spotlight?"

"Why would she do that?"

"Who knows? I'm not sure she's all that balanced after what happened to her."

"I suppose not. And I'm sorry for her suffering."

"Why are you sorry? You didn't know what was happening. It wasn't your fault."

Lynn rolled her head from side to side. "I looked like a fool after Tanner was killed. People whispered about me for years. If they knew *that detail* and that I stayed with him after what he did, what would they say?"

"Why *did* you stay?" Debbie asked.

"I loved him. I would've done anything for him."

Anything. Would she have killed Sandra? Or helped Tanner dispose of the body?

"It's easy to get caught up in a guy's world."

My grip on my cup tightened. Something inside me told me Lynn still knew more about Tanner. Was the point of this conversation to prove to herself she'd been innocent, or was this a reverse alibi?

"This is the last thing I wanted to remember," Lynn said. "I've worked hard to forget him and all that."

"Did you ever see another girl with Tanner?" Debbie asked.

"Once. I pulled up to his house, and when he answered the door, she was standing behind him. She was a teen, really. A sad little creature."

"Oh my God. Who was she?"

"He said she was his cousin. He called her *Cindy*. But I knew he was lying."

I'd seen enough psychologists to know the truth had a way of bleeding out, even if the revelations could be destructive.

"How did you know he was lying?" Debbie asked.

"It's the way his eye contact broke just a little. I saw that look a lot that last month."

Had she seen Sandy or Della? Either way, she'd known he had a young girl in that house.

I blinked hard. An old anger awakened inside me, lifted its head, and looked around for a target to strike. I rose suddenly, bumping my small round table and upending my coffee. Hot brown liquid dripped off the table. I ducked my head and quickly reached for a wad of napkins to mop up the mess.

When I dared to look up, Lynn and her friend were saying their goodbyes. Hugging. Best of friends. Lynn sat back down. So I lingered, taking time to wipe up the last of the spilled coffee. I gathered up the sloppy napkins and cup and tossed them all in the trash can located directly in Lynn's line of sight. As Lynn looked up, her gaze held mine. Surprise gave way to suspicion. Her lips pressed into a frown.

"Lynn?" I asked.

Lynn set her cup down and sat back in her chair. "Scarlett Crosby."

I gave her credit. She wasn't running. "I'm the girl that was locked in your boyfriend's basement."

Lynn reached for her purse. "I don't want to talk to you."

I took Debbie's old seat and laid my hand on her arm. "It won't take long."

"I've got nothing to say to you."

"I don't want trouble." I raised my voice a fraction, catching the attention of a woman passing by us. "I just have a couple of questions."

She yanked her arm back and whispered, "I'm not answering any questions."

"People have pretty much forgotten what Tanner did to me, and I bet they've forgotten you dated him. Neither one of us wants that information to land in the headlines again."

Her frown deepened. "What's that mean?"

I was enjoying her discomfort. "The past will stay the past if we're both careful."

She shoved out a sigh. "What do you want?"

"Tell me about Tanner."

"What the hell? Why would you want to know more about him? Is this a sick game?"

"I want to understand him."

She hugged her purse close as she leaned forward. "He was a sick fuck. That's all you need to know."

"I heard you talking to Debbie. Sounded like you were crazy about him."

"You were listening?" she hissed.

"Why do you think I'm here? You're one of my last connections to Tanner."

"I'm not connected to him."

A smirk yanked my lips. "Yes, you are. Forever. Just like me."

Lynn shook her head. "I'm not playing this game."

My fingers curled into a fist. "Did you know about me?"

"I never knew about you or anyone else," she insisted.

"I don't believe you," I said.

She dropped her voice to just above a whisper. "I didn't know anything about the basement."

"What about Cindy? Who the hell was she?"

She sat back. "Tanner's cousin."

"He had no close family. You just said he was lying."

"It was a feeling. I had no proof." She shook her head. "You give me too much credit. I was stupid to stay with him."

"You had to be curious about Cindy."

"I trusted him."

"What did she look like?" I pressed.

"I didn't get a great look at her." She glanced around the shop, afraid someone might be watching us.

"Don't freak out. We're just two women having a conversation. Nothing unusual."

"It's weird, you and I talking."

Slowly I shook my head. "I stopped worrying about weird a long time ago. Tell me about the cousin."

"She had brown curly hair and a full face. She didn't say anything to me beyond *hi*. Tanner said she was passing through town and he was taking her to dinner before she left that evening."

The description matched Della's. "When was this?"

"Sometime in May."

"2014?"

"Yes."

"Did you tell Dawson about her?"

"He showed me a picture of a blond girl. She didn't look like the cousin."

I wasn't in the basement then. Sandra and Della were in the house, but only Della came close to fitting this description. "Did she look like she was in distress?"

"She smiled a lot. I thought that was weird, but whatever."

"Did Tanner ever mention Della's name?"

"No." She shook her head. "I read about you. You insisted there was another girl named Della. I never saw her."

"You read about me." Of course she had.

"I couldn't believe what had happened. I was trying to wrap my head around his secret life."

Or she was worried about her own public exposure? "What did the papers miss about Tanner?"

She held up a hand. "Are you trying to prove something now?"

"Lynn, I want to know who killed Sandra Taylor."

She shook her head. "I can't help you."

"You were in Tanner's house so many times. Was there any sign of other women there?"

"No! And like I told that cop today, I didn't hear or see anything weird beyond rattling pipes. I'm so sick of telling this story."

"You heard pipes rattling."

She dropped her voice to a low hiss. "Rattling pipes isn't hard evidence."

"The pipes in the basement room were newly wrapped when I was there. Maybe to mute the sound if anyone beat on them again."

Lynn paled. "You didn't know that."

"I had plenty of time to stare at them."

She leaned toward me. "You're stalking me."

"Just grabbing a cup of coffee."

Brown eyes narrowed. "Were you the asshole who came into the hospital and said my house was flooding?"

I didn't blink. "Why would I report a fake burst pipe?"

Her gaze hardened. "You followed me from the hospital to my house."

"Did I?"

"You're stalking me."

"Like I said, I'm here for the coffee."

"Is this payback?"

I ignored her question, letting her wallow in the frustration that oozed from evasive answers. "When did you learn the truth about Tanner? Or were you and Tanner in it together? Did the box under the bed excite you?"

"What box under his bed?" The question sounded as if it had been practiced a thousand times before.

"The box where he locked Della while he made love to you. And for the record, she had curly brown hair."

She swallowed. "Jesus. I'm not a monster."

Had she heard or sensed something when Della was under the bed? I could have pressed, but I was on the verge of driving her out of here. "Tanner could be very charming until he wasn't. I know that better than anyone."

She sighed. "What do you want?"

"What did he talk about? What did he care about? You dated him. I know you two talked."

Her back straightened, but she didn't rise. "I don't know. I've tried to forget all that."

"Tiffany hasn't forgotten you. She remembers you and Tanner talking all the time." I smiled, going for friendly, not feral.

"She would have heard a bunch of stupid dating talk between us. He was sweet. He took me out to dinner and gave me flowers. He wasn't like most guys and didn't rush intimacy." She looked down as if she realized what she'd said. "I don't have to tell you anything."

"No, you don't." I held her gaze, knowing most people were unnerved by lingering eye contact.

Fingers dug into her purse. "When he was killed by the police, I saw his picture on the news, and I called the police and told them I knew him."

"They'd have come to you eventually."

"Tanner was the biggest mistake of my life. I'll never live all that down." How many victim cards could she toss on the table?

"You knew something was wrong. You knew."

"I did not!" Lynn stood abruptly, knocking her coffee over. "Stay the hell away from me!"

The people sitting near us looked up. Without context, they saw a pale, tall woman, fists clenched, face burnished red, glaring at me.

Lynn stalked out of the shop. I sat for several beats and then slowly rose. I glanced at a woman staring at me and smiled. "Show's over."

Outside, I watched as Lynn slid into her car and fired up the engine. The back tires squealed.

Fresh air swirled around me. The summer sun burned bright, cutting through the trees planted in the small patches of dirt dotting the sidewalk.

I slid behind the wheel of my truck, my hands trembling with rage. I could blame Della for my imprisonment, but in the darkest moments in that cell, she'd been more like me than anyone. She'd held me, reminded me to be brave, told me what it took to survive.

Tears welled in my eyes. If Lynn was forever Tanner's girlfriend, I was ever the brutalized basement girl. I didn't want to be that person anymore. I needed to find normal.

My hands were trembling when I texted Luke. Dinner tonight? Believe it or not, I can cook.

His answer wasn't immediate, and I gave up on waiting. As I drove back to my studio, I reasoned it was probably good he hadn't responded. I wasn't sure what a date with Luke would prove. Besides, my studio was filled with drying prints that required preparation for tomorrow's printing. I needed to focus now.

I'd craved normal and thought I'd found it with endless self-imposed deadlines, paintings of Della, and trying to repair the unfixable Tiffany. I thought back to the couple I'd seen walking hand in hand outside the restaurant the other night. They'd been so relaxed and comfortable with each other. Envy mingled with fear.

An hour later, I was mixing paints when Luke texted. Come over to my place tonight?

I stared at the message, half-tempted to ignore it. But this invitation was my chance at normal. My hesitation surprised me. I thought I'd leap at the idea of being with a solid guy.

I spent the next hour going back and forth with myself. If I showed up at his place, how would I react? Would I be calm, or would I freak out? Finally, tired of the worry and questions, I texted him back. Sounds great.

After a moment, he responded. Excellent. I'll cook.

Chapter Thirty-One

SCARLETT

Wednesday, July 17, 2024
8:30 p.m.

I stood outside Luke's condo door, a bottle of red wine in one hand and white in the other. I'd spent a half hour deliberating what he might like, if these bottles were fancy enough, or if stylish graphic labels equated to good flavor.

Inside, the faint sounds of music drifted. Jazz. Which made sense. Luke struck me as a kind of classy individual whose tastes rose above pop. I rang the bell.

Footsteps moved toward the door. I drew in a breath. I'd not been alone in an apartment with a man, well, ever. Doors closing behind me still messed with my head.

When the door snapped open, I flinched. I tried to recover and smile, but he didn't miss my display of nerves.

"You made it," he said easily.

"I did." A smile sputtered on my lips.

He wore jeans, a faded T-shirt, and some generic brown shoes. He smelled of fresh soap, and his hair was damp. I held up the wine bottles as if they were proof that I was excited about the evening. Still, I remained on my side of the threshold.

"Do you want to come in, or are you going to toss those bottles at me and run?" he asked.

"I'm coming in." The words sounded as if they'd been wrenched from my throat.

He stepped aside and held out his hand, giving me a wide berth.

I walked past him, feeling the buzz of energy in his body. His place was neat, furnished in a midcentury-modern style. Lots of teak, slim, low furniture, and light fixtures that were geometric space age. The kitchen was attached and there were two other closed doors. One had to be the bedroom, and I guessed the other was a closet or a spare.

The door closed softly behind me. "You can set the bottles on the kitchen counter."

I moved toward the slate of white quartz and a tray of cheese and crackers. Two pots simmered on the stove—one for sauce and the other steaming water.

"Nothing fancy," he said.

My bottles clinked faintly against the counter. "I live on sandwiches, so this is a major step up for me."

He moved past me into the kitchen and opened a cabinet to a collection of matching wineglasses. That was another step up for me. I was all about mason jars. "Red or white?"

"Red." It was the first of the two offerings, so I defaulted to it. Truth was, I could drink either.

He uncorked the red, poured it through a diffuser, and handed me a glass. "How was your day?"

Stalking Lynn might not be a good dinner conversation starter. "Working on the prints. All colors have been applied."

"If they're anything like the pieces you auctioned off for the Judge, I'll buy one."

"Proceeds go to the recreation center."

"I know."

"Where are you going to hang it?"

"My bedroom."

"Nice."

"Do you see your art displayed often?"

"Almost never." I moved closer to the counter, and he remained on his side. Fear boiled. This felt like that moment I'd stood at Tanner's open van door. My life would change after this.

"Eyes forward."

"Yes." I sipped. "Tell me about your week. Win any cases?"

"No. Lots of prep. Going to trial on a corporate case in a couple of weeks. The hope is that I'll be so sharp and prepared that the other side will settle before trial."

"You don't want to fight it out in front of a judge?"

"Not if I can help it. Always better if these things can be settled privately."

"That I do understand. No one likes their life on display."

"Has it been like that since Tanner Reed?"

"Not much of a tiptoer, are you?"

His gaze didn't budge off my face. "Hard when you have big feet. That a problem?"

"It's kind of a relief."

"Good. Because these feet will never be subtle."

I'd wanted ordinary, and he was dishing it up with a glass of red wine. "It was a big deal in the first two or three years after. It's not fun. You survive a trauma and then everyone else wants to relive it over and over. You want to get beyond it but feel anchored by it." I sipped more wine, realizing I was headed to oversharing. "But in the last few years, I think everyone has basically forgotten. Which is good."

"But." He stared at me over the rim of his glass.

"But? What do you mean?"

"You can tell me to back off anytime. But I have a special radar for the unsaid. Believe it or not, some clients lie to their lawyers."

I chuckled. His radar must be buzzing loud now. "How familiar are you with the case?"

"Versed well enough."

"Remember the girl in the diner?"

"Rescued right before Tanner was caught?"

"That's a kind way of putting it. The girl I tried to lure into a van."

His gaze sharpened. "You called for help, according to the reports."

"Her name is Tiffany Patterson. She connected with me about six months ago. She's a drug addict. And I'm trying to help her. So far, with limited success."

He frowned. "Drug addiction is difficult."

"I've learned that." I swirled my wine. "Detective Kevin Dawson paid me a couple of visits."

"About Tiffany?"

"No. A body was found in the wall of a house around the corner from where my mother and I once lived. It was the body of a girl who vanished shortly before I did. Her name was Sandra and she dated Tanner once."

"Does Dawson have more information on the cold case?"

"If he does, he's not sharing. But he seems to think I know more about the girl and what was happening in Tanner's house." I drew in a breath. "Now, if you're thinking I'm a little too complicated, no harm, no foul."

He set his glass down on the counter. "I'm not scared off. In full disclosure, I have a history with Dawson. I can't get into case details, but we didn't see eye to eye on some of his choices regarding his ex-wife's crimes."

"Crimes?"

"Tiffany isn't the only one with a substance abuse issue."

"And he tried to cover it up?"

"Yes. I wanted to press the issue and file charges, but my boss didn't want me to tarnish Dawson's reputation. He has a solid arrest record. It's part of the reason I left for private practice."

"Now I'm curious."

He shook his head slowly. "He loved his ex-wife. His devotion to her was a blind spot."

"I guess we all have them."

"Maybe."

"Dawson isn't going to let this case go until he closes it." I met his gaze. "Too problematic yet?"

"Not yet."

I shook my head. "The night is young. And you never know with me."

A brow arched. "Is tossing a salad too much to ask?"

Tension melted. "I can handle lettuce."

"Good." He reached in the refrigerator and pulled out a bottle of dressing and a wooden bowl filled with iceberg lettuce. "You toss, I'll set the food on the table."

"Most men would be running for the hills."

He grinned. "As you said, the night is still young."

Dinner proved to be relaxed and fun. Luke told stories from his days in the district attorney's office, and I shared stories about turning my art into a business. I helped him clear the table, but I was still careful not to touch him, and he didn't press.

"Can I make you a coffee?" he asked.

"Thanks, but I won't sleep tonight if you do."

He leaned against the counter, the expanse of his chest pressing against his shirt. "I can drink it 24/7 and be fine."

"And you can sleep?"

"Like the dead."

"That's nice." I'd never been a great sleeper, and I often woke at 2:00 a.m. and found myself staring at the ceiling.

He came around the counter and stood inches from me. He didn't touch, but he could grab me in a second. "Tonight has to be a dating record for you."

"We've set a very high bar."

"I like breaking records." His fingers flexed and relaxed.

He wanted to kiss me. I wasn't so lost in my own head as not to recognize male attraction. His natural reaction normally was enough to turn off my brain. But I didn't want to shut down, so I struggled to stay present.

"Do you want to kiss me again?" he asked.

The stretch of silence was short. "I do."

"I'll let you take the lead on this one. If you want to kiss me, then do it."

I'd broken many of the bindings Tanner had wrapped around my emotions over the years. I'd created a business that was doing well. I volunteered. I displayed my art at the festivals in the NEON district. But I was completely bound when it came to intimacy. Generally, a step forward meant a step back.

I moved toward him. I was so close I could feel the energy emitting from the rise and fall of his chest. The scent of his aftershave wrapped around me. Heat radiated from him. He stared down, as still as stone. My fight-or-flight response was sledgehammering against my chest.

I rose on my toes and carefully pressed my lips to his. They were warm, soft but not soft. He was clean shaven, which meant he must have shaved for a second time today. Tanner often didn't shave. The hair on his face was rough, and he liked rubbing his stubble over the tenderest parts of my body.

Luke was not Tanner.

Not Tanner.

Fear slowly seeped into my bones, but I ignored it. I placed my hands on Luke's sides. Lean muscle remained steady, and his breath didn't hitch or speed up. I leaned into his body. I teased his lips with my tongue, and a growl rumbled in his chest as he leaned into me. When I pulled back, I realized his hands were on my hips.

"That was a G-rated kiss," I said, understanding full well what the dirtiest X-rated versions entailed.

"It's nice." His voice had deepened and developed an edge.

At twenty-five, I had more experience than a sex worker and less than most teenagers. How long would a man like him put up with me? This was going to end. He would realize I wasn't normal. And that would be that. G-rated kisses only sustained a relationship so long. In the past I hadn't been disappointed by men who ran from me, but I suspected this time I might be sad.

"I should probably get going," I said softly.

He didn't move his hands. "Okay."

"It was a great evening."

"It was." His voice was rough with desire as he dropped his hands to his sides. He followed me toward the door. "Do you want to do it again sometime?"

"Do you want to see me again?"

He chuckled. "Is that so hard to believe?"

"Yeah, actually. I'm a lot of work. Eccentricities coming out of my ears."

The hard lines of his face softened with a smile. "I don't mind a few. I'll text you?"

"Okay." I leaned in and kissed him again on the lips and left.

Chapter Thirty-Two

DAWSON

Wednesday, July 17, 2024
9:30 p.m.

The call came in as Dawson was stepping out of the shower. He'd spent the evening rereading all the reports on Tanner, including the job reviews the cops had gotten from the garage where he'd worked as a teen.

Great attitude. Hardworking. Friendly. No real family. And on and on.

As he reached for the towel, *no real family* kept coming back to him. Lynn said she'd met his cousin, but the investigators had found no girl with dark hair. Given the timing, he was more and more certain now that Lynn had met one of Tanner's girls. Sandra had had blond hair, but the mysterious Della's hair was dark.

The phone rang, and he dried off his hands and accepted the call. "Dawson."

"This is Officer Davis. We're in the east end. I'm standing beside a red Honda that's registered to Tiffany Patterson."

"Is Ms. Patterson there?"

In the background, a horn honked. "No sign of her, but we're trying to open the trunk."

"Where's the car?"

"It's parked on Nineteenth Bay Street."

"All right. I'll be there in a half hour. Call Officer Larsen."

"Will do."

Dawson arrived twenty minutes later to a starry sky over the Little Creek. The forensic team had turned on floodlights, and Margo was already on scene, tugging latex gloves on her hands. She appeared cool and composed, ready to take charge. One day she'd be running the entire department.

Summer heat kicked as Dawson rose out of his car. Margo was chatting with Officer Davis, a tall, fit Black man who appeared to be in his late twenties. Her direct gaze was focused on Davis in a way it'd been fixated on Dawson two nights ago.

Dawson reached for gloves in his pocket and worked his hands into the latex as he crossed toward the marked cars and the yellow crime scene tape encircling the red Honda. The forensic crew was on scene, waiting to pry open the trunk.

He glanced in the car and saw fast-food wrappers, soda cans, and snack packages littering the floor along with receipts, and several vivid green pills that he considered might be laced with fentanyl.

"The trunk release doesn't work?" Dawson asked with a nod to Margo.

"No. Key jammed into the lock, and it looks like someone took a hammer to it," the forensic tech said. "We were waiting for you."

Dawson drew in a breath, allowing a quick glance at Margo's stoic face. "Do it."

The technician wedged a crowbar under the lip of the trunk. He shoved hard, and metal crumpled and groaned. For a moment, the lid stuck, and then one final jerk popped open the trunk.

A stale scent rose out of the car; he looked inside to find the remains of a young woman. Her legs were tucked up by her chest and her arms folded at her sides. A splay of red hair covered pale features.

The forensic tech began snapping pictures while also sketching out the scene. All homicides were as unique as they were similar. Manner of death could vary, but the process of untangling the crime came with a checklist. Once this scene had been documented, the medical examiner's technician would arrive and the body would be removed. The trunk and car would be searched for evidence, and the investigation would grind forward.

Margo stood back, her hand masking her mouth as she studied the remains. "We just arrested her."

Wind caught the vivid thick red hair. The medical examiner would have to make a formal identification, but Dawson knew who it was.

"And someone bailed her out, and now she's dead."

Chapter Thirty-Three

Scarlett

Wednesday, July 17, 2024
11:15 p.m.

I'd changed into sweats and a T-shirt and uncovered Della's portrait. As I reached for a tube of red paint, someone rang my doorbell. My first thought was Luke. I wasn't sure whether I was happy or worried.

I hurriedly covered the portrait again and crossed the central space. A fist pounded against my door. Luke did not strike me as the fist-pounding type. I glanced in the peephole. It was Detective Dawson. And my new best friend, Margo. Damn.

I hesitated. They were the last people I wanted to deal with now. I opened the doors. "Detectives."

He'd removed his jacket and rolled up his sleeves past his elbows. Dark hair sprinkled over his forearms down to an old black wristwatch. Margo's cheeks were slightly flushed, but otherwise she looked cool and calm.

"Scarlett, did we catch you at a bad time?" he asked.

He used my first name intentionally to mimic a nonexistent connection between us, I knew. "I was working. What do you need?"

"Can we come in? It's hot as hell out here."

I stepped aside. Tension rippled as they walked past. It felt like a deliberate invasion. They were sending a message that they were in charge. They wanted me off guard.

"You bailed Tiffany Patterson out of jail today," Dawson said.

I glanced at Margo, who studied my place with keen interest. "I did. I gave her a meal here, let her nap while I washed her clothes, and then dropped her off at her car."

"Where was the car?" Dawson asked.

"It was parked off of Shore Drive on Nineteenth Bay Street near a small brick house. What's this about?"

"When did you become her emergency contact?" Margo asked.

"I didn't realize I was until she called."

"When did she reappear in your life?" Dawson asked.

"Six months ago. She was sleeping in the doorway across the street. Like my number, my address is on my website."

"Why did she come looking for you?" Margo asked.

"I don't think she had anyone else."

"If I didn't have anyone, I'm not sure I'd seek help from someone who almost sold me out," Dawson said.

"It was a surprise to me," I said.

"How many times has she shown up here?" he asked.

"Three or four times. I've tried to get her into a rehab program, but she doesn't trust them. Where did you find her car?"

"Close to where you left her," Dawson said. "Did she tell you where she was going?"

I stilled. What did he want? "I'm not in the mood for guessing games."

"You're going to have to play along a little longer," Margo said.

"How did Tanner spot Tiffany? What was it about her that attracted him?" Dawson asked.

The past rolled closer to me, like storm-ripe waves. "He wanted the waitress who had hair as red as fire."

"And when did he tell you he'd taken Sandra Taylor?" he asked.

"I never heard Sandra's name until you brought it up several days ago."

"But you knew there was another girl in the house." He flipped through notes. "You called her *the Other Girl* when you were interviewed ten years ago and when we spoke."

I glanced quickly at Margo, but her face remained stoic. "I'd heard *Della* mention there'd been another girl."

"But Della was never found," he pressed.

"No."

"We're playing games now, aren't we, Scarlett? Looks like you're going to make me work for it. Okay. I like games."

He was square jawed and determined.

"Is there a point to this conversation?"

"You know we still have your DNA on file, right?" he said.

"I'm sure you do."

"The medical examiner pulled hair fibers from a Jane Doe, and when it's tested, are we going to get a match to yours?"

"DNA pulled from Sandra's body must be old and degraded. Testing it will take time. Is this a fishing expedition, Detective?" I asked.

He studied me a long moment, tired eyes sharpening the longer they held my gaze. "Tiffany Patterson's body was found in the trunk of her car."

The news smacked into me. I glanced at the tall glass window, up toward the half-moon. An unsettled feeling rooted in my belly. This moment held echoes of the day Tanner's van doors slammed behind me. I knew I was screwed but didn't know how deep I would fall into hell.

"How?" I didn't recognize my rusty voice.

"We're still waiting on that. But I can promise you that DNA pulled from her body is fresh and easy to test."

"I just told you she was here today. I hugged her before I left her."

"You're saying your DNA is on her body?" Margo asked.

I glanced at her. "Am I under arrest?"

"No," Dawson said. "Not yet."

"Until I am, leave the premises."

"We're going to be talking again soon, Scarlett," Dawson said.

He opened the doors, and Margo followed, leaving me standing in the center of the warehouse. A warm breeze blew through the open front doors. I moved toward them, slammed them closed, and flipped all the locks.

Chapter Thirty-Four

SCARLETT

Wednesday, July 17, 2024
11:45 p.m.

I looked up at Margo's apartment. It was dark.

Dawson's reactions had been expected, but I'd not been able to get a read on Margo. I couldn't tell whether she was on Dawson's side or mine.

As soon as they left, I retreated to the bathroom and turned on the shower. Hot spray splashed the small stall. I quickly stepped in, hoping to wash away thoughts of Tiffany standing lost and alone by her car. I'd waited until she'd started her engine and watched her drive off. I'd thought I'd see her again. I had thought maybe this time I'd helped. But maybe I'd delivered her to her killer.

I dried off, dressed in jeans and a T-shirt, and walked toward the painting of Della. Tiffany had said she'd not listened to conversations in the diner, but I didn't believe her. I'd bet money she'd heard or seen something that years of drug use had buried. A girlfriend accomplice or a reincarnated Della could have a lot to lose.

I stared at the delicate brushstrokes of the face that had stalked me for a decade. I covered it again, lifted it, and after slipping on flip-flops, carried it outside. With it propped against my leg, I locked the warehouse and glanced up again at Margo's darkened apartment window.

I carried the painting across the four-lane road, pausing midway as I waited for the light. When I reached her building, I pressed the buzzer.

"Yeah," the attendant said.

"This is Scarlett Crosby. I was here yesterday with Margo Larsen. I promised her a painting, and I wanted to drop it off."

"It's the middle of the night."

"I know."

"She's not here."

"I don't suppose you could let me put it in her apartment. It's heavy as hell."

"Can't let you in."

"It's worth fifty bucks to me not to carry this back across the street. And she's expecting it."

The door buzzed open. The attendant stood behind his desk, studying me. "I've seen you around."

"I live across the street." To add flavor, I smiled and fished out the fifty bucks.

"You're going to put it in the apartment and that's it, right?"

"You can watch me the entire time."

He reached for keys. "Let's do this quick."

I followed him to the elevator and set the painting down as we waited on the door. When he opened it, I lifted the painting. The paint around the eyes was still tacky, so I was careful not to brush it against my body.

When we reached the fifth floor, he led the way to 512 and unlocked the door with a master key. I flipped on the light and moved past him, carrying the painting past an air mattress to the kitchen counter. Carefully, I set down the painting and leaned it so that it faced the front door. As soon as Margo entered and turned on the light, she'd see it.

"It's pretty," the attendant said.

"Thanks." I walked to the window and stared across the street to my apartment. It was a perfect view for anyone spying on me.

"Now we got to get out of here."

"Sure."

We rode the elevator down in silence. Back in my studio, I reached for my sketchbook and began to redraw Della's face. This time I drew narrower cheeks and shorter light-colored hair. This would be Della #56.

As I stared at the roughed-in face, I glanced toward the building across the street. The lights in Margo's place remained dark. How could she be Della? It was insane to think that she was.

"She's not Della. She's not Della."

And yet the feeling that she was my former cellmate would not leave me alone.

Chapter Thirty-Five

SCARLETT

Then
Ninety or so days in the basement

He'd pulled Della out the door, then shut off a breaker controlling the lights. Upstairs, the radio blared continuously, and I estimated I'd been in the dark three days.

The dark room wrapped around me, squeezing the air from my lungs. He knew I hated the dark. He knew it made me feel entombed. I'd been trying to relax, smile, and not resist, but for some reason he had decided to punish me.

When I finally heard footsteps in the hallway, I was happy and relieved. I'd not been left or abandoned. He'd come back.

However, reassurance faded as the realization of what was going to happen sank in. I pressed my back to the wall. Keys rattled and the lock turned. Light from the hallway streamed into the room, assaulting my sensitive eyes. I winced, turned away, and raised my hand against the one thing I craved more than anything.

Della stood in the doorway, a Mike's take-out bag in her hand. He pushed her inside and closed the door. The lights in the room clicked on.

"You look rough." Her tone was light.

I blinked against the light that reflected on her pale skin peppered with dark-blue bruises. "Where is he?"

She grinned just like she had outside the theater that first day we met. "Gone on a date."

"A date?"

"With the girlfriend. She's kind of a dud."

The smell of burgers drifted around me. "You saw her?"

The smile faded. "I saw her. From the holes in the box."

I'd never been in the box. But the imagined cramped darkness wrapped me in a suffocating shroud.

She reached in the bag and jangled keys. "Look what I found."

"How did you get those?"

"He keeps spares. I saw where he put them."

I scrambled to my feet. "Do the keys work on all the locks?"

"No. Just the front door. We're still locked in here."

"Are you sure?"

"Pretty sure. You need to eat." She tossed the bag at me.

I caught it, savoring the scent of french fries and burgers. Prying open the bag, I found a wrapped burger and a half-empty container of fries.

"I ate a few," she said. "Hard to resist when they're fresh."

The cold fries were tough and greasy, and I couldn't eat them fast enough. "He never leaves you alone upstairs. How will you get a chance to use the key?"

"I have an idea."

"What idea?"

She leaned against the doorjamb, watching me as I ate. "Tanner is going to take you to Mike's Diner, and you'll help him get another girl. There's a redhead he has an eye on. He can't stop thinking about her. He wants to bring her into the fold."

"I don't want to help him."

"If you do, then he'll leave me alone in the house."

"He'll lock you down here," I said.

"He might not."

Convinced she'd lost her mind, I ate the last half of the burger even as my stomach coiled. I had no idea when I would eat again, and I didn't have the luxury of righteous anger.

"Imagine being outside," she said.

I tried to envision sunshine, people, and the smell of food. Freedom. "He's never going to let me loose. And you can steal all the keys in the world, but Tanner's not going to leave you upstairs alone."

Her gaze grew distant. "But if he did and he took you to the diner, would you get the redhead to save me?"

"I'll never help him grab another girl." My hands trembled as I raised the fry to my lips. Was I as strong as I pretended to be?

"Yes, you will. Everyone reaches a point and breaks. Just like I did."

I crumpled the wrapper.

"It's going to be soon." Della folded her bruised arms over her chest.

"He's going to take you," I said. "Not me. It'll be another chance for you to escape."

"Remember, Tanner has wired this entire house with bombs. He'll blow it sky high if he doesn't get what he wants or is caught. If I ran, you'd die."

My gaze looked up toward the ceiling, imagining it falling on my head. "The house isn't wired."

"Yes, it is. I've seen the bombs made from gas cans." Della smoothed her hand over my arm. "Would you miss me if I died?"

"Why do you care?"

"I just do."

I stared into liquid brown eyes that reflected my own.

"Would you miss me?" she whispered.

An impossible truth bubbled to the surface. "Yes."

"Really?"

"Yeah. I couldn't leave you here."

She smiled. "I knew you liked me."

Chapter Thirty-Six

Scarlett

Thursday, July 18, 2024
2:00 p.m.

There was no word from Dawson or Margo all day regarding Tiffany, any DNA results, or the gift I'd left Margo. And waiting was akin to being under the hovering sword of Damocles. Several times I'd almost called Luke to tell him what was going on, but his legal mind wasn't why I was with him. If it came to it, I'd tell him, but I was still hoping the case would settle itself.

Luke texted me and suggested a late dinner at his place, and I was relieved by the distraction. This would be date number five, or six if you counted the reception. In the world of dating, this invitation came with a weight of expectation. He'd been more patient than most men, and for that I was grateful. How long would he linger before the burden of my past became too taxing?

Knowing it would all one day crash and burn didn't mean it had collapsed yet. For now, he was still willing to try, and I needed a friend. I texted back, told him dinner sounded good. I would bring wine again.

Four hours later, when I stood on his front doorstep, the neck of a bottle of red wine clenched in my fist, I felt a sliver of anticipation.

He always smelled good. His hands weren't calloused. There was no scruff on his chin. And though he was physically bigger than Tanner, he moved with care rather than like a bull in a china shop, as Tanner had.

When he opened the door, he was still wearing his suit pants, but he'd removed his tie and rolled up his sleeves. My gaze was drawn to the gold watch on his wrist and dark hair trailing muscled arms up under his shirt cuff.

"Hey," he said.

"Hey."

He leaned in for a kiss. I tensed, but I tipped my body toward his. Our lips touched. He tasted of scotch. "I'm glad you came."

"Me too."

He stepped aside and I walked into his place. "Food smells good."

"Takeout. Again. Can't take any credit." He stood so close, his energy radiated over my skin. He was hungry for me. I knew when a man wanted a woman.

I set my wine bottle on the kitchen counter and faced him.

"Would you like a drink?" he asked.

A drink would buy me time and maybe provide a little liquid courage. But a delay was another chance to lose my nerve. And I didn't want to run this time. I wanted this. I wanted normal.

"No." I stepped close to him and took his hand in mine and threaded my fingers through his.

"What do you want?" he asked carefully.

"To see my painting in your bedroom."

A brow arched. His breathing slowed. "What's that mean?"

"I'm hoping you can show me."

His fingers tightened slightly around mine. "I can show you as much as you want to see."

"Good."

He kissed me on the lips and guided me down the hallway to a bedroom dominated by a neatly made king-size bed. I was vaguely aware of a large dresser, an intricate rug with blues and reds, a chair, and an open closet full of suits. My painting hung on the wall across from his bed.

"We can take it slow," he said.

"I don't want to back out." My desires were too hazy to define.

He traced the line of my jaw. "You can if you want to. It's not a race."

I reached for the hem of my shirt and pulled it over my head. His gaze flickered to the full breasts brimming in the cups of my white bra. I reached for the front hook and unfastened it.

His hand smoothed up my waist to the underside of my left breast. He cupped it while leaning in and kissing me. My heart thrashed in my chest, my cheeks burned with blush pink, and my desire teased to life.

I slid my hand to his chest and along his jawline. "That feels good."

"Tell me if it doesn't," he said.

I touched the buttons on his shirt. When all were unfastened, he shrugged off the brushed cotton with a leashed impatience that was exciting and frightening. I kicked off my shoes and reached for my waistband. I wasn't as anxious for the sex as I was to know how this was all going to end. I wanted to skip to the ending of this story.

His hand returned to my side as if it belonged there, and he pulled me into an embrace. I tensed, but I held steady, and then I slowly relaxed into him. Progress.

This time I deepened the kiss and pressed my body against his. If I left now, I feared I'd be locked in my solitude forever. Carefully, I cupped his ass.

"Still sure?" His voice sounded strained.

"Yes."

I moved to the bed and pulled back the comforter and sheets and climbed in the center. Seconds behind me, he climbed on the bed and planted hands on either side of my face. As his erection pressed against my belly, he kissed my lips, throat, and each breast.

He rose, his eyes dark, wanting. He opened a bedside table and reached for a condom. Tanner had never used condoms. He hated the way they made him feel. Better to be natural. That had skimmed on another layer of fear. What if I got pregnant? Would a baby tie me to him forever? I'd had three menstrual cycles while I'd been in Tanner's room. Each time I'd wept with relief.

Luke slid on the condom. Nothing to bind me to Luke other than a few scattered memories. I closed my eyes.

"Open your eyes," he whispered.

When I looked at him, his face was inches from mine. The intensity of his stare was exciting and daunting.

"I want you to see me," he said.

Not Tanner. Luke. I nodded.

Carefully, he pressed his erection between my legs. I could say no. And he would back off. But I didn't want to say no, so I drew in a breath and arched toward him, pressing closer. He eased into me, stretching and filling. A spark of panic flickered. I gripped his shoulders, my gaze not wavering.

When he slid all the way in, I released a breath, the unseeable coil in my chest unfurling a fraction. Luke remained still, as if sensing the knot loosening. I wasn't so ruined that desire couldn't fill the enduring emptiness for a little while.

"You okay?" Luke's voice was gruff.

"Yes."

Slowly, he began to move. On the edges, ghosts drifted past me. Desire flickered brighter. Frustration for satisfaction nibbled. I wanted the release. My hands slid lower.

As he moved in and out of me, a heat built inside my belly. I began to rub. He pressed faster, harder. What came next was a swirl of sensations. I kept my gaze on him, imprinting this moment and praying it would override all the bad programming.

I lifted my hips, encouraged him to pump harder, faster. I used to do this with Tanner so that he would end it quicker.

Luke resisted, as if he wanted this to last. But I knew how to moan and cup my breasts. He shoved inside me harder, and I rubbed until the rush of sensations washed over and through me. I arched. He plunged deeper. Stiffened.

He collapsed against me, resting his face in the crook of my neck. Like Tanner.

Tanner.

When was I ever going to let Tanner go?

Luke remained inside me as if not ready to break contact. "You okay?"

My smile was as close to genuine as I could get. "Yes. You?"

He chuckled, rolled on his side, and smoothed his hand over my flat belly. He teased the curls between my legs. "I'm very fine."

We lay arms entwined, boneless.

He sighed, rose, and looked at me. "This wasn't the plan. You know that, right?"

"What was the plan?"

He kissed me. "Dinner. More conversation."

I smoothed my fingers along the deep lines bracketing his mouth. "You're indeed a patient man."

"Not really. It didn't take much to crack my resolve."

I laughed. "You aren't complaining, are you?"

"No. Not at all."

Chapter Thirty-Seven

Dawson

Friday, July 19, 2024
2:00 a.m.

Dawson sat with his back to the headboard, staring at the flowered wallpaper. Beside him, Margo lay naked, swirling a manicured finger up and down his belly. His gaze skimmed over her body up to her eyes. She was watching him closely. He'd been up late working when she'd texted to tell him she was outside his door.

"What's that look?" he said.

"I told you I got an apartment."

They'd met each time here in his hotel room because she was waiting on furniture. "You told me."

"I installed a camera in my apartment."

"Why would you do that?"

"Basically, I'm paranoid."

That sparked a smile. "Welcome to the club."

"Someone paid a visit to my apartment after we left Scarlett's warehouse." She rolled toward the nightstand and grabbed her phone. When she sat up, pressing her back to the headboard, her breasts jiggled. She pushed a button on her phone and turned it toward him.

Black-and-white footage of her bare apartment appeared. He leaned closer, discovering he was curious about where she lived. There'd been no talk about what happened beyond this room. She was out of his league, and he should be grateful for what she'd given him. But he was curious about her.

"That an air mattress?"

"Furniture arrives soon."

"I can fuck on an air mattress."

She smiled. "I'll keep that in mind, but that's not the point. Watch." The tape advanced and the front door opened. The first to appear on the screen was an older man wearing what looked like a uniform. A maintenance visit wasn't out of the ordinary.

The front desk clerk moved to the side, and Scarlett Crosby stepped into the apartment. She was holding one of her paintings. She slowly walked into the unit, allowing her gaze to roam the room before she rested the painting against the counter. Next, she moved to the picture window and stared out over the street.

"What's she looking at?" he asked.

"Her warehouse."

He shifted his gaze to the painting. He'd seen versions of it in police files. It was Scarlett's latest interpretation of Della. "She left you a painting of Della."

"Seems we struck a nerve today," Margo said.

"She called you Della before."

"She did. I must remind Scarlett of her," Margo said.

Dawson sat up and reached for his phone. He scrolled until he found the picture he wanted. "This is the police artist sketch of Della."

She leaned in again, studying the image. "Looks like a kid. Not like me."

Margo's nose was slimmer. Her cheeks had a sharper cut. But any good plastic surgeon could've done that for her. Still, he rejected the thought. Oddly, he needed to believe her. "Did Scarlett take anything?"

"No. I talked to the clerk. She was in and out in under a minute. But she's clearly fixated on me."

Spicy perfume swirled around him. That scent would cling to him hours after she'd left his hotel room. "She was also obsessed with helping Tiffany Patterson."

"When are they doing Tiffany Patterson's autopsy?"

"In the morning."

She leaned up and met his gaze even as her hand slid up and down his shaft. "Good. We'll know more after that."

As the sun bobbed above the horizon, Dawson arrived at Scarlett's warehouse and glanced up at Margo's apartment, hoping, maybe fearing she was watching. However, the windows were dark.

When Margo had left his hotel room about 4:00 a.m., she'd said she was going home to shower and dress for work. His gaze lingered on Margo's windows, and he guessed she'd already come and gone.

He imagined Scarlett entering Margo's place and leaning the portrait against the counter. It pissed him off that Scarlett had invaded Margo's space. Her Della fixation had a new target.

With Tiffany Patterson's autopsy scheduled for this morning, he was loaded for bear when he pounded on Scarlett's door and waited impatiently until the steady clip of footsteps approached. They slid open, and Scarlett stood staring at him as she wiped yellow ink from her hands. "I'm in the middle of something."

"This early? Good for you. I'll talk to you while you work."

"I don't like talking."

"We can chat here or at the station, Scarlett. I don't care where we do it."

"Come inside." She stood back as he crossed the threshold, and then she closed the doors behind him.

The strong scents of paint and alcohol permeated the space. She didn't bother a second glance in his direction as she moved toward a table where a large engraved plate rested. She picked up a bundle of what looked like cheesecloth and dabbed it in a dollop of yellow paint. Carefully, she blotted the fabric on a clean piece of paper until she'd removed most of the color.

"What do you want?" She very gently dabbed the yellow paint on the block etched with boats on curling waves.

"What's the deal with you and Margo Larsen?"

"I ran into her on the street, and we had drinks."

"Why did you leave that painting in her apartment?"

Her gaze lifted, tinted with suspicion. "You two are cozy."

Dawson's chest squeezed like it had when his ex-wife's life had started to spiral. "We work together."

"She doesn't look like the type to go running for help."

"She's concerned about your mental state."

Her gaze, filling with questions, lingered on him. "I'm just fine, Detective."

He cleared his throat. "What did you say to Lynn Yeats? She filed a stalking complaint yesterday against you."

Scarlett didn't hesitate as she patted away more paint. "I asked her about Tanner. I wanted to know more about him."

"Why?"

"Finding Sandra Taylor stirred up a lot. I have too many unanswered questions, so I'm trying to make sense of the past."

"Are you a junior detective now?"

Overhead lights buzzed. "I'm looking out for my best interests. The more I know about Tanner, the better."

"Why better? He's been dead a decade."

"You found the body of a missing girl. She vanished, died, and no one missed a beat."

"Do you believe Tanner killed her?"

"Della kept reminding me to be nice to Tanner so I didn't end up like the Other Girl."

"Della."

Scarlett held up her hand. "I'm not debating Della."

"Okay. Okay." Lynn Yeats's description of Tanner's cousin sounded a little like Della. "Did Della have any theories about the Other Girl?"

"Tanner took Della upstairs often, but the woman who had more access to the first floor was Lynn Yeats. Have you asked Lynn?"

He drew in a breath. "She never saw anyone fitting Sandra's description."

"But she did see a girl, didn't she?"

He didn't answer.

"I think Lynn saw what she wanted to see."

"Why wrap the body and hide it around the corner from your mother's house?"

"Tanner was renovating the property. We all gravitate toward the familiar, don't we?" she asked. "He knew the neighborhood. And he knew I lived close."

"Maybe you helped him put the body in the wall?"

"I didn't, but maybe Lynn did. They were dating then, and she said she'd do anything for him."

"When did she say that?"

"Something I overheard while we happened to be in the same coffee shop."

He shook his head, knowing none of this would be admissible. "Tanner didn't kill Tiffany, though, did he?"

Silent tension rippled through her body.

"You were the last person to spend any time with Tiffany."

"But not the last to see her," she said. "Tiffany was a drug addict. Addicts always need money. Maybe she threatened to stir up the past and make life miserable for Lynn. Lynn said it took her years to live down her relationship with Tanner."

"Maybe Tiffany knew more about your history with Tanner. Maybe she was blackmailing you and you got tired of paying."

"It's all guesswork, Detective."

"I have you on video trespassing into Margo's apartment. Leaving her a Della portrait."

Scarlett was silent long enough for him to think she'd shut down. And then: "Did Margo tell you I called her Della?"

"She did."

"Margo reminds me of Della. It's unsettling."

"You've made this mistake before."

"Not like this."

A note in her tone struck a deep chord. His ex-wife had kept secrets, and his denials, and ultimate cover-up, had enabled her addiction and nearly ruined him. Was he on the same path and again ignoring warnings? "How does she remind you of Della?"

"Under the blond hair, I see the dark roots. She's had her nose done, but the eyes," she said softly. "It's always the eyes that give us away."

The comparison soured his gut. Not for the first time, he wondered why Margo had picked him. "Della was never found. She doesn't exist."

"She did and does."

"There's no proof. There's no missing persons report on anyone matching Della's description."

"She said she was initially with him out of choice. And then he kept her locked in the house. And then he locked her in the basement."

"Why didn't she try to escape the night Tanner snatched you?"

"She believed the Other Girl was still alive. She thought if she ran, the Other Girl would die."

"Why would she care about Sandra?"

"Hell has a way of bonding scared, desperate people."

"Is that why you didn't run right away? Were you worried about Della?"

She glanced at her trembling hands. "He beat her up bad the day before. I was scared for her."

"Why did he beat her up?"

"I don't know. She could handle him so well, but she said or did something that set him off."

"Maybe he just lost it."

"Maybe."

"You and Tanner leave, and what happens next? Della sets fire to the house and just takes off?"

"She'd found a set of keys and knew if Tanner left her alone in the house she could get out. After the beating I guess he thought she'd been too injured to run, so he left her upstairs. And the arson investigator stated the house had been rigged to explode. I think she knew where the bombs were and set them off. I think she'd been planning her escape since Sandra vanished from the house."

"Arson report? You read that?"

"I wanted to understand what happened."

Given her friendship with the Judge, he didn't have to ask how she'd gotten the report. "She provoked Tanner so he'd beat her?"

"It explains a lot."

"And then Della reinvented herself into a decorated cop?" He needed her to vanquish his growing doubts of Margo. Because the actions Della had allegedly taken sounded like something Margo might do.

"She was smart. A survivor. Like Margo."

"They look nothing alike."

"The eyes are the same."

Margo had approached him. She'd suggested her hotel room, which happened to be a few floors below his. Had he looked as lost as he'd felt? Nothing like wearing your fuckups on your sleeve. And then Margo had turned the tables for him and put him in complete control in that bedroom.

Scarlett looked up at Dawson. "Why are you so worried about protecting Margo?"

"This kind of baseless rumor could damage her career. Margo isn't your Della," he said.

"Are you trying to convince me or yourself?" She laid a clean sheet of linen paper on the block and another piece of cardboard and then pushed the entire setup under the press. "The woman I knew got under Tanner's and my skin."

He rubbed his hand over the back of his neck. "Margo isn't Della."

She pressed a button and the roller dropped and crushed the paper against the block. When it released, she carefully removed the cardboard and paper and then carried the print to a large table where three others like it were drying. Slowly, she faced him. "Sounds like she's gotten under your skin."

"Don't play head games with me."

Her gaze hardened with amusement. "Are you sleeping with her?"

"She's a coworker."

Scarlett's eyes narrowed as if she could see inside him. "Two things can be true at once."

Chapter Thirty-Eight

SCARLETT

Friday, July 19, 2024
2:00 p.m.

When Dawson left, I was immediately drawn to the new Della portrait. I stared at sketched eyes that were already glaring at me. She was daring me to sharpen the glint in the irises and darken the brows and lashes. This Della wasn't kind or lost or trapped. She understood what she wanted. And she wasn't afraid to cut corners to get it. The gaming master. Those eyes were so real, I expected them to blink. Minutes and then hours passed before I stepped back.

I looked over my shoulder toward Margo's apartment. It was two in the afternoon and the light was now on. "You're real. I know it. I *know* it."

Drawing in a breath, I left the painting and hurried out my front door, slamming it behind me. I crossed the street and buzzed the front door of her building. The doorman looked up as I pressed the intercom button. "I'm here for Margo Larsen. Scarlett Crosby. She's expecting me."

He picked up his phone, spoke for several seconds, and then buzzed the front door open. I pushed inside.

"She's on the fifth floor," he said.

"I know where she lives." The elevator ride was quick, but the small space twisted and tightened my nerves. When the doors opened, the tension didn't release as I moved heavy feet quickly toward Margo's apartment. I knocked.

At first, only silence responded. I shifted my stance, checked the apartment door number to make sure I had the right one. And then steady footsteps moved toward the door. It opened in an easy, languid way. Margo was dressed in black pajamas that skimmed her body, and her blond hair was styled off her face. She wasn't wearing makeup and looked younger.

Full lips broadened into a wide and seductive Della smile. "Scarlett. What a lovely surprise."

"Margo. Sorry for the unexpected call."

"Not at all. Nice to have the company. Come in."

I stepped inside and saw the painting I'd left. It no longer leaned against the counter but hung on the wall.

"Quite the painting," Margo said. "Very striking."

Della didn't run. She was bold. Daring. "I thought you might like it."

"I do. Can't take my eyes off it. It'll go great with the other pieces I have."

The apartment was empty, except for the air mattress, now neatly made with several blankets and white sheets. I thought about the mattress and blanket in the small basement room.

"What brings you home in the middle of the day?"

"I just attended Tiffany Patterson's autopsy. I needed a minute."

The image of a surgeon's blade cutting into Tiffany was jarring. "I can't imagine."

"Probably far worse than anything you can dream up." She moved toward her kitchen. "Can I make you a coffee? A little early for wine. And I need to get back to work."

"How did Tiffany die?"

"I can't discuss that until the investigation is concluded." She set up the coffee machine and hit *Brew*. "Where were you in the last forty-eight hours?"

"I'm a suspect?"

Margo shrugged. "Everyone is at this point. The medical examiner has pulled hair fibers, so fingers crossed there's DNA to be had. That'll narrow the search." Her words rang with the confidence of someone who already had answers.

I'd encountered that brand of self-assurance before. "Dawson came by my place this morning. More questions about Sandra. I smelled your perfume on him."

"You did?"

I moved toward her as she set out two Styrofoam cups on the counter. "Are you doing your magic on him now?"

She chuckled. "Magic?"

I laid my hands on the counter. "Your first meeting with Dawson was random. You just happened by, right? Did you pull strings to get on the Taylor case?"

Her eyes narrowed. "Dawson and I are coworkers."

"It's more, isn't it?"

"Are you worried about the good detective? He's a big boy and capable of taking care of himself."

Della had tied me up into dozens of emotional knots. Hate twisted into fear, into need, into friendship. "I called you Della when I first saw you."

"The girl that lured you into Tanner's lair." She looked toward the portrait. "Is she Della?"

"Yes."

"Counseling is nothing to be ashamed of, Scarlett. You might want to check in with your mental health care provider."

"I'm right about you."

"Or Della is your way of justifying your own bad decisions. Della made you get in Tanner's van when in fact you got in willingly. Della couldn't lure Tiffany, so you did. And when it all went sideways, Della vanished. Della explains away all your poor choices."

"I didn't make her up."

"Memories and truth can blend in ways we can't ever imagine. I think your Della started off as a cover to justify your guilt. But as time went on, Della became real and now you don't know the difference between fact and fiction. I'm not blaming you, Scarlett." Her gaze softened. "Given the trauma you suffered, it's a wonder you function so well."

In a few words she'd painted me as permanently damaged and confused. "How did you get away? He beat you up so badly."

"Honey, I'm not Della," she said softly. "I'm Officer Margo Larsen. I'm a cop. And I'm not sure why you've fixated on me."

"Tanner and his sins have been dead and buried for ten years. And then you arrive in Norfolk, Sandra's body is found, and Tiffany dies."

She cocked an eyebrow, but the hints of amusement were gone. "What's your point?"

"Why did you come back? You were free and clear. Were you bored?"

"I'm not Della, honey."

"You are. And I'm going to prove it."

She folded her arms. "You know what I think? Your mother died recently, and as often happens with a parent's passing, old issues rise to the surface. Guilt over Sandra's death prompted you to call in the body's location. And then you run into Tiffany. A part of you wants to help her, but the other part sees her as another bad memory. Maybe she was pressing you for money to fuel her drug problem. And what about Lynn? She's accused you of stalking. I just happened to arrive in Norfolk as your shit show danced onto center stage."

Della had been so persuasive. She'd coaxed me into the van and convinced me that Tanner was trying to save us and finally to lure Tiffany. She'd made me believe she was a friend. And now the very convincing Margo was trying to put all the blame on my shoulders.

"I'm going to prove you're Della." I turned and walked toward the door. My hand on the knob, I said, "I'm not a lonely fifteen-year-old any longer."

"You're just as vulnerable as that kid." She shrugged. "At least, I assume."

"What's that mean?"

Margo grinned. "I guess we'll see."

Chapter Thirty-Nine

SCARLETT

Then
Ninety-plus days in the basement

My eyes were still adjusting to the bright sunshine when Tanner backed into a parking spot across from Mike's Diner. Della's bruised and battered body and swollen eyes still fresh in my mind, I watched the people passing by the van. They were in the real world, and I was trapped inside this toxic bubble.

The air was warm, and the sunshine on my face should have been intoxicating, but it was terrifying. I didn't know how to act or behave on the outside.

Freshly showered, I wore an old checkered dress that was two sizes too big. I ran my fingers over damp hair. Tanner had forced me into the shower, turned on the hot spray, and handed me soap as he'd watched me wash away the dirt. When I was dry, he tossed the dress at me. Its rough poly blend felt as foreign to me as everything else in my life.

It was seven o'clock in the morning and the diner was filling up with customers. Most looked like tradesmen grabbing a quick hearty breakfast before the day's work.

"Scarlett, go inside and order a plate of pancakes, extra bacon, and scrambled eggs." He fished a twenty out of his pocket. "Also, three coffees and biscuits to go. Della's in rough shape and will need to eat."

"Why did you hurt her?"

He tightened his hand on the wheel, and for the first time I saw a flash of regret. "She made me do it. She knows better. Don't make me hurt her more."

"Is she going to be all right?"

"She's tough. The bruises will fade." He shifted in his seat as his gaze arrowed in on me. "Give any change to that little redheaded waitress and then tell her you saw puppies out back. She loves dogs."

Accepting the rumpled bill, I crushed it in my fist. I looked toward the diner. "I don't see her."

"You will. Hair as red as fire. Her name is Tiffany. Remember, tell her there are puppies behind the diner. She can't resist. I'll be out back."

His beautiful profile had twisted into a grotesque mask. How had I ever seen any beauty in those features? "Okay."

"Remember Della. Don't make me hurt her." His voice softened. "I don't enjoy hurting anyone."

As I reached for the door handle, my heart pounded. I'd dreamed of freedom for months, but the cost was terrifying.

Strong fingers banded around my wrist, anchoring me in place. "I'll make Della suffer so badly that they'll hear her screams in the next state."

"Is that what you told Della about the Other Girl?"

Surprise mixed with amusement. "I'm not shy about killing."

I believed him. He'd kill Della like the Other Girl. I didn't know Tiffany, but I knew Della. She was so battered and could barely move. Could she get her key and get out of that house? I wanted to believe she could, but God, she'd been in such bad shape. My last image of Della was her lying on his bed, curled in a ball, eyes closed.

"Meet me behind the diner," Tanner said.

"Okay."

"Swear."

"I swear."

I took a moment to straighten my dress and smooth the flyaway hairs escaping from my ponytail.

"Pay close attention," Tanner said. "And don't forget to smile. You look like a zombie."

I didn't glance at him as I opened the door and lowered my foot to the asphalt parking lot. My leg felt shaky, and when my second foot landed, it took a moment to secure my balance. I walked slowly toward the diner. A few people crossed my path as they rushed toward the front door and the breakfast they were clearly craving. My stomach grumbled, but my belly was tight with nerves and fear; I doubted I could keep anything down.

I reached the front entrance and walked inside, pausing at the door as I adjusted to the noise of conversations and the sheer number of people. I'd been in near isolation for months and now I was surrounded by noise, light, and sound. This was my chance to scream and yell and tell everyone here that I needed help. I had the power right now, until I thought about Della's swollen face. If she wasn't walking out of that house now, an escape attempt would mean death for us both.

As I approached, the smell of coffee drifted around me. I'd not had coffee in months, and the closest I'd come to a hot meal had been cold french fries. What would it be like to sit at a table and have someone bring me hot food? My mother had never been a great cook, but when we had money, she could order out better than anyone.

I shifted my attention to the waitress. Her hair was a dark red, and she'd pulled it into a ponytail secured with a pink bow. Her tightly tied white apron drew attention to her small waist. She was filling a cup of coffee for a big, burly man and laughing as he spoke to her.

How long would it take Tanner to snuff out that spark?

A uniformed cop walked up to the register, and as he paid his bill, he glanced at me. My throat tightened. If he offered his help now,

Tanner would flee and drive back to his house and kill Della if she hadn't escaped. The cop paid his tab, grabbed his bag, and left.

The girl behind the counter came up to me. "What can I get you, sweetie?"

I tucked a strand of freshly washed hair behind my ear. "Four biscuits." My voice sounded rusty as I struggled to remember what Tanner had told me to order. "Pancakes and three coffees. And two biscuits." Was that right? I couldn't remember.

"You said four biscuits."

"Okay," I said quickly. "Sorry."

"No worries, hon. Coming right up."

I looked behind the counter to the kitchen and the back door. When I looked over my shoulder, I saw Tanner's van slowly pulling away.

"You okay?"

I looked at the man standing behind the bar. He wore a white T-shirt, an apron, and a name tag that read *Mike*. "You look worried."

"I'm fine," I said. "Just hungry."

"You here with anyone?"

I must have looked shady. "No."

He studied me a beat and then returned to the kitchen.

Tiffany filled a stoneware mug for me. "While you wait."

"Thanks." I wrapped chilled fingers around the warm mug and slowly raised it to my lips. I blew on the hot brew and then sipped carefully. Hot, bitter, jarring. It tasted like the real world.

I wanted to be free. I wanted to escape Tanner's basement prison. But Della. I looked at Tiffany's smiling face. "There are puppies out back behind the dumpster."

She grinned. "Seriously?"

I cradled the cup. "Very sweet. Little. Want to see them?"

"I got to work now." She filled mugs with coffee for a couple of customers at the bar.

I tried not to stare at her even as I willed her to return. When she set the pot down and faced me, I said, "It'll only take a second."

Smiling, she motioned me around the counter, and we cut through the bustling kitchen. My temple pounded as amazing food smells swirled. My mouth watered as my stomach grumbled. Out the back screen door, I watched Tanner's van roll slowly into place. He got out and opened the sliding door.

Scream. Scream. Call for help.

I clamped my lips shut as we moved closer. Della had done this to me. *Come with me to my van.* And I'd followed as willingly as Tiffany did now. Was she really trying to save the Other Girl, or had that also been a lie?

"Where are the puppies?" Tiffany asked.

"Hiding behind the dumpster," I said.

"Aw, poor babies."

"They looked hungry."

Tiffany tucked a curl behind her ear. "I can get them hamburger. Mike won't mind. He's a dog lover, too."

"Terrible when a puppy suffers." I glanced toward the van and a smiling Tanner. It was that electric grin he'd tossed my way in the beginning. Now I wasn't charmed, but chilled. "I saw the puppies just a second ago. There are at least three."

Tiffany glanced up and for the first time saw the van. "Tanner. What are you doing here?"

He waved. "Hey, Tiffany."

I moved toward the van and the dumpster on the other side. Tiffany's confident footsteps thudded against the pavement behind me. I pictured what was going to happen. Tanner would shove a needle in her arm, she'd black out, and when she woke up, she'd be lying on the stained mattress in the dark basement room. She'd be like a new toy to him, and he would be excited to play. While Della and I watched, she'd cry, scream, and beg. He would laugh.

I stopped walking. *Della, were you strong enough to get out of that house?*

Clutching my fingers, I froze, whirled around, and my attention shifted to Tiffany.

I'm sorry, Della.

"Run!" My voice was weak, raw, and it took another deep breath and an image of Della stumbling out of Tanner's house to force the word over my vocal cords. "Run!"

Tiffany's smile crumpled into confusion. "What?"

"Run! Tanner's going to kill you."

I'm sorry, Della.

Tanner's smile melted, and he lunged for Tiffany. But she was thin and fast and quickly angled out of his grip. Tanner howled his frustration. "I'm not going to hurt you!"

As she vanished inside the diner, he immediately charged me and grabbed my arm. Calloused fingers bit into my flesh, drawing my startled expression to the white-hot rage tightening his face. I tried to pull free, but he was a strong man, and he easily jerked me hard toward the van's open side door.

I thought about Della running through the woods toward the main road. I thought about the basement room. I'd likely die there. My chest constricted. Who was I kidding? Della wasn't running anywhere. She was as trapped as I was. She hadn't saved the Other Girl, but maybe I could save her.

Balling up my fingers into fists, I struck Tanner in the face. I quickly drew back my arm again and hit him over and over.

Rage darkened his eyes, and he punched me so hard across the face. My teeth felt as if they'd rattled in my head as I fell to the ground.

As he hoisted my body, he said, "I'm going to enjoy cutting you and Della into pieces. It might take me days to finish the job before you die." He threw me in the back of the van, and my shoulder hit the metal floor hard. The door slammed.

He was behind the wheel and jerking the car into drive. "Fuck you. Fuck you."

Tanner punched the gas, and the tires spit up rock as the van lurched forward. I held on to the door as I tried to steady myself. My head pounded and my shoulder throbbed, but I knew Tanner was a man of his word. He would make me suffer.

He took a corner hard, throwing me off-balance, tossing me against the other door. My head struck the metal floor.

"I'll start with your fingers," he said. "The thumb or maybe the pinkie. Which finger will hurt the most?"

I tasted blood, coppery and bitter. "I'm sorry, Tanner. I'm sorry." My voice sounded hollow and distant. I'd just trashed what was left of my life for a stranger.

"Oh, you're not sorry yet. But when we get home, a few obedience lessons will redefine *sorry* for you and Della." He punched the accelerator.

Rage, fury, and fear fused into my belly as the van hurtled down the road. Panic scraped my insides as I rose on my knees. If I accepted this now, I feared Della and I would die. My heart hammered in my chest as I wrapped my hands around his face and pressed my index fingers into his eyes.

Chapter Forty

DAWSON

Friday, July 19, 2024
4:00 p.m.

Dawson drove to the house where Sandra's body had been found. He ducked under the crime scene tape and paused at the front door. The seal was broken. Someone had been in the house. Drawing his weapon, he walked inside.

His footsteps echoing in the empty house, he moved toward the kitchen. The bricks still lay in the haphazard pile fanning around the fireplace. He tried to imagine Tanner standing here a decade ago. He'd taken the time to wrap Sandra's body tight and carried her lifeless form here. How hard had it been to shove the body into the small place? He peered into the narrow space.

He pictured Sandra suffering in that basement while he was at this construction site interviewing Tanner. Shit. He'd known Tanner was slick. The smile was too easy. He was so helpful.

Tiffany's body hadn't been wrapped in plastic, but her purse and identification had been with her remains. Two victims had died a decade apart. Notes from the forensic techs told him Tiffany had also been struck on the back of the head like Sandra. The cases were connected. Lynn. Scarlett. The mysterious Della.

His phone rang, the sound echoing in the house. "Dawson."

"You're going to owe me," Dr. Malone said.

"My favorite medical examiner. I'm so far in debt to you, I'll never dig out," he said, smiling.

"Thank your partner. She can be very persuasive."

He was only just realizing that. "What do you have?"

"As you know, I extracted DNA from Sandra Taylor's back molar. I was able to match Taylor's DNA to her biological mother's, which was still in the penal system. I can confirm her identity."

"Tell me what I don't know."

"I also found dark-brown hair strands on Sandra's body. These fibers were clutched in her right hand."

Tanner's hair had been military short and black and Scarlett's ice blond. "Okay."

"The fibers are old, but the tech at the lab has many tricks up her sleeve, but it's going to take more time, assuming there's a DNA match in the system."

Would DNA from the hair prove Della's existence? "Hair clutched in her hand . . . as if Sandra were fighting," he said more to himself.

"Or reaching for help," Dr. Malone said. "It's not uncommon for victims to grab anything, hoping to save themselves."

Dawson's mind wandered to Scarlett's painting of Della. Dark curly hair. Had Sandra been reaching to Della for help or fighting for her life?

Lynn Yeats had also had long dark hair a decade ago, but hers was straight. The DNA profiles would tell him who'd been near Sandra at her death or handled her body. And if Della was Margo . . . shit.

"Anything else?" he asked.

"June bugs."

"What?"

"I found a June bug under Miss Taylor's blouse. They tend to hatch in Southern Virginia and North Carolina in May and June. Not a hard date, but something."

Sandra had last been seen in April. Dr. Malone's discovery of a June bug indicated that Sandra could have been alive in May or June. If that held true, she would have been in Tanner's house the same time as Scarlett. And there was also the bracelet engraved with an *SC* found with Sandra's body.

Dawson rolled his neck from side to side. "What about Tiffany Patterson? Was her phone ever found on her body?"

"Not that I know of."

"What about any DNA?"

"Light-colored hair strands. Also off for testing for a match."

Basically dead ends. "Thanks, Doc. Keep me posted."

Chapter Forty-One

SCARLETT

Friday, July 19, 2024
11:45 p.m.

The walls of the box were tight. The air inside stale. My muscles ached, cramped. Clumps of dirt hit the outside of the box. Thump. Thump. Thump. Tanner was doing what he'd always threatened to do. He was killing me slowly.

I woke suddenly, my heart racing. My hands trembled as I ran them through my hair and stared into the darkness of the strange room. A hand came to my back and lightly rubbed my naked skin. I flinched.

"Are you all right?"

It took a moment to recognize Luke's voice and for the pieces to fall into place. "Yes."

He sat up, and in the shadows, I could feel his frown. "Nightmare?"

"Yeah." I struggled to steady my hands. "It happens sometimes."

"Do you want to talk about it?" he asked.

"I'm not sure words change much. It's a past I can't always shake."

He laid a gentle hand on my back, running his fingers up my spine. "Words can change everything."

"You don't need to carry my baggage."

"Try me."

I tipped my head back. "Dawson. He's investigating a death that might have been related to Tanner."

Luke clicked on his bedside light. I winced as my eyes adjusted. "Dawson?"

"He was asking about Sandra Taylor. She went missing months before me, and we might have been imprisoned at the same time."

He smoothed his hand down my arm. "What do you think?"

I tried to draw comfort from his touch but could find none. "Della mentioned another girl, but I never saw her."

"Did Della ever mention Sandra Taylor by name?"

He spoke about Della as if she were real. That was touching. "No. She always called her *the Other Girl*." I shook my head. "I know, I know. There was no proof of Della. Just my made-up cellmate."

"I never said that."

"Every cop in the city did. Does."

He touched my cheek. "My money is on you."

I smiled. "I'm not sure I'd bet on me right now. Remember Tiffany Patterson, the girl I tried to lure all those years ago?"

"Yes."

"She was found dead. Dawson said it was murder."

He frowned. "When?"

"She stayed at my place a couple of days ago. Then I dropped her off at her car. It happened shortly after that."

"Dawson has interviewed you?"

"Yes." A slight smile tugged my lips. "Don't bet on me."

He drew in a deep breath. "I'm paid to sum people up. If I had to defend you, I could do it with a clear conscience."

"Thanks. At the rate it's all going, I might need to get bailed out one day."

"Is it that serious?"

"Dawson has wondered out loud if I'd been willingly working with Tanner. I did try to lure Tiffany to the van, and after my release I got into a lot of trouble."

"But you waved off Tiffany, and the rest amounted to a traumatized girl acting out. Once you got the proper help, that behavior ended."

"Boy, you're good."

He grinned. "Like to think so."

I drew in a breath. "There's a new cop in the department. Margo Larsen. She reminds me so much of Della. She doesn't exactly look like her, but I can't shake the feeling they're the same person."

He kissed me on my shoulder. Soft. Delicate. Like Della had kissed me when I was upset. He turned my face toward his. "What about Margo reminds you of Della?"

"Her eyes. Her confidence. And I think she and Dawson are sleeping together."

"Really?"

"I said as much to Dawson. He didn't deny it."

"Not a good idea for his career, especially given what happened with his ex-wife."

"Can you tell me more?"

He smiled. "No."

"Okay." I cupped his face and kissed him. "I'm glad you're where you are."

"Me too." He traced the lines on my forehead. "Now tell me the rest about Della."

"If Margo is Della, she's hard to resist. I could see her spinning her magic on Dawson."

I stared deep into his eyes, looking for doubts. If they were there, I didn't see them. I pressed my lips to his, closed my eyes, and deepened the kiss. Sexual desire was becoming a favorite distraction.

"What's the advantage?" Luke drew back reluctantly. "She's a cop. She's on the case."

"She also found Sandra Taylor's body."

"Doesn't mean she's Della."

I didn't want to chase him away with my obsession with Della. I liked him. And he was the first normal relationship in my life. But Della would have used adoration from a lonely cop. And inside knowledge of this case would have been hard to resist.

"Don't pay attention to me," I said. "There's something about the night that churns up all kinds of crazy thoughts."

"Who called in the location of Taylor's body?" he said more to himself.

"It came from a burner phone placed near a drug dealer's house. I was on the premises at the time of the call trying to pull Tiffany away from the party."

"Did you notice anyone at the party who didn't fit?"

"Me."

"Other than you."

"I wasn't there long and was focused on Tiffany."

"Dawson knows this?"

"Yes."

"Be careful what you say to him. If he presses, insist he call me."

"You don't have to do that."

"I want to."

I wrapped my arms around Luke's neck and pulled him toward me. He moved on top of me, kissing me softly on my lips and then my breasts. Tension radiated in his body, but he still moved with deliberate care. I arched, opened my legs, remembering how Tanner had liked my surrender. When Luke pushed slowly inside me, I embraced the sensations, and for a little while, there was nothing but this.

Chapter Forty-Two

SCARLETT

Saturday, July 20, 2024
6:00 a.m.

Before dawn, I left Luke's and was feeling restless. My phone dinged with a text. It read: I've filed stalking charges. Stay away from me.

I didn't recognize the number but guessed this must be from Lynn. Instead of driving home, I headed down Shore Drive toward Lynn's town house. I parked out front, staring at her darkened windows. I'm not sure how long I sat there, but finally, I realized I was acting irrational.

The drive to the warehouse took fifteen minutes, and as I parked, the sun was edging up toward the horizon. I punched in the front door lock code, but the door locked instead of unlocked. Had I not locked this before I left earlier? I couldn't be that distracted, could I?

I flipped on the lights and entered. Immediately, I realized something was off. Beyond the pink hues of sunrise, I peered into the darkness, but I saw nothing. Buildings in this area were targets, and I'd not been home all night.

I listened for any sign that someone was there. The shadows were still and quiet, but the energy was off, just as it had been the night

Tanner had snatched me. I'd dismissed the feeling then, but not now. The warehouse felt wrong.

I turned on more lights and moved into the kitchen. I checked the back door. It was locked. I inspected the windows. All secure.

There was a rustle in the back of the warehouse. I stilled, the sound of my pounding heart filling my ears, I grabbed a knife from the kitchen and moved toward the back, where my room was located. I glanced over my shoulder. I should leave. Call the cops. Screw Dawson.

A loud thump echoed from my bedroom. Then another thump and another. Gripping the knife, I called 9-1-1. The phone rang and rang. *Thump.* "Shit."

I hung up and flipped on lights, edging past the prints hanging like specters from clotheslines. *Thump. Thump.*

How many times had I pounded on the walls while trapped in Tanner's basement? How many thumps or creaks had I heard signaling his arrival? I switched on the overhead industrial lights, which flickered. It would take a good five minutes for them to fully brighten.

Moving toward the screen that divided off my bedroom, I fought the tension rippling through my body. I quietly angled around the screen, and I drew in a breath as I braced.

When I stepped into the bedroom, my gaze slid immediately to my bed, where a woman was tied to the bed frame. A bag covered her head. She was thrashing against her bindings. Adrenaline scraped through my body, and for a split second I was too stunned to act.

Then shaking off the shock, I hurried across the room and with trembling fingers pulled the bag from her head. Under the cloth, the woman's face was wrapped in plastic. Even through the haze, I recognized Lynn, and she was struggling to breathe. How had she gotten here?

I laid the knife by her head and pried my fingers into the tightly wrapped plastic. The binding was tight, and my fingers slipped over the slick surface as Lynn thrashed. Her bound hands were turning blue as her muffled screams tried to permeate the plastic as she rolled her head from side to side. She was suffocating right before me.

"Hold still." I reached for the knife. "I'm going to cut this off."

Lynn stilled as I wedged the knife tip under the plastic. Very slowly, I ripped through the casing, carefully peeling it away from her chin and then her mouth. The instant her lips were uncovered, Lynn sucked in a deep breath of air. She screamed.

The screen behind me shifted, and I whirled around, knife in hand. Margo stepped into the room. She was dressed in jeans, a dark shirt, black athletic shoes. Her hair was slicked back, and her sidearm was gripped in her right hand. Her eyes were wide and hard, just as Della's had been when she'd asked if I'd damn Tiffany to hell for her.

I almost laughed. No one else might see Della, but I did. All these years of wondering where she was or if I was losing my mind. "Della," I said.

"Scarlett, what have you done?" Margo asked. "What are you doing to that woman?"

"I found her like this."

Lynn gasped for air and railed her head from side to side, trying to uncover her eyes. "Help!"

"You can't help yourself, can you?" Margo asked.

I glanced at Lynn lying in my bed, her face partially wrapped, the knife in my hand and Della's tight grip on her weapon. "You set all this up, didn't you, Della?"

Margo shook her head. "You keep calling me Della. You know she's not real, right?"

Della thought ahead. She was a master at manipulating Tanner and me. All these years, and that had not changed. "You *are* her." I was oddly calm. I felt justified. Not as if my memory were faulty. "You changed yourself, but you *are* her."

"You're paranoid," Margo said. "The cops never proved that Della existed."

The innocent expression and convincing tone reminded me of Della as she lured me to Tanner's van. "Then what the hell are you doing here in my place?"

"Dawson's been trying to get Lynn on the phone for hours. He told me to keep an eye on your house."

She made it all sound so logical. "You always have a good answer."

"It's true. And if you're wondering, the world will believe me. Not you, Scarlett. You're the girl that cried wolf too many times. No one will chase your wild theories. The cops are on their way. I already called Dawson."

I ticked through all of Margo's features and now saw more similarities than differences. "You knew Tanner had a girlfriend. He locked you in the box under his bed."

Margo was silent but her eyes narrowed slightly.

"You met Lynn briefly at Tanner's front door. Did you signal her that you were in trouble? You must have been terrified. If you called out for help, would she have believed you or Tanner? Lynn adored Tanner."

"Did she?"

"It must have felt terrible when Lynn just walked away."

Margo's gaze hardened.

"Is she the reason he started locking you in the basement or the box under his bed? Maybe he was worried she'd come back and figure out you were his prisoner. Or maybe he told her the truth and she kept his secret."

"This is sad," Margo said. "Maybe you'll finally get the help you need."

"Did you help Tanner dispose of Sandra's body, or did Lynn?" I shook my head. "Della knew she was gone and likely dead." I remembered Della's somberness whenever I asked about the Other Girl. I shook my head. "You didn't help him with the body, but you must have heard Tanner talking about it."

She didn't speak.

"That's when you decided to escape. It took time, but eventually you goaded Tanner into beating you before we were all to go to the diner. He thought you were too beat up to move, but you weren't. You found a way out of that house. I thought you looked so bloodied and battered, but maybe that was an act, too. After we left, you got free and burned the house down."

Margo's face was stoic. "Keep spinning tales, Scarlett. It'll entertain us as we wait for the cops."

I glanced at Lynn on the bed. She was breathing. Weeping. Begging to be set free.

"Why did you decide to kill Tiffany after all this time?" Margo asked. "Was she blackmailing you?"

"I didn't kill her. I was trying to help her." My eyes narrowed. "Did you send that text to me this morning?"

"No." Margo looked past me to Lynn. "It's almost over. I'm here to save you. Drop the knife, Scarlett."

"You've been waiting for me. You set this up."

"No. I found you standing over this poor woman with a knife."

I tightened my grip around the handle. "This isn't what you think."

"It's your house. You stalked Lynn."

I realized how terrible this looked. In the distance police sirens grew louder. Margo was a cop, and she was right. No one would believe me. As the cops approached the warehouse, fury and anger rolled inside me. I was going to be arrested and thrown into a cell.

And Margo knew it. That same smile that lured me to the van appeared. Years of resentment flooded through me, stinging my muscles and burning my fingertips. I'd escaped, and now she was back to lock me up again. I'd gone willingly the first time. But not now.

I lunged toward Margo, the knife held high. She raised her weapon, but I was seconds faster. I plunged the knife into her shoulder and sliced across her chest. Howling in pain, she shoved me back hard.

As I raised the knife a second time, I heard a distant command ordering me to drop the weapon. My hands slick with blood, the knife slipped and cut my palm.

And then the zap of electricity seconds before prongs embedded in my chest and a jolt ripped through my body and paralyzed my muscles. I fell to the floor, unable to move or pull in a deep breath.

Strong hands pried the knife from my fingers. Metal clinked around one wrist as it was wrenched behind my back. The second cuff wrapped around my wrist and tightened until metal pinched my skin. My vision blurred as my body convulsed. I collapsed against the floor.

I saw Dawson move to Margo. When he spoke to her, his voice was full of concern. "Margo, hang tough."

"Help Lynn," Margo said. "Her breathing has been compromised."

"You're bleeding," he growled.

"I'll live."

As I lay immobile on the floor, Dawson shrugged off his jacket and pressed it to the wound slashed across Margo's chest. He called for an ambulance. Lynn began to weep.

All the chaos and noise swirled in my brain, just as it had when Tanner's van had crashed. I was getting swept up in a current too strong for me to fight. And I could feel that I was slipping inside myself just as I had in Tanner's basement cell.

Chapter Forty-Three

SCARLETT

Saturday, July 20, 2024
11:00 a.m.

I sat in the gray interview room bathed in shadows, windowless and stifling. Soundproof walls smelled of fear and worry, and the single table and two chairs were both stark and uncomfortable. Glancing up at the ceiling, I noted the wads of paper that had caught in the square white panels. How many people had sat in this chair and waited for someone like Dawson to ask difficult questions designed to incriminate?

I'd waited in a dark room before, but when the door opened, there was always a monster lurking. I closed my eyes, refusing to picture myself locked in a cell for the next three decades. If Della's goal was to reincarcerate me, she was well on her way.

Nerves tightened as my panic ticked up several notches. I had done nothing wrong. Della was the villain of this story. I should be cleared. Anger balled in my belly. Who was I kidding? Life didn't play fair.

I glanced down at the clean scrubs that swallowed my body and at my bandaged right hand. Margo's blood had made the knife handle slick, and the blade had cut my palm. Her blood and mine dotted my hands and neck, and the prongs of the Taser had left two angry red marks. I wasn't sure how long I'd been in this room.

After Tanner, the cops had been kind to me. They didn't keep me waiting in a room like this. They'd brought me water and coffee often when they spoke in soft tones. No handcuffs. They'd not been trying to intimidate me.

When footsteps echoed in the hallway, I sat a little straighter and closed my eyes. The door opened, lights flipped on, and as I slowly lifted my lids, it took a moment for my eyes to adjust. Dawson had a file tucked under his arm and two cups in his beefy hands. He took a sip from one, set the second one filled with water in front of me, and tossed the file on the table. He angled the chair on a diagonal near me and sat. Our knees were inches apart.

I threaded my fingers and sat back. If he thought he was scary, he'd have to try harder.

"How did we get here, Scarlett?"

"I want my lawyer." I was in over my head and needed his help.

"I'll call your lawyer soon."

"I'm only talking to Luke Kane, Detective Dawson."

"It could be a while. I'd hate for you to sit here any longer than necessary."

Maybe. Or maybe he wouldn't come at all. My life had been messy. Now it was a shit show. And my bench was shallow. "I was locked in a basement for eighty-eight days, remember? You'll have to try harder to intimidate me."

Margo must have still been in surgery. That knife had sliced through her silk blouse and into her flesh. I had no idea if I'd hit a major vessel and done real damage. I'd just wanted to stop her.

"Scarlett, let me help you. I want to get this sorted out so you can go home. Talk to me."

We were best friends now? He was my buddy? My pal? I'd sliced up his partner and girlfriend. I had no doubts about his objectives. "Lawyer first, Detective Dawson."

"We have footage of you speaking to your latest victim, and we've also confirmed you were one of the last people to see her alive. You also stalked and kidnapped a second woman. You'd have killed her if you'd not been stopped."

My chest was so tight, I could barely breathe. Had I been the last to see Tiffany alive?

"And I can also link you to the human remains found entombed in a wall." He tipped forward until his knees almost brushed mine. He knew I didn't like to be touched. "What set you off? Why call in the location of the first body that's been hidden for a decade? Why kill again after all these years?"

I didn't respond.

He sat back, as if he had all the time in the world. "Tell me about Della. Tell me how she hurt you."

I leaned back in my chair. "Not talking."

"You and me have history, Scarlett. You don't want another cop handling your case. I've seen you at your worst. Others won't understand you like I do."

"You understand me?" His words buzzed around my head in swirls of bullshit. My anger boiled through the ice and surfaced in my expression.

"Not talking."

"We must talk, Scarlett. You helped kill a woman, murdered another, and tried to suffocate a third. You put a cop in the hospital with a vicious stab wound. You called that officer *Della* multiple times. And this isn't the first time you've confused a woman with this Della."

My fingernails dug into the soft white Styrofoam.

Inhaling slowly, I replayed those last moments. I'd shoved my fingers into Tanner's eyes and the van had veered off course, hitting a ditch and falling on its side. I'd been thrown backward, my body pinging around in the metal van like a bouncing ball. When the van came to a stop, my bones hurt, blood dripped from my temple, and Tanner had been screaming, *I'm going to kill you!* And then he had stumbled out of the van, gun drawn, and shots had been fired. I was aware of Dawson talking now, but I wasn't paying attention until his tone sharpened.

"Nineteen stitches. Your knife left a nasty gash on your victim's neck and chest. The doctor said a few more centimeters to the left and you'd have severed her carotid artery. If she'd bled to death, you would be facing another murder charge."

My fingers tightened around the cup.

I'd passed out on the van floor, crumpling into a heap. I'd never asked who had killed Tanner. I'd simply been grateful he was dead.

"I was there when the van crashed a decade ago. I shot and killed Tanner Reed when he drew on me. I helped pull you from the wreckage," he said. "I'm on your side."

I inhaled and exhaled slowly.

Dawson had killed Tanner. He'd set me free. And now he was trying to lock me away.

"Breaks my heart when I think about pulling you out of that torn metal. What happened to you in that basement should never have happened to any person."

His jaw pulsed as he leaned forward, his knees brushing mine. The contact sent a softening wave through my body, and though I knew it was a ploy, the tenderness was comforting. "Were you always like this?" he asked. "Withdrawn, I mean? As a girl, were you outgoing?"

"You want to talk about my middle school years?" The question was almost amusing.

He tensed. "I want to start a dialogue with you. I want to help you."

"Then call my lawyer."

"At some point you and I are going to have to talk, Scarlett. You need to tell me what you know."

I'd been alone for a long time. I didn't love or embrace it, but solitude kept me safe. Now I realized how removed I was from the world.

"When did you first meet Officer Margo Larsen?"

I moistened my lips. "Is this information for the case or your own personal reference, Detective?"

He tensed and then slid back behind a blank stare. "What does that mean?"

"You know." I smiled, closed my eyes as I released the cup. As I drew in a deep breath, the muscles in my arms and hands eased. He was on the defensive now.

"When did you decide to stalk Margo Larsen?" he pressed. "I've seen the portrait you left for her in her apartment. Odd."

"Her name isn't Margo. It's Della."

"She's Officer Margo Larsen."

"When did you start screwing Della? Did you find her, or did she find you? What itch do you have that she scratched?"

His jaw tensed. "What's that mean?"

"Della found me. Her smile was so bright, it banished all my fears and worries. That smile lured me into Tanner Reed's van. That smile ruined my life."

He shifted and those knees retreated. "Margo Larsen isn't Della."

Frustration scraped under my skin. He didn't believe me and likely thought—like everyone else—that I was confused. "You're wrong. She's Della, and she's come back for me."

"You?"

Dawson didn't see what Margo was doing. His shocked gaze told me he didn't believe me. I sounded crazy, but I knew how clever Margo was and how well she calculated her moves. She'd flawlessly planned her own escape from Tanner's house, even willing to endure one of his beatings for her chance to run. And her vanishing act after the house fire had been flawless. It made perfect sense that she'd plan her return with such careful detail. How long had she been tracking Lynn, Tiffany, me, or even Dawson? Months? Years? "Does Margo know you killed Tanner?"

He sniffed, shifted his stance. "That information is in the files."

All easily accessible to another cop. "I bet she's read it cover to cover. That's exactly why she chose you."

He sat back, his expression blank. "What set you off? You had gotten on with your life and no one suspected you of anything. And then the call about the body."

Slowly, I shook my head. "You should be asking Della that question."

A sad smile tipped the edges of his lips as he reached in his pocket for a plastic evidence bag. He tossed the bag on the table between us. "Does that look familiar?"

I didn't look immediately, but his smug expression lured my gaze down. It was a silver chain hooked into either side of an engraved oval. The letters were *SC*. Seeing the piece of jewelry took me back to the house I'd shared with my mother. She'd given me the bracelet on my fourteenth birthday. It had been a rare moment of happiness for us both. "Tanner took all my clothes and jewelry."

"So, this is yours?"

Yes danced on the tip of my tongue, but I didn't dare utter it. I dropped my gaze and drew in a calming breath.

"Is that a yes or no?"

I didn't respond.

Dawson laid his hand on the bag, slowly dragged it toward him, and pocketed it. My heart sank as the one positive connection to my mother vanished.

"Getting Tiffany alone would've been easy, given your history," he said softly. "But what did you say to Lynn to lure her to your house? We have footage of you parked in front of her house early this morning."

"I thought she sent me a text."

I couldn't say now I'd been with Luke all night. I had been sitting in front of Lynn's house. Luke and I might not survive this, but he was decent enough not to abandon me. I hoped.

Dawson's chair creaked as he leaned back. "There's no record of a text on her phone."

"*Someone* sent me a text. Have you checked Della's phone?"

He sighed. "Margo said you kept calling her Della."

There was no point trying to convince Dawson. "When Luke arrives, then we'll speak."

"You confronted Lynn in a coffee shop. She said you were openly hostile." He stared into his coffee cup. "Hair fibers were pulled from Tiffany's body. DNA test results came back. Guess who's a match?"

I wasn't talking any more. More words led to more distortions and traps.

"Your DNA was found on Tiffany's body," Dawson said.

That wasn't a surprise. I'd driven her to her car, hugged her. However, Dawson fired questions for nearly thirty minutes as I repeatedly asked for and then demanded my attorney.

He chuckled as he shook his head. "How many times have you seen Della over the last decade?"

"I don't care if you believe me. Test Margo's DNA against the samples on Sandra's body. You'll find a match."

He shook his head. "Why would I go to the trouble?"

"Because under all the bluster, you care about the truth. Not many cops would put as much effort into Sandra's and Tiffany's murders."

It was his turn to stew in silence.

"Della was smart. Tanner 'had control' of her initially, but she learned manipulation from him and turned the tables. She had a way of getting in his ear. Maybe she's doing the same to you. She intentionally goaded him, so he'd beat her up. She convinced him she was broken and then waited for him to leave with me. It was her chance to escape. She knew he'd set bombs around the house. She set them off because she knew the fire would erase all traces of her."

Again silence.

"Does she make you feel special?" I asked.

Dawson closed his file folder and stood. "I'll let you know when your attorney calls, if he does."

When the door closed behind him, I stared at the four walls. My breath caught in my chest and constricted into a hard ball. I had survived Tanner. I would survive this.

Another two hours passed before I was moved to a larger room. This one was split in two by a glass wall, and the halves were linked by phone receivers. The door on the other side opened and Luke stepped inside. He was dressed in a dark suit, white shirt, and red tie. His face was stern, with no hint of the familiarity that I'd seen last night. He took the seat across from me and raised the phone to his ear. I did the same.

"Luke, thank you for coming. I know this is a lot to ask."

He shook his head, as if trying to wrap his head around all this. "Tell me what happened."

This meeting was all business, and as much as that stung, I had to suck it up. I needed him. He pulled out a yellow legal pad, and I explained everything I knew about Della/Margo, Sandra, Tiffany, and Lynn.

"Dawson is saying my DNA is on Tiffany's body. I drove her to her car and hugged her before I left. But I haven't seen her since that moment."

His stoic expression was impossible to read. "I doubt he has results yet. What about Lynn Yeats?"

"I looked her up online. I found out where she lived. Followed her to a coffee shop."

His jaw pulsed. "Why did you follow her?"

"I wanted to know what she knew about Tanner. I wanted to know if she knew I was in that basement."

"Do you believe she knew?"

I shoved out a sigh. "She knows more than she's admitted to the police. I don't think Tanner's secrets were that secret from her." I flexed my fingers. "Tiffany thought she heard the two of them arguing at the diner. Lynn said she was tired of helping Tanner with his 'shit.'"

"Tiffany is dead, and anything she told you about something she overheard ten years ago will be torn apart in court. She was an addict, and right now you have every reason to lie."

I shook my head. "I didn't hurt Lynn or Tiffany."

Luke's gaze narrowed into a hawkish glare. "This won't work if you lie to me. The first sniff I have of a lie, I'm leaving."

I raised my chin. "I'm not lying."

He stared through the glass for a long moment, the silence interrupted only by the closing of a hallway door and the tapping of my foot. As physically close as Luke was, the glass, coupled with his cool demeanor, wedged miles between us.

"Margo is Della," I said. "Della was smart, cunning. And not above shattering the rules to get what she wanted."

"Margo is a decorated police officer."

"Who specialized in human trafficking and assaults. Going after criminals like Tanner must have helped her get some sense of revenge against the man who hurt her. Go back and look at her cases. She told me how much she enjoyed watching a human trafficker suffer. There could be complaints against her buried under the arrest records."

"I'll dig into her file. But you understand how this all sounds, right?"

"Her mannerisms, her sense of humor, and her lack of boundaries—it's all Della. I know I'm right."

"Why is she back?"

"Unfinished business. What business, I don't know exactly."

His gaze held mine for a long moment. "I'll arrange bail. It might take time."

"Okay. Thank you."

His gaze lingered, and I could see the scrutiny. He was wondering if he'd been played. He was wise to worry. I'd learned so many tricks from Della.

Luke shook his head slowly before he rose and left.

◆ ◆ ◆

I was released an hour later. When I stepped into the crowded lobby, Luke was waiting for me. He didn't say anything as he guided me out of the building and across the lot to his car. Silent, we got into the car, and he didn't speak until we parked in front of my building. "Why are we here? Your apartment is a crime scene."

"I want to show you something." I got out of the car, walked to the front door, and tore the seal on my back door.

He followed quickly. "I am not seeing this."

I unlocked the doors. When we were inside, I locked them.

His gaze skimmed the locks on the doors, but he said nothing.

I guided him to my art studio, flipped on a light, and uncovered the painting I'd been working on for the last couple of days. He stood back and stared at it. "I just started this one. I've been painting this face for years. I think this is the fifty-sixth version of it. I gave the last painting like this to Margo."

"What do you mean *gave?*"

"I left it in her apartment. The desk clerk let me in."

He muttered an oath. "You entered her apartment without permission."

"I'd told her I'd give her a piece of art. We didn't agree on when."

He faced me. "When did you tell her this?"

"We had drinks a few days ago. It was her idea, not mine. She's moved in across the street from me. Her unit overlooks my place. She came to me."

"Or she moved into a new apartment and her new neighbor began to fixate on her."

"It could be spun that way."

"Is Margo the woman you saw when you fell off the rock wall and also bolted from the restaurant?"

"Yes."

His lips pursed as if he were holding back comment.

I shifted my focus back to the painting, wondering why I hadn't seen the truth earlier. "I've never been able to get the eyes right on all my versions of Della. I always painted her as a kind of victim. But she wasn't a victim. She willingly moved in with Tanner. She knew about Sandra Taylor, and I think she tried to save her by luring me into the van. But Sandra vanished, and when Della ended up with a ringside seat to my suffering, she realized Tanner was a monster she couldn't control. Something in her changed, and she started planning her escape. Maybe she hoped I'd escape Tanner at the diner; maybe she didn't care as long as she had time to get out of the house and set off Tanner's explosives. Either way, when Tanner and I left the house, she set the fires and vanished."

"Why didn't you tell me all this before?"

"Because it sounds outlandish. It sounds like I'm obsessed with a past I desperately can't release. I want to live a normal life. But knowing she was out there made it impossible."

He glanced at me and then back at the painting. "It's a haunting image."

"That's how I remember Della." I folded my arms, suddenly feeling raw and vulnerable. "She wasn't nearly as polished as she is now. She had long dark hair. Now she's cut it short, dyed it, lost weight, and had her nose changed. But it's her. Test her DNA against all the samples found on Sandra, Tiffany, and Lynn."

"You said this is the fifty-sixth version. Where are the other paintings?"

"I burned them. It's turned into a crazy ritual. I paint, obsess over remembering, and then when I can't look at the image anymore, I burn it."

His fingers flexed. "Tell me it's a controlled burn."

That prompted a slight smile. "Metal trash cans are a favorite. I'm odd, but not stupid."

"Why did you try to kill Officer Larsen?"

"When she came toward me, I saw Della. I felt trapped. And I struck out in defense."

"She's an officer of the law who found you with a potential victim."

"How did she know to come to my warehouse? What made her suspect that Lynn was here? I'd been with you the entire night. And then suddenly she appears, gun drawn, and finds Lynn tied to my bed."

"You left my place shortly before six a.m. The police report said the attack happened at six thirty a.m." The devil's advocate in him couldn't let go of the counterargument. "The timeline will not help your credibility."

I drew in a breath. "Margo must have been watching me from her apartment. I've seen her looking this way before. She saw me leave. And I'll bet she followed."

"The prosecutor will say that's guesswork."

"She appears in town just before the anonymous call that led cops to Sandra's body. And then she lands in the investigating officer's bed."

"Again, that's circumstantial. I'd argue that Margo took a new job, you saw her, and it triggered you. You made the 9-1-1 call, killed Tiffany, and kidnapped Lynn."

"No. Margo is orchestrating all this." I shook my head. "Margo has gotten under Dawson's skin. He has a protective vibe for her. You said he bent the rules to shield his wife."

"If they are sleeping together, it wouldn't bode well for him." He shoved out a breath. "And it won't help your defense when it's disclosed that we're sleeping together."

"For the record, I slept with you because I like you. Not because I needed a lawyer."

"I want to believe you and Della aren't playing a version of the same game."

"I'm not playing." I shook my head. "The Della I knew was clever and smart. She knows how to manipulate. She sent me a text luring me to Lynn's town house so she had time to transport Lynn to my warehouse."

"What's Margo's endgame?"

"Clean up loose ends. Lynn, Tiffany, me." The statement sounded outlandish.

"Why wait ten years?"

"Maybe she needed time. Escape, recover from her stretch with Tanner, and build a new life. Maybe working human trafficking cases was enough until it wasn't. She returns out of a sense of guilt or maybe justice for Sandra? I don't know."

"Why move in across the street from you?"

"Obsession? Or maybe she likes elaborate games and living on the edge. I don't know."

He didn't respond.

"Dawson showed me a bracelet. It was found with Sandra Taylor's body, and I didn't admit this to Dawson, but it was mine. Tanner took it from me. Took everything from me."

"Not everything," he said softly.

I wanted to take his hand in mine and tether myself to the present. "I'm sorry I pulled you into this. I didn't know who else to contact."

He was silent for a long moment. "Let me make calls. Find out what's happening."

"I'm sorry."

His gaze met mine. "We'll talk soon."

Chapter Forty-Four

DAWSON

Saturday, July 20, 2024
5:00 p.m.

When Dawson arrived at the hospital, Margo was in recovery and the doctor reported that she had come through the surgery well. The doctor had repaired muscle and nerve damage and patched her up. She'd recover fully.

He thought back to the night they met. She'd come up to him. Her smile had been infectious. And what happened in that bedroom had bonded him to her. Had she read him and summed him up as a lost soul like Della had Scarlett?

Della. Shit. Now he was thinking like Scarlett.

As he stood outside Margo's hospital room, he glanced at his empty hands. Should he have flowers? But if he had flowers, it was proof he wasn't an objective cop when it came to her. They'd see him as the cock-trapped ass that he was.

They'd slept together multiple times, and he'd do it again in a heart-beat. She was a hard woman to quit. But that had to stay in the past until he sorted this all out.

In the dimly lit room, she was lying on her back. Her eyes were closed. Her expression was always so controlled and stern, and now sleeping, she looked years younger. As he sat beside her bed, her eyes fluttered open immediately.

"You're supposed to be sleeping," he said.

"I never really sleep," Margo said.

"The hospital would like an emergency contact." He inched his chair closer to the bed.

"I don't have one."

"No one?"

"Nope." She raised a brow. "Don't look stunned."

"I'm not."

"I'm a big girl." She moistened her lips. "Who's your person?"

He filled a pink plastic cup with water and held it to her lips. She drank, smiled. "Once it was my wife. Now, I'm not so sure."

"I kind of thought for a fleeting second that you could be my emergency call."

"I'm not. I can't until all this is sorted out."

She tried to sit up but winced. "I know."

He arranged the pillows behind her until she appeared more comfortable. "You'll be as good as new in a couple of weeks."

"Where's Scarlett?" she asked.

"Arrested. Bailed out now."

Tension creased her brow. "She made bail?"

"She has a good attorney."

"Have you talked to Lynn Yeats yet?"

"She's next on my list." Odd, he didn't want to tell Margo that Lynn was two floors down in the same hospital. Had the seeds of Scarlett's doubts rubbed off on him?

"Good."

"Why were you at Scarlett's house?" he asked.

"She told me to meet her at the warehouse. She had something to tell me."

"How did she reach out?"

"We passed on the street. I had to run up to my place. When I came back, it all went sideways."

"Why bring Lynn to her warehouse and tie her up? Why not just kill her?"

"She wanted Lynn to confess," Margo said. "All these years of not knowing if Lynn had helped Tanner ate away at her."

"She painted pictures of Della, not Lynn."

A soft smile tipped her lips. "I can't explain all of Scarlett's drama right now. Give me a day or two."

Not drawn in by her humor, he mentally imposed the sketches of Della over Margo's face. The images were close, but close didn't count in court. He'd need DNA proof. "Confess to what?"

"Lynn helped Tanner. She knew what was happening in the basement."

"Why do you say that?"

"I read the original interviews. Gut feeling, but she was lying. But instinct isn't proof."

Margo didn't have evidence. Would she have drugged and bound Lynn for a confession? "Do you want to make your statement now?"

"Are you here for my statement or as a friend?" Margo asked.

"The statement can wait."

"I can give it now," she said. "I don't want to forget a detail."

"I know. But wait. You know it takes a good night's sleep to process a trauma like this."

"I'm fine. I'm not your average victim. I'm a cop."

"Still a human, last I checked, so we'll wait." The nurse came into the room. She was carrying a tray of bland, simple shrink-wrapped food.

Margo grimaced. "Yum."

"Let me refill your water jug," Dawson said as the nurse set the tray in front of Margo. He took the cup and pitcher to the sink. Water, ripe with DNA, glistened on the edges of the glass. If the DNA on Sandra's body was viable, it would answer a lot of questions. He'd pull Margo's DNA in her personnel file so he could put an end to the doubts.

When he turned, Margo was watching as the caregiver opened a cup of broth. She scowled. "Don't suppose you have wine?"

The caregiver shook her head. "No, ma'am."

When the woman left, he handed Margo a fresh cup of water. "Don't look so grim."

"I'm all smiles," Margo said, finding that electric grin.

"I've got to get going." He was tempted to lean in for a kiss, but it felt too civilized for them.

"Talk to Lynn Yeats. I know she must be in this building some-where. She'll have an idea of who took her. And she knows more than she's said about Tanner."

"Gut feeling?"

She shifted, winced. "It's only steered me wrong once in my life."

"When was that?"

She laughed. "For another day."

"I'll return tomorrow."

"Be ready to bust me out of here. If you don't spring me, I'll break myself out. I'm an excellent escape artist. Brilliant with locks."

Like Della. "Your release depends on the doctor."

"I'm outta here come hell or high water, Dawson."

"To be negotiated."

He needed the damn DNA test results to nip his growing doubts. For years he'd had misgivings about his wife, but he'd ignored them. He wouldn't now. And once Margo was in the clear, or not, he'd deal with Scarlett.

Dawson left her staring after him. She reminded him of a trapped animal doing its best to cling to bravado.

He rode the elevator to the third floor and found Lynn Yeats's room and knocked. Inside, a television clicked off. "Come in."

He moved into the dimly lit room and found Lynn lying in her bed, IVs hooked up to her arm. The doctors had told him she'd been heavily sedated and the plastic on her face had come close to killing her. She'd been at the critical stage of hypoxia.

"Detective Dawson." Her voice was rough, jagged.

"Ms. Yeats." He moved to the side of the bed. "How're you doing?"

A romantic comedy played out on the muted television screen. "Okay. Better."

"I hate to bother you now, but I'd like to ask you a few questions." He'd called the hospital and spoken to Lynn's boss. She had a solid reputation as a floor nurse. However, she'd changed hospitals five times in the last decade. Digging deeper, he'd found reprimands on her record. Not enough to trip a criminal investigation but enough to force her out of the job.

"Sure." She sat up and turned off the television.

"Mind if I sit?"

"No, go ahead."

He pulled up a chair, sat, and flipped through a notebook that didn't have many clean pages remaining. "For my own understanding, can I confirm a few facts?"

"Sure."

"You and Tanner Reed met at Mike's Diner in January of 2014."

"January 15. It was cold and windy. I ducked in for breakfast before my morning shift."

"You were a regular at Mike's, correct?"

"Yes."

"A little off the beaten path for you, wasn't it? Opposite direction of your work from your house."

"Not at the time. I worked closer to the diner, but it wasn't super convenient. But I also never ran into doctors or nurses from the hospital. I closed my mind to work completely when I was off duty."

"Was it love at first sight?"

She plucked at the hospital identification band. "I was attracted to him. He was a beautiful man. But I never thought he'd notice me."

"But he did."

"Yeah."

"Magical, right? When I met my wife, it was at a fundraiser for a circus. She was working the dunking pool. I knew the second I met her, I had to talk to her. But she's the one that made the opening line. Who made the first move with you and Tanner?"

"He did. I thought he was talking to someone else at first."

"That's how I felt about my wife. I never thought I had a shot, but I went for broke. How long before your first date?"

"We met in the diner for breakfast several days a week for a couple of months. He asked me out for the first time in late March."

About the time Sandra had vanished. "You two hit it off right away?"

"We did. It all started to feel very natural."

He flipped back pages. "You said you met his cousin at his house."

"Yes. The young girl. Dark hair. Quiet."

"Did you speak to the girl?"

"Just smiled at her."

"How did Tanner react when you met his cousin?"

"A little tense. But he covered it with a smile."

"Her name was Cindy?"

"I think so. But I didn't realize he had no family then. So much I didn't know."

"Did Cindy seem stressed?"

"No. She was just quiet. I didn't stay long, and we really didn't speak." She cleared her throat. "Who was she?"

"That's what I'm trying to figure out."

"She wasn't Scarlett Crosby."

"I know." He shifted. "Tell me about this recent attack. What's the last thing you remember?"

She blinked as if shifting mentally. "I was headed to my car. I'd been out with a friend having drinks."

"What time was this?"

"About two a.m. We'd stayed until last call."

"Who is the friend?"

"Debbie Watson."

"Did she walk you to your car?"

"No. I said goodbye at the bar."

"What bar?"

"Riptide."

"I know the place." It was a middle-range wine bar featuring acoustic guitars, painting nights, and book clubs. His ex-wife had loved it. "The doctors found Rohypnol in your bloodstream. Did you feel woozy?"

"The date rape drug," she said quietly. "I felt buzzed, but I was fine when I got in my car. I keep a water bottle in the side console."

"You drank from it?"

"I guzzled it. I'm obsessed with hydration."

"When did you get woozy?"

"Almost as soon as I pulled up in front of my house. I could barely see straight."

"That was about two thirty a.m.?"

"Yes."

If her water bottle had been spiked, it could have been done at any time after Lynn entered the bar. "What's your last memory?"

Her hand rose to her throat. "Sitting behind the wheel of my car. And then nothing. The next memory, I was struggling to breathe. I couldn't open my eyes. And then I heard a slicing sound."

"When the plastic was pulled free, what did you see?"

"Scarlett standing over me." Tears welled in her eyes. "And another woman. They were fighting. Then you showed up."

Her story jibed with the evidence and what he'd witnessed. "Mind if I backtrack a little?"

"Sure."

Pages in his notebook spun backward. "I checked into Tanner's finances. You cosigned for a few loans for him."

"He had big dreams for his business. I wanted to help him."

"The loans added up to a hefty amount. Fifty thousand dollars."

"I believed in him."

"You loved him."

"I did. I look back and wonder how, but I did love him."

"Sandra Taylor's body was found in the house he was flipping for a client."

"It was charming. Had potential."

"So, you were in the house?"

"A couple of times, when I had a day off."

"Did he demolish any walls?" Dawson asked.

"A few."

"You were head over heels in love with the guy."

She nodded slowly. "Yes. I thought I'd hit the jackpot."

He understood. "You'd have done anything."

"I loved him," she repeated.

He leaned back and did his best to look genuinely curious. "Were you aware of the box under Tanner's bed?"

She paled. "What box?"

"According to Scarlett, Tanner locked another girl in that box while he was with you." Anger surged, but he tamped it down. Lynn Yeats was now on the testing list for the DNA found on Sandra Taylor's body, and he'd know soon if she was lying.

Her eyes widened. She blinked. "I never knew that."

He smelled fear. "Never heard a sound?"

"Nothing."

"Okay. I'm not making an accusation. Just trying to understand. You met Tiffany at Mike's Diner, right?"

"As I told you, I was aware of her."

"Did Tanner talk about Tiffany?"

"No." Her voice sounded low. Childlike. "Not at all."

"But he flirted with her."

"Tanner flirted with everyone." Bitterness edged the words.

"You're right about that. I might have to reach out to you again."

"Sure, of course. What's going to happen to Scarlett?"

"She's been charged and released."

Panic widened her eyes. "She's out of jail?"

"For now. Don't worry. We're keeping an eye on her. Do you have a friend you can stay with?"

"Yeah."

"Bunk with your friend for a few days. Maybe Debbie. I'm close to sorting this out."

"What if Scarlett comes for me again?"

"We're watching her."

"Okay."

"Don't worry," he said, standing. "You're going to be fine."

As Dawson left the room, he dialed the familiar number of former prosecutor Luke Kane. There was no love lost between them, and he wasn't sure the man would take his call. Kane answered on the first ring. "What do you want?"

"I have no favors to call in. And I need several."

"I'm listening."

"I need the DNA found on Sandra Taylor's and Tiffany Patterson's bodies done yesterday. You still have contacts at the lab."

"A few."

"One way or the other, we need to know if Scarlett or Lynn Yeats was involved in either murder."

"Or Della, a.k.a. Margo, right?"

Tension radiated up his spine. "Yes."

"I'll make a few calls."

Chapter Forty-Five

Dawson

Wednesday, July 24, 2024
10:00 a.m.

Luke, good to his word, had pulled a few major strings, and the techs in Richmond had moved his samples to the top of the pile. Answers would arrive any day. Dawson realized he needed the DNA to exonerate Margo, likely just as much as Kane wanted to clear Scarlett.

Dawson arrived at the hospital to check Margo out. She'd been ordering the doctor to release her for days, but they'd insisted she remain in the hospital. He found her dressed in sweats and a loose button-down shirt. She'd washed her hair and applied red lipstick and was sitting in a wheelchair but didn't look happy about it.

"It's a quick ride to the front door," he said.

She arched a brow. "I considered arguing with the nurse, but she looked tired, and she's young. However, I'm perfectly capable of walking out of here. By the way, you look stressed," Margo said.

"I'm always stressed."

"More than usual."

"Maybe."

A nurse arrived and pushed her wheelchair out of the room. They checked out at the nurses' station, and then he angled the chair into the elevator.

Outside, she tipped her face to the sun, soaking in the light. "You have a thing for sunshine," he said.

"Most people do as long as they aren't vampires."

"True."

His car was parked by the entrance, and he opened the passenger-side door. The nurse edged the wheelchair close to the car. Margo lifted herself out of the chair and lowered into his car.

"Good?" the nurse asked.

"Never better."

"Call if you start bleeding or have pain," the nurse said.

"Will do."

As the nurse pushed the wheelchair back into the hospital, Dawson closed the door and came around to the driver's side. Behind the wheel, he started the engine.

She shifted in her seat and rested a hand on his thigh. "How about you stay over? You said you could do wonders on an air mattress."

He shook his head. "You just got out of the hospital."

"I'm fitter than I look."

That prompted a smile. "No doubt."

"Then stay."

"Give it a day or two."

She pouted in a charming way. "You're too good. I need to corrupt you more."

He refused to think about her naked and willing under him. "In a day or two."

When they arrived at her place, he parked out front. She'd not asked once about Scarlett, and as he helped her out of her car, she didn't glance toward the warehouse. Victims of attack generally showed some change in behavior. False bravado, reserved to the point of shutting down, or skittish and weepy. She was none of these. She was who she always was.

As he came around to her side of the car, she'd already opened her door and started to rise. He reached for her elbow, but she brushed him away.

"I told you. I'm fine. Stop fussing."

He stood back, and as she moved around the car, he shut the door. Some might have felt like Judas in his position, but he didn't. Still, he needed to prove to himself more than anyone that he'd not made a mistake with her.

As they rode up the elevator, the soft scent of hand lotion floated around him. She'd left three buttons of her top undone, drawing his attention to the slight side curve of her breast.

The doors opened and he followed her to her apartment. When they stepped inside, the naked floor plan was still stripped of furniture and had a stark, unwelcoming feel. Immediately, his gaze was drawn to the portrait hanging on the wall. Della. He was getting to know that face well.

"Interesting choice of art," he said.

"From my new best friend, Scarlett." She dropped her purse on the kitchen counter.

"Want me to take it down?" He couldn't pull his eyes from the portrait.

"No. I kind of like it."

"Why?"

She shook her head. "It offers me insight into Scarlett. Maybe even myself."

"How so?"

"Della is Scarlett's obsession. If you can identify a person's fixation, you'll understand them better."

"What are you fixated on?"

She laughed. "We don't have enough hours in the day."

Damn, but he liked her. "Are you sure you want to stay here?"

"Of course." A smile flickered on her lips. "Good to be home."

As she moved toward the window that faced the street, she stopped. She sucked in a quick breath and stared down at Scarlett's warehouse.

"Assault charges have been filed against Scarlett," he said.

As if he'd not spoken, Margo pressed her hand to her side as if it hurt. "Why did she choose Lynn Yeats as a victim?"

"Scarlett wanted to know if Lynn was aware of Tanner's activities."

"Lynn's head was wrapped in plastic. She was on the verge of suffocating. Hard to ask questions of a dead person. Whoever took her wanted her dead."

"Or maybe it was a tactic to scare the shit out of her," Dawson said. "Remind her of how Sandra Taylor might have died."

"So she could reveal her secrets?"

"Maybe," he said.

"Fair enough. But why would Scarlett kill Tiffany? Scarlett's gone out of her way to help that woman."

"Manner of death was a blow to the back of the head. Maybe it was a moment of anger and frustration. Tiffany was stalking off and Scarlett lashed out."

"Has the DNA taken from Sandra's body come in yet?" she asked.

"Not yet."

She faced him, looking mildly curious. "When it does, are you afraid it'll prove I'm Della?"

The worry had stalked him for days. Scarlett was so convinced. "Are you?"

Her smile was small, half-hearted. "If I were Della, then I'd have a long and sad story. My guess is that she was a girl with a broken family and was so bruised, she was easy prey for a charming man who promised a family and stability." She drew in a breath.

Was she relating to the combined experiences of the victims she'd helped over the years, or was she talking about herself?

"And then, he stopped being so nice. That's how it goes, right? He became very abusive, making her do terrible things. He locked her in a box under his bed while he ate his breakfast or screwed his girlfriend. Amazing what can be heard from a box under the bed."

Despite all the legal ramifications of what she could be saying, he heard pain burning under the words, and his heart broke for her. He'd have pulled her into his arms if he thought she'd accept tenderness.

"Who are we talking about?" he asked.

She shook her head. "Any one of a thousand different Dellas I've helped in my career. They're all very much alike. Hard to judge a lost soul."

"You've got a reputation. I asked around. You've had a few questionable arrests with human traffickers."

"You mean a few tripped? That's not my fault." She leaned forward. "Do you know one guy who slipped in front of me had just fled from a house where he kept a girl nailed, *nailed*, to the floor?" Her eyes glistened. "A few bruises don't compare. And thankfully for men like that, I'm a cop and I can only bend the law so far."

"You're a ballbuster."

An amused brow arched. "Literally, not just figuratively."

"No judgment here." He shifted his stance, shoving aside a wave of pity for the girl in the portrait. "What would Tanner have said to a girl like Della to convince her to lure another girl into his world?"

"Acceptance, security, threats. That's the standard menu for men like Tanner. Scarlett's no different than Della. She was craving the same things."

"I understand why love is important," he said.

"You can, and you can't. You're an adult male with experience. But a fifteen-year-old girl . . . the world eats them up like candy."

"Would a guy like Tanner tell Della about Sandra?"

"If he wanted to manipulate her. Threats are more effective sometimes if they are against someone else. But as Scarlett said, Della, if she was real, was smart. Della realized there could be others."

"Why did Scarlett target Lynn?"

Margo's expression grew pensive. "Have you dug into Lynn's past as I asked?"

"Yeah. Lynn dated another guy after Tanner. Five years ago. Gus Green. He was arrested for attempted kidnapping. He's serving time now."

"Think Lynn has a type?"

"Or really shitty taste in men."

"Lynn strikes me as selfish, narrow minded, small. She thought she had a good thing and wasn't giving it up, even if her boyfriend had a nasty habit of locking girls in the basement."

"There's no proof of that."

"Unless we can get her to talk."

Sadness rolled through Dawson. He wanted to believe happenstance had brought them together. But the roots of doubt were burrowing deeper. "Are you Della?"

She shook her head, her gaze lingering on his. "Would it matter?"

Vulnerability flashed so quickly in her gaze that he wasn't sure whether it was real. It would take a lot to turn him away from Margo. Hell, a lot might not even be enough. "Let me take the portrait so you don't have to look at it."

"Would it matter?" she asked again.

"No."

She nodded, her frown softening a fraction. "Leave it. I like it. The painting really is very good."

"Are you sure?"

She smiled at him. "Very."

Chapter Forty-Six

SCARLETT

Wednesday, July 31, 2024
9:00 p.m.

It had been a week and a half since I'd stabbed Margo. I kept watch on her apartment, and the light was always on. A couple of times, I'd look up and I'd find her staring down. Once, she waved. I'd not seen Luke since he bailed me out, but we'd spoken on the phone several times. When we talked the last time, he told me that, because of our relationship, he had a new attorney lined up for me to meet the next day. Attorney. Charges. Prison.

Now, as I unlocked my front door, a bag of groceries in hand, I looked up. Margo was there, sipping a glass of wine. Watching.

I closed the door behind me, but like I had all week, I didn't lock it. I put my groceries away and moved to my art studio and stood in front of the canvas, staring at Della version #56. At this stage of the painting project, nervous anticipation electrified my body. I was filled with hope that this time, this version of Della would be just right, and when I looked at her, I could finally let her go.

I mixed paints and began to flesh out Della's face. This version wasn't as full and round as it had been. The angles of the jaw and the cheeks were slimmer, sleeker, like the reinvented Della turned Margo. I shadowed the chin and the cheekbones and then roughed in thin plucked brows.

It was another fifteen minutes before I heard the front door open. My heart rammed against the inside of my chest. I'd spent a decade locked away in this warehouse, and in many ways, I was still trapped in Tanner's basement room.

Gripping the paintbrush, I refused to look away from the sketch, but my strokes slowed.

When I heard clipped footsteps, I stilled.

"You're kind of obsessed with her, aren't you?"

Lynn's ragged voice was coated with smugness. But she wasn't amused. She held up her phone. "You texted me?"

"I always struggle with the eyes," I said, ignoring her question. "I could never understand them. Was she a jailer or a victim? Until I understood her, I couldn't finish the portrait."

"Why do you care? Tanner is dead and gone. His legacy is dust."

"I doubt he'll ever leave my life for good. Same with Della. Same with you. The four of us are fused forever."

"Why did you text me?" Lynn asked.

I studied her quizzical gaze. I had no idea what she was talking about. Was this another lie? Another attempt to cover up her past? Instead of a denial, I played along. "The odd thing about it all is that I hated her, and I also loved her. I missed her."

Lynn didn't speak, but her gaze sharpened as she stared at the portrait.

"For months, it was the two of us." My voice was soft and rough. "Locked in that room. We shared a life no one else in the world would understand."

Lynn stilled. "You wanted to save her?"

"I did. I thought if I rescued her, I'd save myself. We're not so different."

"You didn't turn Tiffany over to Tanner, so you're different."

"I was seconds away from shoving Tiffany into the van. A second or two is all that divides me from Della."

"But you didn't. And you and Tiffany escaped. And Tanner was killed."

"You loved him, didn't you?"

"Very much." She stared at me in silence. Her stillness suggested I'd cut into a nerve and she was afraid to react for fear she'd reveal something important.

"Why are you here? Aren't you afraid of me?" I asked.

"No. And for the record, I'm not paying you a dime. Tiffany tried to blackmail me, and it didn't end well for her."

So, Tiffany had tried to get money out of Lynn. That was motive for murder. "You think I'm trying to blackmail you like Tiffany did?"

Irritation darkened Lynn's gaze. "Yes."

"You think blackmail. The cops think I kidnapped you."

Her gaze hardened. "You did. Or had someone you know do it."

"Why would I do that?" I thought about Luke and how he could shift a conversation with questions. Like Della, he understood strategy.

"To scare me. To make me feel like you did when Tanner took you. You and your make-believe Della blame me for not knowing you were in the basement."

"Everyone keeps telling me Della's not real," I said. "But you know she's real, right? You knew Tanner had a young girl in his house." My anger was rising, and I struggled to keep my voice even. Could Lynn have saved Della or even Sandra if she'd called the cops? "You knew Tanner locked Della in a box under his bed when you two had sex, didn't you?"

Her reaction was oddly calm. "You told that lie to Dawson. And like I told him, I didn't know about the box."

There was no horror or shock. No rush to deny. A normal person would have been horrified. "I think you did know." I dropped my voice. "The box under the bed was an unspoken dirty secret between you and

Tanner, wasn't it? Knowing Della was locked up turned you on. You liked having control over another girl's life, didn't you?"

As Lynn shook her head, her eyes danced with an evil delight. Her hand slid into her pocket. "No. That's sick. I'm not like that."

The denial sounded like it had been crafted for a jury. "You said Tiffany tried to blackmail you. What did she have against you?"

"Nothing." Her confidence flickered a fraction. "She was bluffing."

"Her addiction had gotten bad. She was desperate for money. Did she remember an overheard conversation you had with Tanner at the diner a decade ago? A whisper about Della, Sandra, or me? Were you worried about Tanner's growing collection of girls?"

"Nothing so complicated. Tiffany was a dumb waitress who could barely pour a cup of coffee. She made up shit just to get a reaction."

How many times had I been accused of lying? *Scarlett, you don't know what you're talking about. Stop making up stories.* "Tiffany was always listening at Mike's Diner, wasn't she? No one notices the girl in the uniform behind the counter, do they?"

Lynn's face paled. Her jaw pulsed.

"She did hear you and Tanner talking about his girls, didn't she? Maybe he was worried about having three women locked in his house."

"You're again making up stories that you'll never prove," Lynn said. "I'm the one you stalked. I was the one kidnapped, remember? I didn't attack the cop. That was all you. You're the one going to prison for a long time."

Legally, I was in bad shape. But the more I studied her, the more I saw the truth of what she'd done. Luke would press me to keep asking questions. Get her to talk. Earn her trust. "You killed Tiffany, didn't you? She wanted money to fund her drug habit. If she texted you, her phone records will prove a connection."

"She was a greedy little monster. And no one is going to miss a dead drug addict."

"She didn't deserve to die."

A low chuckle rumbled in Lynn's chest. "You're guessing now. You're trying to get me to say something. But there's nothing to say." The fingers on her left hand flexed into a fist.

"You'll never say anything against Tanner. He had as much control over you as me. You were just a puppet to him."

"He loved me." Her eyes narrowed.

"No, he didn't. He used you."

She tensed and then shook her head as if catching herself. "You're gutsy. What nerve it must have taken to challenge Tanner at the end. I'm certain he would've killed you the first chance he got. He wasn't the kind of guy who bluffed."

"You helped him."

"No."

I moved a step closer to her. Why would Tanner have reached out to a plain woman like Lynn? What could she have done for him? "You're a nurse. You've had access to drugs for years. Whatever he shoved in my arm made me woozy. Did you provide Tanner with the drugs he shoved in my system?"

"He said he couldn't sleep. He needed the drugs to shut off his brain for a few hours."

So, she had provided drugs to Tanner. "Or keep the girl in the box quiet? Or help him grab a new girl?"

"Where are you getting these ideas?" she demanded. "You have no proof."

Luke had said circumstantial evidence was enough for a search warrant. "It occurred to me when I saw you in the coffee shop that Tanner's innocent girlfriend might actually know everything." This dancing back and forth was becoming grating. She was either going to bolt or come at me. I hoped Margo was still paying attention to my warehouse. If she had set all this up, she wasn't the type to miss the grand finale.

Lynn's gaze returned to the portrait. "I bet when you first met Tanner, he made you feel like you were the only girl in the world. That first hit of his affection is addictive. Without the glow of his attention, the world feels flatter, smaller."

"You still miss him," I said. "You really loved him."

"Yes." Sadness dripped from the word. "I loved—love—him."

"There was a moment when we first met that I might have done anything for him," I said. Like Dawson and Luke, I kept my tone even, friendly. I wanted her to believe I understood her. "I know you felt that magic, too. It was so thrilling."

"Yes. It was magic."

And there it was: my opening. "You fell in love with him hard. And then one day you realized you were in too deep with him. You'd seen his cousin. You'd sensed something wasn't right about the basement. But his words could be so sweet. And his smile was so intoxicating. You must have been shocked when he asked you to help him hide Sandra's body. God knows, I'd have been."

"I was shocked. I refused at first."

The dam had cracked and now I needed to bust through the rest. "But he could be so convincing," I whispered. "He fooled me, too."

Tears welled in her eyes as she nodded.

"Tiffany starts blackmailing you, and the house where Sandra's body was hidden was undergoing renovations. The past was coming back in full force, so you decided to get ahead of it, right? Did you call in the location of Sandra's body? Was the guilt just too much?"

"I didn't make that call," she rushed to say. "I thought it was you."

Her genuine surprise was something I didn't expect. "No. It wasn't me."

Oddly, I believed her. But if Lynn didn't make the 9-1-1 call, who did? Della?

Lynn moved toward me, her expression serene—relieved, almost— as if this were a conversation she'd been wanting to have for a decade. Finally, she could share bottled secrets.

Tanner had told me secrets, but that had scared me. He could be honest with me because he'd known one day, he'd kill me. I tensed as

Lynn moved closer. As I stepped back, she pulled a syringe out of her pocket. The point glistened wet in the light.

"If you're looking for absolution, you won't get it."

"I don't need forgiveness. I need to end this." Lynn's voice was steady. "Time to free you from Tanner."

When she lunged, my body coiled with tension. I jumped back, pushing Della's portrait toward her. She shoved it aside with an unholy ease and thrust with the needle. It grazed the side of my arm, but I stumbled left, grabbed the canvas, and batted it toward the syringe.

I'd lamented the damage Tanner had done for years, sure it had crippled me for the rest of my life. But the wounds had healed, and the scars were now fading to a pale white. They would always be there, but they weren't sensitive to the touch any longer. I didn't want to lose the life I had now.

Lynn dived toward me, her face tightening with a determination she'd nurtured at Tanner's hands. The tip of the needle scraped against my arm, this time catching the fabric of my shirt. I stumbled back.

Outside, I heard shouts, and I screamed for help. Lynn barely looked back as she came for me again.

Dawson rushed into the warehouse, his gun drawn, putting himself between me and Lynn. He pointed the gun at her. "Stop."

She halted as shock, confusion, and then acceptance morphed her expression. She looked toward me. "Detective Dawson."

"Put the needle down," he said.

"She came at me," Lynn said. "I just wanted to talk to her. And then she rushed me. I wrestled the needle away from her."

"Put the syringe down," Dawson said.

She shook her head, her eyes now wide with panic before they narrowed on me. "Scarlett just confessed to me that she killed Tiffany. She called in the location of Sandra's body."

I stood still and silent, unable to argue with her lies.

"Drop the needle," Dawson said.

The front door to the warehouse opened, and two uniformed cops arrived, guns drawn.

Lynn looked at him, tears glistening now in her eyes. Her face hardened, but he didn't waver. And then she smiled as she raised the tip of the needle to her neck and jammed it into her jugular vein. She shoved the plunger down. Droplets of blood gushed over her pale neck and stained the collar of her light-blue T-shirt. She staggered. Dawson moved toward her, but she stepped back and then fell to the ground.

Her gaze shifted to me. Tears spilled down her cheeks. She dropped the needle. Color draining from her face, she began to shake.

Lynn looked at Dawson. "I should've killed you."

Dawson reached for his phone and called for an ambulance. He knelt beside her, and I handed him a clean cloth from my workbench. He pressed the fabric to her neck.

"Don't try so hard," Lynn whispered. "Let me go."

"No."

She smiled.

Her face had paled to the color of porcelain, and her skin had cooled to the touch. She began to convulse, and her eyes rolled back in her head before they closed.

The rescue squad arrived and pushed Dawson aside. They checked for vitals, and as one began chest compressions, the other readied a defibrillator. Her shirt open, the paddles were pressed against her chest. They shocked her once, twice, and three times. They worked on her for about ten minutes before they declared her barely stable. Minutes later she was wheeled out on a stretcher.

"Scarlett, are you all right?" Dawson said. "Did she stick you?"

I brushed my hand over the scratch on my arm. "No. I'm fine. Did you hear what she said?"

"Yes. Every word." He shook his head.

Luke had brokered a deal with Dawson. I would act as bait to get a confession from Lynn. All I had known was to expect her to make a move. "You sent her the text?"

"That was Margo's idea."

I shoved out a sigh, not sure whether I was grateful or angry to be set up as bait. I'd bet money Margo had sent me the text that lured me to Lynn's town house to buy time to bring Lynn here. Was this all about coaxing a confession out of Lynn? "Did Margo admit she's Della?"

"No," he said.

As other uniforms arrived, Margo eased through the crowd and came toward me. "You look no worse for wear." She was so easygoing, as if she already knew the ending to this story.

"You knew Lynn was aware of Tanner's secrets, didn't you?"

"I had a good idea," Margo said. "She was obsessed with Tanner, and I suspect still blames you and Dawson for his death. But she'd have blamed anyone for Tanner's demise other than Tanner. The world is a better place without them."

"Who called 9-1-1 with the location of Sandra's body?"

"I don't know," Margo said.

"Who kidnapped Lynn and left her here?" I knew before she spoke that she wouldn't give me a straight answer. Della never played all her cards.

Margo arched a brow. "That's another question I can't answer. Maybe Lynn made the call and tried to frame you for Tiffany's murder."

Lynn's panic had been real when I pulled the plastic from her face. She'd not set that scene up. But it was a Margo kind of move. "I stabbed you."

Margo waved her hand. "Bygones. You were understandably upset. I won't be testifying against you, and I'll insist my wound was caused by an accident."

"Why? I stabbed you. I could have killed you."

"But you didn't, did you? And you did find yourself in a very confusing and stressful situation."

"Did you set it all up?"

Before she could answer, Luke pushed through the front door, his face tight with worry. Relief flooded my body. "Who called him?"

"Me," Margo said. "He wanted to know the moment Lynn appeared here."

"So that's it?" I asked. "I'm off the hook. Case closed?" My hands trembled as the adrenaline raced through my system. All this time, and now it was over?

"As far as I'm concerned, yes. Time we both moved on, don't you think?"

Six hours later, I stood in Luke's shower, hot water pelting my chilled skin and the red scrapes from Lynn's needle trailing up my arm. Old images of Tanner flashed. He'd come as close to killing me a decade ago as Lynn had today. I'd escaped them, but Sandra and Tiffany had not.

The DNA on Sandra's body was too degraded to be viable. It was a dead end, and there was no physical proof of Della or Lynn handling the body. Lynn had admitted she'd seen a girl at Tanner's, but that wasn't proof of Della's existence. If not for the 9-1-1 call, Sandra might never have been found and Lynn's truth never discovered. Cops were already theorizing Tiffany had made the call.

"Scarlett." Luke's voice pulled me out of my trance. "You okay?"

I shut off the water. He pushed back the curtain and wrapped the towel around me. "I'm okay."

He'd remained at my side as evidence collectors poked, prodded, and photographed me. The cops hadn't appeared angry as they'd gathered forensic data, though I saw distrust in several gazes. I supposed there'd always be people who doubted me.

I'd watched Margo talk to the other cops at the crime scene. She moved with the confidence of a master conductor. If there was physical proof that she was Della, she knew it was long gone. She'd won. And for now, we had a truce.

He cupped my face. "You don't have to be."

I looked up at him. "I have to be or I'll fall to pieces. Can't let the ghosts win."

"If you do see a few ghosts and fall apart, I'll help put you back together." Luke wrapped his arms around me, trapping in the shower's heat. "I've got you. It's okay."

I nestled close to him, savoring the strength of his arms. When I finally pulled back, I studied his sharp eyes. "The DNA. You used your contacts to expedite the testing, didn't you?"

He pushed a wet strand from my face. "I twisted an arm or two."

"That was a risk. Were you worried I could've been guilty?"

"I wasn't worried."

"No?" I arched a brow. Any attorney worth his salt would have been suspicious of me. But I wanted to believe him. "I would've worried about me."

He shook his head. "I didn't. I have a radar for the unsaid. I know innocent when I see it."

I leaned forward and kissed him. I wasn't sure I totally believed him, but it was nice to hear. "What am I not saying now?"

He chuckled. "I'd rather you show me."

Chapter Forty-Seven

DAWSON

Thursday, August 1, 2024
12:00 noon

Dawson had no trouble getting the search warrant for Lynn Yeats's town house. He and two other detectives were quickly given the green light to search every crevice of the space. However, he'd not notified Margo because she was still on leave, and frankly, he wanted to see this place without her clouding his insights.

The search team broke into two groups and began to methodically comb through what amounted to a very ordinary town house. Beige walls and carpet, living room furniture that appeared to have been purchased years ago as a matched set, printed posters of the Chesapeake Bay hanging on the walls, and framed pictures of Lynn and her family. Mother, father, sister. There'd even been pictures of a few cats, though there was no sign of any living creature in the house.

He'd learned an hour ago that the text from Lynn to Scarlett had been sent from a disposable phone, and it had also been purchased from the same convenience store where the Sandra Taylor 9-1-1 caller had bought their burner.

After he climbed the stairs to the second floor, he flexed gloved hands as he entered her bedroom. The bed was neatly made. There were two books and a pair of reading glasses on the bedside table. A half-drunk glass of water. The bathroom was clean, the mirror sparkling. Nothing stronger than aspirin in the medicine chest.

In Lynn's walk-in closet, her clothes had been arranged by color and hung on matching hangers. A dozen pairs of shoes lined up like soldiers. He scanned the brown, blue, and white blouses and skirts. There was a stack of neatly folded scrubs on a back shelf, and he saw several pairs of white running shoes. He glanced up toward clear storage boxes stuffed with purses, scarves, and hats. Behind one container, his fingers skimmed over a twelve-by-twelve square metal box. Pulling it down, he discovered a small lock securing the latch.

A half smile quirked his lips as he wrapped his hand around the lock and twisted hard. The lock didn't give, but the latch separated from the box. He opened the lid and realized it was a collection of mementos.

The first was a sketch of a young girl whom he recognized immediately as Scarlett. When she'd first encountered Della on that side street, she'd been trying to sell her art. She'd called her self-portrait *Girl Ready to Escape*. He carefully dropped the paper in an evidence bag, knowing there could be fingerprints.

Next, he found a silver necklace that matched the bracelet found on Sandra's body. *SC* was carved into the single medallion. There were other trinkets that didn't appear to relate to Della, Sandra, or Scarlett, and he feared this could be evidence of more victims.

At the bottom of the box was a white envelope, and in it, three Polaroid pictures. The first was Sandra. She was clearly distressed and scared. The second picture was of Scarlett. Like Sandra, her eyes were red and her face bruised. Dawson rubbed his chin, doing his best to tamp down rage.

The last Polaroid featured a young girl with dark curly hair. Unlike the other two, she stared defiantly into the camera just as she did in the portrait Scarlett had painted. Della.

The girl who'd lured Scarlett.

Who'd thought she could save Sandra.

Who'd been starved.

Locked in a wooden box.

And beaten.

This was physical evidence of Della. And as he studied the eyes and the curve of the lips, all his doubts vanished. Della was Margo.

He slipped the pictures of Sandra and Scarlett into evidence bags and then tucked Della's picture into his side coat pocket. As far as he was now concerned, Della had never existed.

ABOUT THE AUTHOR

Photo © 2015 StudioFBJ

Mary Burton is the *New York Times* and *USA Today* bestselling author of forty romance and suspense novels, including *The House Beyond the Dunes*, *The Lies I Told*, *Don't Look Now*, *Near You*, *Burn You Twice*, and *Never Look Back*, as well as five novellas. She currently lives in North Carolina with her husband and miniature dachshund. For more information, visit www.maryburton.com.